William Fraser

The Melvilles

Earls of Melville and the Leslies, Earls of Leven. Vol. 2

William Fraser

The Melvilles
Earls of Melville and the Leslies, Earls of Leven. Vol. 2

ISBN/EAN: 9783337427429

Printed in Europe, USA, Canada, Australia, Japan

Cover: Foto ©Andreas Hilbeck / pixelio.de

More available books at **www.hansebooks.com**

THE MELVILLES

EARLS OF MELVILLE

AND THE LESLIES

EARLS OF LEVEN

BY

SIR WILLIAM FRASER, K.C.B., LL.D.

IN THREE VOLUMES

VOLUME SECOND—CORRESPONDENCE

EDINBURGH—MDCCCXC

Contents of Volume Second.

ILLUSTRATIONS IN VOLUME SECOND.

VOL. II. *a*

SIGNATURES—WOODCUTS OF

ABSTRACT OF THE CORRESPONDENCE

OF

THE MELVILLES OF MELVILLE

AND OF

THE LESLIES OF LEVEN.

ROYAL LETTERS.

STATE AND OFFICIAL LETTERS.

FAMILY AND DOMESTIC LETTERS.

Rex

Traist counsalouris Cosing in ye cauff of a[sch?]egtmet, making before
Johan marlin[?] of ray[?]t fryst and Johan millzan of merbynis[?]
we greit zou weile, and prayit zou to deif ... makon ... and gude
end, and f[or] gadur in ye eltistum of c[astle?]b... gob begyn before ye
faide g[ois?], and is ye fynd lauff way yt famyp b way of ff
greit Cuntel bot ff yr falt al greteft mod[?]... all for eftar
gtis, and yat ye fulzp to b maid and god ... gurty ... yur
yf may apperaully ftand in guid eftydunt gub fer un ...
vel and under our fignet ... t kirger yt xxie day f
Januar and of b reny yr xxvi ... yer of

Jamys

To ... traist counfalouris
Cumpoftounis Coling and
Lardis of thair Consail

CORRESPONDENCE

OF

THE MELVILLES OF MELVILLE

AND OF

THE LESLIES OF LEVEN.

ROYAL LETTERS.

1. KING JAMES THE FIFTH to the Umpires between JOHN MELVILLE of Raith,
Knight, and JOHN MOULTRAY of Markinch, giving them instructions.
Cupar, 29th January 1533-4.

REX.

TRAIST cousalouris, chosin in the caus of asythtment making betuix Jhone
Mailuile of Raytht, knycht, and Jhon Multray of Merkyinche, we gret you wele :
and prays you to dres that mater to ane gude end, and se quhair the occasioun
of displesour hes begun betuix the saidis parteis, and as ye fynd caus, wey the
samyue to nother of ther gret hurtis, bot quhair the falt is gretest, modefye als
fer conforme thairto, and that ye failze nocht to mak ane gud end thairintyll, that
thay may apperandly stand in concord eftyrwart. Subscriuit be ws, and vnder
our signet, at Cowper, the xxix day of Januar, and of our ring the xxi yeris, etc.

To our traist counsalouris compositouris betuix the lardis of Raith and
Syfeild.

2. King James the Fifth to the Laird of Raith—Marriage of the latter's eldest son to the sister of the Laird of Lochleven. St. Andrews, 3d April [1541].

Rex.

Ratht: We ar informit be our thesaurer and maister of houshald that the larde of Lochtlevin desyris your eldast sonne in mariage to his systyr, and as thay haue schewin ws ye wilnocht end witht hym withtout ye knaw our mynd theriutill, we ar weill conteut that ye contract witht hym rathar nor ony otheris, and that for diuers causes mowyng ws, tharfor our will is that ye end the sammyn. Subscriuit witht our hand at our cite of Sanct Androis, the thryd day of Aprill, and of our reigne the xxviij yere.   James R.

3. King James the Fifth to the Captain of the Castle of Dunbar—Ordering him to cast down the house of Edringtoun. Edinburgh, 15th August [1542].

Rex.

Capitane of our castell of Dunbar we grete you wele : Forsamekle as the house of Edryntovne standis neir Berwik, and in danger to do grete hurt to our realme and it wer takin and strenthit be Inglismen, quhairfore it is thocht expedient that the said hous be castin doun : Oure will is heirfore, and we charge yow that incontinent thir our lettres sene, ye deliuer tua half barrellis of powdir for the dounputting of the said hous, and in likewis that ye caus aue man of maist experience within our said castel to pas to the said hous with William Lauder, for his devise and counsale, for casting dovne of the said hous quhat tyme it salbe thocht expedient. This ye failze nocht to do, as ye will ansuer to ws vpoun your vtir charge, kepand this our lettre and precept for your warrant. Subscriuit with our hand, and vndir our signete, at Edinburgh, the xv day of August, and of our regnne the xxix yeir.   James R.

4. Licence by James, Earl of Arran, Governor, as tutor to David Hamilton, his son, permitting Helen Naper, Lady Raith, to occupy the place of Raith till Allhallowmas. Edinburgh, 7th June 1549.

We, James, Erle of Arrane, Lord Hammiltoun, protectour and gouernour of the realme of Scotland, and lauchtfull administratour, tutour, gydare, and gouernour to Dauid Hammiltoun, our sone, be the tennour heirof grantis and gevis licence to Helene Naper, Lady Rayth, and hir bairnis, to occupy the manes and place of the Rayth quhill the feist of Alhallowmes nixt-to-cum, sua that scho in the menetym may gaddir hir cornes and gudis togiddir, and than remove hir self thairfra at our will, nochtwithstanding the wairning ellis maid, aud remanent ordour to be maid thairwpone, and will and grantis that scho sall commit na violence for occupying of the samin eftir the said wairning vnto the said fest, and the qubit seid to be sawin be quham we pleise. Subscriuit with our hand at Edinburght, the vij day of Junij, the yeir of God I^m v^c xlix yeris.

JAMES G.

5. MARY, QUEEN OF SCOTS, to ROBERT MELVILLE, Resident at the Court of England—Complaining of Randolph's dealings with the Earl of Murray. Edinburgh, 17th February 1565-6.

MALUILE,—It is not vnknawin to yow how before your departing we had grantit oure remissioun to Johnne Johnnestoun, quha cuming hame, and this same day being afoir ws, we inquirit of him the caus of his departing. He answerit that in the middis of August bipast he wes sent for be Mr. Randolphe to cum and speke with him at his ludgeing in Dauid Foresters, quhair he come, and efter sum declaratioun maid to him be Mr. Randolphe, how he was my lord of Murrayis seruand, and ane quhome he wald specialie credit, Maister Randolphe deliuerit to him thre sackettis full of money, selit, quhairin wes contenit (as wes said) thre thousand crownis, quhilkis he at Randolphis desir convoyit to Sanctandrois, and deliuerit the same to my Lady Murray, ressauand hir tickett thairupoun, quhilk he reportit to Randolphe. And fering that mater to be revelit and to cum to knawlege haistelie, durst not abyde, bot departit. And in the verie tyme quhen as we had hard this his declaratioun, Mr. Randolphe be occasioun being present with oure counsell treatand vpoun the bordour materis, we thocht not inconven-ient to report vnto him the report maid to ws, and schew him plainlie that in consideratioun the quene our gude suster, his maistres, had not onlie to our dear-est broder the King of France, and to his ambassatour resident thair, bot alsua to Monsieur Ramboletz, his lait ambassatour heir, and be Randolphe to our self, declarit that neyther she had aydit, nor wes myndit to ayd and support our rebellis with men, money, or vtherwyss to our displessour, quhilk we tak to be vndoubtedlie trew, and will luke for na vther at hir handes, sic accompt do we mak of hir and of hir declaratioun gevin in that behalf, quhilk we can nawyse mistrust, yit that he, hir seruand and minister, occupeing a peciable charge, besides

hir will and meanyng, suld interpryss a thing sa preiudiciall to the peax we
culd not bot think verie strange of it, and had richt gude reasoun to be offendit
with his mysbehavour, that within our awin realme had confortit thame with
money to our displesour quhilkis wer our rebellis, and with quhome we had
sa iust occasioun to be offendit, quhairin, as he had transcendit his maistres
commandment, sa had he schewin him self ane vnfit minister to interteany
amytie, for quhilk purpos he schew him self to abyde heir. At the first he
plainlie denyit that he had ony knawlege of sic a purpos. Bot in our reply we
come neirar vnto him, and schew him our assurance thairin wes procedit of na
lycht report, for we culd evin than cause the self same man quha ressauit the
money of his handes, and convoyit it to my Lady Murray to S[anctandrois]
appeir and mak the trewth manifest, Maister Randolphe, persaving himself nar-
rowlie compassit, begouth to deploir Johnne Johnstonis caiss, meanyng that ony
man in his condicioun wald say far anewch, gif be that meane thay mycht
procure fauour, quhairvpoun we war movit in Maister Randolphis awin presens to call in John Johnstoun, quha thair declarit on his conscience, and as he
wald ansuer before God, that Mr. Randolphe, in the presens of Mr. Thom-
with, deliuerit to him the foirnamyt sakkettis with money, in maner and at the
tyme as of befoir he had declarit to oure self, without variance in onie poynt.
Vnto quhome, quhen as Maister Randolphe had maid na vther ansuer bot that
Johnne Johnstoun mycht speke his plesour as ony wald do being in his caiss, and
that sic a declaratioun was na pruif, yit Johnne constantlie affirmit his report,
with diuerss takynnis vsit in the circumstance of the mater, and gaif the same in
write subscriuit with his hand. Mr. Randolphe at last thocht strange that sic
thingis wer layd to his charge, and said he wald abyde tryall thairvpoun before
the quene his maistres, to quhome onlie he must gif accompt of his doyngis.
Heirvpoun, having at gude lenth avisit with our counsell, finding that sa mani-
festlie he had left the offices of a gude minister and intertenyar of amytie, and
within oure awin realme had in hand this and sic vther vnlefull practizes to our
displesour, we haue fund his abyding heir to be maist preiudiciall to ws and our
estait, and that worthelie he aucht to be removit, and thairfore hes takin resolu-
tioun to send him hame, and gevin him aduertisment to mak him reddy to that
end within four or five dayis. And leist he suld in this meyntyme send thair to
court and mak report of thir procedingis vtherwys nor the trewth is, we thocht
meit with diligence to certifie you of it that is past, willing you, with sic expeditioun as possibillie ye may vse, to pas, and first desir audience of the counsell, to
quhais presens, sasone as ye ar admittit, ye sall declair that we haue assurit
knawlege how Mr. Randolphe, the quene our gude susteris seruand and minister heir,

in the lait rebellioun quhilk our awin subiectis rasit aganis ws, sa fer transcendit
the office of a gude minister and intertenyar of amytie, that he sent thre sackettis
of money quhairin wes contenit iij^m crownis, to the Lady Murray, to the support
of our rebellis in our displessour, quhilk his fact being, as we doubt not, expres
aganis the meanyng of our said gude suster (quhilk we alwayes tak to be inclynit
to amytie), is sa preiudiciall to ws and our estait that we cannot content that he
sall remane within our realme quha haldis vnlefull practizes with our rebellious
subiectis.   And thairfoir hes thocht convenient to send him hame to be tryit of
his mysbehavour be our gude suster his maistres, and ordourit at hir discretioun,
quhairvnto we doubt not bot thay, for the exemplis causs in geving advyse, will
hald hand.   And in particular, that ye expone the occasioun of his hame sending to my Lord of Lecestre, quhais man he is, and hes his dependence vpoun him,
that he sall not find oure proceding heirin in ony wyss strange, seing we haue sa
just occasioun sa to do ; as we doubt nocht, bot efter consideratioun of the caiss,
he will wele considder, and thairefter that ye declair the mater alsua to the quene
our gude suster, and require of hir that like as Maister Randolphe will not avow
his proceding as done be ony commandment procedit from hir (as we ar assuirit
he may not), evin sa she will gif demonstratioun of hir myslyking thairof, and
handle the mater at hir gude discretioun, as mair amplie we mynd to wrait in the
letter quhairof he him self salbe berair.   Thus far we thocht expedient to mak
you privie of afoirhand, or ayther Maister Randolphe or ony of his salbe thair, in
vsing quhairof we wyshe yow schaw diligence.   Subscriuit with our hand at
Edinburgh, the xvij day of Februar 1565.

We haue writtin presentlie to the Fransche ambassatour, to quhome ye sall
pas, and desir him to be present with yow at the report making, quhilk we thocht
meit to do, becaus be his presens the mater wilbe estemit the mair wechty.

Marer

To our seruand Robert Maluile, resident at court, in England.

6. THE SAME to THE SAME—Queen Elizabeth's offer to be gossip to the Queen's
son.   Edinburgh, 11th July 1566.

TRUSTY and belouit, we greit yow weil, we haue receyued great comfort and contentement of the declaration your brother has maid vnto ws, touching the quen

our gud sisters continual affection and constant loue towardis ws, quhilk she causes
appear at all convenient tymes, as now by the great joy she hath taken at our
happy delyuery, and also by the gentil grant she has maid to be gossope, desyring
to send ane honnorable company, both of men and women for accomplissing of the
same, wherof ye sal geue hir in our name maist harty thankes, and say vnto hir
that we wald she suld do nothing therin, bot at hir best commoditie and gretest
aise. Alwais prey hir that he who sal com be such a one as we haue knawen throw
long experience to haue bone tender and familiar with our said gud sister, to the
end we may the more frely oppen dyuers thingis vnto him that we intendit to
haue spoken by our awn mouth vnto hir self, because the tym heirafter wil not
serue so weil vnto the propos. Concerning Onel and Ruxby, we hope that Mester
Killigrew sal satisfie hir anough, quhilk ye may affirme as neid sal requyre, according to the coppies and instruction sent vnto yow, and schaw hir also how we
desire to haue no aduancement in that contre but by hir awn only meanis and
help, nocht douting that our behauour salbe in al pointes such towardis hir, as
she sal haue cause more and more to procure ernestly hirself al thingis that may
serue vnto our weil and preferrement, in this contre, that contre, or any vther
part, vpon the quhilk esperance we mynd to wse al diligent cair to folow such
wayes as may please hir, and to fle and eschew sic as wil offend or displease hir,
with our maist strait command vnto yow also to do the lyk at your power sa lang
as ye ramain ther, and whersoeuer ye be, neuertheles our wil is as before, that ye
entreteau in maist gentil and frendly maner, with many thankes, al thoise that
professes in that contre to bear ws gud wil, and are affectioned vnto our tytil,
provyding alwais that nether they nor ye offend or pretend to offeud heirafter the
quen, our gud sister, in any sorte, and geue ther commes any hasty or seditious
persoune vnto yow, admoniss them gently to cease ; geue they wil not, schaw them
ye wil declaire the matter vnto the quen, our gud sister, and do it indeed or it
fail, by which meanis it salbe weil knawen that all such as go about to saw discord
betuix the quen, our gud sister, and ws, doth it rather apon perticulair respectis
and profit vnto them selues, then vnto the weil of hir, or hir effaires, or for any
loue they bear vnto ther awn contre. Thus leauyng all vther matters vnto your
discretion aud formaire credit, quhilk we haue renewed again in our letter vnto
the quen, our gud sister, we commit yow to the protection of the Almychty,
wreten at our castel of Edenbourgh, the xj day of July 1566.

Marie R

To our trusty seruand, Robert Mcluill, resident at the court in England.

7. The Same to The Same—Recommending Anthony Standing. Edinburgh,
15th February 1566-7.

Trusty and weilbelouit, we greit you weill. This young gentilman, Anthony
Standing, is now returnit to his native cuntrie, quhome we mon recommend to
you, that in caiss in any wyss he haue neid of your commendatioun, fauour, or
furtherance, ye schaw the samyn glaidlie to him, and spair na beneuolence vndone
to him, that ye wald schaw at our commandment to ony of our awin borne
subiectis, specialie gif ony his evill willaris or inymeis wald presume ony thing to
his hurt or disadvantaige, quhilk ye may hynder. It is our will, and we command
you that thairin ye spair na travell nor diligence quhairby ye may releve him or
schaw him plesour, quhilk we will think as gude seruice. Subscriuit with our hand
at Edinburgh, the xvᵗʰ day of Februar 1566.   MARIE R.
    To our trustie and weilbelouit Robert Maluile, etc.

8. The Same to The Same—Desiring him to send her clothes to Lochleven.
Lochleven, 3d September [1567].

Robert Melwyne, ye sall nocht faill to send with this berar to me half elle of
incarnatt satin, and half elle of blew satin ; als caus Servais my conseirge send me
mair twynd silk, gif ther restis ony, and sewing gold and sewing siluer ; als ane
doublat, and skirtis of quhyt satin, ane vthir incarnat, ane vthir of blak satin,
and the skirtis with thame ; send na skirt with the ryd doublat, also ane lowse
gowne of taffateis ; als ye sall send the gowne and the vthyr clais that I bad the
Lady Lidintoun gar send me ; and als ye sall nocht faill to send my madynis
clais, for thai ar naikit, and mervelis ye haue nocht send thame sen your departing fra me, togithyr with the camaraige and lynyne clayth quhairof I gaif yow
ane memoriall ; and gif the schone be nocht reddy maid, caus send thame with
sum vthir eftir ; als ye sall caus Servais send tua pair schettis with tua unce of
small blak sewing silk ; als ye sall caus him send me all the dry dames plowmis
that he hes, togither with the peris he hes. This ye will nocht faill to do, as
doubt nocht bot ye will ; atour ye sall caus mak ane dozen of rasour nedillis and
mowlis, and send me ; and speir at Servais gif he hes ony vthir covering of beddis
to me nor grein, and send me, to put vndir the tother covering. I mervell ye
forgot to send me siluer, conform to promis. Committand yow to God, at Loch-
lewyne, the iij of September.   MARIE R.

9. The Same to The Same—Receipt for jewels.   Bolton, 15th October 1568.

Marev, be the grace of God Quene of Scotilland and Drouriar of France, granttis ws till hef ressauid frome our louit seruitour, Robert Meluill, all owr jouelss, clotying, horss, that we causit delyuer to hym at our beying in Lowght-lewin, of the quhilk geir forsaid and all othyir thing we committit wnto his charge, hes behaiffit hym as ane faythfull seruand to our satisfactioun and content-ment, and dischergis him of the premissis be this our hand, wretin at Bowtoun, and subscryuit witht our hand the yeir of God I^m v^c lxviij yeiris, and the xv of October.   Marie R.

10. Licence by King James the Sixth to George Moultray, younger of Seafield, to sell his lands of Newton of Markinch.   Leith, 14th November 1571.

Rex.

We, with anise and consent of our richt traist cousigne, Johnne, Erle of Mar, Lord Erskene, regent to ws, our realme and liegeis, for diuers ressonable caussis moving ws, be the tennour heirof gewis and grantis our speciale liecence to oure louit George Mowtray, youngar of Seyfeild, to sell, annalie and wedsett all and haill his landis of Newtoun of Markinche, or ony part thairof, to quhatsumeuir persone or persoues he sall think maist expedient, and will and grantis that be doing thairof thair sall follow nor ingener to him or thame na maner of preiudice for foirfal-tour, escheit, or recognitioun of the samin in our handis, vther perrell or daingear quhatsumeuir, nochtwithstanding quhatsumeuir lawis, actis, or statutis maid in the contrair, conditiones, prouisiones, and restrictiones specefiit and contenit in the said Georgeis and his predecessouris auld infeftment of the saidis landis repugnant thairto, anent the quhilk we dispens with him and the persone or per-sonis to quhome it salhappin him to sell and dispon the saidis landis, or ony part thairof, for euir be thir presentis, sua that thai, be his richt, may frelie and peciablie bruke and joise the samin, but ony clame, questioun, contradictione, or impediment quhatsumeuir to be maid or done to thame be ws, or our successouris, be ony maner of way in tyme cuming, and to that effect suspendis oure self fra all persute of recognitioun of the saidis landis, or ony part thairof, as becum in our handis throw the alienatioun foirsaid, be virtew of the said infeftment, pro-uisiones thairin contenit, or vtherwise, and sall move na actioun nor pley thairanent quhilk may tend to the preiudice of the infeftment to be maid be the said George

Marie be the grace of god Quene of Scottland and Dowriare of
France ygrantit ... the ... Scotland fromes ... lant ... s ... we ...
... all the ... thing ... that we tanst down to ... at o...
... in ... them if the ... ... Scotland ... and all other
thing we committ unto ... ... as our hand
full ... to o... satisfactioun and ... ...
of the promiss be ... s ... hand hero... at ... and ... ...
our hand ... ... of ... ... the ... ...

MARIE R

thairvpoun, in maner foirsaid, bot now as than, and than as now, renunces our instance thairof, dischargeing heirfoir the lordis of our counsale and sessioun, our aduocattis and vtheris, our judgeis, officiaris, and ministeris of our law quhatsumenir, of all persewing or proceding aganes the said George, or the persone or persones quhatsumenir to quhome it salhappin him to sell and dispone the saidis landis, or ony part thairof, at our instance, for foirfaltour, escheit or recognitioun of the same in oure handis throw the occasioun foirsaid, and of thair offices in that part simpliciter in tyme cuming. Gewin vnder our signet, and subscriuit be our said rycht traist cousigne and regent, at Leyth, the xiiij day of Nouember, the yeir of God I^m v^c threscoir ellevin yeris, and of oure regnne the fyift yeir.

11. LICENCE by KING JAMES THE SIXTH to JOHN MELVILLE of Raith and others to stay at home from the army at Dumfries. Holyrood House, 28th September 1577.

REX.

WE, be the tennoure heirof, with anise and consent of our richt traist cousing, James, Erll of Mortoun, Lord of Dalkeith, regent to ws, our realme, and liegis, gevis and grantis licence to our louittis, Johnne Maluille of Raith, and Johnne Barclay of Touch, and to all and sindrie our liegis, the inhabitantes, tennentis, and occupiaris of the fyve pund land of Raith and fourty schilling land of Eister Touch and Bogy, liand within our sherefdome of Fyffe, to remane and byd at hame fra our raid and army ordanit to convene and meit our said cousing and regent at Drumfreis, vpoun the tent day of October nixtocum, for persute and invasioun of the thevis and outlawes, perturbaris of the peace and quietnes of our realme, and to remane and await on seruice for the space of fourtie dayes thairefter, according to our proclamatioun maid thairanent : and will and grantis that the saidis Johnne Maluile of Raith and Johnne Barclay of Touch, nor our leiges, the inhabitantis, tennentis, and occupiaris of the landes abonewrittin for thair absence, and not cuming to the said raid and army, sall not incur na skaith nor danger in thair personnis, landes, or guidis, nor sall not be callit nor accuscit thairfoir, criminalie nor ciuilie, be ony maner of way in tyme cuming, notwithstanding oure said proclamatioun, or onny panis contenit thairin, anent the quhilkis we dispens be thir presenttis, dischargeing all our jugeis, officiaris, and ministeris of our lawes off all calling, accuseing, vnlawing, or onny wise persewing aganis thame, or onny of thame, for the caus foirsaid, poinding, troubling, or intrometting with thame, thair landis or guides thairfoir, and of thair offices in that pairt for euer.   Gevin vnder our signet, and subscryuit be our said cousing and regent, at Haliruidhous, the xxviij day of September, and of our reignne the ellevint yeir, 1577.

12. LICENCE by KING JAMES THE SIXTH to JOHN MELVILLE of Raith and his wife to eat flesh on fish days.   Holyrood House, 28th January 1584.

WE, be the tennour heirof, with aduise off the lordis off oure secreit counsall, grantis and gewis lecence and lebertie to Johnne Meluill of Rayth, his wyfe, and aucht persouns with thame in companie, to eitt flesche vpone Wednisdayis, Frydayis, and Setterdayis in Lentrene, and all vther dayis prohibite for the dayis of thame (thaire) lyftymis ; and will and grantis that the said   his said spous, nor the persouns being with thame in companie as said is, sall incure na paine, skaithe, nor danger thairthrow in thair panis (personis), landis, or gudis, uochtwithstanding ony oure actis, chairgis, or ordynancis maid, or to be maid, in the contrair thairanent, and painis continit thairin, we dispence be thir presenttis ; dischairging heirfoir all and sindrie our judges and ministeris of oure lawis within our realme of all calling, accusing, ateiching, summonding, or persewing of the saidis personis, vnlawing, pounding, or troubling of thame thairfoir, and of thair offeice in that pairt.   Gevin under our signat, and subscryuit with our hand at Halyrudhous, the xxviij day of Januar, and of our rigne the auchtein zeir, 1584.

JAMES R.

Rex

Sir Robert we...

James R

13. KING JAMES THE SIXTH to SIR ROBERT MELVILLE, in favour of Robert
    Waldegrave, the king's printer.   *Circa* 1587.

REX.

SIR ROBERT MELVING, ye sall resaue into your companie Robert Waldegrauc,
oure prentar, and deale with our direst sister, the quene, for his pardoun, according to our mony requistis interponit heirtofor in his fauour, that he may thairbe
in surtie provyd him of sic materialis as ar necessarric for our seruice, and also
travell in his vthir lesum offeris in that his native cuntrey without ony maner of
trubill or interuptioun, as we haif mair speciallie govin yow in directiouu.

                                                                  JAMES R.

14. KING JAMES THE SIXTH to JOHN, LORD, afterwards first MARQUIS OF
    HAMILTON—Lord Ross continues in his rebellion.   Linlithgow, 30th
    September 1591.[1]

RICHT traist cousing and counsallour, we grete yow hairtlie welc.   The Lord Ros
being of a lang tyme bigane lauchfullie denunceit rebell, and putt to oure horne
at the instance of Alis alias Alcsoun Ros, now spous to Schir Johnne Meluill of
Carnebie, knicht, and thairvpoun oure vtheris lettres of tressoun being direct and
execute aganis him for randering of his castellis and fortaliceis of Halkeit
    to the officer executour of the same lettres, he nocht onlie still continewis in
his rebellioun be his wilfull remaning at oure horne vnrelaxt, bot to our forder
contempt and dishonnour, he still keipis and detenis his said houssis, fortifeing the
same with men and victuallis, of intentioun, as appeiris be his procedingis, to keip
the same as houssis of weir aganis ws and our authoritie, declairing him selff
heirby a mockar of iustice, and a proude contempuair and disdancair of ws and
oure authoritie; quhairfoir we haue deliberat to see this his rebellioun pvnist, and
himself reduceit to his debtfull obedience, and for this effect haue exped ane commissioun to yow for persute, taking, and assegeing of his said houssis, and recouering of the same furth of his handis, quhilk commissioun we desire yow effectuuslie
to accept vpoun yow, and effectuallie to execute the same in all pointis, conforme
to the tennour thairof, with sic expeditioun as possiblie may be; quhairby as ye
sall testifie vnto ws your gude affectioun and fordwartnes to the repressing of

    [1] Original letter in the Charter-chest of the Duke of Hamilton.

sic oppin and avowit rebellioun, sa sall ye do ws acceptable plesour and gude seruice, meriting oure speciall thankis. Thus luikeing for the coustant and effectuall executioun of our said commissioun without shiftis or delay, we committ yow to God. Frome Linlithquhow, the last day of September 1591.

JAMES R.

To our richt traist cuising and counsallour, the Lord Hammiltoun.

15. WARRANT by KING JAMES THE SIXTH dispensing with the regular attendance of SIR ROBERT MELVILLE of Murdocairnie at Council and Exchequer. February 1604.

JAMES R.

CHANCELLARE, president, and remanent lordis of our priuie counsale and cheker in Scotland, we great you wele: Forsameikle as our trusty counsallour, Schir Robert Meluill of Murdocairny, knight, in regarde of his age, seiknes, and iufirmiteis, is not sa able now as afoir preceislie to keip and be present everie counsale and cheker with you, we haue thairfoir thoght goode heirby to require and desire you to dispence with his not proceis keiping of your ordinare counsale and cheker dayis, and to hald it sufficient that he repair to our counsale and cheker as he pleass or his habilitie may serve, notwithstanding of quhatsumeuir actis sett doun in the contrair, wherauent we dispence in his behalff, and this salbe your sufficient warrand. Gevin at our courte in Whytehall, the   of Februar 1604.

16. KING CHARLES THE FIRST to the EARL OF MAR, Treasurer, directing him to expede the signature of the barony and title of Monymail, subject to the revision of the Commission for Surrenders. 17th August 1627.

CHARLES R.

RIGHT trusty and welbeloued cousin and counsellour, right trusty and welbeloued cousins and counsellouris, and right trusty and welbeloued counsellouris, wee greete yow well: In regard that resignation is to be made in our fauouris by the Lord Meluill of the regalitie of Monymale, and for other good considerations, wee haue been pleased to signe a signatour to him of his lands, barronie, and title of Monymaill, and diuerse other thinges contained therein, which wee haue sent yow herewith; but because there may be things therein which are fitt to be considered off

GUSTAVUS ADOLPHUS, KING OF SWEDEN
BORN 1594; DIED 1632.

by the commissioners for the surrenders, our pleasure is (after yow haue pervsed the said signatour, and vpon the said resignation so to be made), that yow caus the said lord enact himself in your bookes of exchequer, that his signatour shalbe lyable to the said commission for surrenders to abide the order and determination thereof, or of any course wee shalbe pleased to appoint concerning matters of the like nature; and thereafter that with all convenient diligence yow cause exped the same vnder our great seale, for doing whereof these presentes shalbe your warrant, and so wee bid yow farewell. From our court at Bagshote the seaventeene day of August 1627.

To our right trustie and welbeloued cousin and counsellour, the Earle of Mar, our treasurer of Scotland, and to the remanent noblemen and others, the commissiouers of our exchequer in that our kingdome.

17. GVSTAVUS ADOLPHUS, KING OF SWEDEN, to JAMES, MARQUIS OF HAMILTON —That he had sent Colonel Alexander Leslie to assist him.   Frankfort-on-the-Oder, 28th April 1631.[1]

GVSTAVUS ADOLPHVS Dei Gratia Svecorum, Gothorum, Vandalorumque Rex, Magnus Princeps Finlandiæ, Dux Esthoniæ, Careliæque, Ingriæ Dominus : Illustrissimo Marchio, nobis singulariter dilecte ; quod desiderabas in literis tuis, ut quemquam expediremus, cuius tibi opera et consilium vsui esse posset, effectum iam dedimus, expedivimus enim generosum tribunum nostrum, et sincere nobis fidelem Alexandrum Lesle, equitem auratum, ut curarum et sollicitudinis partem tecum sustineret, eaque quæ ad deducenda in effectum negocia tua facere quicquam poterunt, summa industria perficeret ; sufficientibus insuper mandatis ipsum instruximus, ita ut illis observatis, cum nihil desideretur amplius, omnia ex voto nunc confecta iri, non dubitemus ; ne vero a serenissimo Daniæ Rege ullum expeditioni tuæ impedimentum, vel remora iniiciatur, omnis sinistris cogitationibus præcidenda erit occasio ; quamobrem operæ pretium te facturum arbitramur, si serenissimum regem tuum inducere possis, ut antequam exercitus mari committendus, serenitas sua rationem instituti serenissimo Daniæ Regi aperiat, ostendatque expeditionem tuam in nullius amicorum injuriam, vel offensionem, sed in libertatis Germaniæ securitatem et oppressorum libertatem, præcipue directam esse. proinde rogare, negocium hoc, et publice et privatim vtile, omni favore ac benivolentia prosequi velit ; quæ omnia vna cum coeteris, communicato consilio vobis

¹ Original letter in the Charter-chest of the Duke of Hamilton.

peragenda committimus, deque fide et dexteritate vestra securi, non nisi votivum nobis successum pollicemur, et Divinæ protectioni te commendamus. Francofurti Oderæ die 28 Aprilis 1631.

Illustrissimo nobis singulariter dilecto, Domino Jacobo Marchioni Hamiltoniæ, Comiti Araniæ et Cantabrigiæ, Baroni Evindaliæ et Sereuissimi Magnæ Britanniæ Regis Magno Stabuli Magistro.

18. Instructions by Gustavus Adolphus, King of Sweden, to Colonel Alexander Leslie, in reference to the Duke of Hamilton's army [1631].[1]

Instructions for Colonel Lesley.

In regard his Majestie of Sueden hathe thoght Sir Alexander Lesley, knyght, Colonnel of a Brigade of his Majestie's army, fit to be sent to assiste my lord Marquis of Hammiltons expedition, these articles are enjoyned him by his Majestie.

1. In regard, my lord Marquis of Hammilton hathe an army vnder the command of the King of Sueden, his Majestie is pleased to appoint Colonnel Lesley to assiste the lord marquis by action and counsel conforme vnto th' instructions heere set doune: First, Colonnel Lesley is appointed to repaire withe all expedition vnto Hamburg.

[1] Original instructions in the Charter-chest of the Duke of Hamilton.

2. In Hamburg Colonel Lesley is to communicate this our commission vnto Doctor Salvius, our commissary, and aduise withe him what they can conclude with the Bishop of Breme and the toune of Breme, and see what hope there is to haue Graue William of Nassaws army, and of Colonnel Erneryters levies.

3. In respect that wee haue geven to the lord marquis the river of Veser for his rendesvous, and appointed the last of June of this yeere 1631 for his landing, our three regiments of foote and one thousand horse promised vnto the lord marquis shalbee in reddines to joyne withe his lordship, and if Colonnel Lesley do not find these troupes levied then shall hee haue an especial care to haue them lifted withoout all delaye.

4. If Colonnel Lesley do find that Colonnel Erneryter neyther can nor maye make his levies in Holland, then shall Colonnel Lesley haue a care to levie these troupes in Lubec, Hamburg, the city and countrey of Breme. And for this cause, together withe Doctor Salvius, hee shall treate withe the forsaid tounes, and in particular withe the toune and territories of Breme, to the end a place maye be obtained from them for a rendesvous, and mustering of his Majesties troupes, for procuring of whiche they shall vse all sorts of arguments, but the cheefe is, that all shall tend to there safety.

5. And in cace Colonnel Erneryter haue not lifted these troupes iu Holland, then Colonnel Lesley by himselfe, or by other cavaliers, shall levie three regiments of foote, consisteing of Dutche officers and sojours. And if Colonnel Lesley cannot so levie men, then shall hee take Colonnel Gertzkey and Colonnel de Menier regiments for that service : which hee shal not do but in cace of extremity, in regard these two regiments are appointed to come vnto our owne army.

6. And in cace there be no hopes of levies these wayes, Colonnel Lesley, for his last refuge, shall deale withe the lord Marquis of Hammiltou for levieing of three regiments iu Scotland or England : and for that end Colonnel Lesley shall send moneys for lifting of them, or deale withe the lord marquis for advanceing of the same : But vpon this condition that it shal bee in our pouer to exchange these troupes of strangers withe as many Dutche.

7. These levy moneys shall Colonnel Lesleye take of these moneys whiche the States of Holland do contribute : And if the States moneys bee not reddy hee shall receiue them from Errick Larrson, his Majestie's factor, who shall haue sufficient ordor for the delivery thereof.

8. Likwise Colonnel Lesley shall receive from Errick Larrson the munition promised vnto my lord marquis : And if the munition bee not come from Sueden, then shall Errick Larrson buy and deliuer all in Holland, to th' end there bee no defect.

9. In respect the general rendesvous for my lord marquis his army is in and about Breme, whiche must bee his lordship's sedes belli; Colonnel Lesley shall sollicite the Bishop and toune of Breme favorably to receiue my lord marquis his troupes, remonstrating that suche is the necessity, that wee could not thinke of any other meanes of there saftey but the lodgeing of these troupes there.

10. Colonnel Lesleye withe all diligence shal viewe all places vpon the Weser, and considder whiche are fittest to bee fortified: and so soone as possibly hee can send vnto vs the draught of the situation of all places.

11. And to the end the King of Denmarke take no occasion of suspicion, Colonnel Lesley shall strive to dispose my lord marquis to sollicite his Majestie of Great Brittane to write vnto the King of Denmarke not to enter into jealousy, seeing our intentions and actions shall not bee prejudicial vnto the King of Denmarks sonnes pretentions, but shall only tend to the maintaineing of the present Bichop, our oncle, and preparing the best waye of assuring the King of Denmarks sonnes right after the decease of our oncle: And if the King of Denmarke will not actually assiste this enterprise, his Majestie of Great Britaine wold be pleased to desire him not to hinder it, but sit still.

12. And in cace, against all expectation, my lord marquis find any opposition or resistance in landing in the Weser, then by his lordship's ships to make himselfe waye. And that Colonnel Lesleys care be that the lord marquis sedes belli be made sure.

13. Colonnel Lesley shal bee very carefull in the bussines of Westphalia and Lower Saxe. If hee cannot levie forces in our name, let it be done in the name of the toune of Breme, and let him striue to make them resigne there forces vnto him, and that, together withe Doctor Salvius, hee persuade all these troupes to joyne withe my lord marquis, and that vnder his lordship's command : or, if not, vnder there owne general, but vpon this condition that all be done communicatis consiliis et viribus withe my lord marquis, and that matters be so ordered that good correspondence be mutually kept betweene these of the Rhein circuit aboue and the circuits belowe.

14. Colonnel Lesleye shall paye his sojours precisely according to the forme of our chamber ordor ; and trye whether my lord marquis wilbe disposed to a conformity of payement of his lordship's army according to the Suedens custome. But if Colonnel Lesley do find his lordship not disposed to do so, then not to presse it further, but hee shall cause Conrad Falkenberg paye the Dutche troupes in the Sueden manner.

15. And in cace the troupes comming from England shall, by wether, difficulties of forts, or other impediments, bee stayed longer vpon the Weser, Colonnel

Lesleye is to sollicite my lord marquis to bring prouision of victuals not only for his owne troupes, but over and aboue for the whole army.

16. And to th' end no tyme be lost, it is our pleasure that most diligently correspondence bee kept from Colonnel Lesley with my lord marquis about all aggreements and bussines incident, from Hamburg or Holland: and in cace correspondence from this side of the sea do anywaye prejudge the promoting of the bussines, then shall Colonnel Lesley transport himselfe into England, there to meete withe my lord marquis, and personally to conclude of all things.

17. At Colonnel Lesley's arriual into England he shall most kindly salute my lord marquis from vs, and communicate withe his lordship all our descins in this warre, and show our constant resolution to go on in the same.

18. Colonnel Lesleye hathe commission to geue his lordship all possible thanks for being the mover and disposer of his Majestie of Great Brittaine to enter into alliance withe ws, and to desire in our name his lordship to be the honnorable meanes of procuring the sending of an ambassador for concluding of all things, etc.

19. GUSTAVUS ADOLPHUS, KING OF SWEDEN, to JAMES, MARQUIS OF HAMILTON, expressing satisfaction with his preparations and giving instructions. Werben of Oldenmark, 13th July 1631.[1]

GUSTAVUS ADOLPHUS Dei gratia Suecorum, Gothorum, Vandalorumque Rex, Magnus Princeps Finlandiæ, Dux Esthoniæ et Careliæ, nec non Ingriæ Dominus: Illustrissime Marchio, amice nobis singulariter dilecte: Intelligimus ex literis tuis nuper nobis redditis, copias, quas conscribere recepisti esse paratas; quod nobis admodum gratum est, te tanto ardore laudabile propositum tuum prosequi. In nobis autem nihil desideratum iri confidimus, quò minùs et promisso belli adparatu, et eo qui tecum conjungi debet ex parte nostrâ milite tempestivè tibi subveniatur. De illo enim sæpius ac seriò ad ministros nostros perscripsimus, ut tibi eum mittant: Nobisque certò relatum est, eum ad te inmdudum esse expeditum. Ac quamvis rumores circumferantur, eum esse in itinere à Dunkerkanis interceptum, nostri tamen in Belgio commissarii, si id certum est, de alio, ut tibi statim providebunt, iubebimus, ut ita nihil in nobis, quod ad expeditionem tuam pertinere poterit, desiderari debeat. De militibus à nobis tibi auxilio mittendis tribunum nostrum Leslæum, quem ad vos non ita pridem misimus, plene informavimus. Cumque occasionem iam optimam, tum huius belli gerendi, tum tibi

[1] Original letter in the Charter-chest of the Duke of Hamilton.

commodi subveniendi, superato Albi nacti simus; te propterea gratiosè requirimus, ut adventum tuum, quantum unquam potes, acceleres: Tibique persuadeas, eam, quam concepimus, de summo virtutis ac fortitudinis studio tuo, opinionem nostram, te eo ipso valde confirmaturum; nosque ad exhibendum tibi omnia gratiæ ac benevolentiæ nostræ regiæ officia arctius devincturum. Quæ tibi hisce gratiosè offerimus, teque Divini numinis protectioni commendamus. Dabantur in castris nostris Regiis ad Werben Veteris Marchiæ die xiii° Julii anno M° Dc° xxxi°.

GUSTAVUS ADOLPHUS.

Illustrissimo amico nobis singulariter dilecto, Domino Jacobo Marchioni Hameltoniæ, Comiti Araniæ et Cantabrigiæ, Baroni Evindaliæ et Evinæ, Serenissimæ Magnæ Britanniæ Regis Magno stabuli magistro.

20. GUSTAVUS ADOLPHUS, KING OF SWEDEN, to JAMES, MARQUIS OF HAMILTON —Congratulates him on landing on the coast of Pomerania. Werben of Oldenmark, 3d August 1631.[1]

GUSTAVUS ADOLPHUS Dei gratia Suecorum, Gothorum, Vandalorumque Rex, Magnus Princeps Finlandiæ, Dux Esthoniæ atque Careliæ, Ingriæ Dominus, etc.: Illustrissime Marchio, amice nobis singulariter dilecte: Intelleximus cum gaudio singulari vos cum copiis vestris salvos et incolumes ad oras Pomeraniæ pervenisse. Ac etiamsi nobis non ingratum fuisset, si ad Visurgim eas appellere contigisset, quò, occasione nunc, si unquam, favente, purgari totus ille Archiepiscopatus ab hoste et a iugo eius liberari potuisset, cum tamen iter vestrum inopinatò aliter successerit, Deum vobis ducem extitisse, nec minus gloriosa ac felicia, hâc viâ per vos pro sua benignitate exequi decrevisse, firmiter nobis persuademus. Gratulamur itaque vobis de auspicatissimo adventu, perpetuamque felicitatem et omnium deinceps laudabilium actionum atque inceptorum vestrorum successum vovemus. Et ut de mente nostrâ vicissim vobis constet, à vobis benigne requirimus, ut porro faustis avibus militem in terram exponatis, eumque secundum flumen Oderam, Silesiam versus, deducatis, certi, vos in via inventuros ex nostro exercitu, hæc quæ consignari curavimus, peditum quatuor millia et mille equites; illos etiam, qui ex Sueciâ recens advenerunt, ut numerum mille quingentorum explere equites possint; quos omnes copiis vestris adiungemus, imperioque ac curæ vestræ Generalisque vigilum præfecti nostri Leslœi committemus; nec non et omnibus illis copiis, quas successu temporis vobis destinaturi sumus, ut sub vestro Gene-

[1] Original letter in the Charter-chest of the Duke of Hamilton.

ralatu militent, iniungemus. Mandaviuus gubernatoribus nostris et illis qui
annonæ nostræ militaris curam habent, ut quò vos cum copiis iter facere contigerit,
annonam comportari, eisque distribui seriò curent. Offerimus simul illa, quæ a
nobis porro in commoda vestra proficisci possunt. Quod si etiam vobis, relicto
interim Generali vigilum Præfecto nostro Imperio, ad nos excurrere, ac nobiscum
cum de itinere, tùm illis quæ in rem erunt, conferre visum fuerit, certos vos esse
desideramus, gratissimam nobis præsentiam vestram futuram esse, denique nos
Regio affectu benevolentiâ ac favore singulari in vos propensissimos perpetuo
mansuros. Hisque vos Deo optimo Maximo cum exercitu commendamus. Dabantur in castris nostris ad Werbam Veteris Marchiæ 3 Augusti A.D. 1631.

GUSTAVUS ADOLPHUS.

> Illustrissimo amico nobis singulariter dilecto, Domino Jacobo Marchioni
> Hameltoniæ, Comiti Araniæ et Cantabrigiæ, Baroni Evindaliæ et Evinæ,
> Serenissimæ Magnæ Britanniæ Regis Magno Stabuli Magistro.

21. GUSTAVUS ADOLPHUS, KING OF SWEDEN, to JAMES, MARQUIS OF HAMILTON
—That he was sorry to learn the Anglo-Scottish army had lost a third by
disease. Erfurt, 24th September 1631.[1]

GUSTAVUS ADOLPHUS Dei gratia Suecorum, Gothorum, Vandalorumque Rex,
Magnus Princeps Finlandiæ, Dux Esthoniæ et Careliæ, nec non Ingriæ Dominus :
Illustrissime Marchio, amico singulariter dilecte : Qualis sit status exercitus nostri
Anglo-Scotici, in Marchia, id partim ex tuis, partim etiam Dominorum Spensii et
Leslelij literis, satis perspeximus. Tot milites morbo correptos languore, tot
etiam morte sublatos et exercitum tam exiguo tempore tertia sui parte diminuutum,
tantò molestius ferimus, quantò majore de eius robore et virtute nobis polliciti
sumus, eoque semper anxii quo pacto sartus tectusque conservaretur et nobis et
insigni alicui occasioni, quâ gentis istius innatæ fortitudinis documenta daret.
Quæ cura, cum nos etiamnum sollicitos teneat ; jamque Dei auspicio et gratiâ,
victricibus armis nostris nobis in diversa Germaniæ loca, alendis exercitibus,
quantumuis magnis, idonea, viam aperuerimus : Elector insuper Saxoniæ, totius
septemviratus Brandeburgici, cumprimis, locorum ad Viadrum, defensionem in se
susceperit, ex pacto etiam nuperrime inter nos convento, armis Imperatoriis ê
Silesia imminentibus suo exercitu occurrere teneatur ; mutato, quod prius inten-
deramus consilio, valdè tam rationibus nostris, quam ipsi exercitui conducibile
putamus, si ex provinciis istis, diutino bello attritis et rerum inopiâ laborantibus

[1] Original letter in the Charter-chest of the Duke of Hamilton.

in alias magis commodas, et à bellicis calamitatibus immunes deduceretur :
Idcirco, sicuti literis nostris 18 hujus ad te datis et iam tibi sine dubio redditis
poposcimus: ita nunc iterato requirimus ut acceptis hisce statim cum residuis
copiis Anglicis moveas, et nos recta tuta tamen ab inimicis via subsequaris. Id
te pro tuo erga nos affectu, et communis boni studio haud gravate facturum confidimus, et vicissim tibi persuasum cupimus, nos non novas solum, et tot, quot
opus fuerit justo exercitui conficiendo, copias loco nostratium in Marchia relic-
tarum, tibi destinaturos, quæ Scoticis ubi venerint, junctæ sub tuo Generalatu,
nobis merebunt: Sed in omnibus etiam aliis, quantopere honor et dignitas tua,
nec non ipsius exercitus salus et incolumitas nobis cordi fuerit, reapse probaturus.
De infirmorum in Marchia relinquendorum, diversoriis et victu, ad Dominos,
Legatum et Generalem Banerium, perscripsimus, qui, ut omnia secundum mentem
et intentionem nostram curentur, operam dabunt.   Quod super est, te Deo optimo
Maximo benè conservandum, committimus.   Dabantur Erfordiæ 24 Septembris
anno MDcxxxi.   GUSTAVUS ADOLPHUS.

   Illustrissimo amico nobis singulariter dilecto, Domino Jacobo Marchioni
      Hamiltoniæ, Comiti Araniæ et Cantabrigiæ, Baroni Evindaliæ et Evinæ,
      Serenissimi Magnæ Britanniæ Regis Magno stabuli Magistro.

22. GUSTAVUS ADOLPHUS, KING OF SWEDEN, to JAMES, MARQUIS OF HAMILTON,
      desiring him to send Colonel Alexander Leslie to the King.   Mentz,
      26th November 1631.[1]

GUSTAVUS ADOLPHUS Dei gratia Suecorum, Gothorum, Vandalorumque Rex,
Magnus Princeps Finlandiæ, Dux Esthoniæ et Careliæ, nec non Ingriæ Dominus :
Gratiam et favorem nostrum singularem.   Postquam nobis cognitum est, copias
tuas eousque esse imminutas, ut existimemus illas facile abs te ipso, ceterisque quos
adduxisti, officialibus tantis per posse gubernari, donec novis obfirmatæ fuerint
supplementis.   Decumbente autem gravimodo consiliario et Campimareschallo
nostro, Domino Achatio Totten, necessarium nobis sit, ad ducendum eum, quem
eius directioni submisimus exercitum, generalem vigiliarum præfectum nostrum
Dominum Alexandrum Leslei isthuc expediri, quò ægrotanti Tottio auxilio esse,
usuique nostro et rei bene gerendæ copias nostras, quæ sunt in Meklenburgio
accommodare possit : Id inprimis significandum tibi duximus, ut cognitâ intentione
nostrâ præsentique necessitate profectionem istam, Leslæi eò promptius promoveas,
quò magis ea â nobis communi utilitati est destinata.   Quod si nihilominus, aucto
militum tuorum numero, adjungi tibi aliquem denuò cupieris : Non renuemus

<hr>

[1] Original letter in the Charter-chest of the Duke of Hamilton.

tribunum nostrum Helbrunnium, vel alium idoneum officialem cuius consilio et auxilio uti poteris, tibi submittere. Quibus de singulari nostrâ benevolentiâ regia te certum Deo insuper commendatum esse cupimus. Dabantur ex stativis nostris regiis Hostiæ in Archiepiscopatu Moguntinensi, die 28 Novembris anno MDc°xxxi°.   GUSTAVUS ADOLPHUS.

> Illustrissimo copiarum nostrarum ad Oderam Generali præfecto nobis sincere dilecto, Domino Jacobo Marchioni Hameltoniæ, Comiti Araniæ et Cantabrigiæ, Baroni Evindaliæ et Evinæ.

23. KING CHARLES THE FIRST to the PRIVY COUNCIL OF SCOTLAND—The Laird of Raith's taking the title of Lord Melville. 22d May 1635. [Copy.]

CHARLES R.

RIGHT reverend father in God, right trustie and weilbeloved cousins and counsellers, and right trustie and trustie and weilbeloued cousins and counsellers, wee greet yow weile : Whereas the Laird of Raithe, vpon a testamentarie declaration made be the late Lord Melvill, hath assumed vnto him (as wee are informed) the title of a lord and baron of parliament, without acquainting of ws with the reasons thairof, the lyke whereof hes not [been] practised heirtofore : It is our pleasure that yow call the said Laird of Raithe before yow, and discharge him frome vsurpeing anie suche title of a lord heernfter, till he be further warranted be ws, for the whiche these presents sall be your warrant. Wee bid yow fareweill frome our Manor of Greenwich the 22 of May 1635.—Vera Copia.

24. KING CHARLES THE FIRST to ALEXANDER, EARL OF LEVEN—Precedency over the Earl of Calendar. Windsor, 24th January 1642.

CHARLES R.

RIGHT trustie and right welbeloued cosen and councellour, wee greet yow well : Being informed that the patent of the Earle of Calendars title of honour is of a prior date to yours, which is contrary to what wee euer resolued, and which wee finde to have proceeded from a mistake, wee have therefor thought fitt to lett yow know, that as it neuer was our intencioun, so wee doe not intend the precedency to him, but will shortly take such a course for remedying thereof as shall give yow full sattisfaccioun ; whereof desireing yow to be confident, wee bid yow hartily farewell. From our Honour of Windsore, the 24th of January 1642. St. Scot.

> To our right trusty and welbeloued cosen and councellour, Alexander, Earle of Leven.

25. KING CHARLES THE FIRST to ALEXANDER, EARL OF LEVEN—In favour
of the Earl of Antrim. Oxford, 11th June 1643.

CHARLES R.

RIGHT trusty and right welbeloued cousin and councellor, wee greete you well.
Some moncths agone (being then at York) wee wrote our letters scverally both
to you and into Ireland to our justices there, that the Earle of Antrim (then vnder
restraint in Ireland) might either be sent to our citty of Dublin, or to vs, with
the reasons of his committment, as he most humbly implored, hoping that he
should make cleerely manifest his loyalty to vs, and the good offices he had done
to divers of our distressed subiects, releeued and assisted severall times by him in
cases of great extremity at Colerain and other parts of Ireland, as by attestacion
hath since appcared. Wee never hitherto received any account of those our letters.
On the contrary, wee vnderstand he was driven to make his owne way over into
the north of this our kingdom, where, in his attendance vpon our decre consort
the Queene, he so behaued himselfe as became the duety of a good and loyall
subiect. But that, out of an earnest desire to provide for the security of his
estate in Ireland, he, lately repairing thither, was anew apprehended and imprisoned,
and very barbarously treated, and soe remaines at Knockfergus or some other place
vnder the command of our Scottish forces. Therefore that wee may well vnderstand what his fault is, and cause him accordingly to be proceeded against, our
pleasure and command is, that you faile not, vpon receipt of these our letters,
forthwith to give order that the said Earle of Antrim with his attendants and
seruants be sent presently to our said citty of Dublin, together with the particular
charge against him, wherevpon wee shall soone take a course to have him proceeded against according to his meritt. In the interim wee will and require you
to give sufficient direccions also, that the houses, chattels, and other estate of the
said Earle of Antrim in any part of Ireland be saued harmelesse both from the spoile
of the Irish rebels and our owne forces there vnder your command, that soe they
may be found vnimbezlid or otherwise wasted whensoever and howsoever lawe and
justice shall dispose of them: Wee shall expect that you performe your part herein
with that indifferency to him and regard to vs which shall befitt your duety and
charge, and that you give vs a speedy account thereof accordingly, for which
these our letters shalbe your warrant. Given at our Court at Oxford the 11th
day of June in the nineteenth yeare of our reigne, 1643.

To our right trusty and right welbeloved cousin and councillor, Alexander,
Earle of Levin, Generall of our Scottish forces in our kingdom of Ireland,
and in his absence to his seruant Maior Generall Montro [Monro].

My Lord Meluill. Being informed by S. George
Meluill. Kn.t Mr. of my household, that his occasions
and his attendance upon me and my struice doth much
depend upon you at this time: and his struice being
now stredable to me, I thought fitt to recommend —
both himselfe and his occasions to you, w.ch if it worke
any furtherance to him in mouing you to doe what
may be thought iust, fitt, and honorable, I shall —
rectiue it as an acceptable struice done to me

                    Your assured frind

                        Charles R.

Dunfirmling the 6.th
day of May. 1651.

                    For the Lord Melvill of Moneymell.

St Germains Aug: the 4th 1652.

I am promised this letter shall come safe to your handes, and
therfore I am willing that you should know from my selfe, that
I am still alive, and the same man I was when I was amongst
you, I am very much, troubled for what you suffer, and am
vsing all the endeavors I can to free you, and befor many
monthes I hope you will see I am not idle: In the meane time
I cannot but let you know, that I am in greater straights
and necessityes then you can easilye apprehend, and I am therby
compelled to leave many thinges ondone, wch would be of advantage
to me and you; I could heartily wish therfore that by your interest and negotiation with those you dare trust, and whome you
know wish me well, some way might be found out to assist me
with mony, wch would be a very seasonable obligation, and
could never be forgotten by me: I neede say no more to you,
but that I shall be glad to receave any advice or advertisement
from you, that you thinke necessary for me, and shall allwaies
remaine,

Your very loving frend

Charles R

26. KING CHARLES THE SECOND to LORD MELVILLE in favour of Sir George
Melville, Master of the Household.

Dunfermling, the 6th day of May 1651.

MY LORD MELUILL,—Being informed by Sir George Meluill, knight, Master of
my Houschold, that his occasions and his attendance upon me and my seruice
doth much depend vpon you at this time, and his seruice being now steadable to
me, I thought fitt to recommend both himselfe and his occasions to you, which, if
it worke any furtherance to him in mouing you to doe what may be thought iust
fitt and honorable, I shall recciue it as an acceptable seruice done to me.—Your
assured frind,   CHARLES R.

For the Lord Meluill of Moneymell.

27. KING CHARLES THE SECOND [to GEORGE, LORD MELVILLE]. Requesting
the loan of money.

St. Germains, August the 4th, 1652.

I AM promised this letter shall come safe to your handes, and therfore I am willing
that you should know from myselfe that I am still aliue and the same man I was
when I was amongst you.   I am very much troubled for what you suffer, and
am vseing all the endeauors I can to free you, and befor many months I hope
you will see I am not idle.   In the meane time I cannot but lett you know that
I am in greater straights and necessityes then you can easilye apprehend, and I
am therby compelled to leaue many thinges vndone which would be aduantage to
me and you.   I could heartily wish therfore that by your interest and negotiation
with those you dare trust, and whome you know wish me well, some way might
be found out to assist me with mony, which would be a very seasonable
obligation, and could neuer be forgotten by me.   I neede say no more to you,
but that I shall be glad to receaue any aduice or aduertisment from you that
you thinke necessary for me, and shall allwaies remaine, your very louing frind,
                                                                        CHARLES R.

28. KING CHARLES THE SECOND [to GEORGE, LORD MELVILLE]. Requesting a
supply of money.

St. Germains, August 5, 1652.

I DOE well vnderstand the danger you would be in if you were knowne to haue
receaued a letter from me, and therfore I would not write if I were not very

confident that this shall come safe to your handes. I doe assure myselfe your hearte and affections remaine still the same they were to me, how much soeuer you are for the present compelled to submitt to the power and pleasure of your and my enimyes, and I doe assure you I haue the same care of you all which I ought to haue, of which I hope you will finde the effects. Lett all my frindes where you are, and whome you dare communicate with, know that I am well, and tender of them and there sufferinges, and lett them know, too, that I am in so great wantes and necesities that I am not able to prosequte my bussines that way which is best for me and them, nor to doe many thinges which should be done, and therfore if they can with security to themselues find a way to returu any supply to me, it will be a very seasonable obligation, and your care and solicitation in this important bussinesse will be very acceptable to your louing frind,

CHARLES R.

29. KING CHARLES THE SECOND to the PRESBYTERY OF EDINBURGH. That he would maintain the Church. Whitehall, 10th August 1660. [Copy.]

HIS Majesties gracious letter directed to the Presbytrie of Edinburgh, and by them communicated to the rest of the Presbyteries of this Kirk. Receaved the 3d of September 1660.

Sic suprascribitur

CHARLES R.

TRUSTY and well beloved, wee greet yow well. By the letter yow sent to us with this bearer, Mr. James Sharp, and by the accompt he gave of the state of our church ther, wee have receaved full iuformatione of your sense of our sufferings and of your constant affectione and loyalty to our persone and auctorite, and therfor wee will detaine him heir no longer (of which good services wee are very sensible), nor will wee delay to let yow know by him our gracious acceptance of your address, and how well wee are satisfied with your carriadges, and with the generalitie of the ministers of Scotland in this tyme of tryall, whilst some under specious pretences swerved from that dewty and alleadgeance they owe to us; and because such, who by the countenance of usurpers have disturbed the peace of that our church, may also labor to creat jealousies iu the mynds of well meaning people, wee have thought fitt by this to assure yow that, by the grace of God, wee doe resolve to discountenance profainity, and all contemners and opposers of the ordinances of the gospell. We doe also resolve to protectt and preserve the goverment of the Church of Scotland as it is settled by law, without violation ;

St Germain; Aug: 5. 1652.

I doe well vnderstand the danger you would be in, if you were
knowne to haue receaued a letter from me, and therfor I would not
write, if I were not very confident that this shall come safe to
your handes: I doe assure my selfe your hearte and affections
remaine still the same they were to me, how much soeuer you are
for the present compelled to submit to the power and pleasure
of your and my enimyes, and I doe assure you, I haue the same
care of you all wch I ought to haue, of wch I hope you will
finde the effects: Lett all my friendes where you are, and whome
you haue communicate with, know that I am well, and tender of them
and there sufferinges, and lett them know too, that I am in so great
wantes and necessities, that I am not able to prosegate my bussines
that way wch is best for me and them, nor to doe many thinges wch
should be done, and therfore if they can with securityes to themselues
finde a way to returne any supply to me, it will be a very sea=
=sonable obligation, and your care and sollicitation in this impor=
=tant bussinesse will be very acceptable to,

Your louing friend

Charles R

and to countenance in the dew exercise of ther functions all such ministers who shall behave themselves dewtifully and peaceably as becomes men of ther calling. Wee will also take care that the auctorite and acts of the Generall Assemblie at St. Andrews and Dundie in the year 1651 be owned and stand in force untill wee shall call another Generall Assembly (which wee purpose to doe as soon as our affairs will permitt). And wee intend to send for Mr. Robert Douglass and some other ministers that wee may speake with them in what may further concerne the affairs of that Church. And as wee are very well satisfied with your resolution not to meddle without your sphere, so wee doe expecte that church judicatories in Scotland and ministers ther will keep within the compass of ther statione, meddleing only with matters ecclesiastick, and promotting our auctorite and interest with our subjects against all opposers; and that they will take speciall notice of all such who by preaching or privat conventicles, or any other way, transgress the limits of ther calling by endeavoring to corrupt the people, or sow seed of dissafection to us or our goverment. This yow shall make known to the severall Presbyteries within that our kingdom : and as wee doe give assurance of our favour and incouradgement to yow and to all honest deserveing ministers ther, so wee earnestly recomend it to yow all, that yow be earnest in your prayers, publick and privat, to Almighty God, who is our rock and our delyverer, both for us and for our goverment, that wee may have fresh and constant supplies of his grace, and the right improvement of all his mercies and delyverances, to the honor of his great name, and the peace, safty, and benefit of all our kingdoms ; and so we bid yow heartily farewell. Given at our Court at Whythall, the 10 of August 1660, and of our rigne the 12 year. By, etc.

Sic subscribitur   LAUDERDALE.

30. KING CHARLES THE SECOND to the COMMISSIONERS OF THE TREASURY— Francis Montgomery and the liferent of the estate of Leven. Whitehall, 1st December 1674. [Contemporary Copy.]

CHARLES R.

RIGHT trusty and welbeloved cousins and councellours, right trusty and welbe-loved councellours, and trusty and welbeloved councellours, wee greet you well : Whereas wee are informed by some of the nearest relations of the Countesse of Levin that Francis Montgomery, brother german to the Earle of Eglinton, is endeavouring to secure to himselfe the liferent of the whole estate of Levin, not-withstanding that he did restrict himselfe, failing children in the mariage betwixt him and the late deceased Countesse of Levin, to six hundred pounds sterling yearly, or thereabout, and that he had liberty to affect the estate with about nine hundred pounds sterling of debt for providing himselfe with necessaries at his mariage : And whereas also wee are informed that the other burthens lying upon the said estate, by very considerable debts and the liferent of a part thereof to the Countesse of Weems, are so great that if the said Francis Montgomery shall accomplish that his designe the whole estate will soon be exhausted, to the ruine of the heir, and the great prejudice of the creditours : Now, althongh wee will not interpose in the merits of the cause, but leave it to the due course of law, yet wee haue thought fit to signify unto you our pleasure, and wee doe hereby require you to take care that no signatour relating to the said estate of Levin passe the exchequer of that our ancient kingdome in favours of the said Mr. Francis Montgomery, alias Lesly : And if it shall happen to passe there, before the intimation of this our royall pleasure unto you, that the same be by you stopped at the seales, which are not to be appended thereto untill it shalbe determined by the Judge Ordinary whether the conditions conceived in favours of the said Mr. Francis Montgomery can be sustained in law : Seeing they were given by a minor tending to the apparent ruine of the heir, and so much to the prejudice of the creditours. For doing whereof this shalbe your warrant, and so wee bid yow heartily farewell. Given at our court at Whitehall, the first day of December 1674, and of our reigne the 26th year.—By his Majesty's command.

LAUDERDALE.

To the Lords Commissioners of his Majestys treasury and exchequer in his ancient kingdome of Scotland.

31. JAMES, DUKE OF MONMOUTH, to GEORGE, LORD MELVILLE—Thanking him for his trouble in his business.

From Bruxsells the 18 of August 1677.

I WOULD a writt to you sooner, but that this is the first minutt I haue had any time to my selfe. I hope I shall come to London time enofe beefor you goe away, to thanke you for all the troubell and pains you haue taken in my bussines. In seuen or 8 days mor I shall sertenly know when I shall come bake, for our bussines hier must bee oner one way or another by that time ; therfore I hope you will not make soo much heast. Pray lett me know if my wife begins to looke after her bussines at home, and if their be any hopes of her being a good busiue.

from Brussells the 18 of August.

I would a writt to you sooner but that this
is the first minuit I have had any time to
my selfe. I hope I shall come to london time
enofe beefor you goe away to thanke you
for all the troubell and pains you have
taken in my bussines, in seven or 8 days mor
I shall sertenly know when I shall come
bake, for our bussines heer must bee oner
one way or another by that time, therfor
I hope you will not make soe much heast,
pray lett mee know if my wife begins
to looke after her bussines at home and if
their bee any hopes of her being a good
huswife. I shall troubell you now with
nothing ells, for I am sur I have noe
nide to tell you that nobody in the word
can bee mor your humbell servant then
I am— MONMOUTH

For My Lord Melvill

To bee left att his Grace
My Lord Generalls lodgings
att the Cockpitt.

These are to certify that in the time
I had command of his Majesty's forces
in Scotland against the Rebells that were then
in armes I did direct & authorize the Lord
will to send propositions to the Rebells &
receive some from them in order to laying downe
their armes & submitting to the Kings mercy.
In Witness whereof I have sett my hand & Seale
att London this 10th day of June. 1680.

Monmouth

I shall troubell you now with nothing ealls, for I am sur I haue noe nide to tell you that nobody in the world can bee mor your humbell seruant then I am.

MONMOUTH.

For my Lord Melvill. To bee left att his grace my Lord Generalls lodgings att the Cockpitt.

---

32. LAURA, DUCHESS OF MODENA, to MONS. DE CANON, afterwards Brigadier-General Cannon—In favour of Simon Barret, an Irish deserter.

Brusselles, ce 28 Octobre 1679.

MONSIEUR,—La mere de Simon Barret Irlandois soldat dans le regiment Anglois de garnison en cette place de Bergompzon qu'on menace de faire passer par les armes en qualité de deserteur, me priant tres-ardemment de vous escrire en sa faueur, aynsi que uous allez uoir par le memoire cy enclose ie n'ay pas uoulu luy refuser la lettre le caractere de mere me faisant trop de pitié. C'est pourquoy, Monsieur, je uous recomande de tout mon coeur ce pauure miserable d'autant plus qu'on est à present dans une pleine paix, cest à dire, dans un temps qu'on se peut dispenser de quelque chose en faueur d'un filz qui se rendoit icy pour uoir sa mere. Je uous assoure que ce sera un amitie bien remarquable que uous me ferez de luy sauuer la vie, et que ie la reconoittray de uos mains. Je suis de gran coeur, Monsieur.—Vostre bien et bonue amye,

LAURE, DUCHESSE DE MODENE.

Mr. de Canon, Bergompzon.

---

33. CERTIFICATE, JAMES, DUKE OF BUCCLEUCH AND MONMOUTH, to GEORGE, FOURTH LORD MELVILLE.

THESE are to certify that in the time I had command of his Majestys Forces in Scotland against the rebells that were then in armes, I did direct and authorize the Lord Melvill to send propositions to the rebells, and receive some from them, in order to laying downe their armes, and submitting to the king's mercy. In wittness whereof I have sett my hand and seale, att London, this 10th day of June 1680.

MONMOUTH.

34. KING CHARLES THE SECOND to the COMMISSIONERS OF THE TREASURY, to
pass a ratification in favour of the Duchess of Monmouth. Newmarket
23d September 1681.[1]

CHARLES R.

RIGHT trusty and welbeloved cousins and councellours, right trusty and welbeloved
councellors, trusty and welbeloved councellors, and trusty and welbeloved, wee
greet you well : Whereas the Lord Melwill, sole commissioner for the estate and
affaires of our right trusty and welbeloved cousin Anna, Dutchesse of Buccleuch,
hath now for some time had his residence in London, having been detained there
by reason of the said dutchesse her absence from this our kingdome, and the
necessity of her busines; and that wee are by him informed how that the said
dutchesse hath lately obtained a decreit of reduction before the Lords of Session
reduceing certaine deeds done by her in her minority to her lesione, wherby the
charters granted by us upon those deeds might likewayes be thought to be
reduced, and fall in consequence to the dutchesse her great prejudice, if remeid
be not provided ; wee have thereupon thought fit to grant a declaration and ratification under our royall hand for obviating the said inconvenience, and to charge
the said Lord Melwill with the bearing and presenting therof, to the effect it may
be duely past by you, and recorded in your bookes for her full security; and
therfor, wee doe hereby require you to receive and exped our said ratification
and declaration in the best forme, and to cause extracts therof (one or mor as
shalbe demanded) to be given to the said Lord Melwill in behalf of the said
dutchesse : As likewise, that you will give him all assistance in whatsoever other
affaires he may have to doe with you relateing to the said dutchesse her estate ;
seeing wee are fully satisfied that he hath not only been very carefull of all her
concerns (especially at this time of her absence), but that by reason of her absence
he hath been necessarly kept abroad very much to his own prejudice. So wee
bid you heartily farewell. Given at our court at Newmarket the 23th day of
September 1681, and of our reigne the 33th year.—By his Majesties command.

MORRAY.

To our right trusty and welbeloved cousins and councellours, etc., the lords
commissioners of our treasury, and the remanent lords and others of
our exchequer of our ancient kingdome of Scotland.

[1] Copy by Mr. A. Macdonald from original among Treasury Warrants in H. M. General
Register House, Edinburgh.

35. ATTESTATION by JAMES, DUKE OF MONMOUTH, that the offers of mercy to
the rebels in 1679 were by his express warrant. Westminster, 10th
June 1683.

WE, James, Duke of Buccleuch and Monmouth, being appointed generall of his
Majesties forces in the kingdom of Scotland by a commission under the great
seall, and fully impowred to use all means to suppress and extinguish the
rebellion raised in that kingdom in the year one thousand six hundred and
seaventy nine, doe hereby certifie and declare that in persuance of our said commission, wee ordered intimations to be made to the rebells then in arms to render
themselvs in the kings mercie, and the messages and intimations sent to them
for that purpose was by our exprese warraut and allowance. In witnes wherof,
wee have subscryved these presents att Westminster the tenth day of June one
thousand six hundred and eighty three, befor these witnesses, James Vernon, our
secretarie, and William Williams, our servant,   MONMOUTH.
 Ja. Vernon, wittness.
 William Williams, wittnes.

36. KING JAMES THE SEVENTH to the LORDS OF THE TREASURY—To give the
escheat of George, Lord Melville, to the Master of Melville. Whitehall,
21st January 1686-7.[1]

JAMES R.

RIGHT trusty and right welbeloved cousins and councellors, right trusty and
entirely beloved cousins and councellors, right trusty and welbeloved cousins and
councellors, right trusty and welbeloved cousins and councellors, and right
trusty and welbeloved councellors, wee greet you well : Whereas wee haue
been graciously pleased to extend our royall clemency to the Lord Melvill upon
his humble address made unto us for pardon, and have disponed his escheat
and liferent to his son, the Master of Melvill, and are resolved to preserve
that ancient family for serving us and our royall successors, as their prode-
cessors have formerly done to our progenitors with great loyalty and fidelity,
and for that end are resolved to dissolve from our crown what did fall to us by
the forfeiture of the said Lord Melvill, in the next parliament of that our ancient
kingdome, to the effect wee may dispone the same unto him ; it is our will and
pleasure, and wee doe hereby authorise and require you in the mean while to

---

[1] Copy by Mr. A. Macdonald from original among Treasury Warrants in H. M. General
Register House.

passe infeftments to the Master of Melvill on his owne resiguation, with a novo-
damus disponing unto him all title and right which wee haue thereunto, by
wards, marriages, escheats, liferents, recognitions, reversions, disclamationes, and
bastardries, and to cause the same to be expeded in favours of him and the heirs
mentioned in his former charter. For doing whereof this shall be your warrant,
and so wee bid you heartily farewell. Given at our court at Whitehall the 21th
day of January 168⁷, and of our reigne the 2d year.—By his Majesties command.
                                                                                                MORRAY.

>   To our right trusty and right welbeloved cousins and councellors, etc., James,
>   Earle of Perth, our chancellor, and the rest of the lords commissioners
>   of our treasury, and the lords commissioners of our treasury of our
>   ancient kingdome of Scotland.

>   37. LETTERS by KING JAMES THE SEVENTH in favour of GEORGE, VISCOUNT OF
>   TARBAT, for £1500 sterling, the half of Lord Melville's composition.
>   Whitehall, 31st March 1687. [Copy.]

>   JAMES R.

RIGHT trusty, etc., wee greet yow wele. Whereas before our signing lately a
remission and rehabilitation, in favours of George, Lord Melvill, he did agree to
pay the sum of three thousand pound sterline money, as a composition for the
same, besides the sum of two hundred pound sterline out of the yearlie rents and
profites of his estate that became due to us by vertue of his forfeiture ; the just
and equall halfe of which composition wee being resolved to bestow upon our
right trusty and welebeloved cousine and councellor, George, Viscount of Tarbat,
in consideration of his faithfull services rendered unto us, and of the small profites
that he had (as our clerk register) in the two sessions of the late parliament of
that our ancient kingdome : It is now our will and pleasure, and wee doe hereby
authorize and requyre yow furthwith to give the necessarie orders or warrants for
payment of the said just and equall halfe of the forsaid composition, being one
thousand and fyve hundred pound sterline, unto the said George, Viscount of
Tarbat. For doeing whereof these presents (together with his receipt of the said
sum) shall be to yow, and all others respectively who may be therein any way
concerned, particularly to the lords auditours of your accompts for allowing the
same, a sufficient warrant ; and soe wee bid yow heartily farewele. Given at our
court at Whitehall the 31th day of March 1687, and of our reigne the 3d year.
—By his Majesties command. Sic subscribitur   MELFORT.

Followes the precept drawen thereon by the lord of the thesaury. John Drummond, one of the receivers of his Majesties rents, pay unto the above named the Lord Viscount of Tarbat, the sum of seaven hundred and fifty pound sterline, as the one halfe of fiftein hundred pound sterline payed in by the Lord Melvill as halfe of the composition payable by him for the cause within specifeit ; and these presents, with his receipt, shall be your warrant. The other fiftein hundred pound sterline, for which bond is given by the Master of Melvill, being assigned to the said Lord Tarbat and the lord chancellour, who hes right to the other halfe by our assignation. Sic subscribitur PERTH, Cancell.; HAMILTON; GORDON; BELCARRES ; STRATHALAN.

38. ORDER by KING JAMES THE SEVENTH to three troops of the Queen's Regiment of Dragoons to march to Whitchurch and Chester. Windsor, 4th August 1687.

JAMES R.

OUR will and pleasure is that you cause three troopes of our dearest consort the Queens Regiment of Dragoones under your comand to march according to the rout hereunto annexed, one troope to Whitchurch and the other two to our city of Chester, where they are to remain untill further order ; and the officers are to take care that the soldiers behave themselves civilly and pay their landlords. And all magistrates, justices of the peace, constables, and other our officers whom it may concerne, are hereby required to be assisting to them in providing quarters and otherwise as there shall be occasion. Given at our court att Windsor the 4th day of August 1687, in the third year of our reigne.—By his Majesties command,   WM. BLATHWAYT.

> To our trusty and welbeloved Alexander Cannon, Esquire, colonell of our dearest consort the Queens Regiment of Dragoones, or the officer in chiefe with the troopes above mentioned.

39. WILLIAM, PRINCE OF ORANGE, to DAVID, EARL OF LEVEN, to attend the meeting of Estates. St. James's, 5th February 1688-9.

MY LORD,—Wheras the lords and gentlemen of the kingdom of Scotland met at Whitehall, at our desire, to advise what is to be done for securing the Protestant religion, and restoring the laws and liberties of that kingdom according to our declarations, have for the attaining of these ends desired us to call a meeting of the Estates to be holden at Edinburgh in March next, and to make sufficient intimation of the same by our letters to all persons who of right ought to be at the said meeting; we being desirous to do every thing that may tend to the publick good and happiness of that kingdom, in pursuance of the said advice, do by this our letter, desire your lordship to meet and sit in the said meeting of the Estates at Edinburgh the fourteenth day of March next.   Given at St. James's the fifth day of February in the year of our Lord 168⅜.

To the Earl of Leven.
[The letter is a printed form.]

40. WARRANT by KING WILLIAM THE THIRD, to subscribe the docquet of the king's gift to GEORGE, LORD MELVILLE, to be sole Secretary of State. [1689.]

WILLIAM R.

WHEREAS wee have of the date hereof granted a warrant for a confirmation and new gift to passe the great seale of that our ancient kingdom constituting and of new appointing our right trusty and right welbeloved councellor George, Lord Melvill, to be our principall and sole secretary of state for our said kingdome, with power to him to receive all profits and emoluments usually arising therefrom. Therefore wee hereby will and require you to subscrib the docquet of the said warrant which wee declare to be valide to all intents and purposes, and for so doing this shall be your warrant.   Given at our court at   the day of   16   , and of our reigne the first year.

For Sir John Dalrymple of Stair, younger, our advocate for our ancient king-dome of Scotland.

41. KING JAMES THE SEVENTH to the LAIRD OF MACNAGHTEN—To be ready to come to the king's assistance. Dublin Castle, 29th March 1689.

JAMES R.

TRUSTY and wellbeloved, wee greet you well : Whereas the wickedness of our ennemies has reduced our affaires to the necessity of requiring the assistance of our good subjects, these are to will and require you, with all your friends and followers, to be ready vpon a call to come to our assistance, att such time and place as you shall be appointed, and wee do hereby assure you that what expences you may be at shall be fully reimbursed by vs, and that wee will stand to our former declarations in fauour of the Protestant roligion, the liberty and property of our subjects, all which we will fully secure to them, and that wee will reward abundantly such as serve vs faithfully ; and such as doe not their duty as becomes good subjects, wee will punish soe as shall terrify others in aftertimes from the like wicked attempts : Wee expect your ready obedience, and therefore shall send you our commission, with power to you to name your other officers, in the meantime : For what you shall doe in obedience to these our royall commands, and for raising, arming, and training of men for scruing vs, and opposing our ennemies with your vtmost force, these shall be to you and all others a sufficient warrant ; and soe expecting from your loyalty and fidelity all the assistance you can giue vs, wee bid you heartily farewell.   Giuen at our court at Dublin Castle the 29th day of March 1689, and in the fifth yeare of our reigne.—By his Majestys command.   MELFORT.

To our trusty and wellbeloved the Laird of Macknaughton.

42. KING JAMES THE SEVENTH to COLONEL CANNON—Directing him to embark for Scotland. Dublin Castle, 1st July 1689.

JAMES R.

OUR will and pleasure is that you imbarque upon our fregats commanded by the Sieur Du Quesne, and such other boats as shall be provided for you on the coast at Belfast or Carickfergus, and that you go into our ancent kingdome of Scotland, there to obey such orders as you shal get from our right trusty and welbelou'd cosine and councellor, the Viscount of Dundee, lieutenant-generall of our army, for our service, of which you are not to feal.   Given at our court at Dublin

Castle the first of July 1689, in the fifth year of our reigne.—By his Majesties
command.   MELFORT.

> To our trusty and welbeloved Collonel Cannon, to be intimate to the other
> officers and soldiours of our ancent kingdom of Scotland at Belfast or
> Carickfergus.

43. WARRANT by KING WILLIAM THE THIRD to [address wanting], giving powers
to negotiate with the Chiefs of Highland Clans in rebellion. Hampton
Court, 10th July 1689.

WILLIAM R.

RIGHT trusty and welbeloved cousin and councellor, and right trusty and welbeloved councellor, wee greet you well : Whereas wee understand that divers of
our subjects, especially in the North and West Highlands in that our ancient
kingdome, being disaffected, doe daily associate themselves in open rebellion
against us, and being informed that the generality of them are misled by a few
persons who are the cheifs or heads of the severall clanns, and wee being willing
and desirous to prevent the effusion of blood, and if possible by all gentle means,
to reduce our said subjects to their due obedience ; therefore wee doe hereby
authorise and require you forthwith to use your best endeavours to effectuate the
same, and in order thereunto to capitulate with those who are judged the cheifs
and heads of the clanns, or leaders of any parties now in armes against us, giving
them assurance of our gracious pardone, if in due time (prescribed to them by
you) they submit themselves to our mercy, and give surety for the future to
demean themselves as loyall subjects. As also you are to make them such offers
and proposalls as shall be communicated to you by George, Lord Melvill, our
secretary of state for that our kingdome, whose letters to you anent the premisses
wee require you to observe and rely upon as from our selfe. And so wee bid you
heartily farewell. Given at our court at Hampton Court the 10th day of July
1689, and of our reigne the first year.—By his Majesties command.

                                                                MELVILL.

44. WARRANT by KING WILLIAM THE THIRD—For paying to George, Lord
Melville, the sum of £500 sterling. Newmarket, 9th October 1689.

WILLIAM R.

IT is our will and pleasure, and wee doe hereby authorise and require you. out of
the first and readiest of our rents, reveuues, customes, and casualities whatsoever

of that our ancient kingdome forthwith to pay, or cause to be paid, unto George, Lord Melvill, our secretary, or any having his order, the summe of five hundred pounds sterline money. For doing whereof these presents (together with a receipt from the said George, Lord Melvill, or any having his order, as aforesaid) shall be to you, and all others respectively who may be therein any way concerned, particularly to the lords auditors of your accompts for allowing the same, a sufficient warrant. Given at our court at Newmarkett the 9th day of October 1689, and of our reigne the first year.—By his Majestys command.

To the lords commissioners of our treasury of our ancient kingdome of Scotland.

1212670

45. KING JAMES THE SEVENTH to GENERAL CANNON—Encouraging him to greater efforts for the Jacobite Cause.   Dublin, 30th November 1689. An intercepted letter—old copy.

JAMES R.

TRUSTY and welbeloved, wee greet yow well. The conduct yow have shewen in the fall of the late Viscount Dundie has sufficiently demonstrated unto us how fitt yow are to serve us in any capacity. Wee need not therfor exhort yow to courage or loyaltie, which if yow had not been very steady in, the loss yow had in your generall at your very entrance into action, with so great inequality, were eneugh to baffle yow; but yow have shewed your self above surprize, and sufficiently revenged the death of your leader. What wee have chiefly to recommend to yow is that yow would animate all our friends that are in arms there for us to support themselves for some time longer, for nothing could gratifie our enemies more then to see yow affraid of continueing in a posture of defence, which is the only thing they apprehend finding them in, because of the many forces sent into this kingdome by the usurper to invade us, wee could not sooner spare the succors we had destined for your assistance. But God Almighty having made it his own work to destroy and confound the army that was landed upon us, we have resolved to send our right trusty and intirely beloved naturall son, the Duke of Berwyck, to your ayde as soon as the season will permitt the shipping of any number of horse. In the meantime wee will dispatch our right trusty and right wellbeloved the Earl of Seafort to head his friends and followers ; and wee do assure yow that the success wee hope for from their and your endeavours, shall be acceptable to us for nothing more then that therby wee shall shew yow our gratitude, not only by protecting yow in your religion, lawes, and liberties, as wee haue already promised, but by rewarding yow and each mans meritt in particulare out of such forfeitures as shall come to us by the unnaturall rebellion of the rest of our subjects there. Wee must above all things recommend vnto yow a through union amongst yourselves, and that yow look with the greatest indignation upon anybody that, under any pretence whatsoever, shall go about to disunite yow, such an one being a more dangerous enemy to our interest then those that appear in oppen arms against us. We referr to the bearer to give yow a full account of our force, and the present condition of our enemies, which is such as will put our affaires here soon out of all doubt; and so wee bid yow heartily farewell. Given at our court at Dublin Castle, the last day of November 1689, and in the fifth year of our reigne.—By his Majesties command.

To Brigadier Cannon.

(Directed on the back) To our trusty and welbeloved Coll. Cannon, Brigadier of all our forces in Scotland.

46. KING JAMES THE SEVENTH to the LAIRD OF MACNAGHTEN, promising to send over the Duke of Berwick with succours. Dublin Castle, 30th November 1689.

TRUSTIE and well beloved, wee greet you well. The constant loyaltie of your selfe and familie has been all allong soe well knowen to us that wee cann never doubt the continuance of your endeavours for our service, and now that God appeares soe signally to bless our endeavours every where, and that such of our enemies that durst not encounter the iustice of our cause, he has by want and distemper destroyed, wee expect that you and every brave and honnest man will, with your friends and followers, rise and lay holt of soe greate a providence, and tho' the forces you raise for our service may engadge you in an expense farr beyond what you are provided for, yett wee hope you will not decline the charge nor refuse to undergoe the difficultyes, since all things both at home and abroade seeme to conspire to putt us soone into such a condition as will not onely enable us to satisfie the debt our friends have contracted upon our account, butt alsoe to distinguish them from others by particullar marks of our favour; wee have therefore resolued to send imediatly our right trusty and right well beloved, the Earle of

Seafort, to head his freinds and followers, and (as soon as the season will permitt the shipping of horse) our right trusty and intirely beloved naturall son, the Duke of Berwicke, with considerable succors to your assistance, which the present good posture of our affaires here will allow us to spare, and wee doe assure you that the success wee hope for from this and your endeavours shalbe acceptable to us for nothing more then that thereby wee shall shew you our gratitude, not onely by protecting you in your religion, laws, and liberties, as wee have already promised, but by rewarding your and each man's merritt in particullar out of such forfeitures as shall come to us by the unaturall rebellion of the rest of our subjects there. Wee must above all things recommend unto you a thorough union amongst yourselves and a due obedience to your superior officers, and that you looke with the greatest indignation upon any body that under any pretence whatsoever shall goe about to disunite you, such an one being a more dangerous enemie to our interest then those that appeare in open armes against us. Wee refer to the bearer to give you a full accompt of our force and the present condition of our enemies, which is such as will putt our affaires here soone out of all doubt, and soe wee bidd you heartily farewell. Given at our courte at Dublin Castle the last day of November 1689, and in the fifth yeare of our reigne.— By his Majesties command.

Jo. M'Naughten.

To our trusty and well beloved the Laird M'Naughten.

47. WARRANT by KING WILLIAM THE THIRD to DAVID, EARL OF LEVEN, and MAJOR-GENERAL MACKAY, authorising the raising of new regiments. Holland House, 18th December 1689.

WILLIAM R.

RIGHT trusty and welbeloved cousin and councellor, right trusty and welbeloved councellor, and trusty and welbeloved, wee greet you well : Whereas wee are resolved to have our forces of that our ancient kingdome new modelled, and that the regiment of foot may consist of thirteen companies each, and sixty sentinells in each company, and of each regiment one company to be granadiers, and each troop of horse and dragoones to consist of fifty men : Therefore wee authorise and impower you to make up seven regiments of foot, three troops of horse, and three troops of dragoones out of the present standing forces, to be commanded by the persons contained in the instructiones under our royall hand herewith sent ; And wee further impower you to choose and nominate such lieutenant colonells, majors, and other inferiour officers for the foot, and lientenants and other inferiour officers for the horse and dragoones as you shall judge most proper, out of the whole standing army, or such other persones as you shall find well qualified for the stationes in which you are to place them, and to transmitt a list of the same to our secretary that their names may be filled up in commissiones accordingly. And wee recommend to you to proceed in this with such due care and secrecy as the matter doth require, and as you tender the good of our service. For doing whereof this shall be your warrant. And so wee bid you heartily farewell. Given at our court at Holland House, the 18th day of December 1689, and of our reigne the first year.— By his Majesties command.   MELVILL.

To our right trusty and welbeloved cousin and councellor, our right trusty and welbeloved councellor, and our trusty and welbeloved, David, Earle of Leven, Hugh Mackay, Major General of our forces, and Sir George Monro.

48. INSTRUCTION to the EARL OF LEVEN and MAJOR-GENERAL MACKAY, referred to in the foregoing warrant. 18th December 1689.

WILLIAM R.

INSTRUCTIONES to our right trusty and welbeloved cousin and councellor, our right trusty and welbeloved councellor, and our trusty and welbeloved, David, Earle of Leven, Hugh Mackay, Major Generall of our forces, and Sir George Monro.

1. You are to review and modell the six regiments commanded by the Earle of Angus, the Earle of Argile, the Earle of Glencairn, the Lord Viscount of Kenmore, the Lord Strathnaver, and the Laird of Grant, and you are to forme a regiment to be commanded by   Cunningham : Of the said seven regiments three are to remain in that our ancient kingdome, and the other four to be imployed for our service in Ireland.

2. You are to appoint the above seven regiments to consist of thirteen companies each, and sixty men in each company, and one company of each regiment to be granadiers.

3. For making up the said regiments, you are to disband the three regiments of the Earle of Mar, Lord Blantire, and the Lord Bargeny.

4. You are to disband all independent companies, and what officers of them as are fit for our service you are to imploy in stationes proper for them as our service requires.

5. You are to appoint fit persons to be lieutenant colonells, majors, and other inferiour officers to the foresaid seven regiments.

6. You are to imploy what officers you judge fit for our service that were in the three regiments which you are to disband, or in the independent companies.

7. You are to turne out of any of the regiments what officers you think unfit for our service and put others who are well qualified in their places.

8. You are with all expedition to transmitt an account at what places it is absolutely necessary to keep garrisons for suppressing the rebells, and what number of men will be required at each place.

9. For compleating of the above regiments you are to take the men out of such garrisons as are not necessary to be kept up.

10. You are to forme the souldiers of the three regiments, which you are to reduce into companies by themselves, so far as they will goe, and what officers you think fit to imploy of the said three regiments, whether captaines, lieutenants, or ensignes, you are to allow them to command in their severall stationes their own men, that the souldiers may be the better kept together.

11. Being informed that some regiments continue still in the places where they were raised, and may not be so fit there for our service, therefore you are to order such regiments to march to some other place of the countrey where you shall find convenient, and you are to order some of those men that came from Holland to march where they were, if thought necessary.

12. You are to modell three troops of dragoons, each troop to consist of fifty men, and the Lord Cardross to be colonell and captain of one troop, Robert Jackson to be lieutenant colonell and captain of another troop, and Patrick Home of Polwart to be captain of the third troop, and   Guthrie to be major without any troop.

13. You are to modell three troops of horse to be commanded by the Earle of Eglingtoun, the Master of Forbes, and Sir George Gordon of Edinglassie, each troop to consist of fifty troopers, if more troops cannot conveniently be maintained.

14. You are to appoint fit lieutenants and other inferiour officers for the said troops of horse and dragoones.

15. You are to compleat such regiments first as you think most proper for our service.

16. You are to transmitt a list of such officers as you nominate, to George, Lord Melvill, our secretary, that they may have their commissions accordingly. Given under our royall hand and signet at our court at Holland House the 18th day of December 1689, and of our reigne the first year.   W. R.

Instructions to the Earle of Leven, Major Generall Mackay, and Sir George Monro.

49. ADDITIONAL INSTRUCTIONS in regard to the Forces in Scotland.   Kensington,
4th January 1690.

WILLIAM R.

ADDITIONALL INSTRUCTIONS to our right trusty and welbeloved cousin and coun-
cellor, and our right trusty and welbeloved councellors, David, Earle of
Leven, Hugh M'Kay, Major Generall of our forces, and Sir George
Munroe of Culrain.

Notwithstanding of our former instructions, from what you represent wee
find ground to make the following alterations.

1. You are to consider for how many you can find subsistance by methods
within your owne power, and if that fall short of the number proposed by us formerly, you are to advise with our councell (before you proceed to modell and
disband) to know what they can propose for subsistance of the number mentioned
by us, or more if they think fitt, and can find subsistance for them, and after you
have found what the fonds will sustain, you are then to proceed to modell them
accordingly, and to disband the rest for making up of the regiments and troops
that are to stand for your better performance, whereof wee have ordered our privy
councell to give you their concurrence.

2. If the fonds of subsistance money shall not amount to so much as will
maintain the numbers formerly proposed by us to you, you are to appoint the
regiments to consist of fewer companys than what wee mentioned in our former
instructions.

3. And to the effect that the troops which are to stand be compleated, you
are to devide the troops commanded by the Earle of Annandale and Lord Ross
(if the rest are to be kept up) amongst the standing troops for compleating them,
if otherwise to disband them.

4. You are to appoint the company in the castle of Stirling, now commanded
by the Earle of Marr, to continue an independent company, and not to be regimented, and to consist of   centinells, and likewise what numbers
you shall appoint for the garrisons of Dumbarton, Blackness, and the Bass to be
independent, and   Araskin of Alvas company, now in the castle of Stirling, you are to appoint to be one of the regimented companyes.

5. You are not to levy any more foot for making up the seven regiments
untill some new fond be condescended upon for their subsistance.

6. If the ten battalions be so far short of their numbers as you conjecture,
you are to enquire who have been guilty of false musters.

In all other matters wee referr you to our former instructions, excepting in so far as they are hereby inuovated. Given under our royall hand and signett at our court at Kensingtoun the 4th day of January 16⅞, and of our reigne the first year.—By his Majestys command,   MELVILL.

Additionall instructions to the Earle of Leven, Generall Major M'Kay, and Sir George Monroe.

50. WARRANT to MAJOR-GENERAL MACKAY to apprehend certain persons named in a list signed by Lord Melville. Kensington, February 1690.

YOU are to take and apprehend any person or persons that shall be given up to you in a list sign'd by our right trusty and well beloved cousen and counsellour, George, Lord Melvill, as practisers against the government, and keep them prisoners till you deliver them to the governour or deputy governour of the castle of Edinburgh, or of any other our castles, and this shall be your warrant. Given under our royall hand and seall at our court at Kensingtoun the   day of February 16⅞, and of our reigne the first year.

For Major Generall Mackay, commander in chief of our forces in Scotland.

Order to Generall Major Mackay for apprehending persons suspect to be practising against the government.

51. INSTRUCTIONS to MAJOR-GENERAL MACKAY, with reference to the
foregoing warrant. February 1690.

WILLIAM R.

INSTRUCTIONS to our trusty and welbeloved councellor, General Major Mackay,
commander in chief of our forces in Scotland.

Yow are to take and apprehend the person or persons of them who shall be
given yow up in a list subscrived be our right trusty and wel beloved cousin and
councellor, George, Lord Melvill, and any three of our secret councell, as practisers
against the government, and carry them securely prisoners into the castle of
Edinburgh.

Upon what information yow have of any private persons under your command, or otherways, that are delated as practisers against the government, yow
are immediately to secure them, and to keep them closs prisoners till they be
delivered to the councell, or any having their order to receive them; and this
shall be your warrant. Given under our royall hand and seal at our court at
Kensington the   day of February 16$\frac{89}{90}$, and of our reigne the first year.

                                                        W. R.

Instructions to General Major Mackay for secureing or apprehending persons
suspected to be practiseing against the government.

52. WARRANT by KING WILLIAM THE THIRD for engraving the Signet.
Kensington, 26th February 1689-90.

WILLIAM R.

IT is our will and pleasure, and wee doe hereby authorise and require you to
engrave one signet for our privy councell, and another for the justice court of
that our ancient kingdome, and the said two signets, when finished, you are to
deliver to George, Lord Melvill, our secretary, or any having his order to receive
them, to be disposed of for our service. For doing whereof this shall be your
warrant. Given under our royall hand and signet at our court at Kensingtoune
the 26th day of February 16$\frac{89}{90}$, and of our reigne the first year.—By his Majestys
command.   MELVILL.

Kinsington ce $\frac{20}{30}$ de Mars 1690.

Par la lettre jointe vous vaires mes intentions
a l'eguard de l'adjournement de mon Parlement
en Ecosse jusques a ce que celle d'Angletere sera leve
dont la session ne sera que d'environ trois semaines.
Il sera necessaire que vous tachies a gagner Mr. ......
afin que par son moien l'on tache a separer les Rebelles,
et je suis content de donner une bonne somme d'argent,
J'ay fait remettre les 4000 ll. que le Comitée
des affaires de guerre m'avoit demandé pour executer
ce qu'ils ont projette, J'espere que les fregates qui
sont parti il y a si long temps seront arrive, aujourdhuy
est parti flotte avec l'Artl. et Munitions de guerre,
soies asseuré de la continuation de mon Amitie. William R.

53. KING WILLIAM THE THIRD to [GEORGE, LORD MELVILLE]—To try to gain
Lord Breadalbane. Autograph.

Kinsington, ce $\frac{20}{30}$ de Mars 1690.

PAR la lettre j'ecrite vous vaires mes intensions a l'eguard de l'adjournement do
mon parlement en Ecosse jusques a ce que celle d'Angletere sera leve dont la
cession ne sera que d'environ trois semaines.   Il sera necessaire que vous tachies
a gagner M^r. Bredalbin affin que par son moien l'on tache a separer les rebelles et
je suis contant de donner une bonne somme d'argent.   J'ay fait remestre les
4000 ll. que le committie des affaires de geurre m'avoit demande pour executer ce
qu'ils ont projette.   J'espere que les fregattes qui sont parti il y a si long temps
seront arrive.   Aujourdhuy est parti Slezer avec l'artillerie et munitions de geurre.
Soies asseure de la continuation de mon amitie.   WILLIAM R.

54. KING WILLIAM THE THIRD to GEORGE, FIRST EARL OF MELVILLE, Commissioner, appointing Alexander, Lord Raith, to vote in Parliament as one of
the Officers of State. Kensington, 18th April 1690.

WILLIAM R.

WHEREAS the most part of the officers of state are now in commission, and it
being provyded by the Act of Parliament 1617 that the number of our officers of
state who were to have vote and place in parliament and articles, should not
exceed the number of eight, even though at any time there should be more persons employed in the execution of the said offices.   Therefore we do nominate
and appoint our right trusty and welbeloved councellor, Alexander, Lord Raith,
who is one of the comisioners of our treasury, to appear and act as treasurer
deputt, and to have place, and vote in this second session of our parliament,
articles, and in all other judicatures, and occasions as one of our officers of state
during the time of this session of parliament foresaid, and ay and while wee
signify our further pleasure thereaneut.   Given at our court at Kensingtoune the
18th day of Aprill 1690, and of our reign the second year.

To his grace the Earle of Melvill, their Majestys high commissioner for this
second session of parliament att Edinburgh.

55. KING WILLIAM THE THIRD to GEORGE, EARL OF MELVILLE, High Commissioner for Scotland, enclosing the King's remarks upon the Acts for Church Government. Kensington, 22d May 1690.

WILLIAM R.

RIGHT trusty and right entirely beloved cosin and councellour, wee greet you well. We having considered the act anent church government, have returned the same, and the alterations we have thought proper should be made in it; however, we leave you some latitude which we wish you may use with as much caution as you can, and in the way will tend most for our service. Given under our royall hand at our court at Kinsingtoun the 22th of May 1690, and of our reigne the second year.   W. R.

56. REMARKS by KING WILLIAM THE THIRD as to Church Government in Scotland, sent to GEORGE, EARL OF MELVILLE. 22d May 1690.

WILLIAM R.

HIS Majesties remarques upon the act for setling church government in Scotland, which, together with some reasons designed for the clearing of it, and answering those objections that might be made against it, was sent to him by my lord commissioner.

1st. Whereas it is said that the church of Scotland was reformed from poperie by presbyters without prelacy, his Majestie thinks that tho' this matter of fact may be true, which he doth not contradict, yet it being denyed by some who discourse much of a power that superintendents had in the beginning of the reformation, which was like to that which bishops afterwards had, it were better it were otherwise expressed.

2d. Whereas it is said that their Majesties doe ratify the presbyteriall church government to be the only government of Christs church in this kingdom, his Majesty desires it may be expressed thus, to be the government of the church in this kingdom established by law.

3d. Whereas it is said that the government is to be exercised by sound presbyterians, and such as for hereafter shall be owned by presbyterian church judicatories, as such; his Majesty thinks that the rule is too generall, depending as to its application upon the opinions of particular men, and therefore he desires that what is said to be the meaning of the rule in the reasons sent to him may

be expressed in the act, viz., that such as shall subscribe to the confession of faith and catechismes, and are willing to submitt to the government of the church as established by law, being sober in their lives, sound in their doctrine, and qualifyed with gifts for the ministry, shall be admitted to the government, and his Majestie doth judge that the following declaration might be a good test :—
I, A B, doe sincerely declare and promise that I will own and submitt to the present government of the church as it is now by law established in this kingdome, and that I will heartily concurr with and under it, for the suppressing of sin and wickednesse, the promoting of piety, and the purging of the church of all erronious and scandalous ministers, and I doe also assent and consent to the confession of faith and the larger and shorter catechismes now confirmed by act of parliament as the standard of the protestant religion in this kingdome.

4th. Whereas it is desir'd to be enacted that the generall meeting of the ministers doe appoint visitors for purging the church, etc., his Majesty thinks fitt that for answering even those objections, which the reasons sent to him with the act doe suggest, may be made against this method, that what in the mentioned reasons is expressed by a may be, as to the concern of his privy councill in that matter, and the presenting of the visitors to the commissioner, that he may see they are moderate men, be plainly and particularly enacted.

5th. As to what concerns the meeting of synods and generall assemblies, his Majesty is willing that it should be enacted that they meet at such and such times of the year, and as often as shall be judged necessary, provided allways that they apply to him or his privy councill to know if there be any inconveniency as to publick affairs in their meeting at such times, and have his allowance accordingly, and that in all their generall assemblies a commissioner in the name of his Majestie be there present, to the end that nothing may be proposed but what meerly concerns the church, and in case anything relating to the civill government, or that is prejudiciall to it should be there proposed or debated, the said commissioner may give a stop to it till he has acquainted the privy councill and received their direction in it.

6th. Whereas it is desired to be enacted that the parishes of those thrust out by the people in the beginning of this revolution be declared vacant upon this reason, because they were putt upon congregations without their consent, his Majesty desires it may be so expressed as may be consistent with the right of patrons, which he thinks he hath the more reason to desire because in the reasons sent up with the act it seems to be acknowledged that this procedure is extraordinary and not to be drawen into consequence.

7th. The king thinks fitt that the clause from line 30 to 54 be absolutely left out as unnecessary, being meerly narrative, and the act concerning supremacy being now repealled.

His Majesties resolution to be candid and above board in what he does, and his desire that what is now granted by him to the church may not be uneasie to him afterwards, doe incline him to have the above mentioned amendments in the act.

It is his Majesties desire that such as are of the episcopall perswasion in Scotland have the same indulgence that dissenters have in England, provided they give security to live peaceablie under the government, and take the oath of allegeance.   W. R.

57. KING WILLIAM THE THIRD to [GEORGE, FIRST EARL OF MELVILLE]—To assist Major-General Mackay.   Autograph.

Pres de Hylack ce $\frac{9}{19}$ de Juin 1690.

J'AY este informe au long par le General Major Mackay des dispositions qu'il a fait des trouppes, et de ce qu'il a dessin d'entreprendre.   Et autant que je puis juger par la carte, ne cognoissent point le paiis, je croi que sa disposition est bonne, et ce qu'il pretend d'entreprendre est faisable; c'est pourquoy il sera necessaire que vous luy donnies toutte l'assistance possible, et corespondies avec luy en tout ce qui concerne les affaires militaires.   Et puis qu'il les a en main il faudra n'avoir au qu'un reserve avec luy en tout ce qui peut dependre de cett affaire. La derniere lettre que j'ay eu de vous a este du 30 du passe avent mon depart de Kensington d'ou aparament vous aures receu de vostre fils et Sr. W. Lockart divers depesches.   Et aye este informe que j'ay fait arreste Sr. J. Cocheran et Fergeson.   J'espere que vous poures envoyer au plustost des informations necessaire pour les faire transporter en Ecosse sans quoy je crains que selon les loix d'Angletere on sera obligé de les relacher.   J'espere que vous poures bien tost mestre fin a cette cession du Parlement car il me semble pas qu'il convient qu'ils demeurent plus long temps assemble pendent que je seres en Irelande vers ou je m'embarque demain s'il plait au bon Dieu, et espere d'y recevoir de vos nouvelles vous asseurent tousjours de la continuation de mon amitie.   WILLIAM R.

Apres avoir escrit cette lettre je recois la vostre par Castaers qui m'a informe au long dont vous l'avies charge et surquoy il vous faira savoir mes intensions, a quoy j'adjouteres que je suis de mesme sentiment a l'egard de l'expedition de Mackay ainsi que je vous ay escrit icy dessus estant necessaire qu'il l'execute le plus promtement qu'il sera possible.   Je suis aussi confirme en mon opinion qu'il est a present necessaire que le Parlement soit adjourne, ainsi je ne doute pas que vous ne le fassies aussi tost qu'il sera auqu'unement convenable apres que vous aures receu celle cy.   W. R.

58. QUEEN MARY, wife of KING WILLIAM THE THIRD, to GEORGE, EARL OF MELVILLE, Commissioner—That Sir William Lockhart would give him an account of affairs.

Whithall, Jully the 3d, 1690.

I RECEIVED your letter by Sir William Lockhart, as also the others by the scrupulouse persson whom I have seen three severall times to very litle purpose. He has made me promise he shall be no evidence, and has taken care to make me keep my word, for he has named no person, nor told nothing but what was known heer before. Sir William Lockhart will give you a more full acount as he has had it from me. What there is more to be done you will be able to make a better judgment upon the place, but I confess I canot be so aprehensive of the daugers. God has of his goodness revealed enough to make us stand upon our garde, and if it please him to blese the king with successe, I dont dout but all may in time be well setled. I know you will joyn with me heartely in those prayers, and you may be assured I will help you all I can from heauce.

For the Lord Comisioner.

59. PRECEPT by KING WILLIAM THE THIRD to the TOWN OF EDINBURGH to pay £3000 to George, Earl of Melville. Kensington, 15th October 1690. [Copy.]

WILLIAM R.

IT is our will and pleasure, and we doe herby authorize and require you to make payment to George, Earle of Melvill, our sole secretary of state for that our ancient kingdome, the principall soum of thrie thousand pounds sterling, with annuallrent and expences addebted to us by our good toun of Edinburgh, conform to an bond granted by you in name of the said good toun to the commissioners of theasurie for our use. Aud these presents, with his receipt, and your own bond, shall be sufficient exoneration and discharge to you. And for your farther satisfaction, we doe authorize and require the commissioners of our theasurie, or any of them who has the said bond in their custodie, to deliver up the same to you upon payment to him of the sums contained therin. Given at our court at Kensentoun the 15 day of October 1690, and of our reigne the second year.

60. WARRANT by KING WILLIAM THE THIRD to the COMMISSIONERS OF THE
    TREASURY to pay to George, Earl of Melville, the sum of £500 as half
    a year's pension. Kensington, 8th December 1690.

WILLIAM R.

IT is our will and pleasure, and wee do hereby authorise and require you, out of the first and readiest of our rents, revenues, customes, and casualities whatsoever of that our ancient kingdom, furthwith to pay, or cause to be paid, unto our right trusty and right welbeloved cousin and councellor George, Earle of Melvill, our principall and sole secretary of state for that our kingdom, or any having his order, the sum of five hundred pounds sterline money, as one halfe yeares pension due at Mertimass last. For doing whereof, theso presents (together with a receipt from the said George, Earle of Melvill, or any having his order as aforesaid) shall be to you, and all others respectively who may be therein any way concerned, particularly to the lords and others, auditors of your accompts, for allowing the same, a sufficient warrant. Given at our court at Kensingtoun the 8th day of December 1690, and of our reigne the second year.   W. R.

To the lords commissioners of our treasury of our ancient kingdom of Scotland.

61. QUEEN MARY OF MODENA, wife of King James the Seventh [to SIR JAMES
    MONTGOMERY ?]—Mr. Jones had given her an account of the whole affair.

March the 23 [circa 1690].

SINCE my last, which i hope you will haue receiued long befor this, i haue seen Mr. Jones, who has giuen me an exact account of the wholle affaire. i am intirely satisfyed with him, and heard with a great deel of plaisur all he had to say, in whicch ther is nothing mor satisfactory to me then my beeing from many circum-stances fully persuaded that i haue to do with men of honor, who, notwithstanding the consent the king may giue to what is demanded of him, will be as tender of giuing away what so intirely belongs to him as he himself could be : for i cannot beleeue it either the honor or intrest of those who, for succh singular seruices and demonstrations of theyr capacitys, will deserue and may expect the chief trusts in the gouernment, to desire or endeauor the depriuing or abridging what has been once possessed by that power they now so far expose theyr liues and fortunes to establish; and tho' i haue endeauored by my letters to conuince the king that to enable you to serue him, it is necessary he should condescend to what is proposed (as far as he can in conscience do, for i would not for all the world see him go the least step beyond it), yett i do confidently expect and intirely relye upon your good husbandry of what you well know is so valuable for its beeing so absolutely necessary both to a king and his ministers, in the gouernment of a people so inclined to trouble and change as you are in, and even mor aduantageous to them then their owne unsettled wishes could make it. i haue also consulted our friend hear, who is uery well satisfyed, and will do his part in performing what is required of him. i relye intirely both upon your seruing the king and preseruing him that power whicch realy makes him so, and tho i do once mor heartily recomend it to you, yett dont in the least doubt of you, but firmly beleeue you will acte like men of honor in the performance of this great and good worke, whicch once don will make us all happy, and putt me in a condition of shewing you and all the world the esteem i haue for you, and of making good all the assurances i haue sent you by Mr. Jones, to whom i referre myself, hoping he will be with you soon after this.   MARIA R.

62. THE SAME to THE SAME.—£5000 ready for her correspondents, etc.

May the first [circa 1690].

THO i hope you will haue had two of my letters long befor this, and that i think it uery possible for Mr. Jones to be with you by this time, hauing heard from the person he was sent to that he was ready to dispatche him towards you on the 9 of April, yett i resolue to writ to you again, thinking it necessary that you should know what i haue don hear in your affaire, and full as necessary that you should let me know how it gos on with you. i am therfor a sending this bearer to you, to who's honesty as well as memory you may trust intirely, for i haue had the experience of both, and it is uery conuenient to make him learn all by heart when one dares not give him letters.

i hope Mr. Jones will haue brought you satisfaction from that syde wher he was last, and from this i send you all that the care and industry of a willing person could gett for you from one who is now upon the necessity of defending himself against all the world, therfor you must not wonder if you gett not at present so mucch as you deserue uor, i fear, so mucch as you may want, but pray beleeue that it was not possible to get mor at this uery time or i would haue got it, and make this go as far as you can.

In the first place i haue sent orders to the other syde of the water to haue fiue thousand pounds ready for you wheneuer you shall send for it to your friends ther, or to a friend i haue sent thither, who's name this bearer has order to tell you, and desire you from me to keep a correspondence with him, he beeing a person of great prudence and intirely trusted by me and my two great friends. He fully knows our minds, and can keep a secret so well that i haue trusted him with your concerns, and you need not haue any sorte of reserue with him. i ordered him befor he went from hence to find som way of sending to you as soon as he getts on the other syde, whicch if he dos you may hear from him befor this can com to you, but i dare not trust to that, and therfor i am trying this other way, beeing resolued to spare no peines nor any thing els, for persons that i haue reason to beleeue are now taking all the peines imagineable for me and mine.

But to go on with my account, i must tell you that besides the fiue thousand pounds on the other syde whicch i will endeauer to make ten thousand in a short time if you shall want it, i haue hear ready ten thousand pounds mor with as many arms and amunition as this great friend could spare for you at this nick of time, whicch he giues you most heartily, and will be ready to giue mor hearafter if this prooue not sufficient: For i am persuaded, and you will fiud it, that he is uery sincere in his friendship to us, and that he desires nothing mor then to resettle his great friend, a glory whicch i do uerily beleeue God Almighty reserues for him, and will lett you haue a great share in it.   By the last letters i receiued i find you haue already begun to do your parts and long to know what successe you haue had in the first attempt.   i hope you will find som way of letting me hear from you, and aboue all it is necessary you lett me know as soon as euer you haue declared yourselues to whicch place you will haue me sent this succor that will be ready shipt for you at Dunkirke, but cannot be sent till you are ready for it, and till i know wher it may be landed with safety.   All therfor that is to be don at this time depends on your syde, for on mine i shall not loose a moment in sending to you after i hear from you, and when all things are ripe with you and well disposed on the other syde, then this friend has promised to send ouer our great friend wher i hope he will soon be in a condition of rewarding those that haue had the first and greatest part in making him happy, and for my owne part, i shall make it my businesse to conuince you and all the world that i am not capable of beeing ungratefull, and after beeing happy myself yett i shall haue no quiett till i see them happy that haue made me so.

MARIA R.

63. KING WILLIAM THE THIRD to the COMMISSION OF THE GENERAL ASSEMBLY OF THE CHURCH OF SCOTLAND—To admit ministers who had served under Episcopacy. The Hague, 13th February 1690-1. [Copy.]

WILLIAM R.

RIGHT reverend and welbeloved, whereas there has bein humble application made to us by severall ministers for themselvs and others who lately served under episcopacy in that our antient kingdom, we have thought fitt, as well for the good and advantage of that church as the publick justice and welfare of the nation, and the interest of our government, to signifie our pleasure to you that yow make no distinction of men otherwayes well qualified for the ministry who are willing to join with yow in the akuowledgement of, and submission to the goverment both in church and state, as it is now by law established, though they have formerly conformed to the law introducing Episcopacy, and that yow give them no vexation or disturbance for that cause or upon that head.

And in regaird many of these ministers were turned out summarly without any sentence or order of law, if such shall be called to be ministers of any vacant congregations, by the plurality of the heretors and elders, we judge it reasonable that yow do admit and receive them (where ther is no other just cause to the contrary) without making any difficulty.

Whereas some of these ministers do complean of severity and hardships, by severall sentences pronounced against them, we think fitt to give yow this opportunity to review what cases shall be brought before yow, that yourselves may give such just redress as the matter requires before we take any further nottice of these complaints.

We doe assure yow that we will protect yow, and mentain the government in the church in that our kingdom by Presbitery, without suffering any invasions to be made upon it, and therefore we do expect that yow will avoid all occasion of division or resentment, and cordially unite with those who agree with yow in the doctrine of the Protestant religion, and owne that confession of faith which the law has established as the standart of the communion of that church. And it is our pleasure during our absence out of Brittain, and till we give our furder directions, that yow proceed to no more processes or any other business, but dispose yourselves intirely to find out the best means for healing and reconcileing differences, and apply yourselves to give impartial redress upon any complaints that shall be offered to yow against sentences already past; that we be not obleidged to give ourselves any further trouble theranent; and so we bid yow heartily farewell.   Given at our court at the Hague upon the 13 day of February 169⅞, and of our reign the second year.—By his Majestys command,

JO. DALRYMPLE.

    To the right reverend and our welbeloved the ministers and elders commissioners of the General Assembly of the Church of our antient kingdom of Scotland.

64. ATTESTATION by QUEEN MARY, wife of KING WILLIAM THE THIRD—That a Letter reprieving John Macmillan was written by her direction. *Circa* 1691.

MY LORDS,—The Queens Majesty having received and considered the humble petition presented to her by Marion Charters, wife to John M'Millan, shewing that her said husband was sentenced by the lords of justiciary to dy for the slaughter of Thomas Grierson of Bargalton, and likewise humbly supplicating that her Majesty might (for the reasons therein mentioned) be graciously pleased to cause write to your lordships to grant her said husband a reprive untill some short time after the kings returne: Her Majesty, upon consideration thereof, and of the deplorable condition of the petitioner, and her being at so great distance from her husband, and five small children, was graciously pleased, by her royall command, to appoint me to signify, by a letter to your lordships, that it was her Majestys opinion, you should grant a reprive to the said John M'Millan untill the king's further pleasure be known therein. By which her Majesty doth not intend to delay justice against him, if it be acknowledged by himselfe, or proved by others, that he is guilty of any other crime deserving death by the law of the kingdom. I am   .

    Wee do hereby declare that George, Earle of Melvill, our secretary of state for the kingdome of Scotland, did draw, subscrib, and send away the above letter by our speciall command, and according to our direction.   MARIE R.

65. KING WILLIAM THE THIRD to the COMMISSION OF THE CHURCH OF SCOTLAND—Concerning Episcopal ministers.   Aprebaux, 15th June 1691. [Copy.]

WILLIAM R.

RIGHT reverend and well beloved, we greet yow well. By the letter presented to us by Mr. John Law and Mr. David Blair, ministers, your two commissioners,

we doe perceive yow have sufficiently understood our intention containd in our
letter directed to yow from the Hague; and we are well pleased with what
yow wrote, both as to your own unanimous inclinations to redress these that may
be eased, and to unite with such of the clergy who have served under Episcopacy, and fallen neither under the qualification of our act of parliament nor the
termes of our letter; and that yow are sufficiently instructed by the Generall
Assembly to receive them, from all which we doe expect a speedy and happy
success.   And that yow will be so frank and charitable in that matter, that we
cannot doubt there will be so great a progress made in that union betuext yow
before our returne into Brittain, that we shall find then no cause to continue that
stop which at present we see necessar, that neither yow nor no other commission
or church meeting doe meet in any proces or business that may concerne the
purging out the Episcopall ministers.   But we doe not restraine yow as to other
matters relative to the church or yourselves, nor did we ever intend to protect
any in the ministry who were truely scandalous, erroneous, or supinely negligent ;
and therefore we proposed the Confession of Faith as the standart of the C. communion, which takes off the suspition of error.   If any who are truely scandalous,
insufficient, or supinely negligent, shall apply either by themselves or by others,
tho they were willing to acknowledge our authority, and join with yow, yet we
do not oblige yow to receive such.   And in that case, where there is just cause,
yow may proceid to a fair and impartiall enquiry in order to their being received
with you into the C. church, but not in relation to the turning them out of their
benefices or ministry, as the act of parliament has left them to our furder order.
We doe not doubt of the sincere performance of what yow have so fairly promised
in your letter, wherby you will best recommend yourselves to us, and answere the
trust reposed on you by the act of parliament.   And so we bid you heartily
farewell.   Given at our court at Aprebaux the 15th June, and of our reign the
third year.—By his Majesties command.   JO. DALRYMPLE.

66. KING WILLIAM THE THIRD to the COMMISSIONERS OF THE TREASURY—
    Directing them to give Lord Lovat a Lieutenant-Colonel's pay. Kensing-
    ton, 7th February 1695.

WILLIAM R.
IT is our will and pleasure since wee haue granted to the Lord Lovat a lieutenant
colonells act, and for other reasons moving us therto, that the said Lord Lovat
have a lieutenant colonells pay. Wee do therfore require you to order the same to
be duely payed to him from the date of the said act out of the fonds destined for

the payment of our forces. For the doing of which this shall be your warrant.
Given at our court at Kensington the 7th day of February 1695, and of our
reigne the 6th year.—By his Majesty's command.

J. JOHNSTOUN.

To the lords commissioners of our treasury of our ancient kingdom of Scotland.

67. WARRANT to DAVID, EARL OF LEVEN, to set the Earl of Breadalbane at
liberty. Kensington, 16th December 1695.

WILLIAM R.

IT is our will and pleasure that you give orders to the next commanding officer
of our castle of Edinburgh to set at liberty John, Earle of Breadalbane, now
prisoner there, for doing wherof this shall be your warrant. Given at our court
at Kensington the 16th day of December 1695, and of our reign the 7th year.—
By his Majesty's command.   J. JOHNSTOUN.

To David, Earle of Levin, constable and governour of our castle of Edinburgh.

68. JOACHIM FREDERICK of Holstein, [address wanting], recommending
the bearer.

Norbourg ce 3me Fevrier 1697.

MILORD,—Le porteur de cette presente ayant rapporte la protection que vous luy
avès accordè en faveur de ce qui sest reclamè sujet de Son Altesse, mon frere, je
prens la libertè de vous en remercier deuement par ces lignes comme cecy est un
effect de l'amitie que vous aves toujours eu pour notre maison. J'espere que vous
luy accorderes votre faveur dans la suitte ; je suis ravy en mon particulier de trower
des occasions de vous pouvoir assurer de mes devoirs, et je seray entierement
content si je pourray executer vos commandements dans ces pais affin de vous
pouvoir assurer que je suis veritablement,—Milord, Votre tres-humble et tres-
obeissant serviteur,   JOACHIM FRIDERICH, D. de S. Holstein.

69. WARRANT by KING WILLIAM THE THIRD to DAVID, EARL OF LEVEN, to give two pieces of ordnance to the Earl of Argyll. Loo, 22d August 1700.

WILLIAM R.

WHEREAS the lords of our privy council, in pursuance of our letter to them of the 29th day of April last, did order you to deliver up to the Earle of Argyll two peices of ordnance lying in our castle of Edinburgh belonging to him, it is now our will and pleasure that you accordingly give up to the said earle the saids two peices of ordnance, for doing wherof this, with the order from our privy council aforesaid, and the said earle his receipt of them, shall be to you a sufficient warrant. Given at our court at Loo the 22th of August 1700, and of our reign the 12th year.—By his Majesty's command.   RO. PRINGLE.

   To David, Earle of Leven, constable and governour of our castle of Edinburgh.

SEVEN LETTERS from the PRINCESS SOPHIA, ELECTRESS OF HANOVER, to DAVID, EARL OF LEVEN.

   70. (1) Expressing pleasure at the honour he had acquired.

A Hanover, le $\frac{20 \text{ Fevrie}}{2 \text{ de Mars}}$ 1691.

MONSIEUR,—Je tiens a bonheur, que vous voules bien m'attribuer vne partie de vostre fortune. Mais ie suis pourtant persuadee qu'un roy de tant de disernment comme le Roy Guillaume auroit tousiour paie a vostre merite et a vostre nessance ce que vous estoit deu sans que ie vous eusse recommende a Mr l'Electeur de Brandeburg. Cependant il est fort obligant pour moy que vous voules bien m'auoir quelque obligation de ma bonne volonte et de la part que j'ay tousiours pris en toute que vous regard. Ie vous assure que la gloire que vous vous este acquis ma fait beaucoup de plesir, dont les gazettes ont este remplies. Mais j'ay este malheureuxse dans la perte de mes deux fils auquels la guerre d'Hongrie a coute la vie. Lanne passee je perdis le Prince Charle, et auan[t] quelle estoit acheuee le Prince Auguste, ce qui m'accable de douleur. Ie crois que vous me plaindres et que vous continueres tousiours votre affection pour moy et pour ma maison, dont ie

seres for[t] reconnoisante et demeureres tousiour,—Monsieur, vostre tres-affectionee a vous servir,   SOPHIE, P. PALA.
A Monsieur Monsieur le Conte Leuen, a Londre.[1]

71. (2) Death of King William—Her own Scottish descent.

A Hanouer le 21 d'Auril 1702.

MY LORD,—J'ay tousiour este si persuadée de vostre amitie que ie n'en ay pas
doute, quoi que vous ne m'ayez point donné de marque de vostre souuenir depuis
longtemps. Ie suis fachée qu'un triste suiect en a este la cause, car i'ay tousiour
souhaite tont ce qui vous pouuoit faire du plesir. Uostre affliction a este for[t]
grande, aussi de la perte de nostre grand Roy : mais comme il semble que la presente
Reyne veut bien suiuer ces trasses, et mesme le surpasser dans l'affection du peuple,
il faut s'en consoller. On me mende d'Angleterre que sa Maieste veut faire ce quelle

[1] In a list of these letters, preserved in the
Melville Charter-chest, there are mentioned
four others of which no originals have been
found. They are described in the following words:—"During the persecution in
Scotland before the Revolution, the Earl of
Melvil and the Earl of Leven, his son, being
very obnoxious to the then prevailing party,
were obliged to fly from their own country into
Holland. The Earl of Leven went afterwards
to Berlin to push his fortune in the military
way, and applied to Princess Sophia, Electrice
of Hanover, to interpose her good offices with
her daughter and son-in-law, the Electoral
Prince and Princess of Brandenburg, that
they might intercede with the old Elector, so
as his lordship might be advanced in his service. This appears from—
"Letter 1st. Wrote to his lordship at Berlin
in a very obliging manner by the Princess
Sophia, dated Herenhausen, 23 June 1686.
"Letter 2d. This application had a very
good effect. For September 19, 1687, my lord
writes to the electoral prince, then at Cassel,
that the elector had promoted him to be a
collonel, which the prince expresses himself
highly pleased with in a letter to my lord,
wrote from Cassel the 25th September 1687.
"Letter 3d. Wrote to my lord by the Prince

of Orange, from the Hague, the 17th of May
1688, and delivered to him by Mr. Bentinck
(afterwards Earl of Portland), confirms what
my lord has frequently told me of his having
been honoured by that prince to negotiate
affairs at the court of Berlin previous to the
Revolution. This great prince had too much
of the taciturne of his great-grandfather to
commit things of importance to writing. So
he refers my lord with regard to all particulars to Mr. Bentinck. 'En vous asseurant,
qu'en toute sorte d'occasions je vous temoig-
nerai par les effets combien veritablement
je suis votre serviteur.' Sign'd G. PRINCE
D'ORANGE.
"Letter 4th. In August 1688 my lord had
wrote to the Prince of Orange of a proposal
made to him by the Elector of Brandenburgh
to raise a regiment of his countrymen, which
the prince approves of (in his letter from the
Hague of the 19th of August 1688), and bids
him accept ; tho' at the same time, he says
he will find it hard to get a sufficient number
of private men, but as for officers he will find
abundance disperst in different services.
'Cest ce qui j'ai aussi dit a Monsieur votre
Pere qui m'en a parlé. Je suis toujours,
Monsieur, votre très-affectionné a vous servir.'
Signed G. PRINCE D'ORANGE."

pourra pour accorder les deux nations, et quelle a enuoie pour cela le Duc de Quins-
bery en Escosse.   Si cela ce fait ie crois qu'on y aura les mesme sentiments pour
cette maison, qu'on l'a en Angleterre, et ie conte beaucoup sur l'affection des
Escosois, puis que ie suis du sang d'Escosse.   Ie ne scay pour qui pourroit estre
l'autre parti, puis qu'on a tousiour este dans nostre peis fort contre les Catho-
liques; mais vous me le poures dire librement, et enuoier vos lettres au Baron
Schutz, a Londre, enuoie de cette maison, a qui iadresseres celle cy, en vous con-
iurant de croire que i'aures tousiour une tres-grande estime pour vostre merite, et
aussi pour Mr le Conte de Meluil, vostre pere.   Faite luy des remercements de
ma part de l'affection qu'il me tesmoigne, et croie moy tousiour,—My lord, vostre
tres-affectionée a vous randre seruice,

72. (3) Inquiring as to the sentiments of the Duke of Hamilton.

A Lutzenburg proche de Berlin, le 15 de Juliet 1702.
My Lord,—Je n'ay reseu qu'icy la vostre de 10 de Juin.   Sans cela ie suis trop
sensible a l'affection que vous me tesmoignes pour tarder si longtems a y respon-
dre, et vous en tesmoigner ma iuste reconnoissance.   Vous ne me mendez pas a
quel dessein le Duc de Hamilton et ses adherans prenent des pretextes a contre-
carer le parlement, si le Duc de Hamelton est pour le Prince de Gale, ou s'il veut
estre roy luy mesme.   Il me semble puis que la Reyne cousant au gouuernement
ecclesiastique du royaume qu'on na pas suicct d'estre mal contant de sa Maiesté,
et que celon son intantion les Anglois ce gouuerneront d'une maniere plus humaine
enuer les Escossois qu'ils ne l'ont fait iusqu'a present.   On m'a represente my
Lord Quinsburay comme un homme d'un grand merite.   Puis qu'il cet souuenu de
moy fort obligement au Baron Schutis, ie vous prie de luy faire compliment de
ma part, et de me croire tousiour,—My lord, vostre tres-affectionée a vous seruir,
SOPHIE ELECTRISE.

A Monsieur Monsieur le Conte Leuen a Edenburg Castle.

73. (4) Compliments with Baron Schutz.

A Herenhausen, le 12 de Juin 1703.

MY LORD,—Je me sairs de l'occasion du retour du Baron Schutz pour vous assurer que les marque[s] d'amitie que vous m'auez fait parroitre ont este receu de moy avec toute la reconnaissance possible, et que j'ay tousiours les mesme sentiments que je dois avoir pour vne personne de votre probite. Mais, my lord, il semble que je ne suis point a la mode en Escosse, et que dans le dernie[r] parlement on ne ce souuient pas que je suis au monde. Quoi qui arriue vous deuez tousiour croire que a suis,—My lord, vostre tres-affectionee a vous servir,

SOPHIE ELECTRISE.

Mon fils, l'Electeur, m'a charge de milles compliments et amities pour vous, car vostre obligant souuenir luy estoit fort agreable.

A Monsieur Monsieur le Conte de Leuen.

74. (5) Thanks for his conduct in Parliament.

A Herenhausen, le 29 d'Aioust 1704.

MY LORD,—J'ay difere de vous tesmoigner ma parfaitte reconnoisance de l'affections que vous continues a tesmoigner a moy et a ma maison en respondent a vostre tres obligante lettre, de peur de vous dire tousiour vne mesme chose. Mais a present, my lord, vous me pourries croire ingrate si ie tardois plus longtems a vous remercier de l'effect que vous en auez fait parroitre dans la derniere session du Parlement, quoi que cela n'ait pas eu tout le succes que vous en auez souhaite. Ie ne laisse point de vous en estre tout autant obligée, vous assurant que toutes les occasions me siront tousiour infiniment chere par les qnelles ie vous pourres tesmoigner combien ie suis,—My lord, vostre tres-affectionée a vous seruir,

SOPHIE ELECTRISE.

J'ay eu le plesir de voir icy M. Coqborn qui ma parvu vn fort honnet home.

P.S.—Mon fils, l'Electeur, me charge, my lord, de vous faire mille compliments et amities de sa part.

A Monsieur Monsieur le Conte de Leuen.

75. (6) Congratulations on his appointment to Edinburgh Castle.

A Hanouer, le 22 de 9bre (Novembre) 1704.

MY LORD,—A mon retour du voiage que i'auois fait a Lutzburg aupres de la Reyne de Prusse, ma fille, i'ay apris auec beaucoup de plesir que vous estes rentre

A Hanouer le 22 de 9bre 1704

my Lord
                             a mon
retour du voiage que i'auois fait a
Lutsbury aupres de la Reyne de Pruce
ma fille, i'ay apris auec beaucoup de
pleure que vous esties rentré dans votre
premie poste a estre gouuerneur du chantau
d'Edenbourg dont ie vous felicite de tout
mon coeur, et qu'il a pleu a la Reyne
de vous donner cette marque de son Estime
et que s Mte connoit auisi bien votre merite
que moy qui serois raneje de vous pouuoir
montrer par des seruices a quel poin ie
suis
my Lord

                       Votre tres affectionée et
                       vous seruir
                          Sophie Electrice

A Monsieur

Monsr le Comte de Leuen

a Edenbourg

J'ay eté trés sensible, Mylord, à la lettre, que vous m'avez écrite, et aux asseurances, qu'elle contient de votre affection pour moy. Je vous entiendray bon conte, et Je seray tres-aise de pouvoir vous marquer l'estime, et la consideration tres-particuliere, que j'ay pour vous, et combien je suis, Mylord, votre affectionné

L'Electeur de Brunsvic

Hannovre ce 4.e Aougst 1704.

dans nostre premie[r] poste a estre gouerneur du chautau d'Edenbourg, dont ie vous felicite de tout mon coeur, et qu'il a pleu a la Reyne de vous donner cette marque de son estime, et que Sa Majeste connoit aussi bien vostre merite que moy qui serois rauye de vous pouuoir montrer par des seruices a quel point ie suis, —My lord, vostre tres-affectionée a vous seruir,

SOPHIE ELECTRISE.

A Monsieur Monsieur le Conte de Leuen a Edenburg.

76. (7) Marriage of the Prince Elector.

A Hanouer le 27 de 9bre 1705.

MY LORD,—Ce m'est vn plaisir et uon pas vne incommodite de receuoir des marques si obligantes de vostre affection comme il vous plait de me tesmoigner pour moy et pour ma maison en prenent part a l'heureux mariage de mon petit fils, le Prince Electoral, dont ie vous remersie de tout mon coeur, et dois vous dire que nous croyons desia, que nostre Princesse Electorale est grosse si bien qu'apparrament on ne menquera pas de successeurs de ce coste icy, si tout le monde estoit de vostre sentiment et de celuy de my lord, vostre pere.   Mon fils, L'Electeur, m'a for[t] chargé de compliments pour vous deux, et de vous tesmoigner sa reconnoisence des bontes que vous auez pour luy.   Il est de mon sentiment a souhaiter des occasions de faire voir l'estime qu'il fait de l'amitie que vous luy tesmoignes tout deux, et moy aussi a faire parroitre que ie suis tout a fait,—My lord, vostre tres-affectionée a vous seruir,   SOPHIA ELECTRISE.

77. GEORGE-LEWIS, ELECTOR OF BRUNSWICK, afterwards KING GEORGE THE FIRST, to THE SAME—His esteem for Lord Leven.

Hannovre ce 4° Aougst 1704.

J'AY eté tres-sensible, my lord, a la lettre, que vous m'avez ecrite, et aux asseurances qu'elle contient de votre affection pour moy.   Je vous entiendray bon conte, et je seray tres-aise de pouvoir vous marquer l'estime, et la consideration tres-particuliere, que j'ay pour vous, et combien je suis,—My lord, votre affectionné,

L'ELECTEUR DE BROUNSUIC.

78. QUEEN ANNE to DAVID, EARL OF LEVEN—For a draft to Lord Mark Kerr's Regiment. Windsor, 29th March 1706.

RIGHT trusty and well beloved cousin and councellor, we greet yow well. Whereas we have given commission to our right trusty and well beloved Lord Mark Kerr to raise a regiment of foot in that our ancient kingdom, and have ordered our privy council there to give him all incouragement and assistance ussuall in the like occasions; but in regaird it is necessary for our service that the said regiment be compleat and transported abroad, sooner than a regiment all of new men can be levied, we therfor think fit that you cause a draught to be made of good and sufficient men out of our foot regiments and independent companies in that our kingdom, that is out of our regiment of guards, two men each company, being therty two men, all to be imployed as serjeants and corporalls in this new regiment; out of the three regiments commanded by Major Generall Maitland, the Lord Strath[n]aver, and the Laird of Grant, younger, seven men a company, and eighteen out of each of the three independant companies. And you are to deliver them to the said Lord Mark Kerr, at the town of Berwick upon Tweed, upon the first day of May next, for each of which he is to pay three pounds sterling per man. And you are to give strict orders that these several regiments and companies be recruited to their full numbers against the fifteenth day of June following, so that the strength of our forces may not be thereby diminished : For doing wherof this shall be your warrant. And so we bid you heartily farewell. Given at our court at Windsor Castle the 29th day of March 1706, and of our reign the 5th year.—By her Majestys command.   MAR.

To our right trusty and well beloved cousin and councellor, David, Earle of Leven, commander in cheif of our forces of our ancient kingdom of Scotland.

79. THE SAME to THE SAME—Appointing a Convoy for the Draft. Kensington, 15th April 1706.
ANNE R.
RIGHT trusty and well beloved cousin and councellor, we greet you well. Whereas we have thought it necessary for our service to grant a commission to

Lord Mark Kerr to raise a regiment of foot in our ancient kingdom of Scotland, and by our royall letter to you of the 29th of March last, we did, for the more speedy compleating of the said regiment, give orders that you should make a draught of three hundred men out of our standing forces, and to deliver them to the said Lord Mark Kerr at Berwick the first day of May next; these are therfor to authorise and require you to appoint such troops of dragoons or detachments of them as you shall think necessary, to guard the said draughts to Berwick, at which place we have appointed the governour therof to receive them. You are to order the said draughts to march in such numbers as you shall judge most convenient for the country, and securest from giving them any opportunity to desert: For doing all which this shall be your warrant. So we bid you heartily farewell. Given at our court at Kensington the 15th day of Aprile 1706, and of our reign the 5th year.—By her Majestys command.

LOUDOUN.

To our right trusty and well beloved cousin and councellor, David, Earle of Leven, commander-in-cheif of our forces in our ancient kingdom of Scotland.

80. WARRANT by QUEEN ANNE to DAVID, EARL OF LEVEN, for delivering a piece of ordnance to John, Duke of Argyll. Kensington, 28th January 1706-7.

ANNE R.

WHEREAS by warrant under the hand of our royall brother, the late King William of blessed memory, you was ordered to give up to the deceast Archbald, Duke of Argyll, two peices of ordnance lying in our castle of Edinburgh belonging to him, and being informed that one of these peices is not yet delivered, it is now our will and pleasure that you cause the said peice of ordnance to be given up to our right trusty and intirely beloved cousin and councellor, John, now Duke of Argyll, or any having his order. For doing wherof this shall be your warrant. Given at our court at Kinsington the 28th day of January 170$\frac{6}{7}$, and of our reign the 5th year.—By her Majesty's command.

DAVID NAIRNE.

To David, Earle of Leven, constable and governour of our castle of Edinburgh.

81. INSTRUCTIONS to DAVID, EARL OF LEVEN, in reference to an apprehended
invasion. Keusington, 4th March 1707-8.

ANNE R.

INSTRUCTIONS to our right trusty and well beloved cousin and councellor, David,
Earle of Leven, lieutenant generall and commander in cheif of our militia,
and of all our other forces in that part of our kingdom of Great Brittain
called Scotland.

1. You are to repair to Scotland with all convenient diligence, and to take
the advice of our privy council in all things you shall judge necessary for preserving the peace of that part of our united kingdom.

2. And whereas we have intelligence that there are preparations at Dunkirk
for invading that part of our kingdom of Great Brittain, you are to oppose their
landing as much as you can, and in case they shall laud, you are to hinder as
much as possible our subjects from joining them, and to fall upon and disperse
any who shall tumultuously rise in arms and endeavour to join them.

3. You are to make such a disposition of the troops as you shall judge most
for our service in the present juncture.

4. You are to take care to put Edinburgh Castle in such a posture of defence
as your time will allow, and to provid provisions for the garrison for three
months, and to advise with the other governours of garrisons, that they be in
like manner provided, and put in an order of defence.

5. You are to dispose of the ammunition you are to receive to the garrisons
and troops as you shall judge most for our service.

6. You are to apply to our privy council in Scotland for giving the necessary
orders for providing of horses both for the baggage and for the train of artillery,
in case you shall be obliged to take the feilds.

7. You are impowered to call councils of war as oft as you shall think fit,
and to take their advice in any matter of difficulty.

8. You are to advertise us from time to time, either by express or the
ordinary packet, of the posture of affairs there, and of what intelligence you
shall receive of the designs and condition of the enemy, and obey such further
instructions as we shall think fit to give therein.

9. You are, upon the first appearance of any squadron of French ships upon
the coast, to send to Ireland to   to advertise him thereof,
who has orders to send troops to your assistance upon such advertisement.

Given at our court at Kensington the 4th day of March 1707-8, and of our
reign the sixth year.—By her Majestys command.   MAR.

82. QUEEN ANNE to the PRIVY COUNCIL—The apprehended invasion.
Kensington, 8th March 1707-8.   [Copy.]

ANNE R.

RIGHT trusty, etc., Wee did, by our letter of the 25th of February last, acquaint yow with the intelligence wee had of an intended invasion on some part of our kingdom of Great Brittain, and with our royall pleasure on that occasion wee doubt not but yow have used the outmost care pursuant to our commands. We have since further confirmation of our enemies designs. The pretended Prince of Wales is at Dunkirk with some battallions of French and Irish Papists ready to embark for Scotland; and our enemies give out that they have invitations from some of our subjects there. Wee are verry hopefull that this desperrate attempt will, by the blissing of God on our arms and councills, be disapointed and turn'd to the confusion of all concern'd in it. But that nothing be omitted on our part for preventing the leist danger which threattens our people, wee have emitted a proclamation, by advice of our privy councill of Great Brittain, which wee herewith send yow; and wee do require yow to cause the same be published att all places needfull, as proclamations of our ,privy council in Scotland have been published.

Wee think it necessary that the landlords in the Highlands, and chiftains of clanns, be called to Edinburgh to give the security appointed by law for preserving the peace and order, and wee do require yow forthwith to do the same. Wee do again recommend to yow to get intelligence of the designs of our enemies or ill affected people there, and to give present direction for putting our forts, garrisons, and magazines in a good posture of defence, and what shall be expended towards these ends by your warrant shall be repaid, for which wee have already given orders.

Wee take this occasion to lett yow know that our fleet is now at sea, and much encreased since our last. The Dutch fleet is in great forwardness, and both are so disposed that our enemies cannot reasonably hope to escape an engagement. Our troops from Ireland and Flanders, which wee mentioned in our last, are ready to embark on transport shipps provided in those places with all necessaries for that service. The troops from England are all posted in the best way for the releife of our people in Scotland, if our enemies shall have the boldness to pursue their design.

Wee have dispatched the Earle of Leven from hence to command our forces there, and given him such instructions as wee judg'd necessary on this occasion, to whom yow will give your advice, assistance, and due encouragement.

Wee expect that yow will assemble frequently in council, and use such vigour in your proceedings as has been done on like occasions formerly, which shall be acceptable to us, and may prevent the misleading of our people, and their conjunction with French and Irish Papists, the irreconcilable enemies of their religion and liberties.

Wee do also require yow to transmitt to us full and constant accounts of the state of affaires there; and not doubting of your zeal and diligence, wee bid yow heartily farewell. Given att our court att Kinsington the 8th day of March 170$\frac{7}{8}$, and of our reign the 7th year.—By her Majesties command.   MAR.

83. THE SAME to THE SAME—Apprehension of suspected persons.
Kensington, 9th March 1707-8.

ANNE R.

RIGHT trusty and right well beloved cousin and councilour, right trusty and entirely beloved cousins and councilours, right trusty and welbeloved cousins and councilours, right trusty and well beloved councilours, and trusty and well beloved councilours, we greet you well. Whereas upon the intelligence of the invasion design'd by France upon this our kingdom both housses of our parliament have address'd us to secure and apprehend what persons we have cause to suspect, and also ordered a bill to be brought in suspending the habeas corpus acts, pursuant to which address we have thought fitt to give orders and warrants to the Earl of Leven to apprehend diverse persons whom we have cause to suspect, and to bring them before us to be examined; but notwithstanding of those last words in the warrants, we have thought fit to order the said earl to present the persons, when apprehended, before you to be examined in relation to the invasion, or practices against our government, and you are hereby authorized to secure them in such prisons as you think fitt, where they are to remain untill you acquaint us thereof, and receive our further commands concerning them, for doing of which this shall be your warrant, and so we bid you heartily farewell. Given at our court at Kensington the 9th day of March 1707/8, and of our reign the 7th year.—By her Majesty's command.   MAR.

To our right trusty and right well beloved cousin and councilour, our right trusty and entirely beloved cousins and councilours, our right trusty and well beloved cousins and councilours, our right trusty and well beloved councilours, and to our trusty and well beloved councilours, James, Earl of Seafield, our chancelour, and the rest of the lords and others of our privy council of Scotland.

84. QUEEN ANNE to DAVID, EARL OF LEVEN—Sending a blank commission for
a Governor to Dumbarton Castle in the absence of the Earl of Islay.
St. James's, 16th March 1707-8.

ANNE R.

RIGHT trusty and well beloved cousin and councilour we greet you well. We think
it most necessary at this juncture that our garrisons should be provided with
sufficient officers. And considering that our right trusty and well beloved cousin
and councilour, Archibald, Earl of Ilay, governour of our castle of Dunbarton,
may be otherwise employed in our service that he cannot attend to command
that garrison ; therefore it is our will and pleasure, and we hereby authorise and
require you to make choice, with the advice of the said earl, of a proper person to
command in the castle of Dunbarton during the absence of the governour thereof.
For which end we have sign'd a commission, and left a blank to be filled up by
you with the name of the person who shall be pitch'd upon for that station. So
we bid you heartily farewell. Given at our court at St. James's, the 16th day
March 1707/8, and of our reign the 7th year.—By her Majestys command.

MAR.

To our right trusty and well beloved cousin and councilour, David, Earl of
    Leven, lievtenant general, and commander in chief of our forces in
    Scotland.

85. ORDER by QUEEN ANNE authorising Lord Leven to recruit the garrison of
Edinburgh Castle. Windsor, 18th March 1708. [Contemporary copy.]

ANNE R.

THESE are to authorize you by beat of drumm, or otherwise, to raise and receive
so many voluntcers as shall be wanting to recruit and fill up the garrison of
Edenburgh Castle, under your command, from one hundred and twenty to two
hundred private men, servants included ; and for the more speedy raising them,
to receive any such able bodyed men as shall be rais'd and levy'd to serve as
soldiers, by any of our justices of the peace, or other magistrates, and by them or
their order, deliver'd over to you, or otherwise listed by you, in pursuance of the
act of parliament for the better recruiting our land forces and marines. And all
magistrates, justices of the peace, constables, and other our officers whom it may
concern, are hereby required to be assisting to you in providing quarters, impress-

ing carriages, and otherwise, as there shall be occasion. Given at our court at Windsor this 18th day of March 1708, in the seventh year of our reign.—By her Majestys command.   R. WALPOLE.

> To our right trusty and right welbeloved cousin, David, Earl of Leven, lieutenant generall of our forces, and governor of our castle and garrison of Edenburgh, or to the officer or officers appointed by him to raise and receive volunteers and others for that garrison.

86. ORDER by QUEEN ANNE for mustering additional men to the three Regiments of Foot in North Britain.   Kensington, 3d April 1708.   [Copy.]

ANNE R.

WHEREAS we have thought fitt that our regiment of foot guards, and our three other regiments of foot in North Brittain be augmented from their present numbers, and to consist of the numbers following, viz.:—

Our regiment of foot guards, commanded by our right trusty and right welbeloved cousin, William, Marquis of Lothian, to consist of one collonel, one lievtenant collonel, one major, one chaplin, two adjutants, one quarter master, on chirurgeon and mate, one sollicitor, one drum major, one deputy marshall, and each of the sixteen companys in the said regiment to consist of one captain, one lievtenant, one ensigne, three serjeants, three corporals, two drums, and to be augmented from thirtie six to seventy private men, and two companys of granadiers of one captain, two lievtenants, and the like number of non commission officers and private men in each :

And our three other regiments of foot, commanded by our right trusty and welbeloved Collonell Alexander Grant, and our right trusty and right welbeloved cousin, William, Lord Strathnaver, and our right trusty and well beloved Major Generall Maitland, to consist of one collonel, one lievtenant collonell, one major, one chaplin, one adjutant, one quarter master, one chirurgeon and mate ; and each of the eleven companys of every of the said three regiments, of one captain, one lievtenant, one ensigne, two serjeants, three corporals, two drums, and to be augmented from twenty four to fifty nine private men in each, and the company of granadiers of each regiment to consist of one captain, two lievtenants, and the same number of none commission officers and privat men in each :

Our will and pleasure is that as any of the said additional private men fitt for service, shall be produced to you for compleating our said regiments as aforesaid, you do from time to time muster them with the additionall non commission officers into our pay and entertainment, and pass and allow them one the muster rolls untill the whole numbers shall be raised in each company and regiment. And for so doing this shall be your warrant. Given at our court at Kensington this third day of Aprile 1708, in the seventh year of our reign.—By her Majestys command.   R. WALPOLE.

87. SIMILAR WARRANT by QUEEN ANNE to DAVID, EARL OF LEVEN, as to the Horse and Dragoous. Kensington, 3d April 1708. [Copy.]

ANNE R.

WHEREAS we have thought fitt that our troops of horse guards, our troop of granadier guards, and our two regiments of dragoons in North Brittain be augmented from their present establishment to the numbers following, viz.:—

Our troop of horse guards, commanded by our right trusty and right entirely beloved cousin John, Duke of Argyle, to one captain and collonell, two lieutenants and lieutenant collonels, one cornet, one guidon, four exempts, four brigadiers, four sub-brigadiers, one chaplin, one adjutant, one serjean, four trumpeters, one gettle drumer, and from one hundred and six to one hundred and fiftie six private gentlemen :

Our troop of granadier guards, commanded by our right trusty and right wellbeloved cousin, John, Earle of Crawfoord, to one captain and collonell, one lieutenant and lieutenant collonell, one major, two lieutenants and captains, one guidon and captain, two sub-lieutenants, one chaplin, one surjeon, one adjutant, six serjeants, six corporals, four drumers, four houtbois, and from fiftie to one hundred and fourtie five private gentlemen :

And each of our regiments of dragoons to one collonel, one lieutenant collonell, one major, one chaplin, one adjutant, one surjeon, one gunsmith and servant, and the six troops of each of our said two regiments, to one captain, one lieutenant, one cornet, one quarter master, two serjeants, three corporals, two drumers, two houtbois, and from twentie four to fiftie four private men :

Our will and pleasure is that as any of the said additional men with horses fitt for service shall be produced unto you for compleating the saids severall troops and regiments to the numbers aforesaid, you do from time to time muster them in our pay and entertainment, and pass and allow them on the muster rolls untill the whole number shall be raised in each troop and regiment : And for so doing this shall be your warrand. Given at our court at Kensington this third day of Aprile 1708, in the seventh year of our reign.—By her Majestys command.   R. WALPOLE.

88. LETTER by QUEEN ANNE to DAVID, EARL OF LEVEN—Thanking him
for his good service.

Windsor, September the 1st, 1708.

I AM very much ashamed that I have not sooner returned you my thanks for all
the good services you have don me since your last going to Sco[t]land, which I
desire you would excuse, and be soe just as to beleeve me truly sensible of them.
I hope every thing is now soe quiet againe, that nothing will hinder you from
being heare at the oppening of the parliament, where I shall want the assistance
of all my freinds. You may be assured of mine in every thing that lyes in my
power, and that I shall be ready on all occassions to shew you I am sincerly your
very affectionett freind,   ANNE R.

For the Earle of Leven.

89. ORDER by QUEEN ANNE to DAVID, EARL OF LEVEN, to apprehend four
Jesuits, as stirring up sedition. St. James's, 5th May 1709.

ANNE R.

RIGHT trusty and right well beloved cousin, we greet you well. Whereas we
have received iuformation that four Jesuits, commonly called, Durham, a titulary
bishop, Father Chreichtoune, Monsieur la Fray, and Monsieur la Batt, are lately
come from France into that part of our United Kingdom called Scotland, to stir
up seditions among our liege subjects there, and upon other treasonable designs
and purposes tending to the disturbance of our peace, and subversion of our
government: Our will and pleasure is, and we do hereby authorize you, if you
judge it for our service so to do, to cause diligent search to be made for the four
persons above named, or any other disaffected persons in that our city of Edin-
bourg, or elsewhere in Scotland, particularly at the two houses called Nithery and
Dammahoy, or any other houses or places, as you shall have information, or good
cause to suspect of harbouring such disaffected persons and disturbers of our
peace and government, and of the quiet of our good and loyal subjects, and that
upon the apprehending of them, or any of them, you give such directions for the
safe keeping them, as shall be necessary, and immediately transmit an account of
your proceedings herein to one of our principal secretarys of state, that he may
lay the same before us, and receive our further pleasure therein : and for so doing
this shall be your warrant. And so we bid you heartily farewell. Given at our

Windsor Sep: ye 1st 170(?)

I am very much ashamed yt I have not
Sooner returned you my thanks for
all yr good Services you have don me
Since your last going to Scotland, wch I
desire you would excuse, & be soe Just
as to beleeve me truly Sensible of them,
I hope every thing is now soe quiet
againe, yt nothing will hinder you
from being heare at ye oppening of
the Parliament, where I shall want
yr assistance of all my freinds, you
may be assured of mine in every thing
yt lyes in my power, & yt I shall be
ready on all occasions to shew you I am
Sincerly your very affectionett freind

ANNE R

For the Earle
of Leven

court at St. James's the fifth day of May 1709, in the eig[h]th year of our reign.
—By her Majestys command.   QUEENSBERRY.

    To our right trusty and right well beloved cousin, David, Earl of Leven,
    governour of our castle of Edinbourgh, and commander in chief of our
    forces in Scotland.

    90. KING GEORGE THE FIRST, to DAVID, EARL OF LEVEN—To attend the
        King's coronation.   St. James's, 6th October 1714.

George R

RIGHT trusty and our right welbeloved cousin, we greet you well. Whereas the
20th day of this instant October is appointed for the royal solemnity of our coronation, these are to will and command you (all excuses set apart) to make your personal attendance on us, at the time above mentioned, furnished and appointed as
to your rank and quality appertaineth, there to do and perform all such services
as shall be required and belong unto you, whereof you are not to fail. And so we
bid you most heartily farewell. Given at our court at St. James's, the 6th day
of October 1714, in the first year of our reign.—By his Majestics command,
    Earl of Leven.   SUFFOLK, M.
    To the right honourable the Earl of Leven,—these.

    91. KING GEORGE THE SECOND, to SIR HUGH DALRYMPLE, President, and
        SENATORS OF THE COLLEGE OF JUSTICE, to admit Alexander, Earl of
        Leven, as a Lord of Session.   Kensington, 28th June 1734.

George R

RIGHT trusty and welbeloved, we greet you well. Understanding that there is a
place of one of the ordinary lords of our session now vacant by the resignation

of James Erskine of Grainge, Esquire, and it being requisite that a person of loyalty, learning, knowledge and experience in the laws, should be preferred thereto, to the end that in default of the ordinary number of senators of the college of justice in that part of our kingdom of Great Britain called Scotland there be no hindrance of the administration of justice. And we being well informed of the loyalty, literature and good qualifications of our right trusty and right welbeloved cousin, Alexander, Earl of Leven, and of his abilitys and willingness to serve us in that ordinary place ; therefore we have thought good to nominate and present him unto you, requiring you effectually to try, and thereafter to admit and receive him to the said ordinary place, accepting him as one of your number. And we hereby ordain him to have and enjoy all privileges thereunto belonging, with vote among you, and to be participant of your salarys, taking his oath, as use is, as you will have justice to be administered, and as you will do unto us acceptable service. So we bid you heartily farewell. Given at our court at Kensington, the twenty eighth day of June 1734, in the eighth year of our reign. —By his Majesty's command,   T. HOLLES NEWCASTLE.

To our right trusty and welbeloved, and our trusty and welbeloved, Sir Hugh Dalrymple, president of our college of justice, and the rest of the senators thereof.

Edinburgh, 16th July 1734.

Enter'd in the kings remembrancers office in exchequer.

p. W. BOWLES, Depty. K⁸ Remr.

Enter'd in the auditors office, the 16th Jully 1734.

p. JOHN PHILP, D. Aud^r.

92. CHARLES, PRINCE OF WALES, Regent of Scotland, etc.—To protect the house of Lady Dirleton. Holyroodhouse, 1st October 1745. [A printed form— names and dates being filled in.]

CHARLES, Prince of Wales, etc., regent of Scotland, England, France, and Ireland, and the dominions thereunto belonging, to all his Majesty's officers, civil or military.

These are requiring you to protect and defend the estate, house, and effects of Lady Dirletoun from all violence or insults whatsoever, from any person or persons. Given at Holyroodhouse the first day of October 1745.—By his Highnes command.   J. MURRAY.

Indorsed : Young Pretenders protection to Lady Dirleton. October 1745.

93. WILLIAM, DUKE OF CUMBERLAND, to ALEXANDER, EARL OF LEVEN— That
the Hessians and English cavalry were at Perth.

Aberdeen, March the 4th, 174⅚.

MY LORD,—Major Generall Huske gave me your of the 27th of last month,
which gave me great concern to hear that you had been so ill, but I hope it is
now over.

I am very thankfull for the trouble you have given yourself about the affair
that you undertook, and hope that you will have better success from Edinburgh
than Perth has afforded. As the Hessians and some Inglish cavalry will be at
Perth and Sterling, I hope all your uneasiness for the low country will cease. I
inclose with this a draught of some hints for the more effectually preventing a
fresh rebellion. When you have perused it, I should be glad that you would
make the proper remarks in the margin, as I shall be always obliged to you for
letting me know your thoughts on all occasions.—I remain your affectionate
friend,

William

On his Majestys service. The Earl of Leven, at his house at Loch Leven,
Fifeshire. Dispatched from Aberdeen by express, March the 4th, 174⅗,
at eleven o'clock in the forenoon.

(The following is written on the fourth page of the preceding letter.)

Aberdeen, the 3d March 174⅚.

MY LORD LEVEN,—I am very sorry you are kept at home by an indisposition,
as your presence here might be useful, as it would be agreeable to me. The
cause will, I hope, soon be removed, and I shall be pleased with occasions of
giving you further proofs that I am your very affectionate friend.

94. WILLIAM, DUKE OF CUMBERLAND, to ALEXANDER, EARL OF LEVEN, Commissioner to the General Assembly of the Church of Scotland — The
steady conduct of the clergy.

Inverness, the 21st May 1746.

MY LORD COMMISSIONER,—The meeting of the venerable the General Assembly
of the Church of Scotland furnishes an occasion I have wished for, of expressing

publickly the just sense I have of the very steddy and laudable conduct of the clergy of that church through the whole course of this most wicked, unnatural and unprovoked rebellion.

I owe it to them in justice to testifie that upon all occasions I have received from them professions of the most inviolable attachment to his Majestys person and government, of the warmest zeal for the religion and libertys of their country, and of the firmest persuasion that these blessings could not be preserved to the nation, but by the support of his Majesties throne, and of the succession in his royal family; and in support of the sincerity of their professions, I have always found them ready and forward to act in their several stations in all such affairs as they could be useful in, tho' often to their own great hazard, and of this I have not been wanting to give due notice from time to time to his Majesty.

I must desire your grace to assure the venerable the General Assembly of the very sincere acknowledgment I shall always feel for the particular marks of good will and affection I have received everywhere from the clergy, of my regard and esteem for their body, and of my good wishes for all its members.

I heartily wish success to the good work you are upon for the service of his Majesty, and the true benefit of his faithful subjects. I am, my lord commissioner, your graces most affectionate friend,   WILLIAM.

To his grace the lord commissioner to the General Assembly of the Church of Scotland, Edinburgh.

95. KING GEORGE THE THIRD to DAVID, EARL OF LEVEN AND MELVILLE— Summons to attend the Coronation. St. James's, 14th September 1761.

RIGHT trusty and right wellbeloved cousin, we greet you well: Whereas the twenty second day of this instant September is appointed for the royal solemnity of our and the queen's coronation, these are to will and command you and the countess, your wife (all excuses set apart) to make your personal attendance on us at the time above mentioned, furnished and appointed as to your rank and quality appertaineth, there to do and perform all such services as shall be required and belong unto you respectively; whereof you and she are not to fail, and so we bid you most heartily farewell.   Given at our court at St. James's, the 14th day of September 1761, in the first year of our reign.—By his Majesty's command.

EFFINGHAM, M.

To our right trusty and right well beloved cousin, David, Earl of Leven and Malvill.

96. KING GEORGE THE FOURTH to DAVID, EARL OF LEVEN AND MELVILLE— Summons to attend his Coronation.   Carlton House, 27th June 1820.

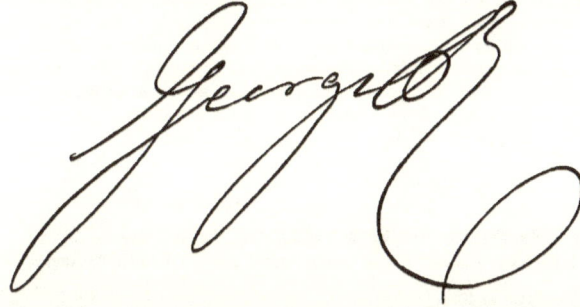

RIGHT trusty and right wellbeloved cousin, we greet you well: Whereas the first day of August next is appointed for the royal solemnity of our coronation, these are to will and command you (all excuses set apart) to make your personal attendance on us at the time abovementioned, furnished and appointed as to your rank and quality appertaineth, there to do and perform all such services as shall be required and belong to you, whereof you are not to fail; and so we bid you most heartily farewell.   Given at our court at Carlton House, the 27th day of June 1820, in the first year of our reign.—By his Majesty's command.

H. T. MOLYNEUX HOWARD, D.E.M.

To David, Earl of Leven and Melville.

97. KING WILLIAM THE FOURTH to DAVID, EARL OF LEVEN AND MELVILLE—
Summons to attend the Coronation.   St. James's, 2d August 1831.

RIGHT trusty and right wellbeloved cousin, we greet you well : Whereas the eighth
day of September next is appointed for the royal solemnity of our and the queen's
coronation, these are to will and command you and the countess, your wife (all
excuses set apart) to make your personal attendance on us at the time above mentioned, furnished and appointed as to your rank and quality appertaineth, there
to do and perform all such services as shall be required and belong unto you
respectively, whereof you and she are not to fail ; and so we bid you most heartily
farewell.   Given at our court at St. James's, the second day of August 1831, in
the second year of our reign.— By his Majesty's command.

NORFOLK, E. M.

To David, Earl of Leven and Melville.

98. KING WILLIAM THE FOURTH to JANE, COUNTESS DOWAGER OF LEVEN AND
MELVILLE—Summons to attend his Coronation.   St. James's, 2d August 1831.

WILLIAM R.

RIGHT trusty and right wellbeloved cousin, we greet you well : Whereas the eighth
day of September next is appointed for the royal solemnity of our and the queen's
coronation, these are to will and command you (all excuses set apart) to make
your personal attendance on us at the time above mentioned, furnished and
appointed as to your rank and quality appertaineth, there to do and perform all
such services as shall be required and belong unto you, whereof you are not to
fail ; and so we bid you most heartily farewell.   Given at our court at St. James's,
the second day of August 1831, in the second year of our reign.—By his Majesty's
command.   NORFOLK, E. M.

To Jane, Countess-Dowager of Leven and Melville.

STATE AND OFFICIAL LETTERS.

99. ALEXANDER, EARL OF DUNFERMLINE, Chancellor of Scotland, to ROBERT, LORD BURNTISLAND, afterwards first LORD MELVILLE—Commenting on the king's letters to the council, especially that relating to Francis [Stewart], son of the Earl of Bothwell, etc.

From Halyruidhouse, 21 Junii 1614.

MAIST HONORABILL GOOD LORD,—I tak occasion to write this to your lordship, to gif yiow present taist in quhat estaitt wee ar heir, in the gouernement off this estaitt ondir his sacred Maiestie, be sic directions as wee resaue daylie frome thence; for this last counsall day wee had in counsall presented to us twa lettirs frome his Maiestie, direct to the haill counsall, quhairoff I send yiow heirwith copies, that yiour lordship may communicat on the same with my Lord Somersett as yie may haue guid opportunitie and occasion; for I assuire yiour lordship thair is na directions cuimis frome thence hither, but (as yie know) the burding thairoff at this present lyis on my Lord Somersett, as he quha onlye has the absolute powar baith be his office and be his creditt.

I sould haue send the saidis lettirs or copies thairoff to my Lord Somersett my self, and my minde thairanent, war nocht I think his lordship[1] with innumerabill greate affaires as I   lasour to reid my lettirs or luike on thame; and I wald be sorie to write my minde friclie in sic maters, and nocht witt quhat sould becuim off my lettirs, nor in quhais handis thay may fall. I am certane thir lettirs has neiuer bein directed be his Maiestie as thay ar wrottin, nor his Maiestie wald neiuer haue signed thame, gif thay had bein red to his Maiestie as yie will parsaue be thame your self, as yie reid thame; for thay ar direct aganist our law forme and practic, and by all rason and in greate pairt foundit upon ontreuth, as yie knaw in the mater, and will considder be sicht off the lettirs.

To the first, the counsall for satisfactioun thairoff, ordourd the kings aduocat to cause summond onye off the parties mentioned thairin for onye particular crimes, offences, or riottis ony man sould giue him informatioun off, and furnish him probatioun. To summond onye persoun upon the generall to ansuir upon his misdemeanour or misbehauiour can nocht stand with our practic nor law, is direct aganist the acts off parlament.

[1] The blanks in this letter are caused by the original paper being torn in various places.

The second lettir sould haue bein direct in guid forme to me onlye, for that lyis to my charge and office yierlie to alter, change, or establish the justices off peace as occasioun may requere. Bot beside that, as yie will parsaue be reiding the lettir, if his Maiestie war weill informed, wald neiuer consent that directioun sould be followed furth. I am determined, neiuertheless, to obey the same if I gett nocht contrair [wa]rrand betuix and Michaelmes, for that lyis to my charge onlye, and this I shiow to the counsall, for I will alvayis obey his Maiestie's commandementis. I think thir lettirs has bein procured to the behoue and at the Laird off Halkertounis desiro; quhilk he neidit nocht for onye thing he has anie raison for your lordship knawis he has the lordis, and off my self in speciall as onye man has. Bot treulie thir forms ar nocht guid, ar eiuill thocht off, wald be remeidit and stayed, or ellis the service will be werie onpleasand heir and diffiicill, if nocht impossibill, to doe guid seruice, and hald all affaires heir in guid frame.

Sence the writing heiroff, thair is ane other lettir cuimed hither to us frome his Maiestie far by my expectatioun. The lettir is to my lord secretair, aduocat, and me, to the behoue and fauour off Francis, sonne to the late Erle off Bothuell, with ane protectioun formed to the said Francis, with command and charge to us to aduyse his Maiestie gif the said forme off protectioun micht importe to him onye thing micht be preiudicial to his fathers forfaltour; and with command to us if it may import that to forme ane other, and send it in all expeditioun to his Majestie, quhilk sould beare na farder, bot his Maiesties acceptatioun off him ondir his protectioun and clemeucie, and restitutioun against his dishabilitatioun be his fathers forfaltour, to import na farder bot libertie to him, butt offence, to marie with ony partie, to enjoye quhat ciuer he may acquire be mariage or otherwayis be laufull meanis, and to haue place, to stand in iugement, to parsew, and defend the same as onye other laufull subject, as gif the sentence of dishabilitatioun had neiuer bein geiuin against him be occasioun off his father's forfaltour. To this wee haue ansuired the best wee could, [and] has send our ansuir to James Douglas to be presented to his Maiestie, [r]efused alluterlie to giue it to the partie quha broght us the kings letter himself, and maed greate instance with us to haue the ansuir deliured to himself; quhow thir things ar sa wroght and broght about, and quha sould be the moyennars and pro   is mistic to me, for I haue na intelligence off   quhilk man mak my pairt werie and difficill in my seruice. I hoipe alwayis, God willing, I sall keip the pairt off a guid skippar. I sall doe all may be done be sic winde and wadder as fallis to me; and if the wadder sould ouer whelme me, I sall perish with the ruidder in my hand, on a dew and honest course. Certanlie it apeiris to me his Maiestie intends be degrees to restore that mannis estaitt, and suim sayis my Lord Somersett is on that course also, suim that it cuimis other wayis.   I hoipe be the nixt occasioun I sall haue to write to yiow to latt yiow knaw suim end off our process with your guid toun of Bruntiland, for we haue presentlie the aduocatioun in hand, and nocht hauing farder for this present, bot to wish yiow all happines, restis your lordships maist affectionat to serue yiow,

   Lord Bruntiland.   DUNFERMELINE.

100. LICENCE by the LORDS OF PRIVY COUNCIL permitting ROBERT MELVILLE, LORD BURNTISLAND, to eat flesh in Lent.   8th March 1617.

THE lordis of secreit counsale gevis and grantis licence and libertie to my Lord of Bruntiland, his lady, and sic personis as sall happin to be at table with thame, to eitt flesche during this forbiddin tyme of Lentrom, and on Wednesdayis, Frydayis, and Satterdayis during the haill space of ane yeir nixt efter the dait heirof, nochtwithstanding quhatsumeuir actis, lawes, statutis, or proclamatiouis maid, or to be maid in the contrar, without ony payne, pairrell, or danger to be incurrit be thame thairthrow in ony wayis anent the quhilk the saidis lordis dispeussis be thir presentis.   Gevin at Edinburgh, the aucht day of Marche 1617 yeiris.   AL. Cancell[e].
                                                                MAR, Th[rs].
                                                                BINNING.
                                                                GEORGE HAY.
                                                                S. G. MURRAY.

101. COLONEL ALEXANDER LESLIE to JAMES, MARQUIS OF HAMILTON—Arrangements for landing the troops.[1]

                         From Hamburg the 12 of Maii 1631.

MY MOST NOBIL LORD AND GENERAL,—I am now cum one vith Mr. Elphinstone and Mr. Meldrome vnto the towne of Hamburge, quher I haue brocht letters of credence vith me from his Majestie of Suedine to the bischope and towne of Breme, quither I mind to goe vith all expeditione, and to tak the kings comissarius along vith me thither to determine of all things quhich may mak suir your excellences randevovs and landing.   Bot if they, as it is to be feared sinc the enemio is so dispersed throch ther lands, be not cabil to giue vs such assistance as

   [1] Original letter in the Charter-chest of the Duke of Hamilton.

is requisit, ve must tak a cours to secure our selfs, quhich is to heastine thos levies quhich your excellence can sie in the instructione, and I vill doe my indevor heir to bring them vp. Bot if ther be heir such difficultie throch the levies of so many princes and townes, that they can hardlie be brocht togither, let me intreat your excellence that I may know if ye vill vndertak your self the leveying of them troups or nocht, and in the mean tyme I vill goe one in effecting all that I possiblie can, not omitting any occasione to acquaint your excellence how ewrie particular goeth. I haue many passages to haue vreatine vnto your excellence, both of his Majesties proceidings, as also of many things done in thir feilds. Bot Mr. Elphinstone and Meldrome can record all to your excellence at large, quho hath cariit them selfs so in this busines that they haue omitted no tyme, bot hes vith gryt deligence givne his Majestie all contentment. As for me, sinc it hath pleased his Majestie of Suedine and your excellence to imploy me in this busines, I assure your excellence my affectione to doe yow servioe is so gryt that ther sall no thing be left vnessayd quhich may tend to your honour or service, aud I sall doe my best to vitnes my self your excellences most humil servant,

A. LESLE.

To my most nobil lord my Lord Marques of Hambiltone.

102. L. CAMERARIUS, agent of Gustavus Adolphus at the Hague, to JAMES, MARQUIS OF HAMILTON—That Eric Larson, commissary, had given assurance regarding pay, etc.[1]

De la Haye, ce 21 de Juin 1631.

MONSEIGNEUR,—Vous entendrez du Colonnel Lesle ce que le Roy mon Maistre luy a commandé, et qu'au regard des deniers le Commissaire Erich Larson luy a donné asseurance. Je m'asseure que vous accepterez son offre, et que le Roy de la Grande Bretagne favorisera aussi volontiers de son costé l'affaire, pour encourager sa Majesté et subvenir a la cause commune. Quant au Commissaire Erich Larson, nous n'avons occasion de doubter de ce qu'il entreprend, veu qu'il a le moyen de lever et fournir des deniers tant en France qu'ailleurs, et que sur tout il ne luy manque de credit a Amsterdam. C'est ce que i'ay pensé vous faire scavoir, et par mesme moyen reiterer le vœu que i'ay fait de demeurer, Monseigneur, vostre tres-humble et tres-fidele serviteur,   L. CAMERARIUS.

A monseigneur Monseigneur le Marquis Hamilton.

[1] Original letter in the Charter-chest of the Duke of Hamilton.

103. G. SALVIUS, agent of Gustavus Adolphus in Hamburg, to JAMES, MARQUIS OF HAMILTON, giving details of the preparations for his reception, and advising that he should land at Bremen, ₁⁴₁ July 1631.[1]

ILLUSTRISSIME marchio, domine benigue : illustris excellentiæ vestræ literas favoris plenissimas de 25 Maii Grenwico, Bremæ ante quindenam recté copi. Ex quibus, quia intellexi illustrem excellentiam vestram circa 5 Julii in Germania pedem figere velle, tantò magis illic negotium ursi, ut animi in illustris excellentiæ vestræ occursum parati essent. Ut autem precor Deum, velit tam generosi consilii expeditionem gratiæ suæ aurâ secundare quâ in portum salva appellatur : Ita cum reverendissimo et illustrissimo principe, Domino Archiepiscopo Bremensi, nomine suæ regiæ Majestatis Sveciæ, in scriptis fœdus pepigi, vigore cujus, quandocunque venerit, accepta grataque futura est Excellentia Vestra. Vrbi autem Bremensi, ob multitudinem capitum (ut in democratia) nolui hoc consilium revelare, ne ad hostem prius emanaret, qvam illustris excellentia vestra appelleret. Præsente exercitu, facile se accommodabit. De constitutione hostis, loco appellendi, et modo procedendi, jam tum statim scripsi ad Dominum Lesle, ut et de copiis Germanicis illustris excellentiæ vestræ jungendis. Nec dubito, quin literas meas jam acceperit ; breviter tamen hæc repeto. Quam primum illustris excellentia vestra appulerit, Rex ipse ò proprio exercitu ad Albim et Havelbergam excubante promissas copias illustri excellentiæ vestræ statim submittet. Scripsi pro eorum transitu ad ducem Luneburgensem, qui, quia respondit me, si venero, responsa grata habiturum ; non dubito (quia nunc ad eum discedo) de eo obtinendo : quinimo, si aliter haberi nequit, summendus est. Gluckstadium bis fui, sed Rex Daniæ non dum advenit ; quamprimum venerit, ei quoque satisfaciam, et satisfactionem ab eo spero. In Episcopatu nulla præsidia aucta sunt ; sed omnia sunt in eodem statu, quo fuerunt cum discessu domini Lesle. Tillius cum exercitu suo ab Archiepiscopatu Magdeburgensi per Thuringiam in confinia Hassiæ usque dispersus est. Quocirca ita mihi quidem videtur non incommode procedi posse, si exercitus illustris excellentiæ vestræ, cum in Visurgim venerit, ancoris ad Blexum fixis, circa Gestendorff terram conscendat, et primò omnium urbem Bremensem amicâ vi, id est, tractatu armis citato, omninò occupet. Tum castris supra Bremam metatis, fronteque in occursum hostis obversâ, expectet, donec Germanicæ copiæ à sua Regia Majestate ad illustrem excellentiam vestram per Albim mittendæ, iunctis provincialibus cùm reliqvum provinciæ purgariut, tum præcipuè, Stadâ occupatâ, ad exercitum illustris excellentiæ vestræ accesserint. Hæc quidem sunt opiniones meæ et quorundam Archiepiscopi consiliariorum, quas etiam scripsi ad suam Regiam Majestatem ; sed omnia illustris excellentiæ vestræ beniplacito, eamque Deo et me suo benigno favori, reverenter committo. Datum Hamburgi die ₇⁴₇ Julii Anno 1631. Illustris excellentiæ vestræ observantissimus quoad vixero,   G. SALVIUS.

Illustrissimo Domino Jacobo Marchioni Hamiltoniæ apud serenissimum Regem Angliæ Magno Equitum Magistro, Domino meo colendo.

104. L. CAMERARIUS, agent of Gustavus Adolphus at the Hague, to JAMES, MARQUIS OF HAMILTON—That he was glad to learn the troops were ready to embark.[1]

De la Haye, ce 7 de Juillet 1631.

MONSEIGNEUR,—Monsieur Ashley allant vers vous, ie n'ay voulu laisser eschapper une si bonne commodité sans vous asseurer de mon service. Je m'asseure que le General Sergeant Maieur Lesle sera desormais arrivé vers vostre Excellence et que Monsieur Helvingston vous aura aussi fait ample rapport de l'intention du Roy, mon maistre. J'ay esté tresaise d'entendre que vos trouppes sont prestes, et que vous faites estat de bientost les embarquer, dont ie redouble mes vœux et prieres vers le Dieu des armées pour le bon succez d'icelles : Vous asseurant que si tost qu'elles seront arrivées en Alemagne en lieu de seureté, et où elles pourront un peu s'arrester, sa Majestie vous tendra tout aussi tost la main, afin que puissiez tant mieux avancer vostre desseing. Cependant vostre excellence sçaura par sa sage conduite et la prudence des siens, le plus seurement acheminer cest exploict, et le mettre en execution au contentement de sa Majesté, le bien public, et vostre eternelle reputation : Vous priant de croire qu'en toute occasion ie m'esvertueray de vous faire paroistre combien ie suis, Monseigneur, vostre treshumble et plus affectionné serviteur,   L. CAMERARIUS.

A monseigneur, Monseigneur le Marquis de Hamilton.

105. COLONEL ALEXANDER LESLIE to [JAMES, MARQUIS OF HAMILTON]—State of the Anglo-Scottish army.[1]

The 21 Agust [1631].

PLEIS YOUR EXCELLENCE,—We arryved at Wkermundt, fond the soiours so weried, being wnaqwainted with mairsching, I wes forced to ly still a day to

_____
[1] Original letter in the Charter-chest of the Duke of Hamilton.

repos them, and to prowyd for schipin to send the seik men be watter, which wer to the number of thrie hundreth; for the hopman of Vkermundt wes apoynted to be comissaries for owr prowissioun, quhilk wes nocht so well as it sould haue for lak of tyme, yit thai wer contentit ressonabill well. But the nixt nicht lodging wes at Mutschellburgh, quhair I fond nothing, bot wes forced to send and seek for it at vther places, for the which the comissarie is to be blamed, as Capitane Weir can schaw your Excellence, and the nixt nycht salbe at Falk in Wald; quhair I hop thai salbe a littill better vsed, and so I sall caus to provyde for your Excellence all the way that I am to pas, bot your Excellence wald do well and nocht to quyt the hopman will he brocht yow to Mutschelburgh, least he serue your Excellence as he has served me; for I will assure your Excellence it is verie gritt trubill to bring them forth and prowyd for them, yit with Godis grace I sall bring them to Stattin. As for the seik, I haue writtin to Charle Banneir, that thaj sall nocht lak thair wnto the rest come.—I rest your Excellenc servant,   A. LESLIE.

106. COLONEL ALEXANDER LESLIE to JAMES, MARQUIS OF HAMILTON—State of Crossen and Frankfurt on the Oder.   20th September 1631.[1]

MONSEIGNEUR,—Je me donne l'honneur descrire a vostre Excellence pour l'advertir en quel estat est la ville de Crossen et ceste ville aussy. J'euvoye ce porteur à vostre Exellence auec vne lettre que le major qui commende la luy escrit; il se plaint de n'avoir pas asses de monition de gerre. J'advertis vostre Exellence qu'il y en a aussy fort peu en ceste ville. Elle donnera, s'il luy plaist, ordro que nous en puissions resceuoir tant pour Crossen que pour icy; je pars aujourdhuy d'icy pour aller visiter la ville affin d'en pouuoir faire vn certain raport à vostre Exellence. J'ay escrit au prince Electeur de Brandeburg affin qu'il mette ordre que nos soldatz puissent estre icy entretenus. J'attendray icy comme en touste autre lieu l'honneur des commendementz de vostre Exellence comme celuy qui n'a autre but que de posseder de se pouuoir dire de vostre Exellence, Monseigneur, le tres-humble tres-obeissant et tres-affectionne serviteur,
                                                     A. LESLE.

De Francfurt, le 20 Septembre 1631.

A Son Exellence, Monseigneur le General Marquis de Hamilthon.

    [1] Original letter in the Charter-chest of the Duke of Hamilton.

107. COLONEL ALEXANDER LESLIE to JAMES, MARQUIS OF HAMILTON—Account
of the death of Gustavus Adolphus.[1]

Stade, the 26 November 1632.

MY MOST NOBLE AND HONOURABLE GOOD LORD,—I haue thought it expedient to
mak to your Excellencie this sad nar[ra]tioun of the lamentable death of our most
valarouse and worthie chiftaine, who, in the sixt of November, did end the constant course of all his glorious victories with his happie lyffe, for his Majestie
went to farre on with a regiment of Smolandis horsemen, who did not second him
so well as they showld, at the which instant ther came so thick and darke a mist
that his owin folkis did lose him, and he being seperate from his owin amongst his
foes, his left arme was shote in two, after the which being shote againe through the
backe, fainting he fell vpon the ground, one the which whill he was lying, one asking
him whate he was, he answeared, King of Sweddin, wherupon his enemies that did
compasse him thought to haue caried him away; but in the meane while, his owin
folkes comeing on, striueing in great furie to vindicate his Majestie out of ther
handis, when they saw that they most quite him againe, he that before asked what
he was, shote him through the heade; and so did put ane end to his dayes, the
fame of whose valoure and loue to the good cause sal nevir end. When his corpes
were inbalmed ther waes found in them fyue shottes and nyne woundis, so ar we
to our wnspeakable greife deprived of the best and most valorouse commander
that evir any souldiours hade, and the church of God with hir good cause of the
best instrument vnder God, we becaus we was not worthie of him, and she for
the sinnes of hir children, and altho' our lose who did follow him salbe greate, yit
questionlesse the churche hir lose sal be much greatter, for how can it be when
the heade which gaue such heavenly influence vnto all the inferiore members, that
nevir any distemperature or weaknes was seene in them; how can it be since
that heade is taken from the body, bot the members therof sal fall vnto much
fainting and confusion. But this I say not, that ather I dowbt of Gods providence or of these whom he hes left as actores behind him, for I am perswaded that
God wil not desert his owne cause, bot will yit stirre up the heartis of some of
his anoynted ones to prosecute the defence of his cause, and to be emolouse of
such renowne as his Majestie hes left behind him for evir, and I pray the
Almightie that it would please his Supreame Majestie now to stirre the King of
Boheme, and to make choyce of him in this worke, which indead is brought vnto
a great measoure of perfectioun, neither doe I think that ther salbe any defect in
these his valorous souldiours and followers, in whome ther is not the least sus-

[1] Original letter in the Charter-chest of the Duke of Hamilton.

picioun of jelousie; bot this al men knowis that a bodie cannot long subsist
without a head, which giues such lyffe and influence, ather good or bade, as it hes
radically in it selfe, when it is present; and when it is cutt away, cutts away
with itselfe all lyffe and influence. As yit this bodie hes done well, for indeid
the victorie was ours, and Papinhamo is killed, Wallenstoune wounded, Corronel
Commargen killed, with many other greatt officers which yit I cannot particularly
nominate. The enemie left the towne of Leipsich, and Duke Ewiene of Lunnem-
berie hes beseiged very hardly the castle, and I think be now it is taken in.
Duke Bernard of Veimers hes persewed Wallenstone with the relictis of the
Emperours armies, and hes so compassed them about that I think also by now
they ar ended. Now it remaines that we turne our sorrow to revenge, and our
hearts to God by earnest prayer that he would stirre up the heartis of such men
as may doe good to his cause, and now tak it in hand when it is in such a case.

I haue no further wherof I can wreit to your Excellencie at this tyme, bot
when occasioun offers I sal not be deficient to acquaint your Excellencie with every
particulare. I intreat your Excellencie to haue me in your remembrance as one
who sal evir be readdie and willing to serve your Excellencie to the verie outter-
most of my power; of which assureing my selfe, and wishing your Excellencie all
health and happines, I rest your Excellencies faithfull servant till death,
                                                         A. LESLE.
A Son Excellence Le Marquis de Hammilthon tres-humblement.

108. THE PRIVY COUNCIL OF SCOTLAND to JOHN MELVILLE of Raith, to attend
      the Council and explain his assumption of the title of Melville without
      acquainting the king. Edinburgh, 4th June 1635.

AFTER oure verie hairtlie commendationis, having by his Majesties directioun
some thingis to impairt vnto you towcheing youre assumeing of the title and
dignitie of a lord of parliament vpoun a testamentarie declaratioun without
acquenting of his Majestie thairwith; Those ar thairfoir to request and desyre
you to mak youre addresse heir to his Majesteis councell vpoun the ellevint of this
instant, at whiche tyme you shall knowe his Majesties will and pleasour in this
mater. And so resting assured of youre preceis keeping of this dyet we committ
you to God. Frome Edinburgh, the fourt day of Junij 1635.—Youre verie
goode freindis,   SANCTANDREWS, Cancell'.
                                             HADINTON.   BINNING.
                                             TRAQUAIRE.   NAPER.
                                             J. HAY.   Sr THOMAS HOPE.
      To our right traist freind the Laird of Raith.

109. GENERAL ALEXANDER LESLIE to JAMES, MARQUIS OF HAMILTON, asking
his influence at Court in favour of Colonel Robert Monro.[1]

Stoltenow, the 16 April 1636.

MOST NOBLE LORD AND PATRON,—I maid bold by tuo several letters of a late
dait to present my service to your lordship with the relatione of such occurrences
as this time doeth affoard; yit occasione presenting it self moveing me to impor-
tunitie, I must still presume to be farther troublesome by intreating your lordship
(that since the beirar heirof, Colonel Robert Monroe, hes commissione frome the
croun of Sweden for levieing of souldiours for the better setting fordwart of our
wars heir, and seing they ar ordainit to serve wnder this armie, whairof it hes
pleasit the quein and directors of thir wars to impose wpon me), that your lordship as a noble patron and protectour of men of our professione, and of me in
particular, will be pleasit to favour him with your lordships mediation at his
Majestie his hands, that he may have libertie to levie and bring forth men out of
his native cuntrie, whiche men, and all who ar or sall happin to be wnder my
command sall be wpon his Majestie his advertisment, reddy to doe his Majestie
service, and I trust if that God blis ws and that by his Majestie his royal per-
missione and assistance we come to any estimatione, that I sall have the wischt
happines to give testimonie of my natural and obliged affectione by doing his
Majestie by my weak labours some acceptable service. Since my last wnto your
lordship thair hes nothing past heir worthie of your lordship. Bot what succes
it sall pleas God give our vther armies, or this wherof I have the command, I sall
not faill to acquaint your lordship thairwith, assuiring my selff that your lordship
will pardone my boldnes and assist the beirar to the obtaining of his Majestie
his gratious ansuer, becaus the fortoun of the gentleman is in his Majestie his
handis at this time, and I as one having interest thairin sall be alwayes dedicated
to pray for your lordships long and happie lyf, and a blising vpon your lordships honourabill affairs and ever to show my selff as becomes your lordships
euer devoted seruant,   A. LESLIE.

To the richt honorable my euer honored lord and patron, my Lord Marquis
of Hamiltoun,—these.

[1] Original letter in the Charter-chest of the Duke of Hamilton.

110. GENERAL ALEXANDER LESLIE to KING CHARLES THE FIRST—Expressions
of loyalty.[1]

Frome our Leager at Herford, the 9th Maii 1636.

MOST SACRED SOVERAGNE,—Being tyed by birth, professione, and affectione, to
imploy the furthest of my endevoirs to doe your Majestie service, and having no
vther present way to expres my willingnes to performe, bot by giving your
Majestie ane accompt of the Germane proceidings, have maid bold (howbeit one
of your Majesties meancst, yit loyall subjects) to give your Majestie the true cer-
taintie of the estait of the proceidings of the wars heir, and fearing the censure of
presumptione, doe remit the relatione thairof to my Lord Marques of Hammiltoun,
whose letter frome me doeth beare the same; wisching my habilitie wold
second my affectione and obedience to the performing of some acceptable service
to your Majestie, or those hes relatioue to your Majestie, whiche I should accompt
my cheifest earthlie happines, and your Majesties long blissed and happie raigne,
the principall desire of him who sall euer pray for the same, and live and dye
—Your Majesties most loyall and devoted subject,   A. LESLIE.

To his most sacred Majestie of Great Britane, France, and Ireland, my most
dred soueragne,—these.

111. GENERAL ALEXANDER LESLIE to JAMES, MARQUIS OF HAMILTON—
Operations of the army in Westphalia.[1]

Frome our Leager, befoir Herford, the 9 Maii 1636.

MOST HONORABLE AND NOBLE PATRON,—Being tyed by dowtie and promise to
give some testimonie of my willingnes to serve your lordship, and for the present
having no other way to expres the same bot by giving your lordship ane accompt
of our German proccidings, have heirby maid bold to give your lordship the true
relatione thairof, wisching the same be not wearisome to your lordship, being my
presumptione proceidis from affectione, and the assuirance I have of your lordships
noble constructions of me, who sall endevoir to entertaine that favour hes pleasit
your lordship conferr vpon me. I have adventured to direct this letter heirin
inclosit to his Majestie, presuming that if the same merit censure, your lordship
as my continowing noble patron will plead pardoun. The particulars of euerie
thing occurres heir, I dowbt not bot your lordship will acquaint his Majestie

[1] Original letter in the Charter-chest of the Duke of Hamilton.

with, to whose relatione I have referrit the same, as namlie, all our bussines goes werie weell hithertillis. Felt Marschall Banncir hes and doeth carrie himself bravelie, as I doubt not bot General Lovetennent Ruthwen will acquaint your lordship, who hes bein ane actor with him. Bot for the present, in respect that Felt Marschall Hatsfeild is come to the Saxon with a great secourse, so that Banncir is not sufficient aneuch to give them battall, Banneir hes besyd [left] Magdeburgh with his footmen, and is reteired to Tangermund, attending our forces from Leisland and Finland, who is thocht will arryve befoir this come to your lordships hands. In the meane time he is stryving to wearie the Saxone by marching to and fro in a waist land where ther is nather intertainment for men nor hors, and thairefter he will tak his best advantage of them. Felt Marschall Wrangle, who commandit in Prussia, is to have the leading of the armie ordanit for Silesia ; he is at this present in Hinder Pomer, attending the proceidings of Marazin, one of the emperours generalis. As concerning this armie in Westphalia, committed to my charge, our beginings, praisit be God, hes beine succesfull. The first rancounter we had with our enemie wes at a castle vpon the Weser, called Petershagen, whiche I unpatronized, and took of prisoners one Baroun Kotler, a colonel, with the compleit officiars of a regiment, and 185 souldiours. Within a day thrie or four efter, by way of a pairtie whiche wes commanded out, we defait tuo regimentis, took certane rutmaisters and souldiours, and aucht cornetis ; thairefter we marcht towardis Osnabrig for the releif of it, whiche is now frie ; then taking to consideratione that Minden, a toun vpon the Weser, wher the Duk of Lunemburgh had his garrisone, wes a pas of great importance, and behouefull to have for the good of the common caus and the better assuirance of our armie, I marcht to it and by a meane acquyrit the same, and hes put in a garrisone into it, with the whiche the Duk is not weell pleased. I am at this present at Herford, within 2 litle myles of the enimies leager, attending the conjunctione of the Landgrave Hessen his forces, whiche I have long solisted for, and wherof now I have assuirance by ane expres whiche the Landgrave hes sent to me, so that so soone as we come togither I intend, God willing, to try the behaviour of the enimie, and if God blis our proceidings, I resolve to uiset Hannow, wher Sir James Ramsay is governour. The 6 of this instant I commandit out a pairtie who, rancountering with another of the enimies and defait them, took a colonel, and certane rutmaisteris and vnder officiars and souldiours, besydis those that wer kilt. What followis heirefter your lordship sall be acquainted. My lord, if it be that the restitutione of the Palatine can come no vther way bot by way of armes, the neirest and most convenient way for his Majesties projectis towardis the advancement of that interest is be Westphalia, wher I sould think myself happie to attend his Majesties commandementis, and to doe his Majestie service with these people committed to my charge. Thus craving pardone for my boldues in impeding your lordships moir honorabill affairs by my long letter, and wisching I may be still honored with the continowance of your lordships patronage, humblie kissing your lordships hands, I tak my leave, and sall never be wanting to approve myself as becomes your lordships most affectionat humble servant,   A. LESLIE.

P.S.—Pleas your lordship, my Lord Forbes can give your lordship the perfyte relatione of our Westphalia bussines.

To the werie honorabill his most noble lord and patron, my Lord Marques of Hamilton,—these.

112. GENERAL ALEXANDER LESLIE to JAMES, MARQUIS OF HAMILTON—State of the army in Germany.[1]

Stockholm, this 15 September 1637.
MOST HONORABLE AND NOBLE LORD,—Being here and hauing the opportunitie of this bearer, I thought it my duetie to let your lordship know in brief the state of affaires in our armies, and how matters are past since our retrait from Torgow : from whence wee being come to Pomerland the enuemie did follow us, and did lodge himself at Tangermund, Neustat, and Sweth ; and when I was come to Stettin and about those quarters, because I found that the warre would turne to bee defensiue, I tooke opportunitie to come ouer hither to sollicit the affaires of the armye. Since that tyme the ennemie is come downe to Anclame upon Felt Marchall Wrangle his quarters, and hath assaulted the same two or three tymes, and is repulsed with great losse ; for to maintaine that post Felt Marshall Bannier did send in due tyme three brigadees of foot to his assistance, and afterward folloued with the bodyes of the armyes which hee and I commandeth ; by which meanes the ennemies attempts haue beene hitherto in vaine, so that when hee would haue passed ouer at Stolp heo was repulsed, and a great many of his folck were drowned in the riuer of the Paine. The multitude of the ennemies is so great that it will bee a hard matter to maintaine those quarters long if they continue in their purpose without any diuersion ; but seeing Duck Bernhard is come ouer the Rhine, wee hope that some forces will be called away from us to hinder his proceedings ; and then if the proportion of the enuemies stronth bee not too farre exceeding, wee are resolued againe to fight them as wee haue done heretofore. It were to be wished that such as haue a mind to helpe us would steppe in whiles

[1] Original letter in the Charter-chest of the Duke of Hamilton.

it is tyme, before all bee lost, for then it may proove too late. Thus I take my leaue, and commending myself to yowr lordship his fauour, I rest, your lordship his most humble seruant,   A. LESLIE.

To my most honorable lord my Lord Marquesse of Hammilton,—these.

113. GENERAL SIR ALEXANDER LESLIE and other Covenanters to JOHN, EARL OF ATHOLE—Remonstrating with the Earl and gentlemen of Athole for their backwardness in paying the tenth penny.[1]

Edinburgh, 25 of April [*circa* 1641].

OUR NOBLE LORD AND YOU WORTHIE GENTLEMEN, OUR MUCH RESPECTED FREINDS,—Whairas their hath come two of your number, with commission from the rest to this great meeting of the estats, to giue in the reasons why your division had not giuen obedience to the generall orders that wer appointed for the whole kyngdome concerning the payment of the ten penny for defraying the publik charges in the late troubles, and for ordering of other matters that wer for the safetie of the kyngdome in this present time, because the had report of your behauiour in all these particulars that wer required had filled the eares of all that honorable meeting befor these gentlemen come, wee that wer your particular freinds, as wee wer glade at their comming (hoping they brought satisfaction with them), soe wer wee the mor carefull to see what their commission was; but when wee looked vpon that paper, and the reasons of your denyall not subscribed by any, and they themselues lesse able to giue any excuse for what was contined theirin: for they alledged they could not goe by that paper: wee cannot think but it proceeds from particular persons, that are disaffected to this common cause of the whole countrey, and wee doubt not but vpon better consideration you will thinke soe yourselues ; for what is that first to alledge that neither you nor the Erle of Athol receaued any of that money directlie or indirectlie, cannot all the rest of the kyngdome and particular persons say soe much, or doe you thinke the publik defence of the kyngdome with soe great ane armie, and manie other charges, hath not taken all that which is craued and much mor, and how should it bee payed, if euerie particular man might alledge I gott none of it : And for the charges that you haue been in your two woyages vnto the north, wee doe beleeue Angus and other parts may alledge much mor, and all the rest of the kyngdome for the south. As for your second reason, of your powertie, wee doe beleeue that is common to you with all the rest of the kyngdome ; if you had anything that might cast the ballauce in

---

[1] Original letter in the Charter-chest of his Grace the Duke of Athole.

your fauours when you shew better ground for your particular exemption then others, wee thinke it will not bee refused vnto you that particular respect bee had vnto your inhabilitie when it appears. As for the third and last, that you cannot send out the fourt man for fear of broken men, this is a weake pretence, for who will trouble you except you sett your selfe against the common safetie of the whole kyngdome, and soe draw the wrath of this whole kyngdome vpon you for shewing soe euill example to all the rest, being situat in the midds therof : for this and mekill mor that wee that are your freiuds, and desires not to presse you ouer sore with this great fault, wee haue thought it fitt not to suffer these men to appeare befor the publik meeting, but haue sent them back in all hast with this our faithfull aduice, and granted them Friday next to returne with your better resolutions, and with others that may giue better satisfactione for your joint concurrence with the rest of the kyngdome. Hazard not all for denyng a part, and for feare of broken men let not all the countrey breake in vpon you. Learne in time from your freinds to distinguish betwixt the generall good of the whole kyngdome, and the particulars of a few euill men that are amongst you. Hast your answer against that time, and know by this that they are your best freinds who giues you this aduice. And soe rest your assured freinds,

A. LESLIE.   KINGORNE.
M. STORMONTT.

To our noble lord, the Earle of Athol, and the rest of the gentlemen of the division of Athol—thes.

114. GENERAL SIR ALEXANDER LESLIE to JOHN, EARL OF ATHOLE, advising him to send forth his regiment. [*Circa* 1641.][1]

MY LORD,—I haue receaued your letter this day from Major Rollock, and hauing acquainted the Committee of State therwith, because it is not ane answer to that which passed betwixt the laird of Inchmartein and the Erle of Rothes and myselfe, whair wee desired that the regiment belonging to your lordship might bee sent furth, according to the common instructions, with all diligence, and that these men which wer named in that warrand subscriued by vs should come . . . [torn] . . . and giue s[atis]faction to the committee their, for giuen (giving) assurance for the people of Athol in time to come for obeying the common instructions of the kyngdome, but your lordships letter goeth quit vpon ane other ground, first excusing the not obeying the warrand that was sent in respect of the

[1] Original letter in the Charter-chest of his Grace the Duke of Athole.

peremptornesse theirof both in condition and dyet, and then requiring a new warrand by the mayor for two or three gentlemen to agent the bussinesse, and that should haue free accesse and regresse both in their persons and goods qbuilk neither your lordship nor they can find in the former. Now for answer to all this I cannot wonder aneugh how your lordship and these men who are not satisfyed with that warrand should thinke that the committee and the great affaires of the kingdome that are dayly craning dispatch at their hands should haue time at their will to grant to a few in Athol who are disaffected vntill they please themselues to come and capitulat, and soe trifle time in comming and returning, your lordship knoweth best how oft they haue been desired to come and giue reasons for their demands, and they should receaue satisfaction, which they did sleight, and now they would begin a treatie when the publique affaires doe strait more, and the burden of keeping men togither: wherfor, my lord, their can be no other thing returned in answer to this letter but that your lordship would bee pleased to send out your men with all diligence, and that these men who wer named in the warrand would come alongst with the regiment or follow them, and by soe doing they shall haue free warrand to come and returne and plead for the necessitie of their countrey, and their owne obedience in time to come what they please, and for this effect it is that the Erle of Argyle hath his commission from the committee and me to see these things reallie performed, and all due obedience giuen to the orders that comes from this, which, if these in Athol bee readie to obey, his lordship will bring no trouble to any, and soe hes lordship is to receaue instructions this night to carie himselfe and his people as he finds their behauiour in Athol, which wee expect now at last they will soe help and amend, that I may, both to them and to your lordship, haue just occasion to continue your lordship affectionat freind and servand,   A. LESLIE.

To my very honnorable good lord, the Earle of Athol,—these.

115. AXEL OXENSTIERNA, chancellor of Sweden, to ALEXANDER LESLIE, EARL OF LEVEN, congratulating him on his new dignity. Stockholm, 12th September 1642.

ILLUSTRIS et generose domine, Campimarschalle, amice plurimum honorande. Postquam ad me allatum fuit serenissimum Magnæ Britanniæ Regem, factâ nuperrime operâ et consilio Illustritatis vestræ accedente, inter Scotiæ et Angliæ regna felici reconciliatione, eum honorem meritis Illustritatis vestræ habuisse, ut eam cum voto et applausu ordinum regni Scotiæ, Comitis titulo et dignitate insignire

Illustris & Generose Domine Consiliarie Marescalle, Amice Charissime honorande.

Gratum ad me allatum fuit, Serenissimum Magnæ Britanniæ Regem, quod quidem audiente, inter Serenissimum & consilij ipsius merita gem. facta nuperrimè, quæ & conciliatione, cum honorem meritis Rex et Angliæ Regni felici reconciliatione, Curiarum Regni Serenissimæ voluisse, ut Eam cum voto et applausu Ordinum, quæ nos Serenissimum Regem habuisse, ut Eam cum voto et applausu insignem voluerit: Obeant, quæ nos tia, (omitto titulo et dignitate insignem amus, amicitiam Eo Nores invicem multis ultro armis compleri amus, amicitiam. Ipsius perauptum Eo Nores totui, quia affectum meum prestatuou Ipsius perauptum suæ querimem ex a Dignitati incrementum, tanquam debitum, reütuli suæ querimem ex a, nims gratulaur.   Quinimo, ut eis Ipsius semi, quæ has magnas, Pc in Electi in cæterum ramallata iam tuem de Beritij Ipsius, Patriæ martissimo quendam Regimeo Serenissimæ Modeonas Regines, Q, sc ut mes ac Caius Comuni spiritibus, Eo testani porum, sancti Eo sic sic nullem non Ipsui ac gloria ut dos fomentum mancantur. Unde nihil ost in Causa Comuni spiritibus, Eo testani porum, monentur. Unde nihil ost. intimaco voluit. quam quod intelligerem. Regm honorem

Ill. V. ...

merito debebatur. — Gratulor proinde Ill. Sti. vorec..., ut quæ

modum ex nove dignitatis in Ill. Dn. facta collatio, Eidem magnis

... meritorum suorum Emolysis et gloria existit, ita ...

... et perpetuatel ejus perpetua ... duturam maiora, induis

... Polonorum incrementa eos se diffundat. Me, et Regno

Sveciæ, nixu quæ patriæ meæ ... omnibus, ... in;

... fructuum ... cupio,

Ill.mi Vri.

... Amicus et Defensor

promptissimus scriptor

... Adolphus
... Torstensson

Dabam Stockholmiæ
12 Septemb. A 1652.

Ill.mi et Generoso Domino
Alexandro Leslao, Comiti,
Equiti Aurato, et Arcis Marechal,
Dno amico meo plurimum
honorando.

Illustri et Generoso Domino Carteri
Marschallo, Amico plurimum honorando.

Postquam ad me allatum fuit, Serenissimum Magnae Britanniae Regem, facta nuperrime, quae et consilio Illmi Vrae auspice, inter Sc.
tiae et Angliae Regna felici reconciliatione, tam honorem meriti
Illmi Vrae rebuisse ut tam cum zelo et applausu Ordinum Regni Sc.
tiae, consiliis titulo et dignitate insigniverolluerit; Obeae, qua vel
in eum multi vitro annis complexi sumus, amicitiae, intermitterem
potui, quin affectum meum testatum IIImi Vrae auspitem Lri Nores
dignitatis incrementum, tanquam debitum virtuti vrae praemium ex a-
nimis gratularer. Eximeno, ut res IIImi Vrae domi forisa magna e.
in civibus in patriam sanctata iam tuen, et Sterilijs IIImae Vrae
meritissimo quondam Reginae Serenissimae Moderoris Regiaris, latius
nas ac cance conacta partitij. Eo testani praem, tanti Re ese, ut
nullum non spur ac glorie redort fomentum mereantur. Unde nihil

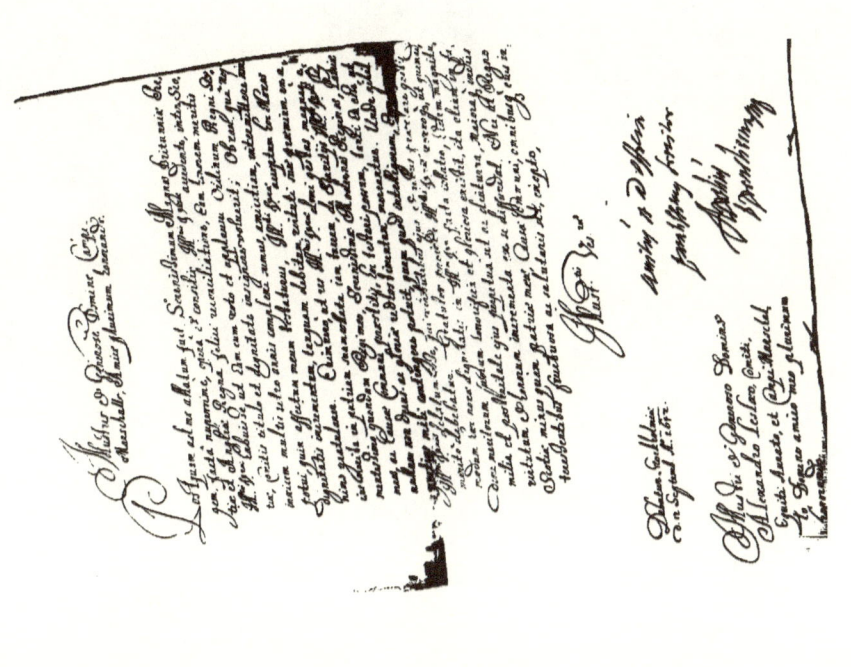

voluerit; ob eam, quâ nos invicem multis retro annis complexi sumus, amicitiam,
intermittere non potui, quin affectum meum testaturus, Illustritati vestræ accep-
tum hoc novæ dignitatis incrementum, tamquam debitum virtuti suæ præmium ex
animo gratularer.   Enim vero, ut res Illustritatis vestræ domi gestas, magnaque
eius merita in patriam suam collata iam taceam, de servitiis Illustritatis vestræ
clementissimo quondam regi meo, serenissimæ modernæ Reginæ, patriæ meæ, ac
causæ communi præstitis, hoc testari possum, tanti ea esse, ut nullum non decus
ac gloriæ redhostimentum mereantur.   Unde nihil gratius mihi contingere potuit,
quam quod intelligerem, eum honorem Illustritati vestræ delatum esse, qui virtu-
tibus ejus et rebus præclare gestis merito debebatur.   Gratulor proinde Illustritati
vestræ, voveoque, ut quemadmodum hæc novæ dignitatis in Illustritatem vestram
facta collatio, eidem magnitudine meritorum suorum honorifica et gloriosa existit,
ita etiam in familia et posteritate ejus perpetua sit ac diuturna, maioraque indies
virtutum et honorum incrementa ex se diffundat.   Nec ut regno Scotiæ minus
quam patriæ meæ, causæ communi, omnibusque eius interessentibus fructuosa ac
salutaris sit, exopto,—Illustritatis vestræ, amicus et ad officia paratissimus servitor,

AXELIUS OXENSTIERNA.

Dabatur Stockholmiæ, die 12 Septembris anno 1642.

Illustri et generoso domino Alexandro Leslæo, comiti, equiti aurato, et campi
marschallo, domino amico meo plurimum honorando.

116. THE SAME to THE SAME—Colonel Lewis Leslie had brought him letters—
Hoping for peace in Britain.   Stockholm, 12th September 1642.

ILLUSTRIS et generose Domine, Campi Marschalle, amice plurimum honorande,—
Gratissimas Illustritatis vestræ literas, datas Edinburgi die 4 Octobris anni præteriti,
recte mihi reddidit opera et consilio Illustritatis vestræ inde expeditus Colonellus
generosus Dominus Ludovicus Leslæus die 20 Novembris ejusdem anni, in quibus
significauit Illustritatis vestra serenissimum Magnæ Britanniæ Regem, reconciliatis
Scotiæ et Angliæ Regnis svadente Illustritate vestra, modo nos in continuando
bello Germanico et promovenda restitutione causæ Palatinatus persistere vellemus,
nobiscum cooperari, et in partes auxilij causæ communis condescendere decrevisse,
ut pax demum honesta secura et universalis tam nobis, quam oppressis per
Germaniam statibus, cæterisque interessentibus obtingat : In eumque finem huc in
Regnum cum regiis literis ablegatum fuisse præfatum Dominum Leslæum nuntia-
tum, in eo stare serenissimo Regi consilium, brevique, qui idem ulterius confirmet,
eiusdem legatum subsecuturum, prout singula hæc in allatis ad serenissimam
Reginam meam, et me literis uberius deducta inveniuntur.   Fuit hoc in clementissi-

mum quondam Regem meum, gloriosissimæ recordatiouis, serenissimam modernam
Reginam et patriam meam continuati affectus studiique præclarum et evidentissi-
mum signum quod Illustritas vestra patriæ suæ curis licet obruta, intermittere non
potuerit, quin propensissimam de hoc Regno ulterius bene merendi voluntatem
suam hac ratione testificaretur.   Et sicuti ego de constanti et perpetuanda hac
Illustritatis vestræ affectione certus semper fui, ita e reciproco eam certiorare possum
nobis non minus cordi curæque esse salutem Regnorum Britanniæ, quam experimur
vobis fuisse patriæ meæ.   Quicquid istius porro est pluribus vobis coram relaturus
est prædictus Dominus Leslæus multis industriæ et fidei suæ documentis hic
cognitus : Quem licet prius hinc expedire voluissemus verum cum eodem fere quo
advenit momento sinistri illi nuntii de rebellione Irlandiæ mox de dissensionibus
inter serenissimum Regem et Parlamentum Angliæ exortis, hic vulgati sint, iamque
eo usque increbuerint ut de bello et aperta armorum concertatione audiatur, itaque
factum est ut expeditio eius spe melioris indies rerum status in præsens tempus
sit protracta, quod sane in expectatum dissidium mihi collegisque meis non potest
non esse ingratissimum cum facile consideremus quantum detrimenti causæ
communi inde accedat ; quod serenissimus Britanniæ Rex discordiis hisce civilibus
præpeditus amicis suis et oppressis evangelicis pro voto et voluntate sua nequeat
subvenire.   Quam ob causam sæpius nominatum Dominum Leslæum hic tam diu
detinuimus, sperantes indies fore ut melior rerum facies illucesceret.   Ceterum cum
spei et voti nostri hac in parte non dum facti simus compotes, coacti demum
sumus, eum cum eiusmodi responso et literis ad serenissimum Britanniæ Regem,
simulque celsitudinem suam electoralem hinc expedire, prout præsentium temporum
ratio permittit et adiuncta literarum copia Illustritatem vestram fusius edocebit.
Nos interim inclitis Britanniæ Regnis felicissima quæque adprecamur, ut ea ope et
consilio cordatorum et pacis amantium patriotarum adiuta suffultaque, in pristinum
concordiæ et tranquillitatis statum quantocyus redigantur, quo serenissimo Regi
et Parlamento Angliæ consveta dignitas, suum ius, suaque utrinque constent sarta
tecta privilegia.   Qua amicabili reconciliatione fiet, quod in votis nobis antiquissi-
mum est, ut consilia et vires suas adversus causæ communis hostes tanto validius
iungere et coadvenire possint ; in quo felici voto et optato rerum transitu præsentes
finio, cætera et quæ rerum nostrarum habitos hoc anno in Germania felices
successus concernunt Generosi Domini Leslæi relationi committens.   De cætero
haut dubius quin Illustritas vestra in coepta amicitia, et sveta erga me bonevolentia
sit continuatum.   De me ex quantalibet occasione experietur quod sim perpetuo,
Illustritatis vestræ Amicus et ad officia paratissimus servitor,

AXELIUS OXENSTIERNA.

Dabantur Stockholmiæ, die 12 Septembris anno 1642.

117. COLONEL ROBERT MONRO to [ALEXANDER, EARL OF LEVEN]—
Campaign in Ireland.

Carrickfergus, the 22 of Maii 1643.

RICHT HONORABILL,—Being returned from our last expedition, for your excellencies information be pleased to know that, being scarce of victualls on the twelth
of May. we marched from Carrickfergus to Drumbo ; the first day at our randisvouz
ther, our partie consisted of two thousand foot, thrie hundereth horsemen and
dragowners, being provyded with ane halfe pound of meale aday for ten dayes
tyme.   I resolued, with the horse and the two part of the foot, to merch towardes
Armach, to find and tutch the enemies pulse ther, and to keip them off from
releiving the castle of Newcastle and Greincastle, both on the soa cost in the countie
of Downe, quher our enemies from England ordinarlie had ther recourse with
supplies to the rebells, which to prevent in tymes comeing, I directed be soa from
Carrickfergus, in thrie birlings, ane hundereth commanded men, with ane halfe
cartow, and two feilding peices, and directed the 13th from Drumbo, Colonell
Hoome with six hundereth men to meit them at Newcastle, for blocking vp and
attacking of both houses, the tyme I suld ly with the rest of the partie betwixt
them and the enemie, as I did, haueing merched the 13th from Drumbo to Sir
Charls Poynt his house, being twentie two myles, and before we settled our
quarter, with the dragowners and commanded horsemen, we beat the enemie from
Tonargie, and immediatlie sent to the Newrie for the troupe of horse and thrie
hundereth musketeirs to joyne with vs at Armach.   The 14th, being Sunday, we
merched to Armach, twelue myles, befor nyne aclock in the morning, and cleired
the countrey before vs, with horsemen and dragowners on both flankes, who
skirmished with the enemie, and recouered bootie, haueing surprysed them
vnawars, notwithstanding of the intelligence sent to them from Carrickfergus and
Antrum.   They were surprysed also at Armach, wher divors of them were cutt off.
After a litle halt made ther, Major Turner joyned with vs, and immediatlie I
resolued to visit Owen M'Art at his owne hous in Lochgall, within a myle to
Charlemont, being the straitest ground in Ireland for defence.   I did heir from
the Newry that he expected Preston with fiue thousand men to joyne with him.
and that he had sent order to Sir Phelimie to bring with him the Tyrone men from
Dungennon, as he did.   I resolued to search for the one before the supplie suld
come, and merched from Armach, be two aclock in the after noone, towards
Lochgall, wherin the entrie the Generall Sir Phelomie and the generalls sone
being joyned togidder, with two troupes of horse and fyftein hundereth men,

rancountered vs in the verie entry with salves of muskett; the want of cariage-horses made vs want feilding peices, greatlie to our disadvantage, since in that ground our horsemen culd doe no service, being all inclosures and hedges, except one highway. The skirmish being begun, whillest some faced the enemie, other were direct about to come on ther flankes, without which it was impossible to make them giue ground. The skirmish continowed thrie houres and ane halfe. Divers were killed and wounded on both sydes; we buried oures on the place, and they brocht off ther dead as they fell. At lenth I discouered, by intelligence, the onlie pass they had to reteire on to Charlomount, and finding them in tyme of hote service to giue ground, I conjectured ther powder would faile them, and if the pass were taken in before them ther retraite behooued to be confused, which moued me to direct these of my owne regiment thrie myles about to take in the pass on the left hand, and directed to the richt hand of the bogg Lawers and Lindsayes men. The enemie, finding our designe, drew off his men in great heast, and qwat the precinct of his house to our mercie. My regiment came short, not-withstanding of all ther speidie merch, one pistoll shott vnbeing maisters of the pass, bot ther horsemen being reteired the foot crossed the bogges towards Charlemount with the loss of some men. The night drawing on, the partie haueing plundered the Generalls house, and brunt it with the rest of the countrey-houses of Lochgall for fiue myles betuixt Charlemont and Armach, we reteired at night to Armach, againe haueing merched twentie two myles that day besydes the tyme of the skirmish. Some of our partie haueing followed kowes were not able to joyne with vs that night, bot having batteired with horsemen on both handes, the nixt day happilie we joyned togidder, at Armach, without anie considerable loss. We lay still all that day, and on the 16th we commanded a partie in our returne to Glencane woodes, who were foughten with, wher Sir James Lockhart receiued deathes woundes, and was brought off to Lochbrickleu, where he died that night, and was buried the nixt day at the Newrie. The 18th, we merched by Ralph Iland and the plaines of Iveagh to Newcastle, of intention to know of Colonell Hoomes success, who ven-tured after shooting without effect threitein shott of cannon at the house; the rebells continowed obstinat, and would heir of no treatie, which moved him in the night to storme ther otter walls and gott away ther kowes. He sett fyre [to] ther gates and windowes, and preased with pikes, crawirones, and gavelock to worke throch the house, but all was in vaine, being forced to reteire from it with loss, some being killed and bruised with stones off the wall-head, and before my returne he drew of his cannon and boated them. Nevertheless I drew vp my whole partie before them, and sent a drummer to invite them to a parley, which, willinglie and happilie for vs, they consented vnto. The tyme of the treatie ane barke from England did cast anchor before vs, and sett one man ashore, who by Godes providence was not hindered to come ashore by our shooting, in reguard of our parley. The man being brocht before me, I knew him to be servant to the Earle of Antrum, who finding himselfe insnared, alleadged he was come from Dublin as a freind, bot being threatined to the death except he would reveile who was in the barque, drawing me asyde he confessed the Earle of Antrum was ther. I told him he behooued to betray his maister or to die instantlie for him. The earle expecting his Irish convey, vpon the first signe he came ashore, and being brocht to me, his letters taken from him, which please receiue, he was immediatlic direct away with a convey of twentie horsemen to the castle of Carrickfergus, wher I hope he shall attend your Excellencies forder pleasure as ane enemie to his Majestie, and to the peace of his Majesties thrie kingdomes, being imployed as a treacherous papist be the Qweines Majestie, with his adherentes for the ruine of Scotland and England both. This service vnexpected to be done be me, we owe God thankes for it, and I hope your Excellencie, and these whom it cheiflie concernes, will be carfull to prevent the devillish consequence of such devillish instrumentes as plotts the ruine of kirk and policie, and the eversion and down throwing, so farr as in them lyes, of the kingdome of Christ and his sacred Majesties throne. As I intend to seaze vpon such as I find guiltie and accessorie to this plott in thir partes, I hartilie wish the lyke may be done at home, otherwayes if the headmen gett leaue to break loose, Scotland will be a spectacle lyke vnto England and Ireland. Our scarcetie of vivers continowes to our great greife, and we ar all of vs civillie dead. The meanes being abstracted from vs which suld weaken our enemies, advance our credites, and make vs a terrour to our foes, being now derided by them. If your Excellency be resolued to returne no answere to my former letteres, I resolue by letteres not to be more troublesome vnto your Excellencie, my patieuce being so exhausted, that now I am out of hopes of gaineing credite by doing of service, the meanes altogidder haueing failed vs, so that I am constrained plainlie to signifie vnto your Excellency that we ar vsed more vnworthie as our deservings hes procured. Howsoeuer, whill I breath, I remaine a reall servant to my countrey and to your Excellencie, hoping that no tyme, occasion, or distance will suffer your Excellencie and others well affected of the kingdome, to neglect and contemne this armie and me.—Your Excellencies humble and obedient servitour,   ROBERT MONRO.

118. HENRY MILDMAY, Speaker of the House of Commons, to the COMMISSIONERS OF THE PARLIAMENT OF ENGLAND IN SCOTLAND—To give a jewel to the Earl of Leven.

Westminster, 9° February 1646.

MY LORD AND GENTLEMEN,—The Howse hath commanded mee to take care that the jewell, together with this their letter inclosed, bee conueyed vnto yow; to the end they may both bee deliuered by your hands to his Excellency the Erle of Lenen as a testimony of their greate respects vnto him, and high esteeme of his fidelity and gallantry. Not doubting of your care of the speedy and seasonable presenting of them, I shall giue yow noe further trouble concerning this busines, nor adde any thing of my owne, but that I am, my lord and gentlemen, your most affectionate freind and seruant,   HEN. MILDMAY.

To the right honourable my lord and gentlemen of the parliament of England, commissioners with the parliament of Scotland. Presente these with speed.

119. GENERAL DAVID LESLIE to THE COMMITTEE OF ESTATES—Lesmoir and Wardhouse reduced, etc.

Lesmoir, 27th March 1647.

RIGHT HONORABLE,—Since my last to your lordships, wherein I acquainted you with the reducing of Strabogy, I haue now thought fitt to give your lordships this further accompt of my proceedings. That after I had secured that place, in maner exprest in my former, I marcht with the army and appointed General Major Holburne, with some horse and dragones, and thrie regiments of foot, to lye doun before Wardhous. The rest of the army wes employed about the house of Lesmoir. Vpon 25th instant Wardhouse wes reduced without much disput, wherein were fourteen Irish and a captain,—all which I caused be put to death, and left a sergeant there with twenty fyue men. Two dayes thereafter I took in the house of Lesmoir—a place of considerable strenth and compassed with water. After the water wes diverted and the close gained with the losse of two or thrie men and some wounded, they burned the low howses and betook themselues to the towr; and finding that the place could not be carried without the losse of men and bestoweing much tyme, I conceaued it most for the advantage and speeding of the service upon a parlye offered by the captain to agree with him upon these conditions, that he should yeeld up the house and all that therein wes,

that all the Irish should dye, and his owen lyfe, with Harthill the elder, should
be spared, but they both to be prisoners untill they satisfyed Church and State,
otherwyse be banished the kingdome.   So I caused hang 27 Irish.   The
captain and Lesmoir, with two or thrie Scottismen, poor sogers, more I haue
prisoners; wherein, if I haue done any thing amisse by sparing their lyues, I
desyre your lordships positive and peremptory orders in tyme coming, that I may
rule myself accordingly.   And becaus the houses and holds in this countrey which
have been formerly guarisoned will but occasion new troubles, if they be not
slighted, I shall lykewyse desyre your lordships orders, for ruining and render-
ing them unprofitable.

My intelligence of the enemy bears that they are at the head of Don Water,
where they are doeing what they can to draw together forces.   But for preuenting
of their dounfalling upon the Mearnes and Angus, I will send 3 troops for
securing of those parts with the generall commissaryes troop, which I shall lykewyse draw out, and with the rest I shall prosecut the busines with all the care
and fidelity that can be, leaving no opportunity of advantage.   The morrow being
the Lords day, upon Monday, Godwilling, I intend to moue to the Boug, for that
place being secured there will be no more places of consequence but Loch Cam-
mure (whereof I shall endeavour to giue your lordships as speedy accompt as can
be).   And so the countrey will be eased of the burthen and danger of guarisons,
and the passage made free.

Having receaued this enclosed, I thought it necessar to communicat the same to
your lordships, and show yow that I have sent a protection to Alexander Makronald
(he submitting himself to your lordships, and conforming himself to publict orders),
and a passe to repair to me; and I shall earnestly desyre to be directed by your
lordships how to deall with him when he shall come to me, that I may so behaue
myself as may be most for your lordships contentement and setling the peace of
that countery.

I have been earnestly desyred by Lues Gordon that he might be permitted to
send two gentlemen to your lordships to offer you what satisfaction shall be requyred; and untill your lordships further pleasure be knowen, to grant him
protection from all violence for 20 dayes or a month.   He hes geuen assureauce
under his hand, upon word of honor, that he shall doe no act of hostility, nor
keep correspondence with the enemy during that space.   And in reguard he is
no person excepted, I haue thereto agreed for that tyme, and expect your lordships
resolutions how I shall further proceed therein.

And now, becaus this part of the countrey formerly under subjection and con-
tributing to the enemy, is not wasted, but able to affoord reasonable proportion

toward the maintenance of the army, I shall offer to your lordships consideratiouu if it might not bear a share of the burthen, now being releeued of the enemy, and if it were not expedient to appoint the collecting thereof. This is all at present can be sayed by your lordships most faithefooll,

DAVID LESLIE.

For the right honorable the lords and other commissioners of the high court of parliameut, or to the ryght honorable committee of estats.

120. LETTER—writer unknown—to LIEUTENANT-GENERAL DOUGLAS—Remark-able interview between Cromwell and his Parliament. London, 20th September 1654.

RIGHT HONORABLE,—Haueing arriued heir, blest be God, thorow a tempestous woyage, I could not rest any longer silent, but salute yow with a gratfull accknowe-ledgment of your noble fawours, and choice intertainments, which were conferred wpon me duringe my abode, cowettinge ane occasione wherin I might expresse those obligationes that were multiplied by your lordshipp and the rest of those honorable persones about his Majestie as a testimonie of my respects, yett find-ing noe other way at present I am necesitated thus to transmitt my high resent-ments of those great courtesies and obliging fawours by presenting your lordshipp with my seruice, longing earnestly to receaue your commands wherin I can be found seruisable or usfull to yow heir, which shalbe my delight, since my arriwall I haw bein receawed heir by his highness the Lord Protector, wnto whom I deliwered the king his letter, who did receaw it, and inquired wery kindly about the king his good health, and the good conditione of his affaires, wher, after seweral other respects expressed to his Majestie, he inuited me to dine with him and used me nobly, for which fawor I am exceidingly obliged to the king his Majesty.   As for the conditione of affaires heir, be pleased to know that the Earles of Glencairen, Athole, Selkrik, etc., with the Lords Dudhopp, Kenmoure, Forrester, etc., are come in and aceptd honourable termes, wiz., that they shall eujoy their estaittes without either forfaulture or fyne, that they shall haw libertie to trans-port a thousand men each of them within six months next ensewinge to any foraigne prince, staite, or king, in coufedracie with this comonwealth, and that all their prisoners shold be liberat.   Heir haue bein some stiffe debates wpon the sitting dowen of the parlament heir about the instrument of government, which consists of 42 articles, but that which was hotliest disputed was wher the being of the supreame power lay, whither in a protector and a parlament or a parlament and a protector, which being highly debated for sewerall dayes caused his Highness send some companies of foott and horse to acquaint them they must not sitt whilest he spok with them, wherupon meitting them in the painted chamber he declaired to them how both God and the people had giwen him the power, and he wold keip it, wher wpon he ordained them to subscrywe a teste or recognitione that they shold neither moue not wotte any alternatione of the forme of the pouer as it is established, which abowe the one half haw signed, the rest refused and are gone, soe those that sitt haw established the power in oue persone, and a parlament whose denominatione is to be further considered, of which causes some imagine wilhe emperor, soe that things are heir peasably and his highness flourishinge, soe that if the king haw ane intentione to haw any men from thence assure his Majestye he shall find me both ready and willing to testifie my obligationes herein to him, for the furtherance wherof I wold hawe his Majestie writte a letter effectualy to the Lord Protector theranent, and I question not but to giue his Majestie a good account thereof, yea auswer his expectatione therein, which is my delight to fulfill. Heir is Colonell Weimes, a wery gallant and braw experienced gentlman, out of imployment, if his Majestie wold desire or stand in neid of him he wold tender his serwice to him and come ower and waitt wpon him ; the gentlman is a wery mire and gallant wnderstanding man of artillerie, and ewry way a compleat souldier. As for your owen affaires I wish I could be found usfull to serw yow heir, but assure yourselff I shall acquaint the Earle of Angus with your noble candor and innatte dispositione, who is not only courteous to all but ane honour to your countrey, I beseich yow lay your commands wpon me and they shall add to my obligationes withall. I pray yow present my humble seruice to his excellencie the chancellor, and to Graw Errick, and Grawe Jane, signifie to them my desire to serv them, whos courtesies canot be forgoten; my seruice to Felt Marshall Kagg, Count Axcleley, Colonell Fleitwood, and Collonell Hambiltone, with my seruice to all other my friends with yow.

I intreate yow will pardoue me for troubling yow thus, and accept of my affectione, which with my choice respects of seruice I present wnto yow, wishing yow prosperous success, which is the desyre of your faithfull friend and humble seruant.

London, the 20 September 1654.

Theiss for the Right Honorable Leutenant-General Douglas.

121. WILLIAM, EARL OF CRAWFORD AND LINDSAY, to JAMES, EARL OF PERTH, Chancellor, asking for a passport.

Struthers, January 20th, 1685.

MAY IT PLEASE YOUR LORDSHIP,—As the great alteration in my health while lately at Edinburgh forced me to pairt from that place somewhat hastiely, so my weaknes necessitat me to so verrie short journeys, as I was three days by the way before I came this length.   But being now in a condition able to write, ame hopefull I may without offence to your lordship mind yow of my passe, which once I had confidently expected along with me. If my circumstances were seriously considered by your lordship they will be found to have no paralel in the nation, so as my passe needs not be denoyed me, in the most ample and credit-able termes, upon the accompt of the preparatiue of it, lest others should deal for the same favour, I being the single nobleman in Scotland that has not some way or other a title to lesse or more of fortune, it is much more my inclination to liue in a remote place of the world, though under the hazard of a want of that supplie so seasonablie from friuds, as I had while amongst them, raither then incurre new displeasures from rulers, for matters that I cannot in anie case help, the place of my retraite (which I named to your lordship), and the few servants whom onlie I take with me, I hope are plain evidences that I designe to displease none that are in trust, in anie thing relateing to that journey, and if my credite amongst rulers is so low, that I cannot have trust in this, I shall not repine that I have a prison in the nation, for secureing them from what they apprehend from so unhappie a creature. Yet if I dare claime to anie favour upon the accompt of the friendship that sometyme I have bene honoured with by your lordship, or the interrest that is betwixt our children, or even from your ordinairie generositie to a person so much the subject of your pitie, I wold humblie begge, that since my wife hes but ten weeks to reckon, and that upon a short wairneing I cannot be provided for such a voyage, I may have your lordships answer with all the convenient hast yow can, for I ame able to doe nothing untill I heare from your lordship, if by your means my desire shall be granted, I may without vanitie assure yow whatever may be my other faults, there is not ingratitude in my nature, and so while I ame incapable of wittnesseing my sence of such a matter otherwayes, your lordship shall for your prosperitie, and that of your familie, have still the earnest wishes of, my lord, your lordships most faithfull and most humble servant,   CRAFURD.

For the Earle of Perth, Lord High Chancellour of Scotland.

122. Sir John Cochrane to Sir Andrew Melville—Announcing the embarkation of the Earl of Argyll's expedition. Amsterdam, 23d April [1685].

Sir,—Although wee have spent much teme in these pairts yett wee have not been idle. Wee ar now readdy with a considerable stoke of armes and ammonitione to goe to Scotland, and if God bliss us wee shall goe aboard the morrow. In a fiwe days the Deuke of Monmoth goes for Ingland, that both keingdoms may oppose this apostate papist, who haith murthered his brother to pave his waiy to the crowne, and as is aparent to all thinkin men, intends to destroy the nations in all ther conserns, religious and civill. But God who has hitherto helped us, will yett helpe to pull down that bloddy tyrante. We have a considerable number of people with us, and all of us in good hearte. I am perswaded wee goe to venture our lives in a good cause, and we have no cause to doubte of Gods assistance. All protestaints in both keingdoms ar longin for us, and will as one man joyne in with us, so that I houpe you shall heare good news from your native countrie. Wee need officers, and therfore I intrytt you to acquaint all our countrie men, who ar in ani foraigne service to cume and take imployment in their own countrie, they shall bee all well provided for. I daire not invite you, although I am perswaded of your good affectione to our cause, the weakenes of your body dissabeling you for the feilds, but if you incline to cume, you shall carve out your own command. Wee shall need men for garisons as well as for the feilds, and I houpe all our countriemen will thinke it their dewty to assist us att this teme. Doe mee the favoure to putt my humble service to Generall Shavott, and when you sie your prince, give my dewty to him, and assure him from mee that I have a deep sence of my obligations to him, and if God bliss mee, I houpe to bee instrumentall in begettiug a good understandinge betwixt the keingdoms of Great Britain and him. Give my service and my soons to your good lady and childering, and to Collonell Lamott, his lady, and hirr sisters. I pray God bliss you all, for the keindness showen to mee. Make it your woorke to send home all men that can bee usefull to us.—I am sincerely, your most humble servant,   Jo. Cochrane.

Amsterdam, 23 Apreill, old steill.

Indorsed, apparently by Lord Melville : "Sir John Cochrans letter to Sir Andrew Melvill, 1685."

123. PERMIT by JAMES, EARL OF PERTH, Chancellor, to ALEXANDER, MASTER OF
MELVILLE, to go about his affairs. Edinburgh, 25th June 1685.

THESE are allowing liberty to the Master of Melvill to goe about his effaires in
freedome, since he hath given band to answer when called, under paine of two
thousand pound sterline, and ordains his former obligationes to be given up to him.
At Edinburgh, the 25 of June 1685.   PERTH, Cancell⁸, I. P. D. S. C.

124. GEORGE, DUKE OF GORDON, Governor of Edinburgh Castle [Address
        wanting.]—Tumult in Edinburgh.

Edinburgh Castle, 11 December [16]88.
MY LORD,—I vould not hawe omitted to vreat to your lordship by the servant
you had last in toune, but that he never did cum neir me notwithstanding I
had called for him severall tyms, now you vill certainly receve your *etuis* from
this bearer, I hawing delyvred it to the gardiner in a seald paper, and backt for
your lordship, which I vish you may recew in mor snifftie as your friend ar for
the present in this toune. Sundays night last ther begoud a tumult in toune about
five aclock at night (after sume litle gathrings vithout hurt for tuo or three days
befor) which lasted till after 12 at night, but the ports being shut few off the rable
could cum that night to the Cannegat or Abay, so sawe sume tumultuous crys
ther was no hurt doune. My Lord Chancellor being frighted therby, vent avay
for Drummond yesterday at 12 of the clock on hors back, accompanyd by a troupe
of the militia hors, and sume gentlemen and my Ladie Perth and Ladie Marie an
hour after in ther owin coich accompanyd by sume hors, but in such heast as
that the hous was left as vsuall : yesternight the tumult begoud agane at fiue
aclock, and befor sevin of the clock at night they possest the Nather Bow, and
vent doune to the Cannegat, breaking severall houses, plundring and spoyling, and
after vent in a great crud, not of boys as formerly, but off all sort of men armd
vith staivs, swords, guns, pistels, and all sort of arms. Captain Valace, who had the
gaird off the abay, after hawing desyred and intretted they might retir, did fyr
vpon them, wherby its said 3 or 4 var kild and mor vounded, which mad them
retir to be reinforsed, as is said they var by the toune militia and Captain Grams
companie, who as they say attack the gaird back and for, so that the captain
and his men var forst to flie, after which the tumult entred the Abay, destroyd
all that vas in the abay church and chapell, and brok vppe all doirs in the whole
abay, and plundred and destroyd all that vas vith[in] the chancellors hous, vppe
and doune, vithout as they say leving any thing, beds, hingins, books, picturs,

cabinets, and all other things, rifled and brunt, but I beeline mor, that his silver plate is gone; and as for my Ladie Huntly I bliss God they did her no harme nor any thing off hers, though they entred her hous; from whence I came to the castle 3 hours befor. Yesternight the tumult lasted till tuo in the morning, and this morning by 8 of the clock its said they var gone, at lest a great manie [to] Wright hous and Nethrie this is abundance off the goodness God knows what ville cum after. Time permits no mor but that I ame

Mr. Dombars[1] newes is literally trew, and mucth off this by the chancelors going outt off town and nott calling the judicatorrys affter him to Stirling. I send yow his Majestys letter to the cuncell. Melford, his ladey, and Craige ar gon beyond seas. I cannott gewes what things may com tooe, butt pray advertis mee if annay thing extraordinary falls outt, and Ill order my frends to reatt off yow. Adiew, my dear lord, my deuttys to the cuntess,   GORDON.

My blessins to my dear ladie, this most serwe in answer to her letter. Wee have keept the bearer to long till this day at on of the clock.

125. JOHN, VISCOUNT OF DUNDEE, to [JAMES, EARL OF DUNFERMLINE?]—
Would be glad to concert with him about the King's affairs.

Coluthie, Apryl 21, 1689.

MY LORD,—So soon as I cam to Clait I wrot a letter giving your lordship acount of my being in this contrey, and desyring to know what way I could wait on your lordship, which Tarpersey undertook to delyver; but befor he was the lenth of the Kirktoun of Inch he mett a servant of your lordships coming to him, by whom he understood that you wer gon to Castle Gordon, so he returned bak and then went towards Castle Gorden, and befor he came this lenth he found on the way a gentleman with your lordships letter to me, which I was extreamly glaid to see : not that I could dout your lordships forwardness for the kings service, but was extreamly pleased that I should have the hapiness to concert with you these affaires, that concerns us all so much. There is no body in this contrey, both on your oun acount and the Duke of Gordons, so proper to influence it. I will send Major Graham from Kieth to know where I may wait on you, or what comands you have for me.—I am, my lord, your most humble faithfull servant,
                                                              DUNDIE.

[1] This paragraph only, is written and signed by the Duke of Gordon. The last postscript is in the handwriting of the writer of the letter, who was apparently a Mr. Dunbar, perhaps secretary to the duke.

126. CHARLES, EARL OF SHREWSBURY, Secretary of State, to ROBERT, LORD
LUCAS, Governor of the Tower—To take Colonel Robert Lundie into
custody. Whitehall, 13th May 1689. Contemporary copy, sent by
post to Mrs. Lundie.

Charells, Earle of Shreusbury, Waterford, and Wexford, and principall secretary of state, and on of his Maiestys most honorable priuy councill.

THES ar in his Maiestys name to authorize and require you to take into your
custody the person of Collonel Robert Lundie upon suspition of treasonable practices against his Majestics gouerment, and keep him safe till he be discharged
by due course of lau, for which this shall be your warrant. Given at the court
at Whitehall the 13th day of May 1689.   SHREUSBURY.

To the right honorable Robert, Lord Lucas, cheife gouernor of the Touer of
London, or, in his absence, to Collonel King, his deputy.

For Mrs. Lundie, at Mrs. Lyons house in King Street, neir St. Jamsses
Squaire, Westminster.

127. GEORGE, VISCOUNT OF TARBAT [to GEORGE, LORD MELVILLE]—Pay of the
forces—Case of Lord Balcarres.

Edinburgh, 21 May 1689.
MY LORD,—I long to heare from you.   Duke Hamilton told my Lord Atholl to-
day that he was on the kings councell, and turnd to me and said, but yow are of.
I said then I hopt his grace and my other good freends in the convention would
no longer fear me in a publick capacity.

I came this day into the convention, and had the honor to be presently named
in a committee to examine the number of forces appointed by the convention, and
to compute there establishment, and to adjust it in comparison with the foond for
payment of the army. The committee mett, and wee computed it will be very near
to quhat I writt, viz. the 9 regiments of foot, 12 troops of horse, 6 troops of
dragoons, and the traine and garrisons will be very near 110,000 pounds sterling.
The foond for pay is the 8 months cess (if all payed) is 48,000 pounds sterling.
The inland excise sett at 31,000 pounds sterling, but will not be effectually
29,000 lb., and the cesse not 47,000 lb., so that $\frac{47,000}{29,000}$}76,000, fals short of the
pay according to the establishment of the Scots pay, be [by] 43,000 lb. sterling at
least, viz. near other 8 months cess, which Scotland is no more able to pay then

to buy the Indies; but then consider that a 3d part almost of excyse and cess will be wanting. The forreign excise and custome, with the litle property, was alwayes dispensed in fees, salaries, pensious, and contingencies.

My lord, yow cannot imagine how much Balcares usage is talkt of. He is a dying, and they would only give him the change of goeing out of the Tolbooth to a close hole in the towne under guard and centry, and 5000 lb. bail, besides the change beeing of no use, and nowayes advantagious to his health. He lyes still in the stinking prison; if what he proposes were dangerous, besides hurtfull to the king, no discreet man woold urge it; but if he give bail on ordinar summes to remove and remaine out of the kingdome, and not to return to any of the 3 dominions without the kings allowance, and haveing his estate to losse to the [king] as goods, what danger can there be to give him these tearms, and all his crim being that another hath writt to him, why might they not to your lordship, and I wonder they did not to me; it would be generous in yow to vindicat our hard dealing by so secure a changing of his condition. He is not allowed to writt nor speak but with two or three, but he intends (as I hear) to begg leave to petition the king.

I did writt to yow formerly of my sonne, who, I think, is weell in Mackys hands. As to myself, I continue still weak. My legs fail me much, so that the baths seemes necessar; therefore I againe intreat for a pass as soon as can be, especially beeing useless heer; but I hope my quietus will cary me allowance to live any where, and to be excused from attendance with the crowd, wher all I can be desyred to doe is to sitt and hold my tounge; but if I goe to the baths I will start to see yow, if yow doe not forbid your faithfull servant and coosigne,

T.

Indorsed: Tarbats letter about the accompt of the cess, Edinburgh, 21st May 1689.

128. Rev. George Walker and H. Baker, to the Officer commanding at Donaghadee—Defence of Londonderry.

Londondery, May 23d, 1689.

Sir,—Wee recceived intellegence by this boy that the kings army of foote were redy to land at the bay of Donoughadee, onely wayted for the horse from Port Patrike, which yow, as the lad informed vs, tould him yow expected this day. Wee have by the blesseing of the Almighty God defended this citty hetherto from the violence of a barborous and cruill enimie, and haue now in this citty, at least, twenty fiue thousand souls, besids the handfull of armed men, therefore deseire yow will

VOL. II.   O spcede to our relife as soone as possable, if yow tender the safety of soe many protestants, and security of this citty. Our succes, since wee had the gouernment of this place, hath not beene vnsuccesfull, wee haue killed, at least, seunty of theire officers and most prencepall men, viz. : two French generalls, Brigadeire Ramsey, Lord Gilmoy, Taffe, and many others, soe they now become old Irish men, and for want of a suply [of] officers to prick them forward, they take the old method of runing away when our men meets them vppon equall tearms, which they seldom dare ingadge vppon.   The councell of warr, held in this place by Collonel Lundie when Collonel Coningham wes here, may suficently informe yow our condicon.   I refer yow to the collonel to giue yow a relation of the said councell, and doe once more request your speedy relife if yow regard the safty aboue mencioned, for the king's aduantage, we remaine, sir. your most humble servants.   GEO. WALKER.

H. BAKER.

To the officer in cheeffe comanding the kings army at or neare Donoughadee.

Inisskellin men has defeated Lieutenant Generall Macarty lately who layde seige to that place.

Indorsed : Londonderry, 23d of May 1689.   Doctor Walker.

129. MARY, COUNTESS OF MAR to KING WILLIAM THE THIRD—Of the deplorable state to which she had been reduced by the death of her husband.   25th May 1689.

Alloa, 25 May 1689.

MAY IT PLEASE YOUR SACRED MAJESTIE,—Tho the deplorable case I am fallen in by the death of my dear lord (who wes knowen to be highlie zelous for the Protestant interest, a great sufferer for it, and a faithfull promotter of your Majesties service) may maik it seim strainge that I move in anie thing so earlie efter that sad stroak, yet the exigence of the familie he hes left behind, and the conditione of his eldest sonne, who is now to represent him, will, I hope, plead my pardon at your Majesties hand, and will allow me humblie to beg that your Majestie will be graciouslie pleased to hear what wilbe offered to your Majestie by my Lord Melvill and my Lord Cardross, who ar near freinds and relationes of the familie, in behalf of my sonne, who is now head of it, which I will not presume to name heir, that it may not be a truble to your Majestie.   Onlie this, my sone, who now runs his 15 years of age, I trust verie speidilie wilbe capable to prosecute what his father began to act in your Majesties service, which he wes resolved to have givin a greater testimonie of, if God had spaired him. But without your Majesties favour and bountie, it is impossible for my sonne or the familie to subsist, which in all humilitie is represented to your Majestie by, may it please your sacred Majestie, your Majesties most humble, most deutifull, and most obedient servant,   MARIE MAR.

130. MARY, COUNTESS OF MAR, to GEORGE, LORD MELVILLE—Requests he will intercede with the king in behalf of her son.

Alloay, 25 May 1689.

MY LORD,—Tho the sad circumstances I am in by the death of my dearest lord may make it appear too early for me to move in any bussines, yet there being nothing now so dear to me as the interest of his family, and thes he hes left behind him to represent it, I have taken the freedom to beseech your lordship that yow may deall effectually with his Majestie for his favour and bountie to his sone, without which it is impossible for this family to subsist. The inclosed note for saving your lordships trouble containes what is thought propper, by his freinds, to be moved for him to his Majestie at preseut. I know my dearest lord had intire confidence in your lordships kindnes and freindship to him and his family, and did formerly give your lordship the trouble of a representatione of his case, and wes so refreshed with the newes of your lordships preferment to be sole secretary of state, that the last letter he wrote wes to my Lord Levin congratulating it. And tho I fear ther may be severall moving for these places which became vacant by the death of my dearest lord, yet being fully assured of your lordships good will to this family that yow have so near ane interest in, and of your pouer at this tyme to save it from utter ruin, I will confort my self to think that your lordship will prevent any such attempts, and secure to the sone what wes formerly enjoyed by his dearest father. Becaus of my Lord Cardross near relatione to this family, I have also writen to him to advyse with your lordship about what is contained in the inclosed note, and to joyn with your lordship for effectuating therof. I am also advysed to write the inclosed to his Majestie, wherof your lordship hes a double, but your lordship may either deliver it or not as yow think convenient. The confusion I am in by this sad stroak will, I hope, both excuse the borrowed hand, and any error hes escaped, my lord, your lordships most humble servant,

MARIE MAR.

131. Mr. Thomas Carleton, to the Earl of Breadalbane. Dublin, 18th
June 1689. [Contemporary copy of an intercepted Jacobite letter.]

Dublin, June 18, 1689.

My Lord,—By this line your lordship has just cause to complaine of my silence
tho it was impossible for me to break it sooner, since I had the misfortune
not to know of Mr. Hay's departure, who promised me to lett me know in good
time, that I might pay your lordship the due respect I ow you. If I be so
unluckie to be blaimed for it, I beg of your lordship to impute it to any thing
but ingratitude, which I can never be guilty of, nor yet worthy of the many
favours received from yow. The king was pleased to tell me he had sent your
lordship his commands, which I answered would be very wellcome. And whenever I have the good fortune to sie yow, I shall tell yow the sequents of the discourse. As to the forme of declaration, there was some of it pleasing enough,
tho other parts of it not very gratefull, yett all was very well received. That
part concerning Lord Argile, I doe assure yow I prest very much, and I found not
without success, for his Majestie answered he was willing it should be done upon
those tearms I spoke of, and I hope gave your lordship instructions in it. What
other commands your lordship trusted me withall, I am certain, tho not alto-
gither, were by times faithfully delivered, and doubt not yow will receive thanks
for them when opportunity serves. Pardon me in leaving what news there is
here to the bearer. I wish your arms success, a merry campagne and a joyfull
meetting with the king, who am with all respect, my lord, your lordships most
obliged and most faithfull servant,   Tho. Carleton.

My service pray to my Lord Dundee and my Lord Dunmore, who I hope is
with yow. I beg the favour of a line from yow by the first.

To the ryght honorable the Earle of Breadalbane—These.

132. Sir James Montgomery of Skelmorlie to [George, Lord Melville]—
Proceedings in Parliament about the Articles. His opinion about the
moderate temper of the Parliament.

Edinburgh, June 22d, 1689.

My Lord,—I have given you the trouble of this line to acquaint you without
disguise what hath passed amongst us in parliament; if it be unacceptable to youre
lordship you shall not haue reason to complaine tuice. The first day wee sat

doune wee did nothing but recognise the king and queens authoritie. The next day there was ane act proposed by the commissioner relative to oure first grievance of the articles; the house did questine whether the vote proposed by the commissioner was ane adeqwate remedie unto that grievance as it was worded, upon these considerationes, 1°, the act proposed by the commissioner supposed a constant committie, which that grievance, as it was worded, did particularlie levell at. It was questioned by some whether ore not the grievance as worded did strike at a constant committie, bot it being voted, the house by there vote found that a constant committie of parliament was levelled at by that grievance; the second considerationie was that the act proposed by the commissioner supposed that committies of parliament should be chosen by the benches and not by the wholl house, contrar to the meaning of the grievance, which expreslie proposeth that all committies of parliament should be chosen by the estaites; the third considerationie was that in the act proposed by the commissioner the officers of estaite were to be supernumerarie in everie committie of parliament, wheras by the grievance all committies of parliament are to be chosen by the estaites, so that officers of staite, qua officers of staite, unless chosen by the house, cannot be members of anie committie according to the words of the grievance, neither can the kings interest suffer anie prejudice by this, for all business being first tabled in the house, all members of parliament having access to be present at everie comittie, and all business being to be brought in from the committies to the house againe, the officers of staite have good access to advert to the kings interest in everie thing that comes before the parliament, especiallie since the commissioner by his negative can shut the doore; this is the true matter of fact, and if anie uther account be given of it or anie bad constructione passed upon the proceedure of parliament it is calumnious, for I ame sure there was never a parliament in Scotland better affected to their princes service and readier to give evident and undeniable proofes of it, and therefor I would make it my petitione that youre lordship would interpose with the king that the several remedies proposed to the respective grievances may quadrate with them. It is of infinite importance to his Majesties service it should be soe, both for the satisfactione of the people and the fixing of his Majestics just and unquestionable right to reigne over us; this may seeme a strange expressione, bot, my lord, if you consider that unless it be granted for a maxime that all laues that are pointed at by anie vote of the meeting of the estaites, whether in the claims of right or grievances, are therby condemned and disabled, dissaffected people may urge that all those positive laues that lay in the way of ane vacating and filling the throne againe continue yet as soe manie nullities in the way of oure proceedure. I find the parliament heiro in a verie moderate temper, and frie of designes against the life and fortune of anie, even of their greatest oppressors, and that the outmost of its heat will amount to a disabling, and this you may be confident of. I doe again recommend to your lordship to mentaine (in soe far as the post you are in gives you access) a good harmonie betwixt king and people, a full redress of those grievances complained of at the tender of the croune is the method, and one my conscience, I doe not sie hou the king can suffer by it in his prerogative. I shall be as much against curtailing of that as anie, for I doe consider that the just prerogative of the croune doeth support the libertie and propertie of the subject. My good intentione in it, I hope, will make my apologie for this trouble given to your lordship by, my lord, your lordships most humble servant,   JAMES MONTGOMERIE.

133. THE SAME to THE SAME, Secretary of State for Scotland—
Regarding the Incapacitating Act.

Edinburgh, July 2d, 1689.

MY LORD,—I designed to have given you more frequentlie trouble by my letters, bot I have bein tormented these ten dayes past with a reumatisme in my right arme that I could not move it. I wrote youre lordship a long letter upon oure differing in votes with his Majesties instructione relative to the articles, and I wrote it with all the good intentiones towards your lordship that could be. I doe not doubt you have bein a good instrument with the king about it, for wee doe consider that instructione to be the effect of one uther mans advice and not of youre lordships. Wee have since past ane incapacitating vote of all such whoe in the former evill government have been grievous to the natione by acting in anie of those encroachments complained upon in the petitione of right to be against lau. This is the materiall point, though there be tuo uthers of less moment insisted upon; beside I doe not questione yow have the vote transmitted from uther hands. I doe take occasione from this to give your lordship my advice about it with all the sinceritie you could expect from the best of your friends. Perhaps I may be suspected to write from designe toe trepan ore wheedle, bot I doe it with all the frankness and ingenuitie of ane honest gentlman and a Christiane. You have it nou in youre hands to endeare youreselfe to youre countrie and to render youreselfe more popular than anie in youre statione ever was, and perhaps you nor noe man else in the same post ever will have the like occasione againe; and that is by thrusting out from under the cover of youre interest and authoritie at court, those persones pointed at by the parliament in that vote. You sie there justice against the nationes greatest oppressors is moderate, bot incapacitating. You can have noe particular concern in it youreselfe; nothing can better satisfie the countrie (and soe consequentlie advance the kings service by binding there affectiones to him) than to secure them against there feares of those persones pointed at in the vote, soe that upon the whol matter, if you neglect this occasione, I will tell it to youre lordship in plaine Inglish as youre friend, you are false to youre oune interest and have slipt the occasione of raising your reputatione, of fixing youreselfe and familie securelie, by doeing that which is good service to king and couutrie, and that which is youre duetie as ane honest man and a true-hearted Scotsman to performe.   I write plainlie, bot I write it from my heart, and if you slight it, assure youreselfe the time will come youre lordship will be forced to confess that James Montgomerie was youre best friend and gave you better advice than all youre uther friends besides.   Pray, my lord, consider seriouslie one it, and ponder it as that which is of weight and importance.—I ame unfeignedlie, my lord, youre lordships most humble servant,   JAMES MONTGOMERIE.

   The right honourable my Lord Melvill, Secretar of Staite for the kingdome of
     Scotland.

   134. SIR JOHN DALRYMPLE to [GEORGE, LORD MELVILLE]—Proceedings in the
        Convention of Parliament—the Bass Rock, etc.

                                            Edenburgh, June 23, 1689.
MY LORD,—Upon Fryday the parliament meett, and after consideration, they fand it was not saif to refuse the overtur I mad in counsell to fall upon such matters only as concerned the house, and needed no articles or committy till the kings pleasur wer knouen, therfor we mad an act ordaining the members to attend under great certifications, then we did proceid to the consideration of thes tuo points whither the committys should be chosen by the whol hous or by the severall stats, conform to the instructions, and whither officers of stat should be of the committy, the commissioner did consider he had bein very slack the last day, and therfor he was very keen, and by fair reasoning we convinct them to quitt the first and delay the last till Tuesday that the records may be perused. I am able to make it appear that for an hundreth and sixty years last, except from the forty to the sixty three, the officers of stat wer alwys member of the articles, and it will be of ill consequence to the crown and consequently to the kingdome if ther be no body at the prepairing the laws.   It's not easy either to discover or amend what hath one gott a wrong sett in the birth, and if the committy could not giv great impressions, why are wee so anxous about them : it's trew the interests of the croun and country can never be trewly oposit, bot they ar seperat and

distinc, and hav different aspects, and as three was of the people, so on was by
the tract of our policy found necessar for the croun if the king do yeeld that the
committys be not constant, and so may be smaller then 24, yett lett a fort part be
still free to the king, that when ther are bot four on a committy lett at least on
officer of stat be necessar. Befor this tim the kings commissioner named all
committys without advice of the hons. From that extreem that the king did all,
we run to the other that he shall hav non for him in the committys when
maters are prepairing. I was this day with the commissioner and told him he
had given that evidenc of his pouer that if he pleasd to do his best, the nation
may be rendred happy by having thes laws mad for which he is instructed,
which ar more then ever was don by on parliament, bot if he did fall back to men
he saw desing to creat truble till they wer gratifyed with places as they pleased,
then I knev ther was not on article of all the gracious concessions of his instructions wold pase or pleas. He took it very weill and promised to do so. I
told him if he did not intend it he had better either tell the king he wold not do
it or desir leav to com up to adjust his instructions, which he mightily presses,
bot to accept so hy a trust and not to do his utmost in it it was nather saif nor for
his reputation. I had occasion fully to convinc him of that freindship that was
mad with my colleagues, which he never knew, and they did deny so much as
ever treaty or meeting. I knov this cannot hold out bot tuo or three days
would turn the opinion of the toun for us, wheras befor Fryday they thought the
instructions quit unreasonable. My lord, I must advertiz you of on thing, they
plainly say the king is ingadged to redress the grivances, and what they pleas
to say was meant in the grivances he is bound to confirm by lawes, and for that
qualification of all just grivances they ar sole judges : they do repent extreemly
the first act that they did assert the king and queens right till they had gott all
their humours satisfyed : they are prepairing and stoking money to com up in
caice of adjurnment, so I hop all will be barred, except the commissioner in
regard of the present stat of affairs. Yesterday in counsell the duke brought
in a draught of a letter from the connsell to the king anent Mr. Inglis gift. I
cleared that I had told him of it, and the man was waiting on. He seemed to be
satisfyed after som storm that the thing was both lawful and at present necessar,
yett he did nrge the consell to a vote and losed it, but still ther is need of mor
counsellour. Sir G. Campbell of Cesnock hath bein a kind friend to your lordship
and a good instrument at this tim. I knov not why he may not pretend as
much as any of our heroes ; the collonels and captans have gotten pay for
many moe men then they hav : the men are trewly right good, I wish they
wer in Irland. It's dangerous to hav that forc in thes hands, and when it coms

to blowes ther must be souldiers, and most of the persons who hav the present
commission wold excuse ther attendanc.   Amongst other things I find D[uke]
H[amilton] will not be satisfyed to be chancellour except he wer first commissioner of the treasury.   I wrott to your lordship last concerning the Bass : if
you indemnify the governour for life and fortun and his brother for correspondanc,
he will deliver it I am sur.   Both ther fortuns are inconsiderable, and I wish it
wer in the kings pouer.   It can hold out, for the sollen gies and other fowls is
mor then sufficient to sustean the garrison, and they send out their boots and take
out meall or provisions from any ship or boott that coms up the firth, and the
place is impregnable.   All thes who hav ther forfaulters to be rescinded ar for the
sitting of the parliment, tho' I cannot say they ar for it's good temper, which wold
secur its sitting.   They complain ther is no instruction about them ; I told them
that was process, and so needed no instruction, but that ther wold be a generall
seperat instruction anent that matter.   Your lordship will remember that ther be
a particular warrand to me not to oppose any of thes restorations upon the kings
interest.   Befor this can com to your hand, yow ar resolved whither to suffer the
parliament to go on or adjurn ; I wish your lordship may be weill directed in it.
I have no other fear nor concern but for the publick.   I'le never doubt the king
will sustean his innocent servants from malice.—My dear lord, adeiu.

Indorsed : Sir John Dallrymple, 23 Junii 1689, in relation to the proceidings
in parliament.

135. DAVID ROSS of BALNAGOWN to MAJOR-GENERAL M'KAY, praying him not
to withdraw from the country.

Invernes, 25 June 1689.
MAY IT PLEASE YOUR EXCELLENCIE,—My being imployed by Collonel Leing-
stoune to interprett the intelligence the Iliolanders gaiv to him annent Dundies
resolutiones, hes giuen me the confidence to trouble your Excellencie with this lyne,
showeing that from soverall certane hands it is confirmed that the morn being
Thursday, ther is ane generall randevozo of thes vnderwrittin to hold at Inver-
gerrie, viz., All the men belonging to Lochele, Glengerrie, Moudart, M'Donald
in the Isles, M'Inlcanes in Kinteir and Mull, etc., with Breadalbinos men and
Athols, Badenoch and the Farquarsones, and all the men in Draemare, and from
ther randevouze they doe intend to march northward and to force all the name
of Freaser and the M'Kenzies to joyne with them, which, as your Excellencie
knowes, will not be ane vnpleasent force to them (and it's feared they wait such

ane pretence). Wherfor, efter I had advised with my Lord Strathnaver and Collonel Liuingstoune, I thought it my dewty to give your Excellencie this accompt by this express, and, joyneing with them in ther judgment which is offered to you by ther letters, I doe humbly, with all imaginable submission to your Excellencie, earnestly intreat that you doe not withdrawe your personall presence at this tyme from this poor countrie, which is now exposed to all the calamity of warr, and will therby be reduced to such povertie and miserie by that cruell enemy of mankind, that at your Excellencies returne from the south they will not be in a capacity to serve ther Majesties tho they be never so willing ; wherns iff your Excellency halt tuixt this and Strathboggie till you be acquanted by my Lord Strathnaver and Collonel Livinstone of the enemies march and progress ; and when they draw to a head, your Excellencie may soon defend and assist this country with your forces and your presence, which will be of more import to the cause then many regiments without you. Ther is methodes laid to bring certaine and dayly intelligence wherof your Excellencie sall be punctually acquanted, so as they cannot sturr without your knowledge, and it is your removeall that they attended, and which I hop in God, by your Excellencies good goverment, assisted by Gods blisseing, will incourage them to com togither so as you may cut them off root and breanch, which is the constant earnest prayer off, may it please your Excellencie, your most affectionat and humble servant,

DAUID ROSS off Balnagoune.

For the right honourable Generall Major M'Kay, commander of his Majestics forces in Scotland—thes.

136. DUNCAN MACPHERSON of Cluny to MAJOR-GENERAL MACKAY—Attachment to the Protestant interest.

Cluny, 25 June 1689.

RIGHT HONORABILL,—I doe not doubt but that the wrong measures your Excellencie charges me and my kinsmen with by your last of the 20th instant is insinuat by misinformation, for your coosen, Captain Hugh Makdonell, to whom I declared my self with fredome, who knew my indisposition of body for the tyme which affects me as yet, and to whom I comitted to shew yow my mynd to the full, might have shewed your Excelleucie, as I doe now declare for my self and my kinsmen, that we are all Protestants and resolve to owin that opinion to our lyves end, and never resolued to raise in arms against it, but rather to suffer burning and harrieing than that we should appere to draw our swords against our consciencies ; and with all I verie much regret that my indisposition at present impeds that I cannot as yet, as I verie much desyre to sie your Excellencie to kiss your hands, to talk of severall matters, and lykwise to remove all these calumnious aspersiones.   I thank God I am recouering partly, and am resolved, how soon it pleases Providence to mak me able to ryd, I will wait on yow when and where yow please, as, right honorabill, your Excellencies most humble and veric obedient servant,   D. M'PHERSON.

    For his Excelleucie Major Generall Makay, commander in cheeff off his Majesties forces in Scotland—these.

137. LIEUTENANT-COLONEL CLELAND to LORD MELVILLE—As to the affairs of his regiment—the Cameronians.   Glenshira, 25th July 1689.

MY LORD,—Being hurried the last tyme I did myself the honor to writte to your lordship I forgot to answer anent Mr. Lockhart and Mr. Karnagie, which I presume to doe by this.   Mr. Lockhart and all his brethren are ill looked upon by this people of Clidsdale, becaus of there violence in persueing those who ware obnoxius in the late kiugs reigne ; for Mr. Carnagie, if he be a verteus man, I dout not but he may be employed verie well in on of the batalions.   The captains are universaly brave men, the subalterns in on of the battallions are all good but on or two, and those I intend to turn out, and evric too hot man, in a litle tyme.   I have brought on of the batallions that hath still ben quartered with me to a verie good condition.   They doe there exercise and fiere as well as many old regiments, but we are lyke to be ruiued with Blackwod, who hath got a comission for paying the regiment from my Lord Angus, and for lifting up all the mony, and goes so about this that if he continue he will ruine the regiment. The councell ordered to advance us a fourtnights pay radie monie, least precepts should not have answered our necessetie, being ordered to the higlauds with Argeille.   This mony, for the most part, he keept up, though I was radie to count for what I had receaved, and had payed the regiment till the 17 day of July, and had only receaved 18 days subsistance in May, and the pay of the month of June, so that officers and sogers are considerably in my debt ; so that out of Blackwods love to keip mony in his hand we lie here above Euneraric without mony, and our sogers radie to desert, except such as will not desert from a principle of love to the cause and there Majesties, of which sort our regiment is mostlie made up.   I should hartilie wish on of the batallions ware given to another, for I find it impossible to have an equal inspection of bothe, being allways quartered in different places. If the former proposal that I made as to the division of the batallions doe not please your lordship, which I wish it might, I hope your lordship shall lett me know your meind, for Blackwood hath taken such a prejudice at me that I can have no peace, and am still diverted by his intrigues from meinding my bussinesse. The ground of his prejudice is becaus I wold not name his son in law eldest captain befor Parkhays son, the sherif of Argeils, and sevral other good gentilmen who had served abroad, he being only a petite gentilman, no soger, and last of all the captaines in raising his companie. All I desired was that I might not have the odium, but that it might be refferred to my Lord Angus, upon which account Blackwod hath still projected my ruine, and falln in with the Duke of Hamilton for that effect. We have intelligence that Athol men, together with Lord William Murray, have declared for Dundee, but, my lord, I can assure your lordship the trimmers are farr more dangerus. There are many of the new raised forces not steill to the back. I begg it of your lordship lett the standing force be in trew mens hands, for the trimming partie will on a litle occasion prove open enemies, and things are caried on deeper and with a further prospect then ever I could have beleveed. The Irish and Macleans are joyned Dundee. They make at present about 3000 men, and are daly gathering, but that signifies litle if those who professe to be friends ware trew. I shall not fail to give your lordship a trew account of what comes to my ears. I recommend myself to your lordships protection and favor, and shall ever continue, my lord, your lordships most humble and ever obliged servant,

Glain Shire, July 25, 1689.   WILL. CLELAND.

138. H[ENRY] FLETCHER to GEORGE, LORD MELVILLE—the Deputy Keeper of the Bass.

Edinburgh, 27 July [16]89.

MY LORD,—One Mr. Dumbar, who is employed to besiege the Bass, tells me that Major General Mackay has recommended him to the king to be deputy governor of the Bass, that he is to have comission and pay as captain, and 36 men in the company. I shal be very well pleased the garrison be increased, neither shal I envy any deputy how great his pay be, but it seems natural that the governors should be greater. I have been informing myself of the profits of the isle, and I find that in my Lord Perths time they were fermed sometimes at one thousand, but most commonly at nine hundered pound Scots a year, which is so mean a thing that unless I have the other smal advantages which have hitherto always depended on the governor, thes are the recommending of a deputy and the modeling and paying of the garrison, I shal not think it worth the keeping. I hope your lordship will suffer no alteration to be made in the nomination of the deputy. Mr. Wood is now in the north of Scotland making his recruits for Holland. I have not yet heard from him, but shal acquaint you when I do. I make no question he will be able to perform the condition required. I know your lordship will not be very foreward in putting the king to any new expence, as the increasing the deputys pay, and the number of the garrison, would be, without which its like Mr. Dumbar will not be very desirous of it, and tho he were, I look upon it as a thing already done and unalterable since the king has signed the commission for Mr. Wood at your lordship's desire. I know no merit Mr. Dumbar can pretend to by besieging it, since I see him often here in town, and that neither intelligence nor provision can be hindered without a diligent attendance both night and day at sea. He was a captain in Dargenys regiment befor, let him be added to it again ; for my part I cannot well trust him. I hope your lordship will think my desire reasonable, and be favorable to, my lord, your lordships most humble and obliged servant,   H. FLETCHER.

This Dumbar was a servant of General Dalzels. He is much troubled with the falling sickness, and thes who know him give him no good character.

139. JOHN, LORD STRATHNAVER, to KING WILLIAM THE THIRD—That his regiment was complete and ready to serve the king.

Invernes, 31 Jully 1689.

MAY IT PLEASE YOUR MAJESTIE,—The meetting of estates in this kingdome haveing thought fitt in Aprile last to appoint me as collonell to a foot regiment, with power to me to nominat my own officiers, though this was done without my knowledge, and that I was sick of a feavor in the time, yett I noe sooner heard of it then the satisfaction I had to think that I was putt in some capacity to serve God and your Majestie in my generation did contribute soe much to my health that in a few dayes, beyond the expectation of many, I was able to goe about the affaires of my regiment, and have now had it compleit at Invernes thir two monthes. I then requested my father, the Earle of Sutherland, to acquaint your Majestie that my ambition to serve your Majestie was such, that seing ther was more forces in Scotland then I hope shall be found needfull, I should therfor be glad to receave orders to march aither to Holland, Irland, or England, or whither else your Majestie pleases, and am perswaded ther is none your Majestie may repose more confidence in then the regiment I command. I am sure ther is naither officier nor sentinel in it but who will esteem it his greatest honour to spend his blood for your Majestie against the French king, or whoever else is your Majesties enimy. I am affraied, out of to great tendernes to ane only son, my father hes neglected to inform your Majestie of my desire, which is the occasion that I take the boldnes and presumption to trouble your Majestie at this time. I wait with the greatest impatience imaginable the happyness of receaving your Majesties commands, and am, as in dutie bound, may it please your Majestie, your Majesties most faithfull subject and most devoted humble servant,

STRATHNAVER.

140. BRIGADIER-GENERAL ALEXANDER CANAN to MAJOR-GENERAL MACKAY—
For exchange of prisoners.

From our Quarter at Kinloch, 5 August [16]89.

SIR,—I receaved yours by your trumpet late yester night, and according to your desire I haue sent yow the enclosed list of those officers wee haue prisoners, for whois releefe wee seek no more but ane equall exchange of those of ours in your prisones, viz.:—ane lievtenant-collonel for lievtenant-collonel, captan for captan, and soe of others conforme to ther station and quality. As for those who were killed in the battaill wee could not know their quality, the night being dark and they stript by the soldiers befor day. All that was possible was done, that is all that were dead on the place were buried, and wee haue freelie set at liberty all the common soldiers. This was not your way of treating those that fell in your hands, who by your ordor were hanged in the north. Your way of defending the Protestant religion (which yow injuriouslie insinuat wee destroy) is nether soe honorable nor Christian as to deserve ansuer, far less imitation, for whatever ambition, state and clergie policy may draw a discontented and enthusiastick rable to doe, yet perjury, treachery, and running away from there king and generall is a new way to honor in men of armes; nay, not soe much as ouned by any confession of faith yet extant in the world. As for your threatening to confine us to the hils with your horse, yow shall have liberty to boast of it when yow have done it. Till then yow must think our forces are better then yours, as all the world knowes our cause is. Those vast armies yow threatten us with, wee hope will in a short tyme be confounded with the vnnaturall vsurper who brybes them out of there honor, religion, and intrest, and makes them actors of the

blackest villanie that ever was.   Sir, wee are in a condition not to fear them.
But I shall not present our forces to yow but in the foild.   Your way of ensnare-
ing people by fictiones and stories lookes like your vsurper, not like the father of
the people, who, for as great a chimera as yow think it, will shortlie call yow to
ane accountt if yow doe not speedily run to your dykes.   It seemes your intelligence is very good, and wee thank yow for telling us that Kirk is in Derry, that
toune being now the kings.   And altho' wee know what yow say of Solmes and
Shomberg, tho yow should join Herbert and M'Cay with them, is such that they
are nether able to face the kings forces nor hinder his landing.   Yet I shall not
make vse of such arguments (as yow doe), as your old comrade, to invite yow and
those gentlmen with yow (whois fate wee regrate) to address to your naturall
prince, and endeavor to make some reparation by preventing the shedding of
more blood.   Otherwise at his Majesties landing (which yow compare with your
goeing to Constantinople) you may prepare indeed for such a voyage as the fittest
for the prince of Oranges reformers.   I shall conclude with mynding that the
mercie of our king exceeds the malice of his enemies, which I wish yow may lay
to heart and returne to your alleagiance, which is the earnest wish of, sir, your
old comrad and humble servant,   ALL. CANAN.

   Indorsed: Cannon's letter to G. M. Mackay, 5 August 1689.

141. COLONEL GEORGE RAMSAY to HENRY, LORD CARDROSS—To bring back his
dragoons to Perth.

                                    Three a'clock in the afternoon,
                                        Pearth, the 19th August [16]89.
MY LORD,—I was uneasie till I heard from yow, but knowing of yow being
there and of yowr good conducke, it quieted me much.   I thing these dragoons
and horse can be of little use in these grounds, so I thinck yowr lordship may come
back here with them.   Liuetenant Colonel Cleland says he will be able to mantain his post if he gett prouisions and amunition.   He will be able, I hope, to do
it, for I haue sent him part of both this day with yowr captain liuetenant, and
shall send him more the morrow.   I am, my lord, your lordships most humble
servant,   GEO. RAMSAY.

   My lord, stay not on that side of the water the toune is on, but stay a mille
on the other side of the water till day and then come to this toun the morrow.

   For my Lord Cardross att Dunkell.

142. The Same to The Same—To retire with the horse under his command.

Pearth, August 20th, [16]89.

My Lord,—I desired yowr lordship last night to retire with the horse and dragoons under your command. Except yow haue orders from some generall person to the contrarie yow most do soe yet or be ansurable for what shal fall out. Major General Laniere knows of Angus regiment being there. I had a letter from him last night which acquaints me of the bodie of the enemy moving towards Atholl, one letts me know he intends to move this way, yet I thinck it fitt yow yet retire, this is from, my lord, your lordships most humble servant,

Geo. Ramsay.

My lord, take such measures that the enemy come not betuixt us and yow and so stop yowr passadge.

For my Lord Cardross att Dunkell. Pearth, a quarter after 3 a'clock, in the afternoon.

143. Sir William Lockhart to George, Lord Melville—Attack on Lord Angus's regiment at Dunkeld.

Edinburgh, 23d Agust 1689.

My Lord,—We had ane account yesterday from Colonel Ramsay, who lys at Perth, that the rebls had falen on the Lord Angus regiment att Dunkell, had kiled the leutenant colonell and severall other officers, and cutt of a grate part of the regiment. Ther being no account com from Dunkell, we wold gladly hope the first acount will prove the worst. Ramsay, at tuelfe att night, Wedensday, marched to ther assistance tuo hours befor Sir John Lanier was comed to St. Jonstoun, and was imediatly to fallou. We wait ane expres with grat impatience, having sent on ther yesterday morning to knou the certintie of the mater. Som say its only the Atholl men and others of that countrie who have joyned them, but its moir generallie believed all Cannons armie are gon that way, and that they have again sliped the major generall. What certenly to believe we knou not till the expres coms. The Master should have been maried this day, but to oblidge the ministers, who wold have them to be proclaimed, its delayed till Tuesday nixt. Ther tuo things on this ocation that peple complain of—first, that that regiment without horse should have been sent to such ane advanced post, and nixt, why Colonell Ramsay, the very day befor the action, should have caled them to Pearth, Cardross commanding ther Polwart and Grubits tronps of horse and thrie troops of his oun dragoons, and its generally thought that Cardross, notwithstanding Ramsays order, should not have marched, he having had som skirmishes with them the day before, and seen the country gathering, which he was to think Ramsay kneu not off. The advocatt may remember that when it was moved in counsell that the Lord Angus regiment should goe ther, my Lord Leven oposed it, and told as plainly as if he had seen it, what wold he ther fatte. The counsell is every day turning out ministers for not reading the proclimation. The duk pairted from this on Tuesday, my Lord Muray only in the coach with him; the Earle of Mortoun, Sir James Ogelbie, Sir William Hamelton, Ricatoun, Pitliver, in a hacknay. The laird of Grange should have made the sixt, but stays for som days. I need not trouble your lordship with what is said hear in relation to the siting or not siting of the parliment att the tyme, nor with the resonings we have had in relation to the dissolution of this parliment, and what interest the king may have in a neu on. The advocat is very capable to give you distinct vieus of the wholl affair. For my oun part, I think, when you have heard all from the advocat, you'll see that you may easily and safly play your oun interest as well as his Majesties service, and be so farr from gratifying thes hott headed peple that are com up, that you have no need of them att all. The expres we waited for is nou com. Sir John Lanier wryts that, having notice of that affair, he had marched his troups for the assistance of that regiment had don so bravly, and that he had sent Durie the inginier to bring such things as wer necessarie for his going towards the Blair of Atholl, to which Colonell Cannon and his armie are retired. Ther is ane other letter from Dunkell, syned be thrie of Lord Angus captains, in which they complin more of ther being ill used then giving anay account of the action, such as Cardross leving them, the want of pouder and ball. The account we have of the action is that they posted themselves in the house and garding of Dunkell after ther horse left them, that Cannons wholl armie, to the number of 2500, entered the toun and atacked them; that they defended bravly, that the enimie brought four peace of cannon, thinking to dislodge them, but wer so ill guners that they did no execution; in short, they forced the enimy to retir with the loss of 200 men on the place. Cleland is kiled, about tuentie of his men kiled and wonded. Hendersons arme brok and ill wonded. Our peple have brunt Dunkell. The major generall with his forces was yesterday att Forfar.—I am, my lord, your most humble and most affectionat servant,   WILL. LOCKHART.

For my Lord Melvill, lord secretarie for the kingdom of Scotland.

144. GENERAL THE DUKE OF SCHOMBERG [probably to DAVID, EARL OF LEVEN]
—King James's army at Drogheda. Contemporary copy. Also copy of
letter forwarding the packet.

From our Head Quarters at Dundalk,
12 September 1689.

MY LORD,—I addressed these letters to your lordship, being perswaded that yow
will willingly take upon yow to send them by express to his Majestie. The contrary winds, which have hindered our victwalling ships from comeing up to us,
have occasioned a great want of bread in our armie, and our waggones for carrie-
ing the bread being not yet come out of England, makes us stay longer here then
wee would doe. I beleive the late King James, being with 40,000 men at Droc-
heda, seeing that wee doe not advance, will incouradge his army to come and give
us battell here. Our army is not all come over. I have wrott twice to his
Majestie that he would ordour us some regiments out of Scotland, and monie to
pay them, but have hade no answear. I beseech your lordship, if there be anything that I can serve yow in here, that yow would command me, who am, my
lord, your lordships most humble servant,

(Sic subscribitur)   SCHONBERG.

Copy letter accompanying the preceding.

Port Patrick, September 15, 1689.

MAY IT PLEASE YOUR LORDSHIP,—The pacquet came this day about 10 acloack,
which instantly I have dispatched. I have nothing to add to my last, saveing
that yesterday 30 saile from England came into Carrickfergus. What store of
men they brought was not knowen when the pacquet came of. A pairt of the
fleet went out of Carrikfergus to Carlingford upon Frydday last, to attend his
graces commands, he being incamped in and about Dundalk, which is all at present from him who desyres to know your lordships furder commands to, may it
please your lordship, your lordships most humble servant,

(Sic subscribitur)   WM. FFULLERTOUNE.

145. WILLIAM, EARL OF CRAWFORD AND LINDSAY, President of the Privy
Council [probably to GEORGE, LORD MELVILLE]—The Earl of Leven
appointed governor of the castle. September 1689.

THIS day, after some little debate, the councill, being well conveened, did appoint
the appending of the seall to the Earle of Levin's command in the castell. All
did agree that the king had made a very good choise, but were in some doubt

what was the councill's power in a matter of that kind; and if it was not an homologation of Mr. Inglis's gift, which they say is a new trust, never heard of before in Scotland, and inconvenient to be in the hand of a subject of that degree. I had yours, daited August 27th, so full of kindness to me, as I am at a stand in what fashion, either verbally or practically, I can make a suteable return. If I know my own heart I sincerely wish well to your selfe and family, and will be ready to evince it att all occasions when your interest falls in my way, either for the vindication of your actions, where people are misledd to mistake them, or to confirm further in a perfect friendship to yon, such as are allreadie favourable to you. If his Majestie is pleas'd to conceive well of my actiones, I have a full requitall without more of all the services I am capable of doing him. But that I be not thought a contemner of his Majestie's favours, or humoursome to have anything by your mediation, or an extinguisher of my family, which the Lord hath made numerous : I shall humbly stoope to whatever his Majestie shall think proper for me, tho' in no fashion I can judge it fitt for me to prescryve to his Majestie, in a matter of his bowntie; nor to you as to what I may be qualified for; but singlely leaves that to discretion. Yea, I have such an aversation in my temper from all selfe seeking, that before I had urg'd anything for my selfe, much less have been speciall in nameing of it, I had rather been reduc'd to the greatest straits, that ever person of my qualitie was trysted with. And should never have grudg'd, tho' his Majestie had plainely overlook'd me, and delt of his favours rather to such whose loyalty cannot be secured but by the dead weight of some rewarde or other. Tho' it be said that paper does not blush, and that there is not plaine effrontrie in what you have now under my hand, yet I may freely say that with great struggling and no small measure of bashfullness you have this freedom from your affectionat friend and very humble servant,

Indorsed : Edinburgh, September 1689 ; E[arl] Crawford.

146. WILLIAM, EARL OF CRAWFORD AND LINDSAY to GEORGE, LORD MELVILLE—Prisoners in the castle examined.

Edinburgh, 26th Nov. 1689.

MY LORD,—You need make no excuse that I have not a return to every lyne I write, not so much as projecting it, and less expecting such exactness, being convinc'd that your lordship hes other wayes a toyle that renders you uncapable of answering all the letters you receave. Your last to me was matter of joy, in that our interest seems yet intire, and enemies have gain'd no ground. Next to his Majestie, in whom we cheefely rely, those of our way do found our hopes on your lordships zeal for the puritie of our establishment, and the use you will make of it with your master, and are not a little sensible that the Earle of Portland, tho not of our nation, hes done us significant service.   This flying pacquet is occasioned by the intercepting yesterday a letter from one Dunbar, a prisoner in the tolbooth, to Lifetennent Collonell Wilson, prisoner in the castle ; upon which two from the council were ordered to go there, and search prisoners, and finding them all in one room (except Wilson), and in their companie, the Lord Lochore, the Laird of Lanton, younger, Walter Scot of Edenshead, and Mr. David Drummond, every one of them signaly disaffected to the government, they search'd their persons and cabinets ; and while they were thus employed, young Lanton tore in small peices a letter that he had on him, and upon no tearmes would then discover either what it contain'd or from whom he receaved it. Upon which he was made closs prisoner, untill this day, that he was examined. That which gave us more ground to proceed on, was a letter wee found this morning, directed to Lantons servant, and designed for himselfe (for wee had waited the comeing of the pacquet and appointed your son Levin and another of our number, to view the letters where they had a suspition).   You have here the double of it, and the examination of severall persons about it.   Wee durst not forbear this haistie way of transmitting it, least David Lindsay, formerly Melfort's man, the writer thereof, should have had warning, and gone out of the way: he is certainly a great rogue, and was formerly twice in prison here, upon trafficking in that manner.   Your lordship will try that matter to the outmost, for severalls where you are will probably be found corresponding here, unto the prejudice of the government.   The prisoners in the castle and tolbooth do generally receave and spread all the unluckie news in the countrey.   It would really be adverted to, for their partie are become extream insolent by it, and ours a little discouraged, the sealled enclosed was about an houre agoe, by Doctor Rule, delyvered to, my dear lord, your lordships most faithfull and affectionat humble servant,

                                                                CRAFURD.

147 GENERAL CANAN to the LAIRD OF GLENCO—To restore the goods taken
         from Glenlyon.   Iron Mills, 22d December 1689.

SIR,—This is ordring yow in his Majesties nam to mak rest[it]ution of what goods was taken from thes men of Glenlyon who is folouers of the Laird of Maknaughton, as yow will answer to the contrair.   Dated at the Iron Mills, December 22, [16]89.   ALL. CANAN.
    Makean.
       To the Laird of Glenco.

148. DUKE OF SCHOMBERG to DAVID, EARL OF LEVEN—A famine threatened—
provisions to be bought for the North-west of Ireland.

Lisburne, Januar 1689 [90].

MY LORD,—I received your lordships letter of the 24th of November at the
hands of Captain Kennedy, whom I am sending to Edenburg to buy provisions
for the supply of the inhabitants of the northwest part of this province, which if
not procured from thence, thousands of souls must inevitably perish. He will
give your lordship full information of his commission as well as the present [state]
of this army. Your countenance in this affair will be very necessary to forward
so good a designe, which is no less then the preservation of many thousand souls.
I heartily congratulate your lordship upon your promotion to the castle of
Edinburg, and shall be ever glad to hear of your further advancement, which is
the sincer desire of, I remaine, my lord, your lordships most humble servant,

SCHONBERG.

Lord Leven.

[Holograph of the Duke] Je uous auais desia fait mes compliments sur le
Chatteau d'Endenbourg ou uous serez obl[i]ge de rester. Le Roy me mande qu'il
euuoyera ici quatre de uos Regiments, j'espere qu'ils seront composes de bons
hommes et pas de garcons trop jeunes.

TWENTY-SIX LETTERS from GEORGE, LORD and FIRST EARL OF MELVILLE,
Secretary of State for Scotland, to WILLIAM [DOUGLAS], THIRD DUKE OF
HAMILTON, Lord High Commissioner to the Parliament of Scotland.[1]

149. (1) News expected of Dundee—The fleet put to sea.

London, Maii 18, 1689.

MAY IT PLEASE YOUR GRACE,—The kings being at Portsmouth hath hindered the
commissioners dispatch, and now they not being ready to goe as yett for Scotland, his Majestie hath commanded me to send the enclosed to your Grace by a
fleeing pacquet, that it might be with you against the meeteing of the estates. I
am but just now come to town, so has no tyme to say much, but to assure your
grace of my readiness to serve you. Wee have litle news heer of moment, but
what wee have from the north, a further account of my Lord Dundee's progress

---

[1] The originals of these twenty-six letters   Duke of Hamilton, and have not hitherto
are in the Charter-chest of His Grace the   been printed.

since he was at Perth, and what is become of Generall Major Mackay is expected and longed for. There is a brave fleett putting out heer, and the seamen now shewes a great deale of willingnes to goe aboord. The Dutch fleet is daily expected on our coasts. Ther is yett no account heer of the arrivall in Scotland of that shipe sent down long agoe with mortars, bombs, and amunition.—I am, your grace's most humble and most obedient servant,   MELVILL.

For your grace.

Indorsed : Dated 18 May. Answered 24 May 1689.

150. (2) The Convention to be turned into a Parliament.

London, 31 of Maii [1689].

MAY IT PLEASE YOUR GRACE,—These lines you honoured me with by the express, came safe to hand. I have done my endeavour to gett him soon dispatcht again to your grace. It surprises me to hear that the pacquett with the king's letter came not till after the meeting of the estats was adjourned. It was sent with a flying pacquet for the heast. I know the commission for the counsell must pass the great scall when it is ready. In the mean tyme I thoght it fitt your grace should have it that you might use it or not as occasion might require. And I hade no further directions from the king about it. In the begining of every reign the like difficulty occurres. Had I altered the style of all former commissions I had not escaped censure ; but I looke on what your grace wreats as other men's thoghts and not your own, and I accept of it as a part of that freedome you promised to honour me with. I remember of no person in the commission who opposed the king's interest in every vote while they stayed, and then deserted. If ther be any such in it, they must have left the meeteing befor I came too it. I thoght the persons most pointed att in the grivances had been left out off the commission. It was in compliance with the address from the states that his Majestie did resolve to turn them unto a parliament upon the fifth of the nixt month. I believe the commissioners sent upe by the states to make the offer of the crown will not refuse that the present exigencie was the reason why the states did desire this to be turned into a parliament with the first conveniencie. The satisfieing the states prevailed with his Majestie, who would otherwals willingly have had your grace heer to have adjusted your own iustructions, and also ther being less to be objected against a parliament of a new election. His Majestie did not communicate to me his resolutions, nor give me his commands, iu order to his answer to what your graces express broght Tewsday at eight a cloake at night at Hampton Court, and on Wednesday he came to Whithall to give audience to ambassadours of the states of the United Provinces; after that, his Majestie was at councel untill he went of town late, which hath delayed the returning your express. I went out this day to Copthall to heasten him, for the king was ther at hunting. His Majestie hath ordered me to signifie to your grace that you might repair to the publick roomes in the palace when you please, as other commissioners used to doe, and said ther needed no other warrant to your grace, who is heritable keeper, if the nomination of the counsell in which your grace is mentioned as president be not sufficient, and if you thinke a separate commission fitt, your grace may be pleased to cause draw it, and I shall present it to his Majestie and be cairfull to have it returned, as also your graces gift of pension, and your allowance of fiftie pund per diem, shall be dispatched so soon as the treasury be's constitute that the precepts can be drawen. I hope your grace will excuse the confusedness of these lines, for I am very weiried. I had not tyme to aske the king concerning the messingers allowance, but shall the first opportunity. The scall was promised to be ready this night, but is not, so I will not delay any longer your messinger, but shall send on with it to morrow whenever it is ready.

In anything else that I can be of use for your service you may command.—May it please your grace, your most humble and most obedient servant,

MELVILL.

For your grace.
Indorsed: Dated 31 May.   Answered 6 Jun. 89.

151. (3) The King's opinion that Major-General Mackay should march southward, etc.

London, 4 June 1689.

MAY IT PLEASE YOUR GRACE,—I waited on the king, and gave his Majesty an account of my being informed from Scotland that severall of the Highlanders were in armes, and some joyned with the Viscount of Dundie, and that many of the standing forces were marched to the north to joyne Generall Mackay, who was in pursute of the rebells. His Majesty was pleased to tell me that he thought it was of greater concern to the country in this present juncture that the Generall Major should march southward with his troopes towards Edinburgh and Glasgow, etc., with all convenient diligence, after having taken some care to secure Invernesse and such other places as he judged convenient for the safety of the country rather than to goe in pursute of Dundie through the Highlands, which would render the horse unserviceable through want of forrage and travelling in

had wayes; and does also expose the south and west countrys to great danger in
case of any invasion, the forces being from thence at so great a distance. This
his Majesty commanded me to signify to Major Generall Mackay, or to Colonell
Balfour in his absence, and to acquaint your grace with the same, and that the
account his Majesty has of the strength of the Highlanders and Dundie's party is
so uncertain that he could not give more particular directions therein, but refers
the same to the councell, on whose prudence and good conduct he very much
relies. Therefore doubts not but they will take such proper methods as may be
effectuall for reducing those now in armes against his Majesty, and securing the
kingdome from any danger of forreigne invasion. The king also commanded me
to tell your grace that what account is sent to the councell of the condition of
the north country, or what else relates to the publick interest of the nation, you
will transmitt the same to his Majesty.—I am, my lord, your graces most humble
and most faithfull servant,   MELVILL.

MAY IT PLEASE YOUR GRACE,—Since the wreateing of what is above I receaved
a letter from you with Generall Major Mackey's letter to your grace from
Badenoch by a flying pacquett, upon which I went immediatly and gave his
Majestie ane account of the same. He was goeing out off town so I had but litle
tyme to discourse his Majestie. But in reguard the number and designs of
Dundee and his associats ar still uncertain, therfor his Majestie could give no
particular derections, but commanded me to tell your grace that, notwithstanding
of what is befor wretten, yett he did referr the matter to his privy counsell to take
such measures with Generall Major Mackey as the present circumstances doe
require, and likewais to secure such persons as they se just cause for. In my
opinion it would be very necessary that some speedy course should be taken for
getting intelligence from the Irish side whither ther be any appearance or present
disposition of an invasion from Irland, and of what number of forces they have
in the north, and if they have shipes and vessells prepared to transport them,
and that the captaines of the two shipes might be ordered to land some of ther
men in Irland, if they may doe it securly, to gett the more distinct informations
from severall places of the coast. Ther ar betwcen 20 and 30 of the Dutch fleet
ar said now to be out, and Admirall, now Lord, of Torringtone is to goe to sea
this wooke with 35 saile. The king is now more confirmed of the necessity of
the sitting of the parliament, and that persons of your graces interest cannot
weell be absent.—I continue your graces most humble servant,   MELVILL.

For his grace the Duke of Hamilton, his Majestys high commissioner. To
be communicated by him to the privy councell of Scotland.

152. (4) The Duke's precept for £50 per diem, to be signed, etc.

London, 13 Jun [1689].

MAY IT PLEASE YOUR GRACE,—By the Monday's packet I had on from your grace of the 4, and designed to have wrett the nixt post, but was not able to doe it, therefor entreats your graces excuse. Yesterday I received another of the 6, with on for the king, which I delivered to his Majestie at Hampton Court this day. I gave his Majestie an accompt how necessary it was your precept should be sent for £50 per diem, as also an other precept for paying immediatly to your grace a sume for your equippage suitable to the character you beare, the king hath promised to doe both, which your grace may rest upon. I thoght to have gott them dispatched this afternoon, but the king went streight from the council chamber to his coach to goe for Copthall, and returns on Saturnday, when I shall wait an oportunity to have them signed. I am very sencible of the trowble and charge your grace must necessarly be at, and I assure you I have not nor shall be wanting in giveing his Majestie a just account of the same.

I shall be sory if what his Majestie hath done with a design only to give satisfaction to his people, and to bring things to a speedy settlement in that kingdome, should meet with such difficulties as your grace seemes apprehensive off. I dowbt not but by your graces caire these will be prevented.

I acquainted the king with your graces letter in relation to armes and ammunition, which he hath promised to send down to Scotland. I shall forward the same as much as I can : I wish England could be moved to send mony too, else I see not weell how your forces can be payed. Your graces representation of the low condition of the nation which is so sencible at home and so litle beleeved heer, might helpe to promove this, which, in my opinion, is much ther own interest. The king hath commanded me to wrett to Brigadier Balfour to forbear his throwing of bombs and shooting much against the castle untill General Major Mackey come south, that amunition may be spared in the mean tyme, and more effectuall waies afterwards may be taken for reduceing the castle. I am very glade your graces sone in laws jurney hath hade so good effects. I acquainted his Majestie, who is weell pleased therwith. Wee long to heare from General Major Mackey.—I am, my lord, your graces most humble and faithfull servant,

MELVILL.

I have been so interrupted that I had almost forgott to acquaint your grace that the king hath wrett to the councell in relation to the election of the magistrats of Glasgow, wheroff I send you a copy.

Indorsed : Dated 13 June 89.

153. (5) The King was well pleased with Lord Murray's diligence.

June 15, [1689].

MAY IT PLEASE YOUR GRACE,—I wrot to your grace last post and acquainted you that I had spake to the king in relation to what you recomended to me, but by reason of his goeing streight from the counsell to his coach to goe to the country I could not gett the precepts signed, but have this day, which heere enclosed I send to your grace. I gave his Majestie an accompt of what your grace and my Lord Murray had wrett. He read both himselfe and is weell pleased with my Lord Murray's diligence, and longs for a good account from the north. I had no more tyme with his Majestie but to gett your precepts signed and that he tooke to read your letters, for he was just goeing to threasury, so have no commands from him att this tyme.

Ther is on thing I presume to recomend to your grace because I was unwilling the king should be put to any such trowble to wrett to the councell concerning such ane affaire, which is this, that the Dutches of Buccleugh is informed that her litle parke and deer are spoiled by putting in some troupe horse in it. Her grace would neither grudge corn nor grasse for the service of the country, but being that the horses might have been weell eneugh provided otherwais, shee thinks it a litle hard usage haveing her deere already spoiled as shee is informed by the liberty given to furnish wood and fagots for makeing upe the batteries att the castle. I take the freedome to give your grace this trowble rather then to any other because of the kindness you have alwais professed to her, not dowbting but you will cause helpe this. I have ordered this to be sent by a fleeing pacquett that it may come the sooner to your graces hands. I wish to hear of the modera-tion and unanimity of the parliament in setling the affaires of the kingdome, which will be of great concern to the king's affaires and to the countries happines and security.—I am, may [it] please your grace, your graces most humble and obedient servant,   MELVILL.

For your grace.

Indorsed : Dated Jun 15, 89.

154. (6) Nomination of Lords of Session, etc.

27 June, Hampton Court, [1689].

I ACQUAINTED your grace in my last that by reason of the king's being so much bussied with multiplicity of affaires I could not return you an answer to yours as

soon as I would.   I have hade but litle tyme to speake with his Majestie since ;
what related to armes and amunition I hope you may have what could be spared
heere ere this come to hand, if the winds favour : as for the prisoners sent south
by Generall Major Mackey, his Majesties pleasure is that they be remitted to a
councell of warr, and that caire be taken to make as full a discovery of this
affaire wherin they have been engadged as may be.   The king remitts the
bombardier's petition bake to your grace and the councell to doe therin what
you shall thinke fitt and just.   His Majestie hath given me no particular directions relating to those who absent themselvs from the parliament, but bid me tell
your grace that he dowbted not but that your grace and the parliament would
dwely weigh and consider what is convenient and necessary for the good of the
government, and safty of the kingdome.   Neither did he question but that the
parliaments procedure in this and other things will be such as shall manifest to
the world that they ar acted by nothing but a sincere respect to the good of
the country and his service.   Your grace knows that hardly any particular
direction could be given at this tyme in this caice ; ther being a great difference
betwixt those who have owned the present government and professes themselvs
willing to serve ther Majesties according to ther capacities, who yett may be
absent upon rationall considerations, and such who have never owned ther
Majesties authority nor countenanced his service, and so may be thought to
absent out of dissatisfaction to the government.

I enquired his Majestie concerning Sr. G. Mackenzie[s] pass.   He told me he
had granted it upon application of some of the English.   I am sorry that anything in my management should give dissatisfaction to any, particularly to your
grace, whom it was never my design to disoblidge.   What hath been the indis-
cretion of others ought not to be impute to me : as for Master Inglis, who is
appointed Keeper of the Great Seale in Entrekins vice, I have no particular
intrest in him, but a freind recomended him, and Entrekin seemed willing to
part with that employment.   I wish he had understood himselfe better then to
append the seal befor the king's commissioner was acquainted with it.   All I
can say is that what he hath done is contrair to what he was ordered to doe.

I receaved your graces of the 23 instant.   I see things at a distance appear
far otherwais then they ar intended ; and if the king's service can allow it I shall
be very glade of personal meeting with your grace, and then you would soon
perceive that I doe not profess on thing and act otherwais ; that neither is, nor
ever was, my way of dealing.   In this bussiness of the Lords of Session, when
considered, your grace and all others may see ther is nothing of my private
interest in the nomination, but many complaining of the want of justice, the king

thought fitt to nominate some judges. He was resolved on the president and in pursuance of his declaration, ther was some obligation to repon such as wer put out for adhereing to ther religion. The instrument of government seemed at present to stand in the way of others who wer formerly in that office. Ther is on Hammilton, on Campbell, and on Murray and Arnestone and on Hume; all persons for ought ever I heard without tash, humaine infirmities excepted, and of good reputation, and ther is a vacancie left for five, thogh all accept that ar nominate. I wish those be no worse filled.

The king's procedure in this may be judged equall and condescending.

I am som what surprised to find the direction to take ther oathes by the president of parliament mistaken as if it wer a want of that respect dwe to your graces character or person, wher as it was considered otherwais: according to my information the chancelor used to take the presidents oath, and the president the others. As I shall study by the assistance of God to doe my dwety with fidelity, and so shall place my selfe, God willing, if not out of hazard, yett out of fear of complaints, so I humbly presume our royall master will endeavour to please and satisfie all his good subjects, and will choose his servants with consideration of ther fittnes for the peoples good and his service. I long for the morrow pacquet by which your grace hath given the account of what hath passed in parliament Fryday and Saturnday. I came heer this day to receave his Majestie's commands, but have not had occasion of speakeing to him yett, so by the nixt post your [grace] may expect the trowble of another letter from, may it please your grace, your graces most humble servant,   MELVILL.

For his Grace the Duke off Hamiltown, his Majesties high comissioner for the kingdome of Scotland.

Indorsed: Dated 27 Jun.   Answered 2d July 89.

155. (7) Waiting on the King at Whitehall.

July 2 [1689].

MAY IT PLEASE YOUR GRACE,—I have litle at present to trowble your grace with, but to lett you know I receaved yours both by Major Simmervaile and by the flieing packett Sabbath night very late.

I went yesterday morning to Hamptown Court, and delivered all you commanded me with to the king, who ordered me this day to wait on him att Whitehall, where I have attended all this day, but his Majestie has been so bussied that I have not yett receaved his answer, but hath commanded me to attend him to-morrow in the afternoon at Hamptown Court. Ther shall be no neglect on my part to heasten a return. Wee have not much of news. I heare nothing of Irland since what your grace sent upe. They talke the Count of Solmes is to goe ther with a reinforcement of 5 or 6000 men to join Kirke untill the army be ready, and the Dutch squadron, being about 30 saile, ar joined the English fleet. Wee long for a good account from Irland and from the North. The secretare of warr came to me two three dayes agoe from the councell desireing I should wrett for ordering the English regiments in Scotland to march on for Berwick, and the rest to Carlisle, but the king hath given me no orders for it yett. Its probable they will now be called away, and I hope ther shall not be much use for them now, only I could wish Leslies regiment staied untill General Major Mackey shall have setled the Highlands, since they ar with him; for a heasty calling all away might encourage the Highlanders if they be not already absolutly broke.—I am, may it please your grace, your graces most humble and faithfull servant.   MELVILL.

Indorsed : Dated 2 July.   Answered 6 July 89.

156. (ℵ) That he should endeavour to allay heats in the Parliament.

July 4 [1689].

MAY IT PLEASE YOUR GRACE,—I am commanded by the king to send this to your grace by a flying packet, being to accompany the enclosed letter from his Majestie to the parliament, and an other to your selfe, with some new instructions. I have also enclosed to your grace a coppy of the parliament's letter, by which you will perceive, as also by your instructions, how willing his Majestie is to give all reasonable satisfaction to his people. I dowbt not but your grace will continue to demonstrate your caire of his Majesties interest by useing your endeavours to allay heats and animosities, which ar apt to retard the setling of the generall concerns of the nation. What is incumbent for me to doe in the station the king has been pleased to put me in, shall according to my ability be most heartily and faithfully performed, and on all occasions I shall be ready to demonstrate how much I am, may it please your grace, your graces most humble and faithfull servant,   MELVILL.

Indorsed : Dated 4 July.   Answered 9 July 89.

157. (9) Apprehension of Sir Adam Blair and Dr. Gray.   Copy of a letter
enclosed.

July 9 [1689].

MAY IT PLEASE YOU'R GRACE,—I receaued yours of the 2 with the enclosed, and on
from the Earle of Crawfowrd by your graces and the councel's order.   I could not
yett have opportunity to acquaint the king therwith, but am just now goeing to
try if I may have it.   That letter your grace mentions you wrett to the Earle of
Selcraige, is long ere this come to his haud, which I dowbt not but his lordship
has acquainted you with.   Ther was nothing but a kind of mistristing in the
caice.   I had an advertisement from the Earle of Shrewsbury that Sir Adam
Blaire and on Doctor Gray, who wer supposed to be guilty of some crimes heere
and under proscription, wer apprehended yesterday, and some letters found upon
on of them, on of which I send your grace the copy sent to me.   His lordship
desired the person to whom it is wrett might be secured untill the affaire wer
enquired unto, and his Majestie's pleasure knowen, if thoght fitt.   The man I know
not, neither have I any commands from his Majestie concerning this, so I leave it
to your grace to doe as you thinke most for his Majestie's service.   I will give
your grace no further trowble at present, but to assure you that I am, may it
please your grace, your graces most humble and obedient servant,

MELVILL.

[The Letter which is enclosed follows.]

Coppie.

Near Dover, 5th July [16]89.

I KNOW you will be impatient to hear from me, but sooner I could not.   This
night I have orderd all things, soe as I hope to be out of this kingdome, and out
of the reach of mine enemyes.   I hope our friends will not be cast down at what
is past.   Lett them trust in God who is able to deliver both them and me.   I
thanke God I fear not what man can doe.   I doe my duetie and that which I am
sure is right, and shall leave the event to him.   The designes of the wicked I
hope will not alwayes prosper.   Men must not forbear acting because there is
danger.   That were hard: if every man were of that opinion our partie should
have an ill game to play, but I hope God will raise up friends to all honest men
and knaves shall at last have their rewaird.   Things I know at first prospect will
seeme desperate to my old friends, but lett them, I begg it of him, take couradge.
I trust God will turne things right about, and then there is noe fear of want.   I
can say noe more to you while I am elsewher, and then you shall heare from me.

Mind my last, and give my humble service to all friends. My best and dearest of friends adiu.

For Mr. James Grahame, ventiner, att his house at the head of Borthwick's closs, Edinburgh, Scotland.

158. (10) To give a pass to a king's messenger to Major-General Kirke.

July 11 [1689].

MAY IT PLEASE YOUR GRACE,—The bearer being sent express by the king to Major Generall Kirke for his more ready dispatch, is ordered to goe by the way of Scotland, and I am commanded to recomend him to your grace that he may have a pass from you, and that a vessell be ordered to cary him to Lochfoile, wher Major General Kirk is supposed to be. I need use no argument with your grace to order what is for his dispatch, it being his Majestie's service. These were his commands upon, may it please your grace, your graces most humble servant,   MELVILL.

I receaued your graces of the 4 instant, and shall doe my endeavour to heasten his Majesties answer.

For his Grace the Duke of Hamiltone, his Majesties high commission er for the kingdome of Scotland.

Indorsed : Dated July 11. Ansuered 13 July 89.

159. (11) The town of Glasgow. Letter to the Privy Council for opening the signet.

July 13 [1689].

MAY IT PLEASE YOUR GRACE,—So soone as I receaued yours of the 6, I went to Hamptone Court to wait on the king, but have not yett had opportunity to acquaint his Majestie therwith particularly, but has appointed me to wait on him again on Monday. I spoke both to his Majestie aud severall of the privy councell iu relation to the petition of Ct Smith, but have not yett receaved any answer. As for that affair of the towne of Glasgow your grace is pleased to mention, I have no particular concern for it. I did represent it to his Majestie befor that letter was wrett, as now your grace does and is mentioned in the Act, but he was pleased wpon the consideratione mentioned in the letter to grant them that liberty. However, I shall represent again to his Majestie as your grace desires.

I heer send your grace two letters from the king to the councell: on for emitting a proclamation declareing the siguet opened: the other for declareing warr against France, the tyme and maner wheroff is referred to your grace and the councell, as you will see by the coppies. It being late befor I came to town, I have not tyme to wrett mor att present least I loose the packett, but that I am, may it please your grace, your graces most humble servant,   MELVILL.

For your grace.

Indorsed: Dated July 13.   Answered 18 July 89.

[The letter for opening the signet follows.]

Copie.

WILLIAM R.

RIGHT trusty and right intirely beloved cousin and councellor, right trusty and right well beloved cousins and councellors, right trusty and well beloved cousins and councellors, right trusty and well beloved councellors, and trusty and well beloved councellors, wee greet yow well. Whereas wee, considering how preju- diciall it is to our leidges that the courts of justice have continued so long silent, wee have thought fitt to name some of the senators of our colledge of justice, and have ordered the opening of our signet with all expedition to the end that law may have its due course. Therefore we will and require yow forthwith to emitt a proclamation in our name, declareing that the signet is opened, that all who are any wayes concerned therein may have due notice of the same. For doing of which this shall be your warrant. And so wee bid yow heartily farewell. Given at our court at Hampton Court the 10th day of July 1689, and of our reigne the first year.—By his Majestie's command,   MELVILL.

160. (12) The king occupied with the Irish expedition.

July 17, [1689].

MAY IT PLEASE YOUR GRACE,—Upon the receipt of yours of the 11 with on enclosed to the king, I went next morning to Hamptowne Court, and as I was goeing I had your graces likewais of the 9 by the ordinary packet. I delivered yours to his Majestie so soon as I had opportunity, but could not speake with him that night. Yesterday I acquainted his Majestie with all your grace had wrett to me; but he being much taken upe with the affaires relateing to the Irish expedition and other business, put off his answer till to-day, and a litle befor he came to town I receaved your graces of the 13, with the enclosed informations relateing to the landing of some forces from Irland, which I did show to his Majestie, as also a letter from General Major Mackey. This affaire, together with what your grace wrett last of some discovery of a plote, puts us to some stand untill wee heare further from your grace. Your grace has heer what his Majestie commanded me to send you, a letter to yourselfe, and some further instructions. I am sory to heare by your graces that heats doe rather encrease then diminish amongst you, when owr present circumstances seeme to call for unity and agreement amongst those who ar embarked in on bottome. I wish your grace had wrett your mind freely to the king in relation to this of the officers of state and articles as they ar called, which makes so much noise. The reason the king gave me in not ordereing a positive instruction at this tyme for the adjurnment, as your grace, it seems, had desired in your former, was, he knew not if in this present conjuncture this invasion makeing some alteration in affaires, if your grace thought it now convenient, seing you had not mentioned it in this last, but refers it to your grace, who, being on the place, can know best what is most fitt to be don in this as most for the kings service and the publicke good. His Majestie depends much upon your graces good conduct and the councells. It is impossible to give particular directions at such a distance in such a conjuncture as this. An good account of affaires with you is much longed for by, may it please your grace, your graces most humble and obedient servant,

For your grace.   MELVILL.

Indorsed : Dated July 17. Answered 23 July 89.

161. (13) The king was gone for London.

25 July [1689].

MAY IT PLEASE YOUR GRACE,—I came heere early this morning to acquaint his Majestie with what your grace did wrett to me to be communicat to him, of the daite 18, which I receaved yesterday. I had immediatly upon the receat of yours come out, but that I knew the king was at hunting. It was 12 o'cloake at night befor he came home, and when he goes, does seldome come home earlier. His Majestie is this morning gone for London, so that I hade not the opportunity of speakeing to him further then to tell him that I had receaved a letter from your grace. I am to wait till his Majesties return and leasure for answer. I assure your grace ther is no neglect in me for not returning answers to yours speedily. The king is extreamly throngd with affaires, must recreat himselfe sometimes. His affaires calls him often to London, and his health in regard of the aire makes it convenient for him to stay heere, and I have no place so much as to retire myselfe in this place, which I hope will pleade my excuse for not giveing your [grace] mor frequent trowble with my letters.

For news, I enquire not much after forraign ons, but the princesse being broght to bedd yesterday morning early of a brave livly like boy, I know will be very acceptable and good news in Scotland as it is heere. I cannot find pen to wrett heare at present, yet would not neglect wretting to your grace with such graith as I could have at present; but probably the king may send a flying packet, which may come as soon to hand as this, so I shall forbeare giveing your grace further trowble at present.—I am, may it please your grace, your graces most humble and obedient servant,   MELVILL.

Indorsed: Dated 25 July.   Answered 29 July 89.

162. (14) Duke of Gordon and Earl of Balcarras not to be kept close prisoners, etc.

London, July 27, [1689].
MAY IT PLEASE YOUR GRACE,—Yours to the king, which I receaved by a flying packet, I deliuered, and communicate to his Majestie all what your grace wrett to me, and what was enclosed. It was farr in the afternoon befor I had his Majestie's return, which heer I send you with another letter to your grace and the councell, which he desired might not be spoke of till you made use of it. All the king commanded me further to signifie to your grace at this tyme, was that he desired that the Duke of Gordon and the Earle of Balcarras might not be kcept close prisoners, but may have the ordinary liberty of the castle; being weell lookt too till his further pleasure wer knowen. He spoke to me a litle of some warrand to be sent in relation to the Dutches of Gordon, but gave me no particular orders concerning it at this tyme, being desirous to heasten this to your grace. His Majestie was once speaking of sending down some officers from this to the castles of Edinburgh and Stirling, because the former accounts of the plott and invasion made him judge all the officers with you might be needed to attend ther charges in the feelds, but he resolvs now to doe in this upon your graces last relation of affaires with you. I know not, yett I am very glade you thinke the hasard is not great now from the Viscount Dundee and the Irish, thogh I be very trowbled with what you wrett, and I heare from others in relation to other things. I wish the adjurnment which the king tells me he has warranted your grace to make, if not already done, may not be made a badde use of by some and misconstrued by the people as many things ar often, but your graces wise management may prevent

much of this. Ther came a flying packet just now from General Major Mackey, and I think from Captain Rooke by the wretting. His letter directed to Earl Nottingham, but have non from [your] grace nor any of my freinds, so have no further news then what you sent me last. I will give your grace no further trowble at present, and hops to see you shortly heere to have an opportunity to evidence how much I am, may it please your grace, your graces most humble and obedient servant,   MELVILL.

For your grace.

Indorsed : Dated 27 July. Answered 1 Agust 89.

163. (15) Recommending Mr. Cairnes, who was for Ireland.

London, 29 [July 1689].

MAY IT PLEASE YOUR GRACE,—This gentleman, Mr. Cairnes, being sent by the king and councell to Irland by the way of Scotland, was desirous I should wrett to your grace that he might have some fitt vessell ordered to transport him ther. I thoght this was needless, being sent by his Majestie to be informed of the state of Irland. However, I would not neglect this opportunity of paying my dewty to your grace and to acquaint you of the receat of yours of the daite this day senight with the enclosed. Yours to the king I delivered, but had no opportunity of speakeing with his Majestie. He appointed me Moonday to wait upon him. So soon as I receave his answers they shall be transmitted to your grace with all diligence.

I receaved an account from some belonging to the town of Glasgow that your grace had demurred upon the towns haveing the benefite of the conventions act for electing ther magistrats because the king's [right] was concerned. This objection was moved to his Majestie befor he granted this warrand to them, but he was pleased (wpon the account of good service done and acknowledged by the convention, and the present conveniency of haveing the magistracy weell setled, which was represented to him by many hundereds of subscriptions) to recomend to the councell that the said town might have the benifitt of the said act of convention, which I suppose as the letter is worded, for I have not the copy presently by me, does not infringe his Majesties right if he incline to make use of it afterwards. This is all I can say of this affaire att present, not haveing occasione to speake with his Majestie since I had this relation. This gentleman being just to take post I shall give you no further trowble att present.—I am, may it please your grace, your grace's most humble servant,   MELVILL.

Indorsed : Dated 29 Jun. Answered 4 July 89.

164. (16) The news of the engagement between Major General Mackay and Viscount Dundee; king's letter ordering troops to Scotland. 1st August 1689.

MAY IT PLEASE YOUR GRACE,—I have showen your graces letter to the king, who, I suppose, will communicate to his councell who ar now sitting. This letter for your grace and the councell of Scotland is all the answer I have yett receaved, which his Majestie desired to be sent with a flying packett. Wee ar impatient heer for a further accompt of General Major Mackey's engadgement. I pray God it may be more favourable then the last. Your grace may easily judge the disorder I am in by these late news, which I hope will procure your pardon for not saying more but that I am, may it please your grace, your graces most humble servant,   MELVILL.

For your grace.

Indorsed: Dated 1 August.   Answered 6 August 89.

[The king's letter follows.]

Copy.

WILLIAM R.

RIGHT trusty and right entirely beloved cousin and councellor, right trusty and right welbeloved cousins and councellors, right trusty and welbeloved cousins and councellors, and trusty and welbeloved councellors, wee greet you well: Whereas wee having seen a letter from our right trusty and right entirely beloved cousin and councellor William, Duke of Hamiltoun, our commissioner, to our right trusty and right welbeloved cousin and councellor George, Lord Melvill, secretary of state for that our ancient kingdome, giving an account that the Lord Viscount of Dundee, with the rebells under his command, had attacked a party of our forces under command of Major Generall Mackay by which the said party did sustaine considerable loss, which perhaps may animate and encourage any who are disaffected to joyne with the rebells against us. Therefore, to prevent the same as much as may be, and to reduce those rebells to their due obedience, wee haue thought fit to order some more troops to march from hence into that our kingdom, and to observe such orders as they shall from time to time receive from you. And in regard there may not be convenient prisons enough to secure what persons you have already taken, or shall think fit to cause to be apprehended, wee hereby authorise you to send what persons of quality you have in custody to be secured

at our tower of London. So relying much on your good conduct in this present
juncture, wee bid you heartily farewell. Given at our court at Hampton Court
the 1st day of August 1689, and of our reigne the first year.—By his Majestie's
command,   MELVILL.

165. (17) Accounts of the battle at Killiecrankie.

London, 3 August [1689].

MAY IT PLEASE YOUR GRACE,—I receaued your graces of the 29 by a flieing
packett yesterday, which was very acceptable heer (after the former bad account
wee had of so great loss) to know that ther wer so many of our freinds safe,
thogh the loss as wee heare it yet is very considerable. The gentleman that came
express was short of the other a good tyme, and I had it not till this morning.
He gives but a very lame, indistinct, and inconsistant relation, but a more cleer
and full on is expected by the nixt. I wish wee be dissapointed of our feares of
Collonel Balfours and Lieutenant Collonel Mackeys [being killed], as weell as of
the others wer thoght to be so.

The king has ordered some Dutch horse and some English foot to march into
Scotland of those that ar lying neerest the border. Your grace and the commanding officers can best cause give them ther route wher it will be fittest for
them to march. I have done all I can to represent the present nakeduess of the
country as to armes, amunition, and otherwais. What will be done I yett know
not. When I shall receave his Majesties further commands, I shall immediatly
acquaint your grace. I am so weary, haveing had litle rest these two three nights
bygone, and but immediatly come to town and about twelve a cloake at night,
that I hope it will pleade my excuse for the confusedness of this.—I am, may it
please your grace, your graces most humble and obedient servant,

MELVILL.

Indorsed : Dated 3 August. Answered 8 August 89.

166. (18) Procedure of parliament—Dundee's death.

5 August [1689].

MAY IT PLEASE YOUR GRACE,—The bearer, Mr. Charles Campble, was sent to
me presently from Mr. Herberd, desireing to be recomended to your grace, which
I know is but superfluous, being employed to make some provisions for Darry, and
is in such heast that I can wrett non to any of my relations, and can only shew

your grace that I have receaued yours of the first August about ane howr agoe with on of the enclosed your grace mentions, which is the copy of that with the white inke. Your letter went to the king, who after he read it sent it bake to me. I am sory for what your grace acquaints me with of the parl[iaments] procedure, and that ther is so litle done for security of the country, for without mony litle can be done, and thogh it be imposed I feare ther may be but badd payment had. I wish your grace had represented fully to his Majestie the low and poor condition of the nation. I doe not remember of that letter to General Major Mackey particularly which you mention. If I had not been extreamly straitned, and ther had been any thing of concern that required concert, I would have undowbtedly sent your grace a coppy, but I suppose it may have been from my Lord Portland, but I cannot be positive, being under phisike, and that I cannot goe presently to looke out my dowbles of letters. I wrott a line to your grace Saturday night by the ordinary packet, the gentleman you sent staies till the king's further answer. I aprehend Dundees death will bridle a litle his party's joy and retard ther progress. I wish nothing may be done precipitantly, in engad[g]eing them untill [ther] be sufficient force to repress them. But this I might spaire, knowing the generall major's prudence and wariness. The king has ordered some Dutch and English forces to march to Scotland. Wee ar expecting an full account of the last action.—I am, may it please your grace, your grace's most humble and obedient servant,   MELVILL.

Indorsed : Dated 5 August. Answered 13 August 89.

167. (19) Engagement between Major-General Mackay and Dundee—State of Londonderry since its relief.

London, 10 August [1689].

MAY IT PLEASE YOUR GRACE,—This gentleman, Levetennat Honiken, whom your grace sent upe express with the account of the engadgement betwixt General Major Mackey and Dundee, was very desirous I should wrett to your grace with him, which occasions my giveing you this trowble. It was very rational and fitt to send on who was in the action to give the ralation of it, but I am sory for the poor gentleman that he had the misfortown not to know things as they wer, by comeing, it seems, to early away, which made his relation differ much from what came about the same tyme, and so has done him no good heer. I shall be sory if his misfortown, which might have fallen in a brave eneugh man's hand (and upon which occasions men ar apt eneugh to see visions when in any consternation), should be prejudiciall to him, which I dowbt not but your grace will endeavour to prevent unless he can be charged with some ill thing.   He not being att Hampton Court when I sent the last flying packet was on reason the letters wer not sent with him, but the chife was your grace desireing to have a speedy return.   The king ordered to send it by a fleeing packet.   I have no other commands from his Majestie since, and was unwilling to detain the gentleman longer from his charge.   Ther is a gentleman who went with General Major [Kirke ?] who has been in London Derry since its relife, who tells the great distress that town was in befor, being reduced to the utmost extreamity, hardly able to keepe out a day longer.   They eat all kind of quike creatures, as rats, mice, etc., and boiled hides, which has occasioned great mortality.   A great part of the town was brunt with bombs.   The Irish drew off a good many miles, and they say has formed a campe.   Kirk has formed a campe neer the town.   A good many men ar come in to him.   He wretts it will not be needfull to send many foot, if any, to that part of the country, but they want horse and dragons, which has put some stope to the goeing of the forces that wer ready to saile with Count Solmes, for the tyme; they report likewais that the Irish in the north committs great cruelties, and ravages the country ther, and have brunt severall towns, and attempted burning the cornes.   Wee have no certain account of the late King James motions.   I shall give your grace no further trowble at present.   Hopeing to have the honour to see you shortly heer, wher you shall be attended by, my lord, your graces most humble and obedient servant,   MELVILL.

I dowbt not but your grace has heard ere this that the Marquiss of Athole was brought heer by a messinger, and I suppose the first relation of that engadgement in Athole has been the occasion.

Indorsed : Dated the 10 August 89.

168. (20) Enclosing the copy of a letter from the king to the council about remodelling the army, etc.

London, December [1689.]

MAY IT PLEASE YOUR GRACE,—I hade the account by the last post of your graces safe arivall in health, which I was glade to heare of after so long a jurney at this season.   Your grace has heer enclosed a letter from the king to the councel (with a coppy of it) in answer to on of thers of the fiftht, likwais giving them an account of his Majesties intentions of modelling the army.   The king designs on regiment for a gentleman of the name of Cuningham, to whom he

has given a commission to be a collonoll. His Majestie hath given the office of
the chanceler to three commissioners, of whom he has named your grace for the
first, and the Earles of Argyle and Southerland for the other two. The commission is not yet sent, but shall be with the other commissions for the threasury,
privy seale and registers, so soon as I shall receave his Majesties commands. I
shall be glade if your grace would lett me know your opinion of the condition
of the country, which also will be very acceptable to his Majestie. If ther be
anything wherin I can be serviceable to your grace I shall be ready to evidence
how much I am, my lord, your graces most humble servant,

MELVILL.

I had almost forgott to acquaint your grace that the king had wrot to the
councoll in relation to the Duke of Gordon's liberty.

For your grace.

169. (21) Dispute between Hamilton and the Earl of Argyll.

London, 9 January 16$\frac{89}{90}$.

MAY IT PLEASE YOUR GRACE,—I receaued yours of the 29 past from Hamilton.
I cannot excuse my selfe from many errors I commit in wretting my letters, as
weell as note dateing them somtimes, but I hope your grace will. I represented
to the king what you desired me concerning that difference fallen out betwixt
your grace and the Earle of Argyle, but could not give his Majestie any distinct account of the grounds of it, not haveing yett learned the particulars from
any sure hand. I am sory any such thing should have fallen out. As for the
great scales being put in commission, I can only tell your grace it was his
Majestie's pleasure at this tyme, and if your grace and the rest of the commissioners have any just exception against the fidelity or ability of the keeper of the
scale, I question not but when its represented his Majestie will be willing he
should be changed. When your grace went from hence the instructions wer not
printed, neither had his Majestie positively ordered they should. I should be
sory that your grace incurre any prejudice on that account. This was not done
in the least to reflect on your grace, but to vindicate the king from the asper-
sions of some ill affected people heere, who did represent his Majestie as if he had
been unwilling to redres the griveances of his people. This opinion, by the
printing of some pamphlets heere, and others means used, came to prevaile a litle
with many ; and when people begun to talke that the instructions given for satis-
ficing the grivances could not abide the light else they would be published, the

king thought fitt they should; and thogh that such a thing hath not been cus-
tomary in former tymes, its no sufficient reason against it, ther being no state
intrigues to be keept secret, but plaine and clear evidences of his Majesties resolution
to satisfie his people's desires.   His Majestie commanded me to tell you that he
expects, so soon as your grace hath ordered your privat affaires, you will attend
the councell, now when both the good of the country and his service requires
your presence.   When I have any further in command from his Majestie it shall
be cairefully communicate to your grace by, my lord, your graces most humble
servant,   MELVILL.

170. (22) With copy of letter enclosed regarding exchange of prisoners.

London, January 16, [1690].
MAY IT PLEASE YOUR GRACE,—I receaved your graces of the 6 instant, with on
enclosed to the king, which I delivered, but have not yett receaved any commands
from his Majestie relateing therto.   I can say nothing at present as to what your
grace writs of some members of councell refusing to take the oaths formerly used
till I heare particularly ther reasons who refused.   Before I did receave your
graces letter the king had signified his pleasure in relation to the president of
councells signing papers that wer in use some tymes to be signed by a quorum,
so that I can add no more on this head untill I shall have further commands from
his Majestie.   This pacquet brings commissions for severall of the offices of state,
and a letter from his Majestie to the councell relateing therto, wherof your grace
has a coppy.   I hope this shall find your grace at Edinburgh, wher your presence
may be so usefull to his Majesties service, and from whence he may have sooner
from your grace ane account of affaires, the returns wherof shall be forwarded by,
my lord, your graces most humble servant,   MELVILL.

To his grace the Duke of Hamilton.

Indorsed : Dated 16 Januar. 90.

[A copy of a letter to the council follows.]

Coppy.

RIGHT trustie, etc., wee greet yow well.   Wheras wee are informed that Mr.
Archibald Riddell, minister of the gospell, and James Sinclare of Freswick, are
prisoners in France, and are very hardly used, whom wee are resolved to have
changed with two preests, now prisoners in Scotland; therefore wee require
you to call for the freinds and neerest relations of the said Mr. Archibald Riddell

aud James Sinclaire, and siguyfy our royall pleasuire to them in exchange of these tuo prisoners with the two prists that shall be condecended upon, and authorize them not only to speak with the two prists but also to write to France anent the negotiating there freinds liberty, and that you cause these two prists to be condescended upon, securely keeped, and make intimation to them that they shall be used in the same way and manner as the Franch king uses the said Scots prisoners, which they may be ordered to acquint there freinds in France with, that the exchange may be the more easyly effectuated : for doeing of which this shall be your warrant.

Indorsed : Coppie of a letter to the councell for releiveing prisoners.

171. (23) With copy of king's letter regarding subscription of papers by the President of the Council.

London, 21 January [1690].

MAY IT PLEASE YOUR GRACE,—All I have to say to you att this tyme is only to acquaint your grace that I could not sooner return you the kings answer, haveing receaved it only this night late. Your grace has heere also a coppy of his Majestie's letter to the councel. His former answer to thers was sent befor he had receaved yours. Ther was nothing in the councel's letter relateing to that oath you mention that was formerly administred to all privy counsellors. I know not the particular reasons why any of the members did scruple it, so can say nothing to it. I will give your grace no further trowble at present, but assure yow that, I am, my lord, your graces most humble servant,   MELVILL.

To his grace the Duke of Hamilton.

Indorsed : Dated 21 Januar. 90.

[The copy of the king's letter to the council bears that, from a letter, dated 26 December last, to the secretary from the Earl of Crawford, president of the council at that time, the king understood the council had made an Act appointing the president to subscribe, in name of the council, all such papers as were in use to be subscribed by the whole council or their quorum ; which Act the king had approved of ; but it having since been represented as an iunovation and of dangerous consequence, the king ordaius the council to cause the records to be inspected, to know what methods were used in the reigns of his predecessors, the reasons for and against to be transmitted to the king, that he might intimate his further pleasure. Kensington, 21 January 16$\frac{89}{90}$.]

172. (24) The west country to be put into a posture of defence.

Edinburgh, July 11th, 1690.

MAY IT PLEASE YOUR GRACE,—I am sorry that yow are keept by indisposition from attending the parliament, and do heartily wish your recovery. I need not acquaint yow with the dissorders that the country is in, nor use any arguments to excite yow to use your endeavours for preventing the confusions that malecontents would involve us in; only I most tell your grace that it is thought necessare that the west country be put into such a posture as that it may be in a capacity to act for defence of the government, as occasion shall require: and orders being given to that effect, I doubt not but your grace will take care that they be effectually and speedily executed in the places where yow are concerned.—I am, my lord, your graces most humble servant,   MELVILL.

173. (25) News from Flanders—Macmillan's reprieve.

London, 12 July [1691].

MAY IT PLEASE YOUR GRACE,—I have heard litle here since you parted from this, worthy of giveing your grace the trowble of a letter. Ther is litle of news at present but what you will have in the publick accounts. Quher our fleet or the French fleet ar is yett uncertain. All I have from Flanders [is] this, which of the date the 6, is the confirmation of the French retireing from the seige of Conie in Piemont with some precipitancie upon the aproach of the Savoy troopes. They wer Vadois, and French troops wer in it. So the French wer in no hopes of prevailing by mony. They left ther seek men, much of ther baggage, and some of ther cannon, behind them, and have lost severall hundered of ther men at the seige. The duke is now come bake to Turin, and its expected shortly he may be able to give the French battle. The Duke of Saxony has crossed the Rhein, and its thought if Caprara had come to him as he expected, the whole French infantry ther had been routed. Generall Fleemen, with a party of two hunder horse, fell upon a party of 400 of the French by surprize, killed 90 on the place, tooke severall prisoners and a good many horses. Its thought at the campe the peace betwixt the Emperor and the Turke will very quickly be concluded. Ther was a design in Brussels and in Bruges to have fired these places in severall parts, and the French wer to have forces nigh to have attacqued in the confusion, but it was happily discovered. It was said likewaies that ther was some kind of confusion in the Duke of Luxemburghs campe, which was thought to proceed

from the news out of Savoy, and that of the peace from Vienna.   Luxemburgh had
been moveing his campo severall tyms.   Our kings was still at Gemblours quhen
this last pacquet came away, but it was thought they would move soon now that
ther great cannon ar come upc.   I doe not heare of any alteration in our affaires,
or to be, in our counsell at present, though ther was a discourse of it latly.   Wee
ar expecting the news from your airth now, and what effects the Earle of
Bredalbans negociation has produced.   I have had non from Scotland these
severall pacquets, so I suppose my sons must be out of town.   Ther was a fleing
pacquctt sent, I heare, by Sir William Lockart to the Earle of Nottinghame seven
or eight dayes agoo, but I have not heard the least what its in relation too.   I
thought that when the king had a councell, and a president, or any officer of state,
or a comander of his forces in Scotland, that an inferior servant who was no
counceller had not been the dispatcher of fleeing pacquets, neither did I thinke
till my Lord Staires brought it in practice, that so long as the king has a Scots
secretairy here a packett should be directed to an English minister.

    I am glade to heare your grace is arrived weell at home.   I heard, though
but by second or thrid hand, that you wer much concerned about the reprive
Macmillan has gott.   I can say nothing except I knew particularly what wer
saied.   My part has been faire eneugh in it.   Nor did I anything without warrant.   Your grace and I may possibly differ in our sentiments in the matter, but
I can say I have no byass.   I never see any of the persons.   Quhat the queen
ordered me to doe in it was upon the Atturny Generalls opinion.   Whatever
solicitations might be, thogh I know non, neither was I on further then to give
account of the affaire so farr as a knew of it, but no advice.   Its off my hand.
Matters of blood is what I am tender in, either to absolve a guilty man, or con-
demn an innocent.   What seemes most neglected in this affaire was that the
process was not sent wpe tymouslie to the king, which he desired might be severall
months agoe, but did not come till ten or twelve dayes after his Majestie went
last to Holland.—I am, my lord, your graces most humble and obedient servant,

MELVILL.

For his grace the Duke of Hamilton.
Indorsed : Answered 21 July 91.

174. (26) Breadalbane's negotiations, etc.

July 29, [1691].

MAY IT PLEASE YOUR GRACE,—Yours of the 21 I had by yesterday's pacquet,
and am sory to heare you wer so ill of the gravell.   I have given an account of

the councels orders for the marching of the army, the best I could, which has been, as I suppose, misrepresented.   It was alledged there was a kind of alternative in the king's letter, as if Bredalban's negociation tooke effect it was not to be.   I remember no such thing in the copy I see for I have no dowble my selfe.   I said that Bredalban's negociation was a thing on foot, presently after the king went from this, if not before; that the queen a litle after desired Sir Thomas Livingston to forbeare goeing to the Highlands to encampe his men, as was designed befor that; that the king was acquaint with this stope, and yett after this his Majestie, by his letter to the councell, had ordered them to encampe wpon the borders of the Highlands, so the councell had done but what was ther dwty : tho I confess for my own part I see not great use for it, things managed as they are, but only to fatigue the forces a litle, which is not much to be considered. It will helpe to keepe them in excercise, and to be some trowble and expence to the country, which is impossible to avoide, and they have no need of.   However, the councell[s] part was very faire, and they ar not to blame that the expedition might not be very usefull.   Wee have keepe upe an army these two yeeres at a great expence to the countrie ; not much done yet to the setlement of by them. And now, when ther was a greater proba[bi]lity of succeeding in it than ever, a stope put to the endeavoureing it upon a solide fundation, I know not by quhat representations or misrepresentations : the cess will be soon exhausted, the army in the mean tyme lying idle.   The Highlanders no dowbt overlaueing themselvs and possibly thinkeing doe what they please, they can make such terms for themselvs as they please when they will, and others not only haveing no reparations for ther losses by them, but still obnoxious to them.   This is what I understand not.   I wish the king and country have no prejudice by it.   Wee have the account this day of the surrender of Gallaway ; from Flanders that our campe lies still at Gerpins.   They say the French ar so strongly encamped they cannot be weell attacqued without dissadvantage.   Ther ar many deserters from the French. Severall prisoners wer brought in severall dayes to our camp befor the last pacquet cam off.   The Duke of Berwicke is endeavouring to make upe a regiment of Brittish at Lisle, called the Prince of Wales regiment, but its very thin.   The Archbishope of Naples is chosen Pope.   I have forgott his name, but he is saide to be of the Spanish faction.   The Marquiss of Castinago is to quite his employment, and its reported the grand Signieur is dead, but wants confirmation.   Wee have no account of our fleet that I heare of yett, but its said the Barbadoes fleet that wer reported to be fallen in the French hands ar gone on ther voyage. Your grace seems dissatisfied with Macmillan's reprive, but I would begg of you to be as litle concerned as I am, and wee will soon agree in it.   I am of your grace's opinion that all concerned should be for keepeing the thron free of blood. Ther hath no remissions past ih my tyme for blood, but what others procured. This fellow, I know him not, nor ever see him. If I had don less then I have done I could not but have blamed myselfe if he had died; now its off my hand. If that had been as your grace takes it, that the king had refused a reprive after he had gotten the process which he had ordered long befor to be sent, it had altered the caice much. But the king was in Holland before it was sent out of Scotland; for that which [your] grace mentions of being encroachment upon our Courts of justice I would be as tender of any thing of that kind as any man, but I doe [not] thinke at first veiw ther is much of that in this caice, it being a mater of grace and favour competent to the prince, and he cannot be blamed for adviseing with any of any nation or quality to satisfie his own conscience in dispenseing his favoures, especially in such a caice quher the judges wer interposers. But I have said enough for my own exoneration, and hopes it will not be mistaken. I am afraied to loose the pacquet so can add no more, but that I am, with all respect, my lord, your grace's most humble and obedient servant,   MELVILL.

For his Grace the Duke of Hamilton.
Indorsed : Answered 3 August 1691.

175. LEWIS, LAST VISCOUNT FRENDRAUGHT, to GENERAL CANNON—The state of the Jacobite cause. Bedendalloch, 1st March 1690. [An intercepted letter.]

SIR,—Tho the many affaires you have in hand hinders you from sparing so much tyme as to give your friends here incouragment from your newes, yet I will not forbear to give you such as comes to my hand. I had no sooner returned from Baydinoch then I was assured that our enemies had seized my Lord Oliphant, Ogilvie, younger of Kempcairn, his brother, and Thornybank, who are all prisoners att Aberdeen, and its thought they will have them to Edinburgh. Immediatly after Lieutenant Collonell Buchan with ane troup of horse and ane other of dragoons came to Frendraught, and took the Countess of Arroll prisoner, who is caried to Edinburgh close prisoner, none being admitted to come near her bot her maid. The reason of her being taken is as followes. One Bell att Glasgow, who, under pretence of loyalty, keeps correspondence with the king, and under hand betrayes him to his enemies, for the king having sent over one Strachan (who had ane commission in my regiment), with letters to my Laydy Arroll, and being reccommended to Bell, under hand made him be seized, who after being putt to the torture confessed they were for the Countess of Arroll. This accident gives me a great deall of trouble upon the account of the loss wee sustain by the want of her intelligence, and particularly the pain I am in att present how to gett your return to her Majestie safely convoyed to the gentleman that should be the bearer. However, I shall doe all that lyes in my power. I most advertise you that our enemies are very bussie in seasing all the persones that they suspect will joyn us, and unless there be some methodes fallen upon for preventing this apparent loss to the kings service wee will in short tyme have more of our friends in prison then in armes with us. I signified something of this in my last to Major Generall Buchan, and desired to know his will thereanent. Therefor I hope you will further him to give me a return as soon as possible. My service to the Earl of Dunferling and all your friends.—I am, sir, your most humble servant,

FRENDRAUGHT.

Bedendalloch, first of March [16]90.
For Major Generall Cannon—Thes.

176. SIR THOMAS LIVINGSTONE [probably to MAJOR-GENERAL MACKAY]— Account of the battle at Cromdale. [2d May 1690.] Contemporary copy.

HONORED SIR,—As I have in severall letters befor given yow nothing but ill news, so I am glad I have now the occasion of sending yow some what better. The General Buchan, Brigadier Canon, with his Highland army, having for a while marched up and down this countrey, increased as a snow ball daily, which affrighted and discouraged the countrey so farr that, upon Sonday last, I resolved to march out of Inverness with a detachement of 400 men of Sir James Leslies, six companies of Grants, the Highland company of Captain Mackays, three troups of my dragons and Yesters troup of horse, and camped that night near Bro[dies?] uher I was forced to stay 2 days for my baggage,   coming in very slow from the country, as likways the 2 other troups of dragons from Elgin, and Captain Bur   troups of horse. The enemy was at this time in Strathspy threatning to slay and burn all that would not joyn, wherupon I resolved the 30 April, about 12 aclock of the day, haveing then got certain intelligence uher they camped, and of uhat number they were, to march towards them. Wee marched the whole night in as bad ground as Lochaber may be, till at last, by 2 a'clock in the morning, we got to Balla-castoell, wher, being arrived, wee discovered by the enemies fires their camp. I informed my self of the nature of the ground, and the depth of the river, and notuithstanding they told me the ground was somequhat boggy, I formed a designe to attack them by surprise, for they did

not know of my being arrived, but my men and horse being so extremely uearied
I gave them about half an hour to refresh themselves.   After uhich time I called
the officers together and told them my resolution, so that they might examen their
souldiers if they were able to do it, who unanimously told me they would stand
by me to the last man, and desired earnestly to go on.   I having got guids by this
time in readiness, wee passed the river by 3 a'clock in the morning at a ford
uher ther was a church, and they keeped a strong guard, uhere I sent some foot
and few dragoons to fyre upon them and amuse them, and in the mean time
passed the river at another ford below it.   Tuo troups of dragons and Captain
M'Kay's company was already passed befor the enemy perceived us, and then wee
see them run in parties up and doun, not knowing which way to turn themselves,
being surprysed, so I commanded all the horse and dragoons to join and persue ;
which affrighted them so, that they took themselves to the hills, and at the foot of
Cromdell, we overtook them, attacqued them, killing betuixt 3 or 400 in that place ;
and about 100 prisoner, the great part of them officers, and the rest cutt of by a
mist that came just at that time upon the top of the hill, so that wee could scar[s]ly
see one another, otherways the slaughter should have been much greater, so I caused
beat a retreat, our horses being ready to fall doun under us upon the low ground,
prisoners being brought to me from all hands.   Buchan, uhen he took the alarm
first, had commanded a nephew of his uith some mo officers and souldiers in an
old castle, who at first seemed to be oppiniatre ; I caused surround them, and
finding the ground proper, undermind them, which they finding surrendered
themselves to the king's mercy.   Buchan got of uithout hat, coat, or suord, aud
uas seen that day, and in that posture, aud in Glenlivet, very much fatigued,
tarryed in a cussins house of his : Canon got away in his nightgown.   Dumferme-
lyne had gone from them about some business the day befor.   Wee have taken
all their baggadge and amunition, and the shouldiers have got more considerable
plunder then I thought off, they carryed about with them their kiug and queens
standard, uhere they cited the country people to repair to, are taken.   They are said
to be people of nott who are killed, but of this I can give yow no certain account,
being that when we came to visit them, they were all naked ; by uhat we could judge,
ther was some appearance of it.   The resolution and forwardness of all the
troups is admirable, and although the foot could not get up to us, yet they marched
after us with all diligence possible.   It is remarquable that in this whole business
ther is not one man lost, 3 or 4 uounded, and nothing dangerously either, and
about 12 of horses, but many horses disabled.   This night we have had one of
the severest could bee, I designed to pursue this and see if I can disperse uhat is
of them yet, uhich uill bee but a small number, being that they run to all airts ;

but the uather is soe horrible, that I fear [I] shall be obliged to get it over, expecting further orders, I am, sir, your, etc.,   THO. LIVINGSTON.

A list of officers taken at the battell of Cromdell May 1, taken in the field, Captain Hutchings, Captain John McClean, Captain Allen McClean, Captain John Colloe, Captain John McClean, Captain Alexander Halliburton, Cornett Andrew Baird, Ensigne John McClean, Eusign John Macknougton, Ch. Collonel Volontiers. Taken in the castle of Lethendy, Captain Jam Buchan, Captain Broun, Lieutenant Seraher, Lieutenant Middleton, Lieutenant Brandie, Lieutenant Sevell, Lieutenant Haghamotie, Lieutenant Drumer, Ensigne Dunbarr, Ensigne Rosse.
                                                       THO. LIVINGSTON.

177. LETTER to GEORGE, EARL OF MELVILLE, Commissioner to the Parliament of Scotland, concerning the plot, 1690. Contemporary copy.

                                            London, May 30, 1690.

SIR,—Having the good fortun of your acquaintance, I made choyse of you before any other person, knowing you to be both a good protestant and a truely honest man, to make a discovery to you of a most helish and damnable plott against your religion, king, and country.   My acting so conterary to the principles I was both bred and born in wil inclyne you to look upon me as a very ill man, but my future behaviour, I hope, will convince the world it is not intrest that engages me any way.   I lay under great obligations to King James, which, out of gratitud, laid a tye upon me to doe him all the service in my pouer, and which I did till I found there was such a designe on foot as will certainly extirpat the protestant religion, whatever specious pretences may be made to the conterary, the conviction of which hes induced me to make to you the following discovery, and yet I must keep so closs in this matter that I must be still unknowen except to your selff, with whom I resolve still to keep a correspondence of what I can learn, that you in a prudent manner may comunicat it as you shall see fitt.   I pray God when King William goes for Ireland he may be brought back saife to Brittain, and then I may cast myself at his feet.

I shall endeavour from the beginning to inform you hou this plott was layed. When King James found he had Ireland inteirly fixed for his interest, he went thither and sent to Scotland to his friends there to take heart, for that he would send men for their help, which had gon but for his ill fortun at Londonderrie, by which, and his parties ill success in Scotland, he saw he could not gain his point by force of armes, therefor resolved to trye what policie and Frensh gold

could doe.   To effectuat which he made most of his partie in England joyne with
King William, and to make great offers in caice he gave no further encouragement to the dissenters, and that he should have whatever he could demand ;
upon the other hand, the dissenters were imposed upon to suspect King William.
At this time the adress from a considerable party of the parliament of Scotland
was brought up to be presented to the king.   Annandale, Ross, and Sir James
Montgomery, who went up with it, for some time were not alloued access to the
king, which so incensed them that they were not unactive, but added much to the
ill temper the parliament of England was in.   This fare King James suceeded
to his wish.   The nixt thing to be done was to engadge the dissafected persons
in both kingdoms, and to amuse them King James seemed to be convinced that
the other partie non joyned in to King William were men that studyed nothing
but their oun interest, and ingaged never to trust them.   And upon this, and his
engagement to doe all that was requyred of King William in both kingdoms, the
heads of both the parties in England and Scotland seigned a paper to engage with
him for reducing the kingdomes to his obedience, which paper was sent over to
France to the queen, and comunicat by her to the Frensh king, and therafter
sent over to Dublin to King James, where he seigned it and sent it back to
London.   They being thus engaged, the scheme layed donn for his restouration
is thus, that King James should leave Ireland and goe to Brest, in Monsieur de
Lozins hands, he not to fight upon any termes till he had advertisement from
King James or his master.   All endeavours were used by King James partie to
persuade King William to goe to Ireland, and when he is there King James
intends for England with ten thousand men, with armes, amunition, and pay for
tuenty thousand more.   At the same time there is five thousand to be landed in
Scotland from Dunkirk, with armes and money for ten thousand more.   The Earle
of Arran is to command in chieff in Scotland, and with him are joyned by a commission from King James, for managing affairs at present, Earle Annandale, Lord
Ross, and Sir James Montgomery, by whose advyce and direction all things are
to be ordered there ; and beside this, those who have been still for King James,
and in opposition to King William's government, are also manadging for him in
their own way by the Earle of Arran's privat directions, without the knouledge
of Annandale, Ross, and Sir James Montgomery.   The Highlanders move as they
have direction from the Earle of Arran, who designes a cessation, and to hinder
any forces goeing against them, that they may be in a better condition to joyne
with the Frensh when they land there.

There is a considerable sum of money in persons hands here for managing of
King James affairs, and some of it is sent to Scotland, from whence we have

expresses every week giving an account hou King James affairs goes there, and getting intelligence from this place.   There is an indemnity sent to Scotland to the Earle of Arran, wherin are excepted the Earles Crnfurd, Melvill, and Leven, Stairs, Generall Major Mackay, Livetennent Generall Douglas, and Sir Coline Campbell of Aberurchall.   There is an indemnity also for England, but who are excepted I doe not knou.   But the greatest persons here are concerned for King James.   There hes been great endeavours used to engage the Earle of Argyle, and when Sir James Montgomery was at London he undertook to secure him, but upon Sir James return from London he found Argyle so fixed to King William's intrest that he acquainted King James that there was no hope of bringing him of, tho King James, to my knouledge, would seign a blank to be filled up as Argyle should think fitt.

Upon the Frenshes landing in Scotland, the regiments commanded by Glencairn, Kenmure, Cuningham, and Grant, and the troup of guards, are to joyne them.   I am goeing to King James, and will be very shortly back, and then you shall hear from me at length if I be not disscovered, and therefor trust non till King William be acquainted.   Its advyseable that som of your forces were removed whom you see you have ground to suspect, and that others may be called in to you that may be trusted.

I have exonered my selff, and I pray God Allmighty that there may be speedy methods used for preventing blood and the ruine of the protestant religion, and the dreadfull storm that threatens these poor distracted nations, for which night and day I shall pray, who am, sir, your friend and servant.

Indorsed: Coppy of a letter sent to the Com[missioner].   June 1690.

178. COLONEL HILL to GEORGE, EARL OF MELVILLE, Lord High Commissioner—
In treaty with Glengarry and Locheil.

Inverness, 2nd of June 1690.

MAY IT PLEASE YOUR GRACE,—I hope my letters haue reacht your hands, wherein were the coppies of two letters from Glengary and one from Locheil.   The partie (mentioned in my former) whom they sent to speake with me is gon backe to know particulerly what they desire, and alsoe to fetch their possitive resolucion, for I have assured them I cann admitt of noe more delay; that the army will speedily be vpon them, and then there will be noe tyme or roome for treatie.   This person hath promised me to hasten with his best dilligence back againe, and to acquainte me truly how all things stand with them, which when I haue gotten (if they comply not) I shall thinke of returning; but it were very well if

the Major Generall were upon his march, for that would much facilitate this affair and anticipate their preparacions. I find they are prettie ripe for setlement, were it not for the romantick storys they weekely get out of Ireland, some wherof from the late King James himselfe (as your grace will perceive by the inclosed coppie of his letter lately brought ouer to them). They haue made many of the silly people beleoue that 30,000 men out of Ireland, and 20,000 French, are allready landed in England, and that Berwicks army will be ten thousand, and will speedily land in this countrey. The newes we first had of my Lord Seaforts ship being a vessell of 36 guns, proues to be but sixteen, and is said to be one of the two privateers of this kingdom that were taken by the French men of war; nor did he come west aboute Ireland (as was said), but from Dublin, through St. George his Channell, and when hee was upon the coast of Scotland, was by contrary windes driven back upon the coast of England, and plyed too and againe, three dayes, but in all this tyme saw neither ship nor boate upon the sea, and now the ship is gon back againe. If the kings ships looke noe better to their duty, they may send owr whom or what they will. I doe not find that Seafort will make any great progress in raising men; the people are willinge (for the most part) to doe noe more then what is by compulsion, and refused his vncle a few days before his arrivall to stir with him at all. One Mr. Donald McRa, the minister of Kintayl, is the emissary my Lord Seafort makes use of to inveagle and corrupt the people, and severall other ministers (of the Episcopall way) neere this place, and yet continueinge in their places, are very great incendiaryes and evill instruments amongst the people.—I am, may it please your grace, your graces most humble and obedient servant,   Jo. HILL.
    For his grace the lord commissioner of Scotland.

179. SIR JAMES MONTGOMERIE of Skelmorlie to GEORGE, EARL OF MELVILLE, High Commissioner for Scotland—In reference to the accusations against the writer. Hirst, 18th June 1690.

MAY IT PLEASE YOURE GRACE,—It hath beine noe small trouble unto me since first I heard of it, to find that I stand accused and suspected of designes to bring in King James to the prejudice of the Protestant religione and the interest of my countrie in its libertie and propertie, I can in all sinceritie of heart take God to be my wittness that those great interests of religione and libertie have bein alwayes deare unto and valued by me since ever I came to have anie knowledge in the world, and I have had a speciall eye to both in all the publick appearances

that I have either willinglie entred ore bein brought upon ; nay, it was a tender
regaird to those great concernes that induced me to take my life and fortune into
my hands, and embarck soe earlie in the beginning of this great revolutione, and I
daresay that in as far as ductie can be folloued and performed amidst soe manie
weaknesses, my steps and measures have bein suitable and ansuerable unto that
motive to this verie minute. When first I heard of a designe to seise me, I
believed it upon the account of those measures I tooke in parliament, which though
honestlie and faithfullie designed, have bein constructed other wayes, and considered it best for me to withdraw untill that storme bleu over, though at the
same time it was not without a great daill of griefe I did sie that my former
services, which sometime agoo were neither unusefull nor unpleasant, could not
secure me against the effect of such groundless suspiciones ; bot when I find that
the malice of my enemies flyes soe high a pitch as to accuse me of designes to the
prejudice of the Protestant religione and my countrie, by indeavores to bring
them both into the same dangers and difficulties they laitlie labored under from
poperie and slaverie, I find myselfe obleidged not to be silent, bot, if possible, to
undeceive the world, and wipe of such a calumnie by all the methods that a man
of honor can be capable of acting, and therefor it is that I doe in a more speciall
maner applye myselfe unto youre grace, whose temper and integritie I have
alwayes had a value for, to implore youre good opinione, and to desire youre
protectione amidst those reproaches I ame fallen under, and withall to beg it as a
pairt of Christiane charitie due unto me, that youre grace would believe noe such
thing untill it be maid appeare against me ; and in ordor to a speedie discoverie
of the trueth of it I shall come presentlie to toune if youre grace will assure me
of a speedie tryall, that soe a prisone, which in the present conditione of my
health would certainlie kill me, may be avoided ; nay further, though the lying
under such a reproach uncleared be grievous to ane innocent man, yet if more
time be neidfull either for ane cleare probatione, ore untill the return of this
invisible messenger whoe is gone to Brest and whose sham letter hath given that
disturbance to the government he designed by it, if youre grace will assure me I
shall not be sent to prisone in the interim, I will come to toune and wait upon
youre grace, and give good securitie not to depairt from toune for such a competent time as may be judged necessar for attaining to a clearer discoverie of the
trueth ore falshood of what is alledged against me. I venture to make this
proposall unto youre grace purely from a desire to be vindicated, and in such a
method, to shun imprisonment that would certainlie occasione death in the
present stait of my health, which I ame confident youre grace would not contribute unto. Whatever returne youre grace thinks fit to give to this, if sent to

my wife, will reach my hands.—I ame, as in all duetie bound, my lord, youre grace's most humble servant,   JAMES MONTGOMERIE.
Hirst, June 18, 1690.

180. COLONEL RICHARD CUNINGHAM to [GEORGE, EARL OF MELVILLE, Lord High Commissioner]—That he is commissioned to reduce Braemar to obedience.

Aberdeen, the 15th day of September 1690.

MAY IT PLEASE YOUR GRACE,—I am just now marching out of this towne with six hundred foot, ninety hors, and a hundred and ten dragoons, to goe to the head of this shire, to settle and put in some meall in Aberyeldy and Aboyne, and reduce the head of Braemarr to their Majesties obedience, or lay it in ashes. My party is stronger than any they can bring to the feilds, and this is the only time in the year to ruin their countrey, just when they have taken in their cornes, which is the most part of their subsistance for the winter time. I will give your grace from time to time an accompt of my proceedings per express. I shall be somewhat troublesome to them blades in the hills, if they have any thing to loose. I think likewise fitt to tell your grace of a minister that preaches here in one of the greatest churches in towne, that does not acknowledge the government, and downright refuses to pray for King William and Queen Mary so long as King James lives. It is a great encouragement to the ill affected men of this countrey that is by farr the stronger in number. If your grace please that I may hinder him to preach, it shall soon be done. To shew the inclination they have for him here, when he preaches the church is pact so full that there is hardly room to stand in it. I still recomend me to your grace in all cases, and hopes yow will not see us suffer for want of money. The Major Generall designes me for the garrison of Inverness and Buchan here, as the fittest man to rule these parts. I referr it all to your graces care, and rests your graces most humble and most obedient servant,   Rd CUNINGHAM.

181. THE COMMISSIONERS IN ENGLAND FOR TAKING INSPECTION OF THE ACCOUNTS OF THE ARMY to GEORGE, EARL OF MELVILLE—Regarding the pay of the English regiments in Scotland.

From York Buildings this 14th day of
March 1690 [91].

OUR VERY GOOD LORD,—Wee, being entrusted by act of parliament to examine, take, and state the publick accompts of the kingdome, are thereby to take an accompt, amongst other thingis, of their Majesties regiments and troops which are paid out of the publick revenue of England (whereof some part are now in Scotland in the charge of Sir Alexsander Bruce, Muster-Master-Generall of that kingdome).   And in pursuance of the trust reposed in us by the said act, wee have directed the inclosed precept to him, which wee intreate your lordships permission to recommend to your lordship's conveyance, and to take from him his acknowledgment of the receipt of it.   Wee have further to acquaint your lordship, that because wee would make his returne of this service to us (which is to be upon oath) easy to him, wee have directed him to make oath of his true performance thereof before the Lord Provost of Edenborough, which wee pray your lordship to signifie to him, and desire his lordship to administer to him upon this occasion if he offers himselfe, to take it of him.   The necessity of this duty, and the confidence wee have of your lordship's readiness to promote their Majesties service, is the best apology wee can make to your lordship for this great trouble, which wee pray your lordship to take in good part from, our very good lord, your lordship's most humble and affectionate servants,

R. RICH.	THO. CLARGES.
PAUL FOLEY.	ROBT. AUSTEN.
MATH. ANDREWES.	BENJ^N. NEWLANDS.
SAM. BARNARDISTON.	RO. HARLEY.
P. COLLETON.	

To the right honorable the Earle of Melvin, principall secretary of state for their Majesties kingdome of Scotland.

Indorsed: Letter from the comissioners in England for takeing inspection of the accounts of the army.   March 1690.

182. COLONEL JOHN HILL to GEORGE, EARL OF MELVILLE, Secretary of State ---Arrival of French ships in Skye with Lord Dunfermline and others.

Fortwilliam, the 9th May 1691.

MY LORD,—Since my last ther are four French men of warr come from Ireland to Sky (whereof one off fyftie guns) who have brought with them the Earle of Dumfermline and some officers, with armes, amonitione, provisions, and some money, and cloaths, but no men; but they give out that the Duke Gordone and the Duke off Berwick are speedily coming with five thousand men from Ireland to land in the north.   Buchane and Glengary are gone to Sky.   I have given my Lord Argyll double notice hieroff that he may take care off his people in Mull.

and have given his garrisone there notice off it, for that these ships intend thither. I have also sent advice to any off their Majesties men off warr that I heare are in Clyde water. It is probable Sir Donald M'Donald and Glengary may stirr (though Sir Donalds people are willing to be quiet), as alsoe Sir John M'Laine, but the rest of the clanes (except a very considerable force come) will nott stirr. As I gitt any further intelligence of their proceedings your lordshipp shall have ane accompt theroff from, my lord, your lordships most obliged and most humble servant,   Jo. Hill.

Since I began to write I have further that the ship said to be of 50 guns, will prove a great merchant man, who soe soone as vnloaden, is to returne, and the small frigots with her, who are in the meantyme cruisinge out at sea, and have taken severall prises, and they further say that there are 5000 men detacht out of the army in Ireland for this countrey, besides the men above mentioned, which are to be 4000 foote and 1000 horse.

For the right honourable the Earle of Mellvill, principall secretary of state for the kingdome of Scotland, Londone.

183. LETTER to REV. WILLIAM CARSTARES—Proceedings in council as to calling out the militia—Election of a Provost of Edinburgh.

Edinburgh, 16th June 1691.

REVEREND AND WORTHIE SIR,—I am glad to hear by a friend, that my letters goe safe to your hand, and that you use them as is designed. The calling out of the militia did take up the council about a fourtnight agoe, for several dayes togither; and when the proclamation went to the vote, the members were 5 and 5. Those for it were the Earles of Morton, Forfar, Viscount of Stairs, Lord Beilhaven and Stevinston. Those against it were the Earle of Crafurd, Lords Cardross, Ruthven, the Justice Clerk, and Sir John Lauder of Fountainhall; the Earle of Leven, that day chosen president, demurring, in a matter of that import, to give his casting vote either way. The Viscount Stairs, who was the first projecter of that matter, and all along carried it on with a great solicitude, practised thus with the dissenting members. My Lord Cardross, sayes he, I know where your scruple lyes. By the priviledge of the mint, you are exempted from attending the kings host, and cannot be forced to it but by consent, and are unwilling to wrong your successors in their rights: besides, your modestie prompts you to declyne being collonell to the regiment of the militia in Edinburgh, which a provost, if he were once chosen, may probably claime. Therefore you may cause mark it in the minuts, that your signing the proclamation is no homologation of your acceptance of that trust, nor yet a parting from your priviledge in the mint. Upon which my lord was prevailed on to sign the proclamation. The same wise man then addressed the Lord Ruthven in thir tearmes. By your temper your lordship is not willfull, nor are you commonly wedded to your own opinion ; and as Abraham, in his pleading for Sodom, would have prevailed if there had bein ten righteous in the city ; so it was hoped that for a few ill men that might come out in the northern shires, he would not reject the western, southern, and inland counties, who would be such a defence to the nation in case of invasion ; upon which that honest nobleman concurred. The discourse was then to the Lord Justice Clerk ; that his lordship had been long sick, and it would be understood peevishness if he were further dissentient ; upon which his lordship likewise complyed. My Lord Fountainhall was then told, that being no souldier, it was expected he would not be tenacious, and that as he was a nottable countrey man, and tender of putting the country to any unnecessar charge, his lordship should be gratified, and whatever money was sav'd of the 40 dayes loan, should go into the payment of the current cess. Upon this his lordship was likewise proselyted. The Earle of Craufurd proved stiffer then the rest, and freely told that board, that his hand could not contradict his head and heart, and unless his arguments were plainly answered, could not subject his reason and conscience to the practise or will of others, and gave the following reasons for his dissent. 1st, That the legality of some things in the proclamation was much questioned by him, as is contained in the enclosed paper, to which I referr you. 2ly, That it appear'd at this juncture ill policie, except there were more probable grounds of an invasion, to impress the countrey by fears, and put them to so vast a charge, which would amount to full five months cess, and that men without principle would be for or against a government, as they found themselves easie under it. 3ly, That it appeared dangerous to call out the militia in those shires benorth Tay, who were generaly so disaffected to the present establishment that we could not have 4 or 5 in a whole county in whom we could repose the least trust, and for proofe of this, desired the excepting commissioners for uplifting the supply might be counted, and how armes should be put in those mens hands, who last year were disarmed, appeared strange. It was answered to this by the wise man at that board, that it was no way fitt our friends should be burdened, and our adversaries escape free, nor could legaly a burden be laid on a part of the nation, and not on the whole. To this it was duplyed, that it was commonly practised otherwayes in the late times, and if there was difficultie in law, there was at least no scruple in this, to appoint the rendevouz of those ill affected shires about Michelmass next, when the danger of an invasion might be over, and that there was no such ready access to run in to the enemie as there might be at this critical juncture, and especialy if it trysted with a landing; and that the western and other well affected shires may be ordered to be ready upon a call. 4ly, That as the western shires would inclyn to be under the conduct of such as were favourable to them, so they would look upon the northern shires as a designed dead weight on them, and would not willingly joyn issues with them, tho under commanders of their own choise, in whom they confided. They would pleasantly ventur their lives, and all that's dear to them, for King William's interest, and take directions from Sir Thomas Livingston, with an intire trust in him. 5ly, It was urged that in the meeting of estates, when the friends for the government were more zealous than now, and the appearing enemies far fewer, and under great discouragement for the time, the project of the militia, tho' moved by the Duke of Hamilton, was not seconded in that great assembly. When the counsel became more numerous, and many representations were made from the countrey, and the discourses of an invasion had less beliefe, a proclamation was issued out, dischargeing the militia untill further order, which by somes dayes prevented the queens letter to the same effect.

The affair of Aberdeen is found very durtie, and the probation distinct. It is warrantably suspected, that some of high quality, and in the government, had a deep share in the contrivance of that foule matter. There is likewise a sort of bond of association, subscribed by all the disaffected in the place, not only undertakeing to stand by their ministers, but protesting against any thing the commission should do. I presume his Majestie will not approve them in such a procedour to a commission of the assembly, delegat by that venerable meeting, consented to by his commissioner, and carrying the authority of parliament with it. Some wise men are like to putt a faire face on it, as only a protestation for remead of law, which is still lame and ought to referr to the parliament as well as king. It does not sound well that Presbiterian government, being the legall establishment, their judicatories should be appealed from, which is a consequential if not a direct disclameing the authority of king and parliament; but I will not enlarge on this theam. The deprived Episcopal men are every where transgressing the law, preaching without qualifieing themselves before the council, and cross to the act of deprivation preaching in their own paroches; yea, many of them setting up for calls, and mustering all the disaffected in the countrey for hearers to them. His Majesties former letter to the commission is the pretence for this behaviour; if some speedy course be not taken to remeady this, I am much affraid itt will shake both church and state. It is of no little prejudice to the government, that the deputs of sherriffs, stewards, and baillies of regalitys, do officiat without their constituents being qualified by takeing of the oaths; for besides that in law there can be no deput, where the principall hes forfeited his right, so they are still men of freedom who are placed in those trusts, and only swallow oaths that more effectualy they may prejudge the state ; and the most necessar dispatches in the nation commonly miscarry in their hands.   There is still an opposition by some in this place to the sequestrating the estates of such as were out in rebellion in harvest last upon this critical pretence, that in law they ought to be cited before sequestration.   It is the wish of others that there were nothing other at the bottom of this then a real scruple in poynt of law.   Many find a want in that such as have been nottourly in armes are not intercommuned, which would involve in guilt all such as corresponded with them, tho' they themselves did not fly to armes.   It were well the kings mind were known anent the baleing of such as have been in rebellion, for his name is used by some, as inclyning to it, which others do presume is great mistake, the law makeing such unbaleable, and our present circumstances evinceing it to be ruining to the state.   It is no less urged that the Earle of Perth be enlarged upon bale, tho' he be under a process of treason before the parliament, was imprisoned in the late government for his streaches while in the management of affairs, and guiltie of three or foure of those articles in the claime of right, for which the late king forfeited his right to the crown : tho' he will not own the government, names our king still Prince of Orange, and hectors such as do not still tearm him Lord Chancellor of Scotland.   Now, at such a juncture, to address for a liberation, in the season of action, when the Highlanders are likely to move, and the Duke of Berwick said to be amongst them, hath not the appearance of good.   The same addresses are for the late Bishop of Glasgow, and too much entertained.   It were a great reloof to the council of Scotland, if his Majestie would give warrand to seaze the horses and armes of papists and other disaffected persons, for tho' it be represented law and necessary for our present circumstances, it sometimes meets with this answer, that those methods are not suted to our king's inclination.

The late struggle anent the provost of Edinburgh was managed in this manner.   Upon the demitting of Provost Hall, Baillie Graham, as first baillie, without being elected, claimed as dew to him the priviledge of proceeding in the town council, and upon that same title usurped two votes, a thing only dew to the provost; yea took on him a negative, and refused a vote, anent both the time and maner of liteing a provost: upon which unwarrantable procedour, two instruments were taken by the major part of the council, yet he proceeded to the

chooseing proxies for old counsellors, tho' in the town, and not called, notwithstanding the dyett was not intimat, and that their right to vote was as good as
his own. This practise made such a discourse as he found himselfe necessitat to
address the secret council, and by this application sustained them judges. The
adverse partie in common justice was allowed to sie and answer, and the second
of June assigned them for that effect, the council being adjourned to that time.
Beyond the ordinary forme, that there might be no ground of clamour, Baillie
Graham and his adherents was allowed to sie, and answer the answer given to
his former bill; which produced no other effect then the raiseing a summonds of
declarator before the session to have thrust in that matter before that judicatory.
However, the major part of privy council not declyning themselves in a business
once tabled before them, by consent of both sides there was an earnest appearance, one way or another, in all the members of that board; for no less was insinuat
then that the issue of this matter would determine the continuing or disolveing
of this parliament, a significant step indeed, unto the ruining or preserveing King
Williams interest in this nation. The Earle of Crafurd being chosen president
no sooner had taken the chair, and shortly narrated the occasion upon which that
extraordinar council was called, when the Viscount of Stair endeavoured to bring
some other thing on the feeld; however, that shift did not take, and the members,
for 6 houres togither, were very attentive in reading of papers, hearing lawiers
plead, and reasoning among themselves without heat, but yet great earnest-
ness. The matteriall things said were a jest from the Lord Beilhaven, that
this was a family competition betwixt the Earle of Melvill and the Lord
Viscount Stair, which put some to smileing, others to blushes, and some
to their vindication. The Lord Fountainhall urged the Earle of Crafurd
thus, that Baillie Graham and his adherents procedour was either legall or
not; if legall, there was no access to review it; if not, the city of Edinburgh
had lost their priviledges. It was answered, that where the major part were
regular, it could be no ground to devest Edinburgh of their priviledges, for the
male administration of a few; ells it were in the power of any ill man to ruine a
corporation : besides that government which had extended mercy to the greatest
criminalls would never ruine a societie for a smal informalitie in law, and since
the late king was put from the throne for streaches to that thrid estate, it was
not like King William would devest them of their rights upon narrow escapes.
The Lord Stairs then reasoned thus, either the matter in debate was a thing of
right, or meerly of possession ; if the first, it belonged only to the session, if the
last, he offered to instruct that the possession was on Baillie Grahams side, and
that since the dimission of Provost Hall, Baillie Graham had exercised the two

votes, without reclaiming in the other partie. It was answered by the president, that he denyed every matter of right did belong only to the session, for matters of government and policie more truely was the work of the council, and Baillie Graham in the entry had thought so, by tableing the matter before that board. Besides, tho' the council should only meddle with the possession, they were not to be cast as judges of that, because right was in with it, for by consequence one could involve in every possession somewhat of right ; and lastly it was instructed by two instruments, that Baillie Grahams usurpation of the two votes, and of a negative voice, was reclaimed against as unwarranted. The Lord Boil-haven then made an overture, that the candidats for the provostrie on both sides should be laid aside, and the magistrats ordered to make a 3d choise, which he said was an evidence of a peaceable temper on the one side, and that it would import humor and peremptorness if it were refused by the other. It was answered by the Earle of Crafurd that this overture minded him of the discourse of the two harlots with Solomon anent the liveing childe. She who was not the true mother desired it might be neither the others nor hers, which was plaine evidence that she had no interest in it ; so Baillie Grahams offer did not proceed so much from an inclination to peace, as the conviction of the want of a title. There was another argument used by Fountainhall, that it were pitie and dangerous in so critical a time, to have a division continuing betwixt the magistrats of the cheefe city in the nation, which could not faile, if any one of them had intirely their will. To which it was answered, that after mariage, commonly the rejected rival came at a temper, and that it would be so in this case. The vote was then stated and carried in the affirmative, that they should proceed of new unto the chooseing of their proxies and liteing of a provost, which in the issue terminat in the election of Baillie Muire, who since hath taken his place in council, and is believed will manage to satisfaction. The post goes, and I am wearied, so adieu.

For Mr. William Carstares, minister of the gospel, and one of their Majesties cheplains.

184. JOHN TILLOTSON, Archbishop of Canterbury, to [GEORGE, EARL OF MELVILLE]—Mr. Fuller had spoken with his son.

November 5th, 1691.

MY LORD,—This day Mr. Fuller sent againe to speake with my son, and tells him, now, there is no need of his goeing, because Captain D. will be in towne to-morrow or Saturday. He still wants more monyes, and I very much doubt now whether there be anything of reality in the whole business, but two days more will put an end to our expectation one way or other. I have return'd your lordship's letter to Captain D., there being no occasion for it, and am, with great respect, my lord, your lordships very faithfull and humble servant,

JO. CANT.

185. COLONEL JOHN HILL to GEORGE, EARL OF MELVILLE, Secretary of State—Cameron of Locheil submits to the Government.

Fortwilliam, the 28th December 1691.

MY LORD,—This acquaints your lordship that on the 25th instant Lougheil came in to me and submitted to the gouernment of the king and queen, is gon to Arkinlosse (who is sherife) to take the oath appoynted by the kings proclamacion, and soe straight for London, to giue the king further assureance of his fidelity and resolucion to serue his Majestie for the future to the vtmost of his ability. Hee has broke the ice, and I know more will follow if not prevented by the elaps of the day appoynted (if they may not be afterwards accepted). As for me I will obserue orders, and if any of them be ruined they must thanke themselues.—I am, my lord, your lordships most humble servant,   JO. HILL.

[To the right] honourable the [Earle of] Melvill, [secr]etary of [state for] the kingdome [of Scotla]nd.

186. THE SAME to THE SAME—Submission of Glengarry and other Highland Chiefs.

Fortwilliam, 31 December 1691.

MY LORD,—My last on the 28th of December acquainted your lordship off the comeing in of Locheil, whose breaking the ice and leading the way hath made a good impression on the rest, for on the 30th December came to me Ranold M'Donald off Aughtera (neare kinsman to Glengary, and one off the best bred and most significant men for sence amongst the M'Donalds), who, being comissionat from Glengary and the rest there (to the effect in the enclosed),[1] in behalfe of themselfes, friends, and followers (amongst whom Keppoch and Glenco are included) did subscribe the paper whereof the inclosed is a true copie (the originall is re-

---

[1] For the submission here mentioned see vol. iii. of this work, No. 161.

served by me for feare of miscarriage), by which your lordship sees what is desired. They ask noe mony, but seem rather to rely on the kings royall pleasure, but the great mater they stand upon is safe passes for those officers mentioned (and say they are bound in honour rather to dye then desert them till they see them safe), I presume not to propose, but finding it their resolution to stand out on that accompt (unlesse safe passes be given to them), and yet to do what is proposed and promised in the inclosed (iff granted) I humbly conceive it adviseable to consider the proposall in regard the house off Invergary is strong, and strongly fortified and victualed, soe as not to be taken without great guns, at least eighteen pounders, which are not any way to be transported thither at this time of the year (the wether being excessive bad) and by that a great many men will loose their lifes, and doe nothing to effect, in regard they cannot continow any time there, I say I humbly think it worth consideration what is proposed, that they may be soe taken in as offered : and then there will be ane end off all the Highland troubles, and mony and men saved, and his Majesties greater affaires vninterupted, and then nothing is wanting to a compleat setlement but the fixing a civil jurisdiction here (which the Highlanders themselfes greatly desire), but what orders I receive shall be obeyed to the utmost off my ability, who am, my lord, your lordships most obliged humble servant,   Jo. Hill.

Since I writ on the other side I haue an accompt that Collonel McDonald of Keppach hath gon to the sherife of Invernesse, and hath taken the oath of alleageance, and soe haue the Stuarts of Appin with the sherife of Argyll, only the laird (haueing been sicke these two monethes past) is not able to goe, but hath written both to the sherife and myselfe that soe soone as hee is able hee will doe itt, soe that (if Glengary be admitted) there will be none out but Mull, the Captain of Clanrenald, and Sir Donald McDonald, for the McLaines in Morvern and Argour haue submitted and sworne long since, and those who are not yet come in in Sky will soone comply, especially if Cannon (who hath lyen there all this tyme) haue his passe granted to goe away, soe that their will be noe need of the armyes marching further, there being nothing left to doe, and the fatigue of marching now at this season (which is very bad) would be much damage to the army, but I shall obey orders, who am, my lord, your lordships most obliged humble servant,   Jo. Hill.

For the right ho[nourable the] Earle of M[elvill, secretary of state for the kingdome of Scotland].

187. REPRESENTATION of the Losses sustained by the EARL OF MAR during the Rebellion. *Circa* 1691.

A REPRESENTATIONE of the losses sustained by the Earle of Mar in the burning of thrie castles belongeing to him, in the north of Scotland, in the Highlands, and upon the borders of it, which was done by the Highlanders that wer in rebellion against the king for preventing of garisones to be putt in them for the kings service, and of his other losses in burning of his other lands.

Their was first burnt, to the Earle of Mar, his castle of Braemar, consisting of a great body of ane house, a jam and a stair case, being fyve storie high, with the furnishing within of bedsteads of timber, tables and chairs, which cannot be repared in the same conditione under eight hundred pound sterline.

In the nixt place was burnt to him his castle of Corgarf upon the water of Don, consisting of a tower house and jam, thrie storie high, which cannot be repared in the same conditione under thrie hundred pound sterline.

In the nixt place was brunt to him a great castle belongeing to him in the mouth of the Highlands, called the castle of Killdrumie, sourrounded with great walls, wherein their was much building, and being for the most part totaly burnt and destroyed, the reparatione of it cannot be under nyn hundred pound sterline.

Item, the Earle of Mar has been debarred from his rent about the castle of Bramar, which is about tuo hundred pound sterliue yearly, by the insurrectione of the Highlanders for the years 1089 and 1690, and now his propper lands in Braemar being totally burnt, and his saw milnes there made totally useless and laid idle, he cannot expect to have his land there in tennendrie for thrie years to come; att least his loss these thrie years comes to one thousand pound sterline.

All which loss amounts to thrie thousand pound sterline, as shall be sufficiently instructed.

> It is therefor humbly beg'd that his Majestie may be mov'd to give order that the forfeiturs and fynes to be imposed, on any of the Earle of Mar's vassalls that wer in the rebellione may be applyed to the reparatione of his losses above named in the first place, and that all remissiones to them may be stopt till that be done, especiallie since they took up armes agaiust his Majestie, and contrare to the Earl's express order, and tenor of their chartors.

188. COLONEL JOHN HILL to [GEORGE, EARL OF MELVILLE]—The Glencoe men
settled again in their country.

Fortwilliam, the 8th off August 1692.

MY LORD,—Hearcing that your lordship is now at Edinburgh, I thinke high
tyme to renue my acknowledgments for all former kyndnes and favors, which I
must ever owne to have been very great.

I have now (by the good providence off God) effected my bussines with the
Highlanders, notwithstanding all the opposition I meet with ; and now I have the
request I made, grauted by the king, off recciueing to mercy the Glenco men,
and setloing them again in their owne countrey, which is a very seasonable
mercy to them, and to the setlement off the countrey. I have (since your lordship left your former station) met with some difficultyes by some who are opposite (without just cause), but I hope I have wethered their designes, and I know
they cannot hurt me with the king, and my Lord Portland is my true freind. It
is the goodnes off God to me that (being a stranger) I have soe many freinds of
the best sort, to whom I shall ever adhere. And iff my methods have not been
soe vindictive (as some would have had them), yet they have effected, and iff
they have broken the designes off others, it was but in the way off my duty, and
hath been to my masters advantage ; and I rest satisfied whilst I doe walke in
the way off my duty, as becomes an honest man. Let others say and thinke
what they please, and let the world goe which way it will, I shall allwayes be
fonnd your lordships thankfull servant, whilst I am, my lord, your lordships most
obliged and most humble servant,   JO. HILL.

189. THE LORDS OF SESSION to KING WILLIAM THE THIRD—About the nomination of the Clerks of Session.   Circa 1692.

MAY IT PLEASE YOUR SACRED MAJESTY,—Having so recent assurances that your
Majesty will not be short of any of your royal progenitors in vindicating and
asserting the honour, authority, and priviledges of this your judicator of the
session, it hath emboldened us to signify to your Majesty that the clerks of this
court, having the greatest trust of the nation reposed in them, not only by having
the custody of your peoples evidents, bot in the extracting and giving furth of
their sentences and decreets ; they must necessarly be persons of great integrity,
probity, and breeding, for mantaining and keeping up the reputation and con-

fidence your subjects ought to have in this court. For effectuating wherof your royal predecessor Charles the Second of glorious memory, by his letter in June 1676, aunexed the nomination of the clerks of session to the senators of the colledge of justice in all time therafter, and to be subject to their censure, and the clerks of register are ordained to give deputations to such as the lords shall nominat from time to time : and any variation that has been since bears expressly to be on personal respects and favor to those who obtained that office for the time. And now, seeing in the gift granted by your Majesty to the present commissioners for exerceing the registers office, yow have with that same wisdome and justice which is refulgent in all your royal actions, reserved and retained the nomination of our clerks ; it hath furnished your Majesty with an occasion of reponing your judges to the nominating and bringing in their own clerks, which certainly will prevent many abuses which otherwise may fall out, and will fill these important offices when they happen to vake, with persons of integrity and knowledge, which will make it one of the properest seminaries for this bench, being conferred on lawyers tho' no great baristers, yet being otherwise judicious, have greater advantages of learning from what they hear argued within doors than others. This will exceedingly tend to the comfort and satisfaction of all your people, and to the speedy and equal distribution of justice, where the tentations arising from the venality of these offices are wholly cutt off ; and as this takes away non of the other emoluments of the registers office, so wee have no other prospect in it, save the general good of the nation, the obligation lying on us to mantain the priviledges of this house, and your Majesties honour, which shall be dearer than all other temporal concerns to, may it please your Majesty, your most faithful, most humble, and most obedient subjects and servants,

A. Hope.	Ihone Baird.	Stair.
Jo. Lauder.	Ja. Falconar.	R. Hamilton.
W. Anstruther.	David Home.	Jo. Lauder.
Ja. Murray.	J. Hamilton.	Ro. Dundas.
	A. Suintoun.	C. Campbell.

190. Rev. William Carstares to George, Earl of Melville—Reputation of King William.

At the Camp at Limbeck, Agust 7, 1693.
My Lord,—Your lordships of the 25th last moneth came safe to hand, the king revieued his armie upon Saturday last, and it is much stronger then before the

fight by the re-enforcement it hath had.   We marched four leagues this day, and are, as is reported, within lesse then three of the enemie, who some talk have a design upon Charleroy, but it is not at all probable, it being certain by what we hear from some of our generalls that were prisoners and are now returned, that their infantrie suffered extremelie by the late action, and they have 1500 officers lying wounded at Namur alone.   It is reported that the D[uke] of Luxemburgh did discourse in privat with Monsieur Luylenstein when his prisoner, and askt if it was not possible there should be an aggrecement betwixt their masters, who might divide the world betwixt them.   He said also that he saw our king still where the greatest heat of the fight was, and did declare that he had the highest value for him, and that if he might have the honour of one minutes discourse with him, he would be content to die the next.   It is a sicklie time here.   My Lord Elphing-ston gives your lordship his service and will pay his respects to your lordship by a letter so soon as his commission is signed, I know your lordship will communicat my news to friends in Fife, to whom, as to your lordship, I am a very faithfull servant.   I forgott to tell your lordship that the king, haveing sleept an hour or two in his coach the night before the battell, did earlie the next morning send for Dr. Meinard, the French minister, and desired him to pray, which he did in the coach ; it was a conceived prayer and no form, and allwayes when he goes upon action he makes this minister pray.

191. The Same to The Same—Death of the Archbishop of Canterbury.

London, November 22, 1694.

My Lord,—I had the honour of your lordships yesterday, and doe think that so long as a new order is delayed it will be fitt your lordship aggrie with the town as you can.   As for the mastergunner of the castle I think it will be fitt E[arl] P[ortland] be wrote to in a few lines about it, and I shall deliver it.   The arch-bishop of Canterburie [Dr. John Tillotson] died this day ; your lordship knows how great a losse it is.   The king hath had a slender fitt or two of an ague, but is, blessed be God, well.   Our affairs are not yet come to be discoursed of.   I am in all dutie your lordships without change.   Sir Thomas Livingston is not yet arrived.   The parliament hath aggried to supplie in generall, though argued against by Jack How, Sir Edward Seymour and some few others.   There is a generall satisfaction with this years mannagement.   The house of commons hath been this day upon the businesse of the Lankishire gentlemen that were tryed, and all witnesses are ordered to be before them.

192. THE SAME to THE SAME—Attack on Namur.

At the Camp before Namur, July 11, 1695.

MY LORD,—I have the honour of all the letters you mention in yours of July 2d. and make that use of them you desire; I also communicat what your friend writes to those concerned, and to none else. It is hardlie possible to gett any affairs done at present, which is the only reason he hath not had an answer ere now. What I wrote to your lordship before, will give as much light as to your carriage as it is fitt for me to give till I have your cypher, which I exspect every day with my trunck ; the want of it vexeth me not a litle. The bringing in that 3000 lib. bond will not rellish well here, for it does indeed seem unfitt to take up the parliaments time with things of that nature; it was exspected here that the parliament would not have sitt after the last of June, for though an order was sent allowing it to continue till the 26th instant yet if it came too late it was not thought that the session would be continued in exspecting it after the time, but this to yourselfe only and your friends, for I am not to medle in those things. We made a vigorous and successefull attack upon the outworks of the town upon Munday last, our men carried with such resolution as that some of them entred the town with the enemie and are there prisoners ; the French had 8 battallions and 4 regiments of dragoons engadged in this action, but nothing stood before our men. The enemie lost a major generall, briggadier, three or four collonells, besides inferior officers. Maitlands regiment lost poor Melvill, Lievtenant Arret and Gordon is sore wounded. This is all at present.

193. THE SAME to THE SAME—Surrender of Dixmuyd.

Before Namur, July 22, 1695.

MY LORD,—I have the honour of yours of the 12th, a part whereof was written with another hand which I know. What I have wrote formerlie will serve at present for an answer to all. It is a notorious untruth that I was at Rotterdam with the Master of Stares, for he did not goe that way as he tells me, nor did I see him till I came hither, nor knew anything of his comeing over, but any thing that may be thought to tend to blemish my reputation with some honest men must be made to runn current, true or false it seems it serves a turn, but I have been prettie much accustomed to such usage. I can say nothing against 85 his conduct ; I wish your lordship would send me a short account of the falshoods that you find in the information of the town of Edinburgh. As for our news, upon Fryday last the D[uke] of Bavaria did upon the side of the castle attack a very strong trench of the enemie which did runn from the Maes almost to the Samber, and did it with such successe as that he beat them into their walls. Boufflers lookt upon this to be of such importance that the night before, when exhorting his men to defend it vigorouslie, he said he would rather lose the town then that trench. This day one of our bombs fired a mine of bombs and carcasses of the enemie, and blew up severalls of them, but this good successe is allayed by the base surrender of Dixmuyd, in which were 8 battallions and one regiment of dragoons who all gave up themselves upon discretion, and are carried prisoners to Iper; there must have been villanous treacherie, but we have not yet a full account of the particulars. Deinse is also surrendred but the garrison that was in it is marched to Ghent. This is all at present.

194. The Same to The Same—Capitulation of Namur.

Before Namur, July 25, 1695.

My Lord,—All I have to say at present is that this day the capitulation for surrendring the town of Namur is signed, and we in possession of one of the gates, the garrison hath two dayes allowed them to send their sick and wounded to Dinant, and to carrie their own baggage into the castle; this makes aminends for the infamous surrender of Dixmuyd and Deinse. The garrison of the last are prisoners of warr for three moneths as well as the first, but the governours and officers did foolishlie as well as baselie capitulat for their baggage, and D'Offarrell, governour of the last, did send his baggage to Ghent, which Prince Vaudemont sent to the provost. Sir Charles Graham, who was one of the collonells in Dixmuyd, came to Ghent, but how I can not tell, but he is made prisoner there. The king is well. Lievtenant Carrou in Maitlands regiment is killed.

195. The Same to The Same—His lordship to visit London.

London, October 17, 1695.

My Lord,—Since my last it hath been confidentlie reported here that your lordship would be by this time upon the road thitherward, so that I did not think it fitt to urge for a positive allowance, which your lordship can not much wonder at, present circumstances being considered, but your lordship knows there is nothing like a prohibition of any. Earl Annandale hath kist the kings hand in order to his

return to Scotland ; I am apt to think that the kings affairs did not allow him time
to speake to him in his closet. I saw my Lady Weems in prettie good health this
evening, she complained a litle that she had gott a litle cold which your lordship
knows is scarse evitable in the winter here. I heard that Earl Leven too was
comeing up, which I am heartlie glad of. My Lord Raiths post, I know, makes
his presence absolutelie necessarie at present where he is, he is in good esteem
here for his sense and conduct. I must presume to tell your lordship, and you
may rely upon it, that reports amongst you as among many here of our affairs
are uncertaintie and conjecture, and therefor I easielie judge your lordship
will suspend your judgment of them, all I shall add is that wherever I am you
and yours have a faithfull wellwisher and servant, without a parade of words
and complements. I write this at a venture of finding your lordship.

196. JOHN, LORD MURRAY, Secretary of State, to GEORGE, EARL OF MELVILLE—
        the King's purpose to make him President of his Council.

                                            Whittehal, May 8, [1696].
MY LORD,—The king has thought fitt to apoint the Lord Polwarth to be chancelor, at the same time did designe your lordship to be president of his councill,
but delayed itt untill he knew your lordship woud be satisfied of the change as to
which you will be pleased to lett me kno your opinion as soon as your lordship
can. I can say that none does designe any inconvenience to your lordship by itt.
For my own part I never had thought you shoud be out of the post you are in
except you had a better, and if your lordship does not think the presidents post
better and more honourable, others doe ; there is no hurt done, but its like the
king will prefer another to itt.—I am, my lord, your lordship most faithfull
humble servant,   J. MURRAY.

197. SIR JAMES OGILVIE, Secretary of State, to GEORGE, EARL OF MELVILLE—
        That if his Lordship wished he might be President of the Council.

                                            London, May the 8, 1696.
MY LORD,—The king hes thought fit to make my Lord Polworth chancelour.
He did alwayes, and I hope uill stil live weal uith your lordship and your
familie, if your lordship think it for your interest, I belive you may be præsident
of the councel, and this would make way for doing for the Duke of Queensherry

and Earl of Argyl. The prœsident's place is more honorable and of æqual profite.
Bot doe in this as your lordship pleases, for I shal neaver propose any thing præ-
judicial to your lordship's interest or that is contrarie to your inclinations, for I
wish your familie al happiness. I doubt not your lordship will use your endeavours to make good agreement amongst al the king intrusts in the government. Wee can neaver expect ane ful setelment in the kingdom whilst thos
imployed in the publict doe not agree.—I am, my lord, your lordships most
faithful and humble servant,   JA. OGILVIE.

   I give my humble service to the Earl of Leven and my Lord Raith.

198. REV. WILLIAM CARSTARES to GEORGE, EARL OF MELVILLE—
        About being President of the Council.

                                            Rotterdam, May 12, 1696.
MY LORD,—It is like your lordship will have heard ere this can reach you of
changes designed to be in the government with you, and that a proposeall hath
been made of your lordships being president of the councill, and I have not the
least reason to think but that it was done both with a sincere respect to your
lordship and for the advantage of the kings service ; but the king hath delayed
to doe anything in it till he hear what is your lordships own mind in the matter,
which was indeed very kind. Your lordship may be pleased to communicat your
thoughts about it so soon as you shall think fitt. I shall not presume at present
to trouble your lordship with a long letter, for there is nothing of moment to
write. We have much discourse here of a peace, but upon what grounds I know
not. The king goes to the camp in a few days. Whatever is amisse as to any of
your lordships affairs, I know your lordship will not blame your faithfull servant,
and reallie I can not say but both the secretaries are your lordship's friends.
Your lordship shall hear frequentlie from me.

199. GEORGE, EARL OF MELVILLE, to SIR JAMES OGILVIE—Declining the office
        of President of the Council—Draft.

                                            Monymaill, May 15, 1696.
MUCH HONOURED,—By yours of the 8th instant you are pleased to inform me of
the Lord Polworths being made chancelour, and that if I thought it for my
interest I might be præsedent of the councill. I neither question the honour nor

profite of it, but I never much liked changes, and since I am informed that his
Majesty haith left it to my choice, I am resolved to serve the king in the station
I am now in. I heartily wish a good agreement amongst all honest men and good
subjects, and am bold to say I ever endeavoured to live well with all, especiallie
those entrusted by his Majesty. I thank your lordship for your expressions of
kindness and for your good wishes to my family. I wish you hade been more suc-
cessfull in procuring from the king what once his Majesty had done and was
pleased to say should be done for me. I never heard any thing since I see
you of that warrant you speak to me of at pairting for the lord advocats
delivering up to me that paper he haith in relation to the toun of Edinburgh,
which he profest himselff willing and ready to doe. If non of these things be
yet done I recomended to you, I hope and expect you will minde them, whereby
you will oblige, my lord, your lordships most humble servant,

MELVILL.

Indorsed : Copie of my Lord Privy Seales answer to Sir James Ogilvie.

290. JOHN, LORD MURRAY, Secretary of State, to GEORGE, EARL OF MELVILLE—
    Further about being President of the Council.

Whitehall, 26 May [1696.]

MY LORD,—I receaved your lordships acquainting me that you doe not incline
to change the place you have for that of president of the councill, in which I
shall not pretend to advise your lordship, but I hope you will allow me to assure
you that none that proposed itt did it out of any designe to prejudge you, but
for your advantage, for it being a more honourable and, I belive, as beneficiall a
post, it was thought you coud not but agree to itt, which perhapes you still may,
especially since it will be an obligation put on those who have apeared and don
theire indeavours to serve you, and which will ingadge them the more to continow so, and for my owne part I 'll assure your lordship I shall doe my best you
be secured in continuance of the presidents place if you think fitt to accept it, in
which I belive you will litle need the assistauce of your friends becaus I am persuaded non can doe your lordship prejudice with the king, who dos not doupt
but you will always continow to apear firm and zealous in his servess.—I am, my
lord, your lordships faithfull humble servant,   J. MURRAY.

201. JOHN, LORD MURRAY, Secretary of State, to GEORGE, EARL OF
MELVILLE—Regretting he had not become President.

Bath, June 27, [1696].

MY LORD,—I have your lordships acquainting me of your inclinations to continue
rather in the post you are, then to have that of the president of the council. I
must say for myself, my designe in wishing your lordships accepting the one for
the other, was never out of any prejudice to you, but on the conterar, since that
of president is lookt on as more honourable, and the difference of the benefitt
betwixt them inconsiderable. I had not opurtunity myself to speake to you of itt
before I left Edinburgh, because I had no opurtunity to waitte on you after it
was motioned, because, as I remember, you went out of toun before me. Be
pleased to give my humble service to my Lord Leven and my Lord Raith, to
whom I am an humble servant, as I am, my lord, your lordships faithfull humble
servant,   J. MURRAY.

For the right honorable the Earle of Melvill, Lord Privy Scale.

202. REV. WILLIAM CARSTARES, to GEORGE, EARL OF MELVILLE—
About being President of the Council.

At the Camp at Gemblours, July 2, 1696.

MY LORD,—I delivered yours to Earl P[ortland] and acquainted him with your
lordships reasons for not changeing your post. He said he would write your lordship an answer. I doe not find that you are under any mistakes either with the
king or him, as to the matter in hand, and I have reason to be assured that the
only ground of their being inclined your lordship should be president of council
is because they judge it fitter for one of your lordships years and experience then
for a young man, nor can I indeed say that the secretaries had any other reason
then this for their proposall, and if I thought otherwise I would not write thus
to your lordship. I did indeed think that your lordship had been acquainted with
the matter, but my Lord Murray writes to me of late that at that time your
lordship was out of town, otherwise he would have concerted the matter with
you. The discourse that we have had of peace is now more warm then other,
and not without ground, for some, as I hear, were sent from the French king to
the Hague to make proposalls to the allies, and one of them is returned with the
finall answer of the confederats, to which he is to bring a cleer and satisfactorie

answer from the French king against the 8th of this moneth, or the treatie is to
be broke off. A litle time will cleer this matter. 33 must bear the reproaches of
30 ; I can say he is loaded with much more than in justice comes to his share. I
am in all dutie your lordships.

203. WILLIAM BENTINCK, FIRST EARL OF PORTLAND, to GEORGE, FIRST EARL OF
     MELVILLE—Regretting that he had not become President of the Council.

Du Camp de Giblours ce 16 Juillet [1696].

MONSIEUR,—J'ay bien receu la lettre que vous m'avez fait l'honneur de m'escrire.
Je suis marry que vous ayez de la peine a vous resoudre d'accepter la charge de
president du conseil, la difference du profit siil y en a est si petitte, et la difference a lesgart de l'honneur de la direction aus affaires, et de la confidance du Roy
est si grande, que je vous advoue que je ne croyois pas que vous y auriez balancé,
et vos amis a qui j'ay parlé estoit du mesme sentiment, et vous voyez que c'est
une chose que la souhaitteroit quoyque pourtant il vous laisse l'entiere liberte de
faire ce que vous trouverez bon. Je vous prie de me croire tousjours, monsieur,
vostre tres-humble et tres-obeissant serviteur,   PORTLAND.

     M. Ld. Melvill.

204. THE SAME to THE SAME—Compliments.

Du Camp de Diegone ce $\frac{29}{19}$ May [circa 1696].

MONSIEUR,—Je vous suis tres-oblige de l'honneur de vostre lettre, et de la part que
vous prenez dans ma guerison, je vous asseure que serois tres-aise si elle me fournit
les occasions de vous rendre service, monsieur, puis que je suis tres-veritablement,
Monsieur, vostre tres-humble et tres-obeissant serviteur,

PORTLAND.

     M. Ld. Mellvil.

205. REV. WILLIAM CARSTARES to DAVID, EARL OF LEVEN—Would receive
     his lordship's commands before going to London.

Edinburgh, March 10, 1698.

MY LORD,—After parting with your lordship, I have considered that by going to
Fife I shall be detained for some days longer in this countrey then I know my
lord president would desire, considering that upon my lord chancellours going up
and Earl Tullibardins design to enhance him, it may be necessarie I be above. It

is a great presumption in me to think that my lord president should have any the least trouble upon my account, but it may be he will think that the sooner his faithfull friend and servant be at London, it may be so much the better, how insignificant soever he be, but I am resolved not to part from Scotland till I see his lordship, but I must first return hither, and then I shall receive your lordships commands. Pardon the confusion and freedom of these lines to my lord, your lordships most faithfull and most humble servant.   W. CARSTARES.

To the right honourable the Earle of Levin.

206. SIR JAMES OGILVIE to GEORGE, EARL OF MELVILLE—Condolences on the death of Lord Raith.

Whitehall, 28th Aprile 1698.

MY LORD,—I ame extreamly troubled for the death of your sone, my Lord Reath. I hade alwayes a great esteeme for him, and I was under particular obligations to him. Bot it is our deutie to submitte to Providence, and I beleive to your lordshipe it was not a verie great surprize, for he hes bein ille of a long time. The king hes not as yet resolved concerning the disposing of his place. The pretensions of your lordshipe and your famely shall be known. Bot it is verie probable that nothing will be done towards the filling of the vacant places for some time. It is reported that ther are some, particularlie Colonel Buchan, Patt Grahame, Maxwell of Litlebarr, and some others who are presently in France, are designing to returne privately into Scotland, and therfor his Majestie hes ordered the letter to the councill herewith inclosed, and wherof I send your lordshipe ane coppie. The king is this day gone to Windseour, and my Lord Portland is expected the nixt week, or the week therefter at furdest. I give my humble service to your lordship's sone the Earle of Leaven, and to Maister James. —I ame, my lord, your lordship's most faithfull and humble servant,

JA. OGILVIE.

207. REV. WILLIAM CARSTARES to GEORGE, EARL OF MELVILLE—The death of Lord Raith.

London, May 10, 1698.

MY LORD,—Though I have not presumed to give your lordship any trouble of late, haveing written to Earl Levin, yet I have had a sincere sympathie with your lordship under your heavie affliction. God hath been pleased to exercise your lordship with many troubles in your pilgrimage, but He hath in His goodnesse given you many proofs of His care of you, and concern for you, amidst many of them, and it is my sincere desire that your lordship may be supported under your present heavinesse, and that the God of all consolation may give you inward comforts in proofs of His favour to your soul under outward troubles that are of such a nature that without strength from Him cannot easielie be born aright. As for what Earl Levin did me the honour to write of, I can say that I am not inconcerned in any concerns of your lordship, but the king seems to be resolved to come to no determination as to supplieing of vacancies till after the parliament. As for the bond, I doe and will act in it what I can. Earl Portland is to be here it is thought next week, and I judge it may not be improper your lordship give a return to his last letter. I am your lordships in all dutie.

122 is a great friend to 85 so farr as I can see.

208. Rev. William Carstares [to David, Earl of Leven]—Filling of vacancies in the administration.

London, January 31, 1699.

My Lord,—I did think it fittest for me to leave my Lord Seafield to acquaint my lord president and your lordship with the manner of supplying the vacancies in the government. He told me that he had desired the favour of the Duke of Queensberrie to acquaint you both with the design of the last flying packett, and I doubt not but he writes by this that brings commissions for filling of vacancies. The Earl of Selkirk is putting in hard for the tithes of Dunfermling, but the secretarie resolves faithfullie to represent both your lordships and the Countesse of Rothesse her concern in this matter, and the inconveniencies in granting such a gift to any but the persons so nearlie interested. I judge it may not be amisse that your lordship send up a gift of that forfaultur you were speaking of when here, your lordship may with all freedom command me as to what is in my power, for I am heartilie your lordships to honour and serve you.

I had the honour of my lord presidents letter, and doe presume to return my heartie dutie to his lordship. I shall mind Captain Coult when the establishment comes to be drawn, which will be very shortlie.

209. JAMES, EARL OF SEAFIELD, Secretary of State, to GEORGE, EARL OF
MELVILLE—Of the need of union among his Majesty's servants.

Whitehall, December 26, 1699.

MY LORD,—We have had occasion this day to give his Majesty full information
how faithfully and vigourously you and your son, my Lord Leven, acts in his
Majesty's concerns, and I shall not faill from time to time to let your lordship
know what his Majesty desires to be done, and I will take it very kindly that
your lordship do writ frequently to me, and let me have your opinion in anything
that occurrs ; and I doubt not but the chancellor will also advise with your lordship and his Majesty's other servants in matters of consequence, and difference in
opinion is as much to be shund as is possible in publict orders, for it takes of
their weight and influence when they do not come out with unanimity, and
meeting togither beforhand is the surest way to prevent mistakes. If we do
continue unite amongst ourselves we will be capable to signify to his Majesty and
to one another, but nothing will give so great advantage against us as division.
I know your lordship will excuse me for useing this freedom, for you cannot
but be convinced that ther are a great maney who act under a popolor pretence
of a national concern when their own interest is only at the bottom. I am obliged
to writ a great maney letters this night, and so I cannot writ to my Lord Leven.
I intreat your lordship may give him my humble service, and I am, my lord,
your lordship's most faithful and most humble servant,   SEAFIELD.

   Earl Melvil.

210. Rev. WILLIAM CARSTARES [to GEORGE, EARL OF MELVILLE]—The king's
resentment at the ill-usage of his servants.

Hampton Court, June 26, 1700.

MY LORD,—The king hath heard what insolent usage your lordship and others of
his servants did latelie meet with, and does highlie resent it, and is very desireous
it should be searched to the bottom, being resolved to encourage and stand by
his servants in the vigorous prosecuting of it ; the king was acquainted with
what 85 did write about the sitting of the parliament, and he is much inclined it
should meet in Agust, if it may be hoped they will be in any kind of temper.
Pray lett 33 know 85 his thoughts of this. The king goes the end of the next
week to Holland. I am ordered to attend him. Your lordships commands shall
be acceptable, for I am faithfullie your lordships.

211. JAMES, EARL OF SEAFIELD, Secretary of State, to DAVID, EARL OF LEVEN
—Death of King William the Third.

Whithall, March 10th, 1702.

MY LORD,—Your lordship has had a particular loss this winter, for which I was
much concerned, but did forbear giving you any trouble about it.   I know your
lordship will now again be very much afflicted with the death of our king, who
has done so great things for these nations.   It is ane unspeakable loss to all
Europe, and it will not appear now so much as afterwards, for his influence abroad
was fully as great as that he had over his subjects.   However, wee must submitt
to the providence of God Almighty, though it is impossible not to be deeply concerned under so great a stroke ; and all that remains for us to doe is to follow
out those measures he has laid downe for our own preservatione and security.   The
present queen is all that wee have now betwixt us and popery and slavery, and
therefor I hope honest men will unite in the supporting her government, and
I cannot doubt but she will follow the example of our king in protecting us in our
religion, laws, and liberties.   I shall not trouble your lordship with ane accompt
what wee have done since, that being so fully written to the lords of the privy
council.   I shall be glade to have your lordship's advice in this criticall juncture,
for there is no doubt as soon as wee are a litle recovered wee must propose some
measures to her Majesty for the security, government, and advantage of the kingdome.   Excuse my useing ane other hand, being that I cannot yet write with my
own.   I am afraid I have entertained your lordship too long with this melancholy
subject, and therefor shall only add that I am, my lord, your lordship's most
faithfull and most humble servant,   SEAFIELD.

Give my humble service to my Lord President of the Council.
Earl Levin.

212. JAMES, EARL OF SEAFIELD, Secretary of State, to DAVID, EARL OF LEVEN—
The Duke of Queensberry to be Commissioner, etc.

Wheithall, March 19, 1702.

MY LORD,—Your lordships friends here are most sensible that your lordship has
acted very vigorously and faithfully in the presentt juncture, and now that God
Almighty has deprived us of the king, wee have nothing under God to look too
but to support her Majesties government, for after her reign wee have a prospect of
nothing but popery and confusion, and she seems att presentt very well inclined

to follow out his Majesties measures both as to the government of church and state, and it is evident that it is the interest of the Presbiterians to concurr in her service, for she has given them already reiterated assurances of her protectione. She has named the Duke of Queensberry her commissioner, and has plainly and positively declared that the parliament shall meett att the day to which she has now adjourned, so that the objections of many will be over, that they were afraid of a dissolutione. The parliament of England here seem mightely inclined to ane union. It has carried in the House of Commons to bring in a bill for enabling her Majesty to name commissioners to treat, and the lords are all most unanimous for it, and if wee be unite among ourselves wee cannot miss to prevail in the union. I hope your lordship will be active with the members of parliament not to engage themselves in rash measures till wee come down to Scotland, and have occasion to let them know the true state of affairs, and that nothing will be demanded but what is for there security and happines. This is all that I shall trouble your lordship with att presentt, but that I am, my lord, your lordships most faithfull and most humble servant,   SEAFIELD.

    Earl Levin.

213. JOHN, DUKE OF MARLBOROUGH, to DAVID, EARL OF LEVEN—The Castle of
                    Edinburgh in want of repair.

                                                February 10th, 1704.
MY LORD,—I haue receiu'd the honour of your lordshipes letters of the 21st of December and 25th past; the former did not come to my hands til more then three weekes after its date, and the other but 4 or 5 days since, however I shou'd haue acknouledged them sooner if I cou'd haue given your lordship any light into your affaires in Scotland; they are not yett setled, but will be soon, since her Majesty thinkes it absolutly necessary for her service that the parliament shou'd meet early this spring. I am sorry to see the castel of Edenborough is so much out of repaire, and that you are in such want of powder. I hope you may be able to find some in Scotland, or mony to provide itt; however, her Majesty has thought fit to order a present supply to be sent to Barwick for any emergincy that may happen, and if you cou'd find a fond for the repaires of the castel vpon the first notice I shal be glade to let you have an enginier.

    I haue moved the queen againe in relation to the place of master of the ordinance, and can assur your lordship that as soon as her affaires will admit of the disposal of it, you may depend vpon her Majestys making good her promis to

you. If any thing else shou'd occure while I am in England, either with reference to yourself or the publique, I pray your lordship will comunicate it to me
with the same fredome you wou'd to your own brother, and beleiue I shal make
it my constant endeavours to assure you on all occasions of the true vallu I haue
for your friendshipe, being with truth, my lord, your most obedient humble
servant,   MARLBOROUGH.

214. JOHN, SECOND DUKE OF ARGYLL, to DAVID, EARL OF LEVEN—The
distribution of offices.

London, February 20, 1704.
MY DEAR LORD,—Till Sunday last I knew no more of our affairs then the man
in the moone, and this day only have learnt what I shall tell you, but if you dont
hear it from others, which I believe you will, take no notis of it.   I am told Lord
Seefeld is to be chancelor, Lord Tuedal presedent of the council, Lord Anandel
secreterry, that you are to have the ordinance, and that I am to be commissioner.
I have advisd that the four gentlemen that were last added to the tresurey
should be turnd out to make place for sum of our friends, and the Whigs here
ar positive that Mr. Jonson must be out, so that will be five vacancys.   Pray
take no notis of this, for I have told it no mortal, but the Duke of Queensberry
and Lord Annandel. The tresurer tells me the queen is resolv'd to be much
advisd by you, my Lord Annandel, and myselfe; so I wish you would give
him your opinion as to this. I have desir'd my Lord Anandel to doe the saime.
I have writt my lord my opinion as to the filling them, which he'l tell you. Pray,
my dear lord, lett me hear fully from you, and pray command me as you would
your best friend and servant, and whoe will ever be so.

Indorsed : Letter, the Duke of Argyll to the Earle of Leven, the 20th of
February 1704.

215. SIDNEY, LORD GODOLPHIN, Lord Treasurer of England, to DAVID, EARL OF
LEVEN—The remission desired by Lord Leven—the queen's purpose to
defend her servants.

Windsor, June 28th, 1704.
MY LORD,—I am sorry to find by the honour of your lordships letters that
since your arrivall in Scotland you are still more confirm'd in the apprehensions
you had here of the malice of your enemys. I have acquainted the queen with

the substance of your lordships letter. It was not for want of kindness or con-sideration of your lordship, as you may have seen by other proofs, that her Majesty declined to give you the remission desired by your lordship, but that she thought it both reasonable in itself, and for her service, that all things of that nature should bee left free for a just consideration of the parliament, and in hopes that, among other things, that fairness of proceeding might bee one means of bring-ing mens minds to be more moderate, and into a better temper, and her Majesty is willing to hope it may yett prove to have that effect, to which purpose I have written to my lord chancellor very plainly by this post, and I am very sure, as I have told him, that the queen will always bee disposed to interpose her authority in your lordships favour against any violent and unreasonable prosecution of your enemys. Your lordship has a very good friend here, Mr. Secretary Harley, with whom I shall always bee ready to join in what you shall have occasion to propose for yourself and for the queen's service according to the accounts you give us from Scotland: being with great respect and truth, my lord, your lordship's most humble and obedient servant,   GODOLPHIN.

Indorsed : Letter from the Earle of Godolphen to the Earle of Leven the 28 of June 1704.

216. ROBERT HARLEY, Secretary of State, to DAVID, EARL OF LEVEN—That he was sorry his lordship was badly treated.

June 29, 1704.

MY LORD,—I am honord with your lordships letter of the 20 instant, which came not to my hand til the 27 at night. It came not with any post mark, so your lordship wil judg whether I should have had it sooner or no.

I am heartily sorry your lordship should meet with any mortification at home, but I know your firmness and penetration is too great to suffer any of those little arts to have effect upon you : It is, I confess, a matter of great concerne that those who have the benefit of her Majesties service wil not treat your lordship and such others well, who serve her Majestie out of principle and gratis ; but I hope the notice that is taken of it heer wil quickly make a change in their behavior to your lordships advantage. I send your lordship enclosed a letter from lord treasurer, which I hope wil give your lordship intire satisfaction, and there-fore supersede my repeating anything to your lordship upon that head ; only I cannot forbear often telling your lordship, because I often hear it, that no person in Scotland hath a greater share than your lordship of her Majesties favor and good opinion. My lord treasurers letter I doubt not wil give your lordship so ful satisfaction, that I should but mispend your tyme to add any more than that I am, with great respect, my lord, your lordships most humble and most obedient servant,   RO. HARLEY.

I shal troble your lordship again as soon as I heear anything material for your lordships service.

Erle of Leven.

217. ROBERT HARLEY, Secretary of State, to DAVID, EARL OF LEVEN—The Settlement of the Succession.

July 20, 1704.

MY LORD,—When anything doth not go as it ought in your kingdom, I am heartily sorry for it, because I love your nation, and as I am a servant to your lordship as wel as a welwisher to the kingdom, I am concernd when your lordship is hors de jeu, because I am so fully satisfied of your ability as wel as zeale for the public, and I can never beleive things wil succed wel wherin your lordships aid and assistance is not made use of. I must own that what we hear from thence is incomprehensible to me, and I cannot solve the phænomenon, to see so many persons of different partys, understandings, inclinations, and interests, al joyne to oppose; what? why, the only thing which can secure that kingdom, or not deliver them over, as we do dead carkasses, to undertakers and projectors to practice upon, viz., the settling the sucession. The two things from Scotland we have yet seen are proclamations of warr against England, and nothing of good to Scotland. Can Scotland live by negatives? or is England to be whip'd into that which was voluntarily offerd at the union? when the greatest advances which ever were made by England were then agreed, and have been since (by an unparraleld instance) scornd and refusd. Are those gentlemen in earnest to do good to Scotland who have endeavord to ridicule an union, and yet now pretend to be for it? who have pretended to beleive poor Mr. Hodges his chimerical book, and yet at the same time would have us beleive they are true Scotsmen, and would be glad of a real union, by which they mean somewhat either very imperfect or very impracticable. Wil not the example of Poland carry some instruction with it and shew how far faction and avarice can carry people to the destruction of their country, and at last find themselves deceivd, and make a very sorry retreat? Wil not the nation, when they are cool (which wil quickly happen), make reflections that they might have had everything which was reasonable, even their losses about Darien repaid, and nothing askd but for their own good? I say, wil they not, as soon as their eyes are open, be apt to turne upon their misleaders and give them their just doom ? But I have said too much ; your lordship will please to forgive the overflowing of my zeale and affection to the noble Scots' nation, whose ruine, if heaven be not more merciful, wil be upon their own heads. The firme beleif I have in your lordships true zeale for your country, in your unmoved affection to the common cause of religion and liberty, and your lordships great candor, hath encoragd me to use this freedome to which I have no other call than as being a zealous lover of your nation, and, my lord, your lordships most humble and most obedient servant,   Ro. HARLEY.

Your lordship may depend upon the good opinion of her Majestie, and al good offices from my lord treasurer.

Indorsed : Letter from Mr. Harly to the Earle of Leven, the 20th of Jully 1704.

218. SIDNEY, LORD GODOLPHIN, Lord High Treasurer of England, to DAVID, EARL OF LEVEN—Acts in the Scottish Parliament regarding the Succession—the queen pleased with Lord Leven's behaviour.

                                        Windsor, July 27, 1704.

MY LORD,—Since I had the honour of your lordships letter with the resolves passed against the succession, I have other letters from Scotland with an account of what passed in parliament the Friday following concerning a cess, for the speedy obtaining of which the hopes given the queen by these letters will, I beleive, prevail with her Majesty to continue the session till she hears how that will end ; and not much longer, I hope, whatever bee the event.

I reckon it will bee no ill effect of the queens having declared herself as she has done for this measure, if it proves a means of uniting all those in her Majesty's service for the future who have sincerly concurred in it on this present occasion, and it is only from such a union that I can have any prospect of better success hereafter. In the mean time I hope this session cannot now continue long enough to do anything that will be disagreeable to your lordship, of whose proceeding the queen has all the satisfaction that you can desire. I wish I were able to say the same for others from whom her Majesty might with reason expect much more.—I am, with great truth and respect, my lord, your lordships most humble and obedient servant,   GODOLPHIN.

Indorsed : Letter from the Earle of Godolphen to the Earle of Leven the 27 of July 1704.

219. THE SAME to THE SAME—The queen had restored him to the
governorship of Edinburgh Castle.

London, 15th of October 1704.

MY LORD,—I have forborn to acknowledg the honour of your lordships letter till
I might at the same time bee able to give you some account of the queens
intentions in her affairs of Scotland in generall, and particularly in what relates
to yourself.

Upon the report of her servants called from thence her Majesty is fixed in the
resolution of being firm to the measure proposed in the last session of parliament,
and by endeavoring to cement and unite all those who concurred in that measure,
to remove from her service, and discountenance all those, and those only, who
have endeavoured to obstruct and oppose it. What effect this may have in Scotland, either now or hereafter, I cannot pretend to judg, but I dare affirm to your
lordship that the queen will continue as steady to this measure, as she has done
to her promise of restoring you to bee governour of the castle of Edinburgh, for
which her Majesty has given the necessary directions ; and as to the place of master
of the ordnance, she resolves to keep it vacant till the Duke of Marlborough
comes over, which I also look upon to bee a decision in your favour, since it was
by him that these applications were made to her Majestie in your lordships
behalf.

The queen was willing and ready to have given you the privy seal which the
Duke of Atholl had, but the time not allowing to stay for a return from Edinburgh, she thought it was better to stick to what your lordship had desired, and
she had promised.

As I have always been desirous to serve your lordship to the best of my power,
so I shall continue in the same intentions upon any occasion that offers, being,
with much esteem and respect, my lord, your lordships most humble and
obedient servant,   GODOLPHIN.[1]

[1] Lord Treasurer Godolphin's letter was enclosed in one from James, Earl of Seafield, dated 18th October 1704, which simply congratulates Lord Leven on his re-appointment, expresses a wish for concurrence in the queen's service, and announces his own settlement as joint-secretary with the Earl of Roxburghe.

220. SIDNEY, LORD GODOLPHIN, Lord High Treasurer of England, to DAVID, EARL OF LEVEN—The queen desired a scheme by which her measures might succeed.

May 7th, 1705.

MY LORD,—I have the honour of your lordships of April 26th by the flying packett, and tho your lordship appears to have a just sense of the queen's favours to you, I am very well satisfy'd they were not all necessary to engage you in her Majesty's service and measures to the utmost of your power.

The queen has written herself so fully to my lord commissioner upon the subject of the removes, that I need not give your lordship any trouble upon that head, not doubting but he will communicate to your lordship what he has received from her Majesty, who desires nothing more than to see a plain scheme by which her measures may succeed, and in that case whoever desires the publick good so much as she herself does will have no difficulty in submitting their own private concerns and advantage for the good of the whole kingdom. I shall bee glad to receive your lordships comands upon all occasions, and shall always remain, my lord, your lordships most humble and obedient servant,

GODOLPHIN.

Indorsed : Letter, Earle of Godolfin to the Earle of Leven, the 7th of May 1705.

221. DAVID, EARL OF LEVEN, [probably to LORD GODOLPHIN]—Application for the office of commander-in-chief in Scotland.[1]

Edinburgh Castle, September 10 [1705].

MY LORD,—Pardone me if I give your lordship the troble of this line, altho' I did my selfe the honour to wreat to yow yeasterday by the post. This is occasioned by the death of Leivtenant Generall Ramsay ; and as therby the command of the queens forces in this kingdom is become vacant, so I have presumed to lay my pretentions to that vacancy befor her Majesty. My lord, I am the nixt in command, and therfor I hop her Majesty will be pleased to doe me the honour to give me a new mark of her royall favour in preferring me to the command of her forces when she shall think fitt to fill up that vacancy ; and I most humbly beg your lordship's favour and assistance in recommending me to hir Majesty. I dare say nothing of my oun fittnes for this employment, but that what may be

[1] Original among Laing MSS. in the University of Edinburgh. Historical Documents, Letters, etc., Division I. No. 194.

wanting on way, I shall endeavour to make up by my zeall, application, and fidelity; and by your lordship's assistance, and that of his grace my Lord Duk of Marleburrough, to whom I am also to address my selfe, I am very hopfull to succeed, and then to oue it to his grace and your lordship. I beg pardone for this presumptous freedom.—I am, my lord, your lordship's most obleidged, most humble, and most obediant servant.   LEVEN.

222. LORD GODOLPHIN to DAVID, EARL OF LEVEN—In reply, explaining any delay in the appointment of a commander-in-chief.

September 20th, 1705.

MY LORD,—Upon receiving the honour of your lordships letter with the notice of Lieftenant Generall Ramseys death, and letters at the same time from the commissioner, and others of the queens servants, wishing her Majesty would not take any finall resolution of filling that vacancy till the Duke of Marlborough came over, to which the queen is of herself inclined, and the rather because she thinks she is very secure by your lordships having the chief command by your post in the intervall, I think your lordship has no reason to doubt of his graces inclinations to serve you, nor of those of, my lord, your lordships most humble and obedient servant,   GODOLPHIN.

Indorsed: Letter from the Earle of Godolphen to the Earle of Leven, the 20th of September 1705.

223. JOHN, DUKE OF MARLBOROUGH, to DAVID, EARL OF LEVEN—He had written to the queen in Lord Leven's favour.

Au Camp at Calmpthout, the 25th of Octobre 1705.

MY LORD,—Upon the receipt of your lordshipes letter I have not failled to represent to the queen in the most feavourable maner what you desire, and do not doubt but her Majesty will have a due regard to your merit and the justice of your pretentions.

I am now going to vndertake a jorny to Vienna, and if her Majesty should not haue declar'd her pleasure before my return, I shal then be very glad to give you any farther markes of my friendshipe, and of the truth wherewith I am, my lord, your lordshipes most faithfull humble servant,   MARLBOROUGH.

Indorsed: Letter from the Duke of Marlburgh to the Earle of Leven, the 25 of October 1705.

224. JAMES, FOURTH DUKE OF QUEENSBERRY, to the EARL OF LEVEN—Requesting the sword of state.   Edinburgh 8th November 1705.

MY LORD,—Having recieved her Majesties warrant to represent her royall person for conferring the most noble Order of the Thistle on the Marquis of Lothian, and it being necessary to have the sword of state to knight his lordship with, I doe therefore desire of your lordship to deliver up the same to Mr. Francis Montgomery, one of the lords commissioners of her Majesties treasury.   For doing of which this shall be your lordship's warrand.   Sign'd at Edinburgh this 8th day of November 1705.   QUEENSBERRY.

   To the right honorable the Earle of Levin, constable and governour of the castle of Edinburgh, etc., and in absence, to the deputy governour.

225. SIDNEY, LORD GODOLPHIN, Lord High Treasurer of England, to DAVID, EARL OF LEVEN—That the queen would not appoint a commander-in-chief in Scotland till the Duke of Marlborough returned.

                                                          4th December 1705.
MY LORD,—In answer to the honour of your lordship's letter I can only say at present that I have all the inclination that can bee to doo your lordship the best service in my power as to the chief command of the army in Scotland.   I beleive the Duke of Marlborough has the same, but he not being yet arrived, tho expected now in one week more, the queen will not determine that affair till he comes. Which coming being not like to bee much longer deferred, I hope your lordship will soon find this matter decided to your satisfaction.—I am, with great esteem, my lord, your lordships most humble and obedient servant,   GODOLPHIN.

   Indorsed : Letter from the Earle of Godolphon to the Earle of Leven the 4 of December 1705.

226. JOHN, DUKE OF MARLBOROUGH, to DAVID, EARL OF LEVEN—His commission as commander-in-chief to be despatched.

                                          St. James's, the 15th January 170⅚.
MY LORD,—I must now acknowledge the favour of three letters from your lordship, and at the same time ask pardon for deferring to answer the former.   I easily persuade myself you will impute it to nothing else than the continual hurry I have been in vpon my first coming over, and not to any want of friendship.

You will soon hear from the secretarys of the dispatch of your commission to command in chief the forces in Scotland, a trust I am sure her Majesty cannot repose in better hands, and you may depend vpon my earnest solicitations that you may keep at the same time your commission of master general of the ordnance, with the government of the castle of Edenborough. I shall likewise move her Majesty that you may have leave, as soon as her service will permit, to come vp to London as your lordship desires, being with great truth, my lord, your lordship's most faithfull and humble servant,   MARLBOROUGH.
Earl of Leven.

227. DRAFT LETTER, JOHN, EARL OF MAR, to DAVID, EARL OF LEVEN, intimating his appointment by Queen Anne as commander-in-chief of the forces in Scotland. 17th January 170⅚.[1]

MY LORD,—I was unwilling to trouble your lordship with letters, letting you know what past here concerning the affair of your being comander in chife of the forces in Scotland, until I cou'd tel your lordship something to purpose of it. I spoke often to the queen of it, as the rest of her servants did likewise, and severall times to the Duke of Marlborough and the treasurer, particularly yesterday I had occation of speakeing to the queen, and her Majestie was pleased to tel me that she was resolved to give the comand to your lordship, and to continow you in the posts you alreddy haue. This she ordred me to let your lordship know, and that very quickly she wou'd order me to draw the paper for that effect that she might signe it. This is not yet publick here, so I leave to your lordship to comunicat it to whom you think fit in Scotland. I think I may now wish your lordship joie, as I doe with all my heart. I am to be yet some time under your lordships comand, for all other Scots bussiness is delay'd until the Duke of Queensberry arive, but very soon after that I belive my regiament will be disposed of, tho whatever station I be in your lordship shall alwayes find me most sincearly, my dear lord, etc.

228. JAMES, EARL OF SEAFIELD, to DAVID, EARL OF LEVEN—Congratulating him on being made commander-in-chief.

London, Januarie the 24, 1706.
MY LORD,—I had the honor of a letter from your lordship about the time the Duke of Marlbrough came, and since that time I had two letters from Sir

_____
[1] Original draft in the Charter-chest of the Earl of Mar and Kellie, at Alloa.

Alexander Ogilvie giving me ane accompt of what past betwixt your lordship and him.   I did wreat to Sir Alexander that your prætensions wer fullie laid befor the queen and the Duke of Marlbrough, and that they wer favorablie receaved, and that soon your lordship would have reason to be satisfied.   I did most willinglie receave the assurences of your friendship, and I have served your lordship faith-fulie ackording to my pouer.   The Earle of Mar did by the last post accquant your lordship that the queen had determined to give you the command in chief of her forces in Scotland, and to continou with you the two posts of the castel and ordinance.   I am satisfied that none would have served her Majestic more faith-fulie, and that you had the best prætensions.   I heartilie wish your lordship joy of them, and in the station I have the honor to serve, you shal have al the con-currence in my pouer, and [I] shal be readie to intertain ane intier good correspond-ence with you.   What further concerns the armie is delayed till the Duke of Queensborries arraivel.   He is expected on Moonday or Twesday nixt.   The secre-taries wer also friendlie, so that I hope by chearfulie concurring together wee may be the more capable to serve her Majestie and our couutrie effectualie.   I am, with al sinceritie, my lord, your lordships most humble and obedient servant.

SEAFIELD.

The Duke of Marlbrough was most readie to serve your lordship.

229. DAVID, EARL OF LEVEN, to JOHN, EARL OF MAR—Thanking him for his services in obtaining his appointment as commander-in-chief of the forces in Scotland.   24th January 1706.[1]

Castle, Edinburgh, January 24.

MY LORD,—I have the honour of your lordships of 17th, with very particular expressions of your lordships frindship, and which is more, with reall proofs therof, for which I return your lordship my most humble and hearty thanks. Hir Majestys pleasour notifyed to me by your lordship in designing to honour me with the command of the forcess, as it is most acceptable, so I doe assure your lordship I have a most gratefull sence of hir Majestys great and undeserved bountie; and wer my zeall capable of being enlarged, I must oun ther's great reason for its being so.   I hop your lordship, who has been so good ane instru-ment in this matter, will not grudge a litle more truble in finishing therof, by expeding in dew time my commission, and I must beg that you will take the first opportunity of delyvering a letter to hir Majesty which I am to inclose to your

¹ Original in the Charter-chest of the Earl of Mar and Kellie, at Alloa.

VOL. II.   2 B

lordship by this post. I am glad that your lordship thinks the Duke of Queens-
bury is so weell stated at court. I hop his grace is safely arryved befor this.
I shall be glad to know wherin I can serve your lordship, so pray be so kind as
to command freely, my dear lord, your lordships most obleidged, humble and
obediant cusing and servant,   LEVEN.

230. MEMORIAL by DAVID, THIRD EARL OF LEVEN, to the LORDS OF THE
     TREASURY, in reference to the military stores in the castle of Edin-
     burgh. 5th February 1706.[1]

                                         Edinburgh, 5th February 1706.
   Memoriall—The Earle of Leven, master of ordinance, to the lords commissioners of her Majestic's thesaury.

THAT wheras I am oblidged by my office to consider the condition of the magazines,
and represent the same to your lordships, I find myself obliged at present to
informe yow that the magazine is in a very bad condition, their being little or
noe cannon pouder, noe flint stones, few or noe chests of ball cither for firelock or
pistoll, and but a small quantity of cartrage paper and match. And for arms
their are not above tuo thousand firelocks, and these the refuse and worst of all
the arms provided for many years, and soe consequently very bad. Their are
noe pistolls nor carabins but such as are old and insufficient. Their are few or
noe bajonets, and the patrontashes and holsters that are in the magazine are very
insufficient, being made up with paper. Their are noe planks for making new or
mending old carriages.
   Their is no providing of any of these things here except the ball, the bajonets,
and patrontashes and holsters; and therfore it is hoped your lordships will
give order for the homebringing of such quantities of each as your lordships shall
judge proper.

231. JOHN, EARL OF MAR, Secretary of State, to DAVID, EARL OF LEVEN—The
     Marquis of Annandale's refusal of office, etc.

                                         Whythall, Februarie 22, 1705-6.
MY LORD,—I hope your lordship will forgive my long silence. I knew your
lordship was sure of my cair in delivering your letter to the queen, and I waited

   [1] Original in the Charter-chest of the Earl of Mar and Kellie, at Alloa.

from post to post alwayes expecting to have something worth your while of wryting
to you, but our affairs have been for some time at a kind of stand. Your English
friends and ours spoke nothing of my predecessor (the Marquis of Annandale)
until the Duke of Queensberry came up, and then they show'd a desire of
haveing him brought again into the service, but withall said they thought
it cou'd be no otherwayes, but by giveing him the post that was formerly
offred him. This we all consented to, and spoke to the treasurer and the
Duke of Marlborough of it, who both went and viseted him, our English
friends spoke to him also, but he stile persisted in denying to accept. This
treatie put a stope to all our affairs, and particularly to the comission for the
union, but at last it cou'd be put off no longer, so the queen ordred Loudoun
(the secretary in waiting) to go to Annan[dale] and tel him she had keept the
place she had offred him all this time vacant to give him time to consider of it,
but now she thought it for her service that that place shou'd be fill'd, therefore
had sent him to get his last and positive answer. He said he had formerly given
it, but since the queen had been pleased to send her secretary to him, he desir'd
he might let her Majestie know that he acknowledg'd she did him a great dale of
honour in offreing him that post at first, and now too, but he did not think he
cou'd serve her Majestie in it, so cou'd not accept. This answer my Lord Loudoun
cairied to the queen, so ther's an end of the affair, and my lord sayes he is now
going home. Every body must own the queen has not taken my lord short, and
no body cou'd expect more condesention in the queen's servants, that after all the
stories my lord has been pleased to talk of every one of us since he came here,
yet we were willing to have received him, forgot bygones, and served friendly
with him : however its to be presum'd my lord knows his own intrest best, and
on the other hand I hope the queen's affairs are not so low but she can be served
without his lordship, or any one or more of us. Our English friends who show'd
a desire of haveing him imploied again are satisfied there cou'd not more be done
for that end either by the queen or her servants. I thought your lordship wou'd
be desirous of a true account of this affair, which made me give you this trouble.
Now since this affair is over, I belive the queen will very soon name the comissioners both for Scotland and England, and the Scots comission will very
quickly be sent down. We were so uncertain of our selves til now that we
cou'd not wryt to people who we design'd to recomend to be on the treatie, and
now it is past time to have answers from them, but we hope none will excuse
themselves from comeing up, when so much depends on the isue of this affair,
as the preserveing the pace of the two kingdomes and sattling them on one Protestant bottome. We all hope your lordship will be with us very soon. I'm

sure you will be of good use to the generall cause, so I hope your lordship will lay aside any inconveniencies you may have by it in your private affairs. We hear the justice clark talks as if he wou'd excuse himself, which I shou'd be very sorie for. I belive the queen will admit of no excuse, and I wish his friends may keep him from makeing any. I'm sure his friends here, either Scots or English, will not take it well if he do. The queen has ordred my Lord Loudoun to let my Lord Glasgow know that she is resolved he shall represent her person in our nixt assemblie. I hope by the accounts I have from Mr. Carstairs and other ministers of the good disposition amougst the ministers in Scotland there will be no troublesome thing in that meeting, and I question not but my Lord Glasgow will be very acceptable to them.

Your lordship may be sure that your comission's not being yet sent down proceeds not from any stope or demur in it, but the queen inclin'd to have the comission for the treatie first finisht before she did any more in relation to the armie, and she resolved to signe your lordships comission when she sign'd some others.

I had a letter some time ago from Livtenant Collonel Grant of the Highland company, teling me that one of his livtenants was dead, and that his comission some years ago was put in his handes (meaning himself) blank, and that he never had fill'd up his livetenants name in it til now, since his livetenants death, that he had fill'd it up with a friend's name of his own, which he hopt I wou'd not take ill. This seem'd to me a very odd thing, and tho I fancied it was a sin of ignorance in Willie Grant, yet I thought my self oblidg'd to lay it before the queen, which the rest of her Majesties servants thought too. Her Majestie was indeed surprised at it, and had not I given it a favourable turn, she had certainly ordred him to be broak, however, she resolved that he shou'd be made sencible of his fault, and therfore ordred me to wryt to your lordship to suspend him during her pleasure. I hope upon your lordships wryting in his favours and others of his friendes, the queen will be pleased to pardon him, and the sooner this be done the better. The queen has made Gordon of Barns, livtenant in the regiament I yet comand, livtenant to the Highland company in place of him thats dead, and Abercrombie of Glasough livtenant in Gordons place, the first of thirr two comissions is sent down this post, and the chancelor has got the other, to send it or not as he pleases, either now or after the election of his shire is over, for he intends to make this Glasough parliament man in room of Braco, who's dead, so if Glassoughs comission be not sent down now I belive the chancelor desires it not to be spoke of. I shou'd have wryten to your lordship the end of the last month anent Livtenant Colonel Grant, but the queen's servants here thought it wou'd be a loss to the service to suspend Grant until once the livtenants comission was sent down, that so he might take cair of the company, and it cou'd not be sent down sooner because of something about it that the chancelor and I had to adjust. It was mightily my concern to have one I knew to be livtenant to that company considring my intrest in that countrie where that company very often have ado, and the chancelor prest for his friend, so this is the way we adjusted it. I'm sure I've wearied your lordship with this long letter, so I'll say no more now, but in a post or two I belive I'll wryt to your lordship again. A compliment wou'd give you more trouble of reading, so without any, I am, my dear lord, your lordships most affectionat cousin and most obedient humble servant,

MAR.

I doubt not but your lordship is very glade of the happie conclusion is like to be to this session of parliament here. 'Tis thought it will rise next week. The Duke of Queensberry's lage continows stile so ill that he is not able to go abroad.

E. of Leven.

232. HUGH, EARL OF LOUDOUN, Secretary of State, [to DAVID, EARL OF LEVEN] —The Commission for the Treaty to be expede.

Whitehall, February 23d, [1706].
MY LORD,—I have delay'd till nou the acknoledging the honor of your lordship's of the 26th ultimo, because I had litle to say worth your lordships while. The farder procedur in the affairs of the armie has been delay'd till that of the nomination of the treaters for the union be over. This is the reason why I ha'nt had the good fortune to send your lordship your commission as commander in cheif, in which your lordship is so well secur'd, not onlie by the unnanaimitie of the queens servants, but likeways by her Majesties promise, that I hope yo'll not be uneasie at the delay that has hapn'd, which I recon in a verrie few days will be over. I hope in the beginning of the nixt weeke the commission for the treatie will be exped, which was delay'd by the throng of bussiness in the parliament here, which will now have a happie conclusion, the Whigs, who in the House of Commons were divided upon the Regencie Bill, being again united, and have carried that affair to their satisfaction. Wee have been for a long time uncertain wither the Marquis of Annandale was to be in the queens service or not. There has been a great dale of time given to my lord to consider of it, and endeavors were used by sume freinds here to persuad him to accept, till at last it came to be necessar to bring that affair to a point, in order to which her Majesty

sent me to my lord to let him know that she thought it was for the interest of
her service to have a president of the councell, that if he had a mind to serve in
that post her Majestie was willing he shou'd have the commission she had sume
time ago sing'd in his favors. My lord said the queen did him a great dale of
honor, bot that being persuaded he cou'd not be usefull to her Majestie in that
post, he cou'd not serve in it, and allou'd me to tell her Majestie so, which I did,
so that this affair which contributed to the delay of the nomination is now at ane
end. Our freinds here think it was manag'd with all the condecension upon the
queens part, and all the disinterestedness and good natur upon that of her
servants that cou'd be desir'd. I hope your lordship and our freinds in Scotland
will likeways think so. Her Majestie has allou'd me to tell the Earle of Glasgow
that he is to be commissioner to the assemblie. I doubt not but he'll be verrie
acceptable, and will have an easie assemblie. Mar is to write to your lordship
concerning Gordon and Glasoughs commissions. I hope you'll be preparing
to take journie as soon after the nomination as you can, your being soon here will
be of great use to your freinds and the common interest. I'm verrie glad you
doe not mistake me in the affair of your signatur. I assure your lordship I shal
upon all occasions serve you with the sinceritie and plainess of ane honest freind,
for I am, my dear lord, your lordships most faithfull and most obedient cussine
and servant,   LOUDOUN.

233. JOHN, EARL OF MAR, Secretary of State, to DAVID, EARL OF LEVEN—
    The Marquis of Montrose made President of the Council.

                                              Whythall, March 2, 170⅚.
MY DEAR LORD,—I wrote to you two posts ago, which I hope you got, and by it
you wou'd know my Lord Annandales storie, and how business is going here.
Since that time the queen has nam'd the comissioners for the treatie (of which I
send you a list incloased), and sign'd the comission, which is sent down by this
express. Your lordship will see that the first dyet of the treaters meeting is the
middle of Aprile, by which they will all have time to prepair themselves for their
jurnie, and be here some time before the meeting, which the queen expects, that
we may consult togither before we meet with the English. Her Majestie expects
also that upon this occation non who she has nam'd will decline comeing up, and
realie it wou'd look odd if any did. Since your lordship is to come, I wish, and
so does the rest of your friendes here, that you may come as soon as posiblie you
can for a great many reasons, and I hope it will be no inconveniencie to you, but

will certainly be an advantage to the generall intrest and your friendes. I hope your comission will be with you in a few postes, so that needs be no stope, for you'll have it before you can posiblie be reddy. I hope your lordship has disswadded the justice clark from declincing this jurnie, as I wrote last we heard he intended. If he did, it wou'd look very odd, do harme to the generall intrest, himself, and his friendes, so I hope he'll be advised. The queen thought it absolutly necessare that the place of precident of her councill shou'd stand no longer vacant, so she has sign'd a comission for it to my Lord Montrose, who has given all the assurances for his being on the same intrest with us, that can be ask'd from a man of honour. This I hope will strenthen the intrest, the queen's service and her present servants, so I doubt not but your lordship will be well pleas'd with it. He did not incline to be of the treatie because it wou'd oblidg'd him to come up here, which in his present circumstances wou'd have been inconvenient to him, so his comission will not be sent down for some posts, that the comission of treatie may be in Scotland some time before it. When his comission is sent down there will also be sent a letter adding severalls to the councill and exchequer, most of whom were formerly of them. I hope e'er long there will something be done for Weems, but I'll say no more of this until I be surer of it. If I cou'd tel you as much for North[esk] I wou'd be pleased, but things cannot all be brought about at the same time as people who wish them inclines; however, I hope that may do afterwards. I'm a letter in his debt, and will pay it as soon's I can. I'm sure he'll neither doubt my good wishes and endeavours to serve him nor my coleges, and I belive he has no reason to doubt any of the queen's present servants.

There has been talking here a good while of a regiaments being to be leavied in Scotland upon the English esteablishment, as M'Kertnies was, but not to have quit so many drawghts, and this regiament to go abroad under Lord Mark Ker's comand. Tho this has been a considerable time talkt of, yet we were never so certain of it, that I thought it worth your while to wryt of it, til now that the Duke of Marlebrow spoke to the queen's Scots servants of it, and told us it wou'd be for her Majesties service abroad, and that he inclined to it for that, to provide Lord Mark, and he thought it might be for the queen's service also in Scotland, therefore desired we might have our thoughts of it, how to make it conduce most for this last end, which we have done, and are to speak to him of it in a day or two. There are severalls of the captains in the two regiaments comanded by Lord Strathnaver and me, that we know are more desirous of serveing abroad than at home, and those we are sure of inclines this way we are to propose to be of this new regiament, and so make vacancies in Scotland. By this we think there may be five or six companies in Scotland to dispose of, which we wou'd advise the queen to bestow to people of intrest, which wou'd strenthen her service and her present ministrie, without preferring any of our own particular friendes. If we be not sure of five or six of the captains of the two regiments who are willing to go abroad, we think to advise to send so many of the five or six comissions as we are not sure of to your lordship to fill up with any of their names you think fittest, and they not to know but that they had been fill'd up here. As to the rest of the captains of this regiment there are more people recomended for them than there will be room for by the half. My brother, who served captain in Row's regiment all this warr is proposed to be livtenant colonel, and Clephan, captain in my regiament and an old good officer, major. Your lordship may be sure if we had been certain of this affair's being in earnest in such time that we might have acquented you of it, and got your return before we were oblidg'd to give the D[uke] of Marlebrow our scheme of it, we wou'd not have done it without your advice, but he told us the regiament behoved to be reddy in six weeks time, and he wou'd expect our scheme of it in two or three dayes. The subalterns recomended for this new regiment are inumerable, and all the blaime from those who are dissapointed, and those who recomended them, will fall upon the secretaries. We have need of broad shoulders to bear all the blaime both upon this accompt and others that people will give us, tho we be very inocent, and has as little the doing of things as any of the queen's servants.

I wou'd have wryten oftner to your lordship had I knowen or been certain of anything how our affairs wou'd go, and I doubt not but you windred at my silence; but as soon 's I knew my self I gave you an account of them, and til my last letter I was as ignorant what shape our affairs wou'd take as any body in Scotland. I have a great many letters to wryt, so I'll trouble your lordship no more now but to assure you that I am sincearly, my dear lord, your lordships most affectionat cousin and most obediant humble servant,   MAR.

Earl of Leven.

234. DAVID, THIRD EARL OF LEVEN, to JOHN, EARL OF MAR, Secretary of State for Scotland, in reference to proposed draught from the Scottish regiments. 7th March 1706.[1]

March 7.

MY LORD,—I had the honour of your lordship's letter of 2nd, with a list of the persons named on the treaty. Your [lordship] lets me know also that ther is a

[1] Original in the Charter-chest of the Earl of Mar and Kellie, at Alloa.

regiment of foot to be raised in Scotland, and that ther is a designe to make a draught out of the forces here.   This makes it necisary for me to represent to your lordship, as secretary in waiting, how prejudiciall this method will be. Your lordship knows how weak the regiments are, and what necisary detachments ther are.   I shall begine [with] Major-Generall Maitland; he has so many out-garrisons that your lordship must be satisfyed he can spare non: and for your lordships and Lord Strathnavers regiments, affter the detchements in the west attend Mr. Patrick Ogilvie and those that must goe on board the friggotts, what number will remaine, judge yow.   I need say no more, but its impossible to think of anie draught.   I need say nothing of my jurnay.   That depends on your lordship dispatching my commission.—I am, my lord, your lordships most humble and most obediant cusing and servant,   LEVEN.

235. JOHN, EARL OF MAR, to DAVID, EARL OF LEVEN—The Queen had signed several commissious for officials in Scotland.

Whythall, March 9th, 170⅚.

MY DEAR LORD,—I hope your Lordship got mine by the flying pacquet.   Since that time the chancelor, my Lord Loudoun and I waited of her Majestie and laid before her the affairs of the armie and peoples pretensions.   She ordred me to prepair your lordships comission, Lord Carmichails, and Grants, but told us since there were severall pretenders to the Guards, she behoved to have more time yet to consider of it.   Within a few dayes we are to wait of her again about that affair, but we are uncertain of its being determined.   I have wryten to my Lord Lothian and beg'd he may have patience, for that will be the way to bring it about as he wou'd have it.   The queen has been pleased to signe a colonels breviat for Colouel Bruce, and declaird at the same time that it was the last of that kind she wou'd grant.   Thirr comissions are sent by this post, and also a letter to the treasurie ordring your lordships pay as major generall.   Thers a particular storie concerning this last which I forbear teling your lordship til meeting, and then I hope you'll be convinced there was no omission on my pairt.   My Lord Montrose comission for being precident of the councill, and a letter adding him to the treasurie as those of that office formerly were, my Lord Weymes comission for being admirall with a pension of six hundred pounds, and two letters adding severalls to the council and exchequer, are also sent by this post.   In a little time my Lord Glasgows comission for being comis-sioner to the Asemblie will be sent down, and also his instructions, and then I think we will be very near idle until your lordship and others come up to the treatie. Ther's no more hapned since my last of Lord Mark Ker's regiament, and perhaps it is yet a question if it go on. Ther's a paper to be presented in exchequer under the queen's hand in my name, tho it will put little in my pocquet, but I beg your lordships friendship in it. The whole valow of it one year with another does not amount to ane thousand pound Scots by the rentall I have seen, and it is pay'd in so many smalls that it deminishes the valow. Tis for keeping in repair the roof of the palaice in Stirling Castle.

When any thing else occurrs your lordship shall know it. In the mean time I have nothing else to trouble you with, but to wish you joie again, and to beg of you to haste up.—My dear Lord, I am your lordships most affectionat cousin and most humble servant,   MAR.

It is probable that Grant will now be desireing his regiament to be quartred somewhere in the north. Your lordship knows how necessar 'tis to have a regiament at Stirling, and this is best acquent in that place. But I leave this intearly to your lordship.

E. of Leven.

236. DAVID, THIRD EARL OF LEVEN, to JOHN, EARL OF MAR, Secretary of State for Scotland, acknowledging his Commission, and intimating that he was coming to London, 14th March 1706.[1]

March 14.

MY DEAR LORD,—I have this day the honour of yours of 9th, wherein you are pleased to tell me that my commission is sent doun, for which I retorn your lordship many thanks. Your brother has also been with me with my commission and letter to the Treasury. I shall be sure to take care of all your lordships concerns whenever they cume in my way. But as to the particular yow recommend to be passed in Exchequer, I fear wee shall hardly be able to make a quorum in toun. However, I will try what can be done to gett a meetting. I am very glad ther is no further advance in the project of a new regiment by way of draughts, because realy its not practicable without the utter ruine of the troups here. But I wish the gentlemen very weell that are to be concerned in it, and therfor shall be very ready to assist them in ther levies if the regiment goes on ; and a moneth or two more, with what help may be willingly gott from us here, given of more time, may. be equall in my opinion to anie draught that can be made.

I recken myself by your lordships last at liberty to begine my jurnay when I please, and therfor the Earle of Weemys and I are to sett out nixt week. Your

---

[1] Original in the Charter-chest of the Earl of Mar and Kellie, at Alloa.

lordship did recommend to me sume time agoe to speak with my Lord Justice-Clark concerning his jurnay, which I have done, and I doubt not of his readynes to obey hir Majestys commands in that matter.

My lord, since I am now to be with you so soon, I have not offered to give the queen anie truble by wreating, but does delay making my acknowledgements until I have the honour to kis hir Majestys hand. However, if it fall in your lordships way, I must beg yow may make it understood why I wreat not—wherby you will very much obleidge, my dear lord, your most affectionat cusing and most humble servant,   LEVEN.

237. JOHN, DUKE OF MARLBOROUGH, to DAVID, EARL OF LEVEN—To draft 300 men for Lord Mark Kerr's regiment.

Whitehall, the 26th March 1706.

MY LORD,—It is not without some reluctancy that I trouble your lordship on this subject while you are on the road, being sensible that the draughting of the troops must be of prejudice to them, however, the queens service requiring that my Lord Markerr's [Mark Kerr's] regiment should be raised as soon as possible, I cannot help praying your lordship will be so kind as to give him about three hundred men out of the standing forces in Scotland ; and I do assure your lordship it shall be the last favour of this kind I shall desire from you.—I am, with truth, my lord, your lordships most faithfull and humble servant,

MARLBOROUGH.

Earle of Leven.

238. ROBERT HARLEY, Secretary of State, to DAVID, EARL OF LEVEN—The Union just and advantageous to both nations.

October 7th, 1706.

MY LORD,—I cannot leave this town without kissing your lordships hands, and assuring your lordship you have no servant readier to express a just sence of your lordships firmness to the true interest of both kingdomes than myself. I must own I think the Union as agreed upon by the commissioners of both kingdomes to be just and advantageous to both nationes, and as such it is the only visible foundation of settlement and peace between us, and delaying it or putting it off, as well as making alterations, can tend only to loos this golden opportunity, and to create jealosies and distrusts, which every good man will endeavor to heale. I

shal be very glad to receive any commands from your lordship whereby I may shew in obeying them how much I am, my lord, your lordships most humble and obedient servant,   Ro. HARLEY.
Earl Leven.

239. JOHN, LORD SOMERS, Lord Chancellor of England, to [DAVID, EARL OF LEVEN]—The happiness of the nations depends upon the Union.

London, 26 October 1706.

MY LORD,—I return my humble thanks to your lordship for the honour of your letter, and the account you have bin pleasd to give of your happy beginnings, and yet more, for your promise to let mee know, from time to time, what passes. I interest my self in your prosperous proceeding very sincerely, beleiving the peace and happines of both nations to depend upon it, which I wish with all my soul. Your great majority gives vs a most hopefull prospect. I hope there will be no time lost, because delay gives the public and concealed enimies to the Vnion oppurtunities of working, and because the meeting of our parliament will be soon coming on, the publick affairs of Europe not bearing that it should be long deferrd.—I am, with all possible sincerity and respect, my lord, your lordships most obedient and most humble servant,   SOMERS.

Be pleasd to let my Lord Melvil know how much I am his humble servant, and that I very heartily wish his health.

240. LORD CHANCELLOR SOMERS [No address]—About the Union.

London, 26 October 1706.

MY LORD,—I am sensible I ought not to trouble your lordship with letters of complement at so busy a time, but realy I cannot forbear to congratulate with your lordship upon your majority, which afford vs so hopefull a prospect that things will conclude well. I have it constantly in my mind of what consequence you thought it to have one person kept in good humour, and therefore I was not wanting to do my vtmost to have his new request complyed with, and am become an vndertaker in some manner that his freinds in Scotland shall do their best to improve this favour, so as to engage him to act with zeal, and I promise myself your lordship will not be wanting. I am very sensible how easy it may be to obstruct proceedings in an affair of this nature, which consists of so many parts.

But, on the other hand, I hope no delays shall be suffered which shall not be found absolutely necessary. It seems of very great consequence that the main difficulties should be over before the meeting of our parliament, and besides, there are some in the world who perhaps will vnderstand the natural effects of this Vnion better than now they do, and than will not fail to strengthen the opposition.—I am, with much respect, my lord, your lordships most obedient humble servant,   SOMERS.

241. SIDNEY, LORD GODOLPHIN, Lord High Treasurer of England, to DAVID, EARL OF LEVEN—The queen satisfied with his care in preventing the violence of the mob.

                                                        October 31st, 1706.
MY LORD,—I have acquainted the queen with the substance of your lordships letter by the flying packett. Her Majesty is very well pleased with your lordships care and diligence in preventing any ill effects from the violence of the mob, and will take the best measures she can to have some forces drawn nearer to Scotland both in England and in Ireland, to bee in a readines in case this ferment should continue to give any farther disturbance to the publick peace.—I am, with much respect, my lord, your lordships most obedient humble servant,
                                                                GODOLPHIN.

    Indorsed: Letter from the Earle of Godolphen to the Earle of Leven, the 13th [31st] of October 1706.

242. JOHN SMITH, Speaker of the House of Commons, to [DAVID, EARL OF LEVEN]—The progress of the Treaty of Union.

                                                        November 14, 1706.
MY LORD,—I am extreamly delighted with the honor you have done mee by your letter, and am very glad to hear that you have hopes of a happy agreement to the Vnion. Wee are here under great apprehensions by the slownes of the proceedings, and the opposition you meet with, which wee could not apprehend, the termes appearing to us soe very advantageous to Scotland. I have great reason to hope, if it comes to us, that it will have an easyer passage, provided it does not come clogged with additions. Let the successe be what it will, I am very glad to find wee have soe many wellwishers to Great Britaine amongst you, of whom I shall ever retaine the greatest esteem, and as you have been pleased to honor

mee with your favor, soe I shall with utmost endeavor approve myselfe your most humble servant.   I am very sorry to hear that a honourable freind of mine acts soe different a part from his old freinds, and could heartily wishe it were otherwise, but I must submitt.   I begge leave to adde but one word more, which is that dispatch amongst you is not only advantageous to the common cause abroad, but will be a means of making it lesse difficult in its passage here, many wellwishers being not only surprised at your delay, but thinking it very hard that the very great advances they have made should meet with soe warme an opposition from some persons that they have had reason to expect otherwise from.   Your lordships zeale, however, has appeared soe eminently for the common interest of Great Britaine that it has most justly gained the affections of all good men, for which noe one more heartily rejoyces then myselfe, who am with the greatest respect, my lord, your most obedient and most humble servant,   J. SMITH.

243. LORD CHANCELLOR SOMERS to [DAVID, EARL OF LEVEN]—The question of the Union.

London, 15 November 1706.

MY LORD,—I was in the country when I had the favour of your letter, which, to vse your own phrase, I confesse I thought very full of greivances; but your lordship told mee I was not to despair; and since I came to this place I find our freinds are all persuaded that if the freinds to the Vnion continue firm in Scotland, it cannot fail. The management of the opposers shew plainly they mean to terrify, and I hope they will be disappointed. The queen (as I am told) is every day more concerned the Vnion should take place, the violence of the proceeding of those who are against it convincing her of the evident necessity of it.

Your lordship was pleasd to hint at some explanations, which, if admitted, might make the passing the treaty more easy. Since that I have seen a memorial which states the particulars more largely. I assure you I would most readily endeavour to promote the agreeing to anything which would facilitate the passing of the Vnion in Scotland, which would not manifestly stop it here, for that would be alike fatal. I have not the memorial by mee, and therefore what I shall say to your lordship is not likely to be in any method, but as well as my memory will serve, I will offer some thoughts as to the several heads mentioned.

One thing proposed is, that the two penny drink in Scotland should pay as small beer for the excise. Wee have talkd with some of the commissioners here, and also with the gentlemen employd in stating the equivalent, and they assure vs of two things. The first of them say they are well informd that that sort which is called two penny beer in Scotland is as strong as the ale that is generaly sold in all the publick houses in England. If that be so, than there will not be an equality of excises, which your lordship knows was the principle which the English commissioners thought themselves bound to proceed vpon throughout, and which was the only thing could excuse them for agreeing to so very low a quota for the land tax. The other sort of those gentlemen said that the two penny drink was the general drink in all the publick houses in Scotland, and if that was made small beer, the excise in Scotland would fall by the Vnion, instead of being raisd by becoming liable to the English duties, and that it would considerably alter the equivalent. What ever case can be given, or is given in the way of management of the duty in England arises from the commissioners observation, that it is best for securing and ascertaining the grosse of the duty to be as gentle as may be reasonable in the collection, and that reason will hold much more strongly in Scotland, and therefore it may well be depended vpon that it will be practised.

As for the encouragement to be given vpon the exportation of oates, etc., I hope it will not be found difficult to be obtained in the parliament of Great Brittain, because it seems to stand vpon the same reason, as what is already law with respect to other species of corn; and as that premium does in a manner only concern some of the maritim counties in England, and yet was agreed to by the whole parliament of England, so there is no reason to suspect but the parliament of Great Brittain will be willing to comply with a proportionable premium to the oates, tho' it will perhaps principaly concern but one part of the Vnited Kingdom. But that which makes it in a manner impossible to be an article in the treaty is this: The calculation of the equivalent, as to the proportion of the customs of the two kingdoms, was made vpon the neat produce of both. This premium for exportation in England is paid out of the customs, and the English customs were calculated at a neat sum after these premiums and all other drawbacks deducted. Now, if such premiums should be agreed to be paid out of the Scottish customs, your lordship sees it will alter the whole equivalent, and that very considerably. So that both these things can never be calld explaining, but are a manifest altering the articles.

I remember only one other particular, which is the apprehension of inconvenience from importation of oates, etc., from Ireland, which (as I take it) is proposed to be remedied by levying a higher duty on Irish oates. All that I shall say as to this (besides that it is an alteration and therefore to be avoided) shall be, that, in my opinion, matters of trade, which in their nature are variable, should not properly be made the subject of articles of Vnion, which are to remain for ever sacred and immutable.   But on the other side, as this is not a subject of any of the articles, nor was touched vpon in the treaty, if any great weight be laid vpon it, I should hope it might be got through with vs.   But I should wish it might be let alone, because it may give occasion for like things to be started here.

I am quite ashamd of this tedious scrible, but I hope your lordship will beleive mee to mean very well, and I wish I had time [to] express myselfe in fewer words.—I am, with much esteem, my lord, your lordships most obedient humble servant,   SOMERS.

I doubt my letter is not legible, but I have not time to read it over.

244. ROBERT HARLEY, Secretary of State, to DAVID, EARL OF LEVEN—A eulogy upon the conduct of those who support the Union.

Whiteball, November 21, 1706.
MY LORD,—I receiv'd the honor of two letters from your lordship, the first just as I was taking coach to begin my jorney out of Herefordshire hither, the other came to my hands a few days since.   I need not tell your lordship the opinion that all whose opinion is valuable have of your lordships conduct, the true sence your lordship has shewn for the interest of your country, your firmness not to be shaken by popular insults, nor influenced by those who are professd enemies to the liberty and interest of Britain.   I say all this is abundantly celebrated by common fame.   And I must confess that your lordship and the rest of you, tho you have had a very hard game to play, yet it is a glorious one, and I think I can defy all the historys you have left to shew a paralell instance of so steady virtue. Your ancient kingdom has indeed inumerable instances of valour, of fierceness, of the excesses of courage, and the excesses of rage, but this, my lord, is an example of true, sedate, cool, determind steadiness, such as neither the whirlwind of the mob, the continual dropping within the house, the allurements from the other side of the water, nor the mistaken zeale and ill informd heat of the ecclesiastics have, tho united, been able to remove from the true interest of their country both as to religious and secular concernes.   I have namd the mistaken zcale of the Church in the last place, because it gives me a very particular concerne to see those who profess to be ministers of the Gospel breaking through the positive laws of our ever blessed Redeemer, and acting the parts of Jewish zealots, so much declard

against by Peter, James, and Jude in their Epistles, instead of being clothd with humility and possessing their souls in patience, and this to please the enemies of their constitution and discipline in oposition to their true friends and firme adherents. The hundred part of this foly in King Williams time so far sunk the credit of the Presbyterians in England, that the Independants and other sectarys have scarcely left them a remnant ; but I hope better things yet from them in Scotland, and that they will returne and repent and do their first works, else ——. But I must ask your lordships pardon for this excess which my zeale and love for your country has carried me to. I wil troble your lordship no farther than to assure you that I am, with very great respect, my lord, your lordships most humble and obedient servant,   Ro. HARLEY.

The Earl of Leven, etc.

245. CHARLES, LORD HALIFAX, to [DAVID, EARL OF LEVEN]—Anxiety for the Union—Stringent stipulations about trade should be avoided in the treaty.

23 November 1706.

MY LORD,—I was extreamly delighted with the honour you do me in remembring one who has a real esteem and value for your lordship. I should have been very proud to have had any share in the great work you are carrying on, but since I could not set my hand to the treaty, I shall more freely espouse it when it comes before our House. The opposition it meets with in Scotland is not more then I expected ; tis the last throw some people have for their game, and the consequences of the Union will be as fatal to them as Ramellies or Turin. In such a case you must allow them to make the utmost effort, but one cannot forbear lamenting the blind zeal of some who cannot distinguish between the certain good and the imaginary dangers they aprehend. What frightens me most is the expectation you seem all to have entertained, that every thing that you can think of for the advantage of your trade should be granted you now, as an explanation of the treaty. If this notion is pursued I know not whether it may carry us ; if wee depart from the agreement, and change the equivalent, every thing is unsetled, and wee are at sea again. On the other side, I am confident there is no occasion of such distrust ; in my opinion, the parliament of Great Brittain will give all the ease, and all the encouragement to your trade that you can desire. You need no more doubt that wee shall assist your fishery for herrings, then the southern parts fear the care wee take of their pilchards ; that trade is peculiar to one or two countys only, but there's as much favour show'd to it as if it concerned the

whole island. Wee shall have the like reguard for any trade that more immediately concerns Scotland, and to think otherwise is to suppose us not so united as
the English affect to have it. My lord, upon my word and honour, this is my
sentiment as to the whole article of trade, which is so changeable in its nature
that it should not be setled among the fundamentals of the Union ; and if you
should think fit to leave it as it stands in the treaty, I would answer, as far as
one can answer for a parliament, that you would not repent the confidence you
put in us.—I am, with great sincerity, my lord, your lordships most humble and
most obedient servant,   HALIFAX.

246. LORD CHANCELLOR SOMERS to [DAVID, EARL OF LEVEN]—Of the Articles
of Union—a tumult in Edinburgh.

London, 26 November 1706.

MY LORD,—I have with very great trouble heard you have not bin very well,
which is a great misfortune to vs all at so busy a time. I hope I shall soon hear
your lordship is perfectly recovered. I congratulate with your lordship vpon the
passing of the three first articles. But not only I, but every one who hears of
the tumults are astonished at them ; and I am told the queen looks upon that
behaviour as the highest affront to her government and the greatest indignity to
parliaments, and would shew her displeasure iu any manner her servants in Scotland should judge proper.

My lord, I doubt not you have heard from all hands of the great apprehension the freinds to the Vnion here have of the making alterations in the articles
of the Vnion. Besides the delays which such alterations, when begun, will cause
in Scotland, they will beget difficulties here, and give oppurtunities for such delays
as wee know not how to get over, and will cause the treaty to be sent back to
Scotland, as is apprehended here. Your freinds here think everything they have
yet heard mentioned as what sticks with you, will be taken away by the management of the commissioners of excise, as they now collect the duties in England,
or else are such things as can not be denyed by the parliament of Brittain.

But if you will not be persuaded to trust in Scotland, without at least making
some claim to what is desired, might it not suffice, without altering the articles,
to state the matters which are desired to be explained, in an address to the queen,
praying her to interpose that those matters might be complyed with at the same
time when the treaty is ratified in England. Many of your lordships freinds here
think (if there be an absolute inevitable necessity of doing something to gratify
people in Scotland who will be jealous) that this way would be more safe, and

more likely to prove effectual than a direct change of the articles.   I submit this to your thoughts, and am, with great respect, my lord, your lordships most obedient humble servant,   SOMERS.

247. JOHN, DUKE OF MARLBOROUGH, to [DAVID, EARL OF LEVEN]—Intimating the military precautions he had taken.

December 7th, 1706.

MY LORD,—I haue receiu'd the favour of your lordships letter, and am very much concern'd att the ill state of your health, particularly at a time when the queens affaires requier your most active assistance in Scotland.   However, I am persuaded no care will be wanting on your part to promote her Majestys service. I now acquaint my lord commissioner with the march of the regiment of horse gardes towardes Barwick, and that all the troops on your borders, as well as those in the north of Ireland, will hasten to your assistance vpon the notice they may receiue from his grace or the privy councel, tho, as your lordship well obsarves, this aught not to be requier'd but vpon the most vrgent necessity.   Her Majesty has likewise giuen derections to suplie your [lordship] from Barwick with amunition out of the small stores we haue, vpon the like orders; but we hope the late vigorous procedings of the parliament in suspending the act that allowes the country to arme, will intierly dissipate the cloud that seemed to be hanging over you, and that the parliament wil soon go through this good work so much to be desir'd by all well wishers to these nations.—I am, with truth, my lord, your most obedient humble servant,   MARLBOROUGH.

248. THE SAME to THE SAME.—A regiment to be raised for Lord William Hay.

St. James's, the 4th January 170⅞.

MY LORD,—The queen, intending to raise three new regiments of foot this spring, is enclin'd that one of them be raised in Scotland in favour of the Lord William Hay, provided it may be done partly by draughts out of the standing forces, in the same manner as the regiment was raisd for Lord Mar[k] Kar, vpon which I should be glad to receive your lordships advice, with the names of such officers as you may judge proper to be employ'd in this service, reserving some of them to be taken out of the regiments abroad.—I am, my lord, your lordships most faithfull and most humble servant,   MARLBOROUGH.

Pray pardon my being oblig'd to make vse of Mr. Cardonels hand.

Earl of Leven.

249. THE SAME to THE SAME—The regiment not to be raised.

St. James's, 13th January 1706-7.

MY LORD,—I take the first opportunity of acknowledging your lordships letter of the first instant, by which I am heartily glad to find you have made so good a progress in the Union. Your lordship will have seen, by what I wrote to you some days ago, that the queen was enclin'd to raise a regiment by draughts out of the standing forces in Scotland, in favor of the Lord William Hay, but since your lordship gives so very good reasons against it at this juncture, you may be assur'd her Majesty will have no further thoughts of that matter, and for my own part, you may depend upon it, that I shall readily be govern'd by your opinion in everything that may relate to the troops under your command.—I am, with truth, my lord, your lordships most humble and obedient servant,

MARLBOROUGH.

My head eake must be my excuse for making vse of Mr. Cardonels hand.
The Earl of Leven.

250. THE SAME to THE SAME—The new regiments.

St. James's, the 7th February 170⁴⁄₇.

MY LORD,—I have receiv'd the honour of your lordships letter of the 21st of the last month, and am very glad you are satisfyed with my answer to your former. It seems yet vncertain whether the queen will raise any new regiments, but if she should, your lordship may be sure her Majesty will have all due regard to your lordships recommendations.—I am, with truth, my lord, your lordships most faithfull and most humble servant,   MARLBOROUGH.

You will be so kind as to excuse my being oblig'd to make vse of Mr. Cardonels hand.
Earl of Leven.

251. THE SAME to THE SAME—Lord Leven to go to London.

St. James's, the 4th March 170⁴⁄₇.

MY LORD,—Tho' the leave you desire to come to town be already sent down, yet I would not omit acknowledging the favor of your letter of the 14th February. I shall be very glad to see you here before I go over to the army. In the mean-time you may be sure the queen will do nothing in relation to the vacant regiments till my lord commissioner and your ministry come up, and that her Majesty have their advice in it, so that then you will have an opportunity of recommending those who have distinguisht themselves by their zeal for the publick service. I wish your lordship a good journey, and am, my lord, your lordships most faithful humble servant,   MARLBOROUGH.

Earl of Leven.

252. DAVID, THIRD EARL OF LEVEN, to [JOHN, EARL OF MAR, Secretary of State for Scotland]—Intimating arrival of the Equivalent.—Affairs in Scotland. 5th August 1707.[1]

MY LORD,—I have the honour of your lordships of 29 July, wherin yow give account that its hir Majestys pleasure I should attend sume time at Edinburgh. My lord, I receve hir Majestys commands with great pleasure, and to be sure shall use my utmost endevours for preserveing off the peace. I am only affrayed that its not knoun that I have attended clos here ever since my retorn to Scotland, wheras, except to goe out of toun of a Saturday and retorn on Munday, I have been still here.

Yeasterday ther was sume fear of a mob occasioned by sume of the brewars servants who run about and put out all the fyres of such who continued to brew aille. But this soon went over ; and in my humble opinion those litle disorders are better passed over then noticed, unles they goe to a greater hight For I am very woell assured that thers nothing the Jacobit party wish so much as to see the government and the mob goe by the ears together. This day the Equivalent arryved safe in the castle. Ther was a vast number of spectators, and sume of the mob threw stons at sume of those who drove the waggons, but ther was litle harm done. I have done all I can to accommodat those who have the charge of the mony so far as even to give them my oun lodgings in the castle. I intreat your lordship to be so kind as to assure hir Majesty that nothing shall be wanting on my part to promot hir Majestys interest and to preserve the peace of this part of the kingdom.

Ther has been a great talk of a Highland hunting, which has occasioned me to give out as if I intended to send a regiment of dragouns towards the north without giveing anie reason for it ; and I hop this has had a good effect, for I am told this day by Collonel Campbell of Finnab that ther is now no word of anie such hunting. Your lordship knows my allowance for intelligence is very small,

[1] Original in the Charter-chest of the Earl of Mar and Kellie at Alloa.

and perhaps if I had more it wer not mony ill spent; but I was a great deall out of pocquet last winter and cannot affoord allways of my oun on that account.—I am, my lord, your lordships most obediant and most humble servant,

LEVEN.

253. [SIDNEY, EARL OF GODOLPHIN, to DAVID, EARL OF LEVEN—Directions to apprehend John Murray.   Copy.]

St. James's, 30th August 1707.

MY LORD,—I am commanded by the queen to acquaint your lordship that her Majesty has very certain intelligence of John Muray, who was mentioned in Frasor's plot, being nou in Scotland, probably in the north, because the Duke of Gordons following are buying up horses and makeing preparations to go to a hunting in Athole.

The speedy discovery and apprehending of John Murray is of the greatest importance at this time, he being the soul of this whole affair.

Her Majesty therefore hopes no dilligence will be wanting in the government of Scotland to defeat and disappoint these mischeivous designs.—I am always, my lord, your most humble servant,

254. JOHN HAMILTON, LORD BELHAVEN, to DAVID, EARL OF LEVEN— Remonstrating against seizure for high treason.

Beil, 16 March 1708.

MY LORD,—I am verie much supprysd to receive an order under your hand as impoured by her Majestie and the cowncel of Brittain, to seazo upon me for suspition of high treason and treasonnable paractises. In ansur therto, my good lord, I am affraid your lordship will be found more faul[t]y than I am, in the executive pairt of your duty, for if yow have only a general warrant from her Majestie and cowncell to seaze all suspect persons, than I doe boldly assert yow have exseeded your commission. For whatever your lordship or any other subject thinks of me it is without aney manner of ground ; since my actions at and ever since the Revolution have been as loyal as any who pleases themselvs with greater thoughts of ther own meritts then I doe. Bot if your lordship has a particular warrant (as your order to Captain Richardson seems to import), for seazing my person for high treason and treasonable practises, then I think you have failed in not sending such a force as might have compelled me to obey your orders. Bot, my good lord, a letter from your lordship would have been as effectual for your designe, and

much more acceptable to me, for as I hate to be a treator, I doe not like verie weel
the name nor manner of treating of treators. Therfor, my lord, to let your
lordship see that I shall doe willingly that which your lordship did designe the
world should beleive was don by force, I shall wait upon her Majesties privie
cowncell once upon Thursday nixt, God willing, wher I hope to exculpate myself
as weel and all boldly as I did befor the parlament of such like malitius calumnics.
—My lord, your lordships most humble servant,   BELHAVEN.
     For the right honorable the Earle of Leven.

255. JOHN, EARL OF BREADALBANE, to [DAVID, EARL OF LEVEN]—Expressing
     surprise at his lordship's orders concerning him, but that he could not take
     the journey for age and sickness.

                                        Taymouth, the 20th of March 1708.
MY LORD,—I am very much surprysed with your lordships orders to Livtenant
Collonell Campbell of Fonnabs concerning me, who am a very inocent man, and
free of such practices, and since the tyme that your lordship dismissd me out of
the castle of Edinburgh I have not medled with any publick bussincss, and my
great age should liberat me from such toylesome journies as is required of me,
altho' I hade health, but my last journie hes brought upon me such diseases and
indispositione as renders me uncapable of goeing out of my romes, which I hope
your lordship will beleev to be truth from, my lord, your lordships most obledged
and most humble servant,   BREADALBANE.

256. JOHN, LORD BELHAVEN, to [DAVID, EARL OF LEVEN]—Protesting his
     innocence, and craving to be liberated.

                                        Edinburgh, 21 March 1708.
MY LORD,—I am informed your lordship taks it veric ill that I should have wreit
such a letter to you, and yet worse, that I should have published it in the coffe-
house with a great dale of noise and clamour. My dear lord, I doe think for these
verie reasons your lordship should raither have estemed me an honest man, and
valwed me as on who uses his outmost indevor to let the world see that nothing
can be so provoaking and injurius to me as to be reputed amongst the herd of
these disafected Jacobitts. I am sure if I had used policy at this tyme, it had been
better for me to have been quiet and silent, since I know I am in no manner of
danger and no wayse hardly treated that I might have made my court the better

upon all events, and reckoned amongst the sufferers a name your lordship knous which goeth a great way with any pairty.

Doe not think, my lord, that I am such a dog as to snarle at the ston. I have no manner of resentment against your lordship. If my imprisonment or any other designe against me had been any otherwayse intended than to calumniat me, and attack my reputation, I would have made no noise, no clamor at all; your lordship would have writ me a privat letter by your footman, and I would have keept silence and obayed, bot as your lordship most obay your orders, so pray, my lord, allow me also the liberty to doe what an honest man aught to doe in my circumstances. This is the second tyme I have been thus wrong'd in my reputation, and as little probabilitie of having a fair tryal as at the first, so that I have no other remedie to recur to, save to cry, complean, make a great dale of sputter and noise, as wrongd, injured, lesed, and what not, yea even to that hight as to brag, bost, and value my self of past services and merits, and what not. Should this offend your lordship, no, my lord, I know yow know better things. Ther is a tyme for all things ; a tyme to gather stons, and a tyme to throw them away.

Your lordship may remember that I did commend your behavior when yow wer laied aside by her Majestie and another substituted in your place. Yow gatherd up the stons, yow were patient, silent, had your stons and amunition laid up in store that you might make use of them when yow saw cause, as it fell out afterwards to your advantage, bot my circumstances ar quit contrarie : my good name is attackd, I am called unfaithfull to my God, and treacherus to my queen ; I must throw my stons abroad, I must cry and not spare ; and yet, after all, if her Majestie and your lordship and goverment doe not some signal and remarkable thing for my vindication, the world who hears of my accusation will never hear nor beleive my exculpation.

Upon this head I have wreit to the quein yesternight that her Majestie would wreit to the privie cowncell a letter for my liberation, without bail, parol of honor, or any other suspicius ingadgment. I have not insinuated the least reflection or complaint against your lordship, for I am not altogether so ignorant as not to know something from whence this rigorus calamny against me proceeds, and for what end I did inclose that to her Majestie vnder cover to the secretary of state, and now I thought it my duty to aquaint your lordship of this, and send my son to yow, who is to intreat your lordship's favor that I may be confined to my country house till the queens pleasur be knowen. He will tell your lordship also that I will make no application any more to the cowncell save what your lordship thinks fitt to doe for me, and that I am verie desirus to have some particular favor granted to me above the rest of my fellow prisoners ; besyds, my lord,

its knowen to all my relatious that I never have on days compleat health in this
place; and if any rural arguments have any weight with your lordship, I must tell
yow my self, without commission to my son, who possibly thinks ther is no great
strenth in this argument, I have eght plows goeing.   We have had a verie bad
season, I am greive my self, and they neither plow nor sow bot by my particular
direction; besyde I have a little lough to drain in order to make midow ground,
and the workmen cannot work bot when I am present, being cheiff ingeneer
myself.   Thus I have opend my breist to yow, and most conclude with the poet—

Nil mihi rescribas attamen ipse veni,

for I expect your lordship will doe my bussines, and come and liberat me yourself,
wher yow shall be heartily weelcom.—I am, in all sinceritie, my dear lord, your
lordships most obedient and most humble servant,   BELHAVEN.

257. SIDNEY, EARL OF GODOLPHIN, to [DAVID, EARL OF LEVEN]—Recommending
De Foe.

March 22th, 170⅞.

MY LORD,—I give your lordship the trouble of this letter by the bearer, Mr. De
Foe, only to recommend him to your protection as a person employed for the
queens service in Scotland relating to the revenue, etc., by, my lord, your lordships most humble and obedient servant,   GODOLPHIN.

258. JOHN, DUKE OF MARLBOROUGH, to DAVID, EARL OF LEVEN—Sir George
Byng had brought in the Salisbury—the troops were at Berwick.

St. James's, the 23d of March 170⅞.

MY LORD,—I am very thankfull to your lordship for the accounts you have given
me of what passes in your parts.   Sir George Byng's bringing in the Salisbury
afforded us great matter of joy, and as we hear nothing of the enemy since,
we hope their design has been entirely defeated, and that they are returned to
France.

We hear our troops from Ostend are past by Tinmouth, so that they must be
now at Berwick or nearer you.   We have nothing directly from them since their
sailing, and I now begin almost to wish they were safe landed again on the other
side, which will depend on the advices you send them, as your lordship will have
seen by what I sent you some days ago express.

I am going over to the Hague to concert with Prince Eugene, who is come

on purpose from Vienna to meet me. I design to be back, God willing, in less
then tenn days.—I am, with truth, my lord, your lordships most faithfull humble
servant,   MARLBOROUGH.

Pray forgive my making vse of Mr Cardonels hand.

Earl of Leven.

259. JOHN, LORD BELHAVEN, to DAVID, EARL OF LEVEN—Petitioning that his
wife might live with him in the castle.

Edinburgh Castel, 25 [March 1708].

MY LORD,—My weife, who hath been my bed fellow these thirty and four years,
taks it much to heart to be seperated from me now.   The experience I have just
now received of your lordships distinguishing keindness to me by allowing me
to be so weal and commodiusly lodged and seperated from the bulk of ——
doeth incouradge me to beg your lordships asistence as to procure a liberty to
my dear old weife to be inclos'd as a prisoner in the same manner with me in
evrie thing; bot if your lordship will take it upon yourself to grant me this
favor, I had raither it cam that way as any other.   I want my cook, being I have
conveniency of dressing meat.   I hope your lordship will allow him and on
single servant more to myself, and on woman for my weife.   I pray, my dear
lord, grant my supplication and finish the favours your lordship have so weal
begun, which will be most ingadging to, my dear lord, your lordships most
obedient and most humble servant,   BELHAVEN.

For the right honorable the Earle of Leven, commander in cheiff of her
Majestics forces.

260. SIR JOHN MACLEAN of Dowart to [DAVID, EARL OF LEVEN]—Intimating
his own surrender at Dowart Castle and protesting his loyalty.

Dowart Castle, 26 March 1708.

MY LORD,—Upon the recept of your lordships orders, signified to me by Captain
Were in his letter, I immediatlie in obedience to them repaired hither, and putt
myself under his custodie.   My lord, I shall never be wanting in any testimonie
I am capable to give of my deuty to the queen, yet I can not forbeare regreteing
my misfortune in being debarred the opportunity of showeing actively my zeale
for her Majestics service.   Whatever follies I have been guilty of I never was
capable of a treacherous or base action, and besides the deuty I owe the queen,

I have all the ties of gratitude that can bind a man of honour. If her Majestie has any ocasion to trye the fidelity of her subjects, I pray God they may be as reddie to sacrifice there lives for her interest as I am, and that those who would injustlie give sinistrous impressiones of me, as perhapes they are more capable to serve her, may be as reddie to spill there blood for her service as I would be. I have given instructiones to all those of my family with whom I have interest to testifie there zeale, if ocasion offers, for her Majesties service, and I can assure your lordship yow may depend on them in there meane capacitie, and for me, my lord, all her Majesties commands shall be chearfullie obey'd.—I am, my lord, your lordships most obedient and most faithfull servant,

MACLEANE.

261. JOHN, EARL OF BREADALBANE, to DAVID, EARL OF LEVEN—He could not travel to Edinburgh—the Council might garrison Kilchurn Castle.

Taymouth, the 30th March 1708.

MY LORD,—I receaved your lordships and returns you my many thanks for your civilities. It is a great trouble to me, besydes the disorder I am in with my descas, that it renders me altogether unfit to treavell, that I might vindicat myself to the councell from such aspertions as have been unjustly cast upon me, I hade noe oppertunitie or ocasion of serveing the queen or the countrie, since I was out of imployment, except that of liveing peacablie at home, which I have done to all intents, the long habite whereof is nou made it my inclyneatione, and my great age, attended with descasos and infirmness incident to it, oblidges me nou, for the short tyme I have to live, to make it my choise. I hear the councell is pleasd to order my house of Castlekelchorne to be garisond ; it shall be at there service when required, if the representations I have made of its uselessness for that pur- pose, to be shouen to your lordship by my cousen the bearer, does not prevent that trouble and expence to the goverment and countrie.—I remain, my lord, your lordships most oblidgd humble servant,   BREADALBANE.

I can not sitt so long as to writ with my oun hand.

For the right honnourable the Earle of Leven, commander in chief of her Majesties forces in Scotland—these.

262. LIEUTENANT-COLONEL WILLIAM GRANT to DAVID, EARL OF LEVEN—Lady
Huntly—State of Braemar, etc.

Castle Grant, Aprill the 3d, 1708.

MY LORD,—I hop befor now all thes noble persons that I hade warrant from
your lordship to secure have acording to ther word of honour presented themselues
to your lordship. I hop they cannot complain of anie rudnes from me, nor was
I wanting to tell them all that I hade speciall comands from your lordship to
treat them with all maner of respect.

My Ladie Huntlie wold not at anie rate pairt with my lord till her ladyship
recover a litle health. Your lordship will receiw my lord marquisis letter under
this cover ; he hes givin me his word of honour that he shall take jurney soe soon
as my ladie is in anie condition of health, and that he shall continue the gover-
ments prisoner till he vaites of your lordship, and that he will not be out of the
uay, if I have new orders to call for him befor the tym he apoynts. This is the best
I cold make of it, without offerring force to noe purpose and perhaps disobbey a
ladie that declaires herself a sincere well wisher to the queen and goverment.

I cam straight from Perth to Bramar to offer my advyce to the leding men of
that countrie, being my neir relations and nixt niboures, and told them as I have
done all uthers the danger they vere in that seemd to make anie apeirranc against
the goverment, and what fore was readie to com to subdue and demollish them. I
found som people verie heartie for the goverment that is thought to be utherunys,
perticullarlie Ferquhareson of Inverrey is fullie resolud to joyn the queens
friends if ther be a landing. I was in all the seaport towns from Monross to
Spey mouth to inform myself all I cold ; ther was tuo big ships and a small frigat
that cam up the Murray Firth till Spey mouth, and neir Cullen took a fisher boat,
boght the fish, and carid som of the men abord. They carid a rid flag till they
vere anent Gordon Castle as neir the shore as possable they cold com, and then
put out Frensh collars and sett anchor for som tym. They cam ashore, fortie of
ther number in a pairt they call Buckie, in the Eanyie, boght som fresh provisions. A verie honest gentlman neir that place informes me that all the
armes cam from Franc was abord thes ships, and is not sure but ther was a
pairt of them landed and left in the Eanyie. The Duke of Atholl wrot to Grant
desyring ane apoyntment to consert measures upon this drumlie ocasione, but Grant
sent his excuse. I am informd he wrot to the leding men of the name of Fraser
how have also sit his graces call. My lord, acording to your orders my companie
are com of ther posts, and are now in the bracs of this countrie, quher I hop

to make a veric considerable pairtie, if ocasion offers, for I fynd Grant veric forward and frank.   I shall be with my companie betuixt the braes of this countrie and Badenoch to vaite your orders, and upon sex houres advertishment, if I doe not march as good a companie of fyftie men as is in Briton, Ile nather deserw nor desyr the queens Majestie nor my Lord Levins favour, and thats the last two things that I shall willinglie dispenc with.—I am, in all dutie and respect, my lord, your lordships most humble and most faithfull servant,   WILL. GRANT.

Indorsed : Letter from Leiutenant Collonell William Grant, the 3d Aprill 1708.

263. ALEXANDER ROSE, Bishop of Edinburgh, to DAVID, EARL OF LEVEN—
        Begging for leniency, while under suspicion of treason.

                                                    Canongate, April 6, 1708.
MAY IT PLEASE YOUR LORDSHIP,—Seing I have lived these many years bygon altogether abstract from all publick business, I am extremly surprised to find myself considered as being under suspition of treasonable practises ; and tho I am not in the least apprehensive of the strickest tryall, nor am I to use any indeavours whereby to avoid it, yet seing my health is much impair'd, and that my condition in the world is so low, that I can hardly enough live in conjunction with my family, and much less in separation from it, therefor I humbly beg that through your lordships means and favour no measure in the meantime may be taken with me, which may infer ane insupportable charge or expose my self to certain ruine ; and as I am perfectly satisfied that your lordship has no inclination to be hard upon me, so I doe depend upon your lordships goodness for what ease and favour, prudence and the present circumstances shall permit to be allowed to, may it please your lordship, your lordships most ductifull and most humble servant,   ALEXᴿ. EDINBURGEN.

If your lordship have any commands for me at present, my wife, the bearer of this, will humbly receive them.

Indorsed : Letter from the leat Bishop of Edinburgh, the 6 Aprill 1708.

264. JOHN HAMILTON, EARL OF BELHAVEN, to DAVID, EARL OF LEVEN—
        Beseeching liberation.

                                                    Edinburgh Castel, 6 April 1708.
MY DEAR LORD,—As ever your lordship would oblidg a prisoner, both upon my healths accompt and my other specialities which I can not bot alwayse insist upon,

I must most earnistly intreat your lordships personal favor and interest in order to my liberation. I know yow can doe it if you will take it in hand. Confine me to Beil, and on mile round it, for all my days if you please, only let me be bot fred of this miserable condition. I shall not multiply arguments. Doe frankly that which will oblidge perpetualey your servant, and take your own way, bot by all means haist, haist, haist. Qui cito dat, bis dat. I depend upon yow only, only, only.—My lord, your lordships most obedient and most humble servant,

BELHAVEN.

For the right honorable the Earle of Leven, lieutenant general and commander in cheiff of her Majesties forces in Scotland.

265. JOHN, EARL OF STRATHMORE, to [DAVID, EARL OF LEVEN]—Thanking him for obtaining the Council's leave to stay at home.

Glamis, Aprill 8, 1708.

MY LORD,—I return your lordship my most thankfull acknowledgments for procuring me the councills leave to stay att home. I shall allwayes retain a most gratefull sence of your lordships kindnes and favour to me.

My lord, I doe assur your lordship, upon my word of honour, I shall keep myself under confinment to my house of Glamis and two miles round the same, and shall present and deliver up myself to your lordship or any haveing your order whenever I shall be required soe to doe. I am soe much oblidged to your lordship that I am not able to express it.—I shall ever be with all sincerity, my dear lord, your lordships most obedient humble servant,

STRATHMORE.

266. ANDREW FLETCHER OF SALTOUN, [to DAVID, EARL OF LEVEN]—To mention his case when writing to London.

Sterling Castle, 22 April 1708.

MY LORD,—I received your lordship's this morning, in which you are pleased to express yourself so obligeingly. You make me hope good things, and I dout not but they would be effectualy so, if they depended upon your lordship. I can not but be easy considering this first step. All I fear is that so inconsiderable a man as I may be forgot, and no further orders given about me. This I hope may be remided if your lordship shall bestow one line of the nixt letter you writ to London upon my affair. For I doubt not that having befor this time examined

Stralough and Mr. Scot, they will see there is nothing can touch me in these letters.—I am, with all respect, my lord, your lordships most obliged humbel servant,   A. FLETCHER.

Indorsed : Letter from the laird of Saltoun, the 22 of Aprill 1708.

267. JOHN, EARL OF BREADALBANE, [to DAVID, EARL of LEVEN]—Enclosing certificates of his illness.

Taymouth, the 30th Apryle 1708.

MY LORD,—I could no sooner get the phisicians brought together hear, they are soe much imployed ; be pleasd to recive inclosed the certificat signed by them and my minister, in form acording to coustom and law, which I hope will serve, and satisfie the government that your lordship hes done your dutie in obeying your orders, and that it frees you from being accessorie to the takeing of the life of ane inocent man, and free of all these crymes led to his charge, and my great wish uere to be in a condition to attend her Majestie, for vindicating of my self off them, but that being impossible, I must now recomend it to the justice and kindness of my friends.—I remain, my lord, your lordships most oblidged and most humble servant,   BREADALBANE.

268. JOHN, EARL OF BREADALBANE, [to DAVID, EARL OF LEVEN]—The bail-bond for his liberation—Gratitude to the Earl for his kindness.

June 24, 1708.

MY DEAR LORD,—Yow heap obligations vpon me uherof I can never free myself. Your kynd uay of intimating my liberation is most acceptable, and many thanks for the trouble yow giv yourself to send it so early after your order. I uonder uhat can be the particular quarell ther is to my nighbour, that he is made the single example of severitie, uho uas once so great a favorite that he dayly uears the token of it. I uish to know it, and how it uas that Earle Selkirk should hav had but my vote alenarly, and his 2 brothers so many, if it has not been a concerted business betuixt the 2 pairties, and that my vote could not be got scord out, it being in faithfull hands. I hav orderd my writer, Coline Kirk, to wait on your lordship and receav your commands directing the maner of the bail. I can not apply to the cationers intill I know the nature of the bond. If it be lyk the old bonds, Broomhall, now Kincardine, uas my cationer 40 years agoe. I am now soon baild to keep the peace. I doubt not but D[uke] H[amilton] uill soon

follow these lords. I know your lordship can not goe. I never desyr to see ane
other in your place. I know not the effects or import of these protests uhich uer
made, if it be to contravert the elections in parliament. I shall try for bail.
The sume is great, but the hazard litle. If I got non, your lordship has keept me
in the best prisson for me in Christendome, and Ill not leav it uith my uill.
Adiew, my dear lord, adiew. Your comands at any time to me. Be pleasd to
send them to Cartluns house, at the court of Gaird, Coline Kirk is his servant.

Indorsed : Letter from the Earle of Breadalban, 24 June 1708.

269. JOHN, EARL OF BREADALBANE [to DAVID, EARL OF LEVEN]—Interceding
for the liberation of his neighbour (John, Duke of Athole).

June 28, 1708.

MY DEAR LORD,—I receavd yours of the 23d. I know I shall hav by this
express ane ansuer to my last, which I sent by your lordships express. I beseech
you vse your endevours for my nighbour's liberation. I uish he did owe it to
you. Its a shame to his grace, who pretends to hav the pouer of the keyes, to
suffer his brother to be the only prisoner, he having uith difficulty been brought
to insert him in his list, but I beleev his pouer as much as that of St. Peters
successour, which time uill tell. I can say nothing about my bail intill I hav
your lordships returne. I uish I uer alloued to bail my nighbour. Adiew, my
dear lord.

Indorsed : Letter from the Earle of Breadalban, 28 June 1708.

270. JOHN, EARL OF MAR, to DAVID, EARL OF LEVEN—His exertions on behalf
of the Scottish prisoners in London.

Darlingtone, Wednsday morning,
Julie 15th, 1708.

MY DEAR LORD,—We came here last night, and the Duke of Q[ueensberry] holds
out very well, so I hope our jurnie will not be so tedious as I once expected. I
doubt not but Sir David Nairne has wrote to your lordship that the queen
frankly agreed that the Earl of Glasgow shou'd have the Regesters posto as soon
as it was vacant, so I expect the comission very soon. I sent a flying pacquet
from Anwick on Munday night with the account of poor Philops death, and as
soon as that arives the new comission will be sign'd and dispatcht. I hope this
will convince people of the queen's inclinations.

I was sorie I did not see Auchterhouse when at Edinburgh, for I hear that he sayes the Earl of Su[nderlan]d told him that it was your lordship who inform'd of the prisoners from Scotland, and that I gave in the list of them to be brought up. If this be true, his lordship has saild pritty near the wind, and had he gone one step further it had been a down right falshood. I shou'd be mighty glade to know certainly how Auchterhouse tels this storie, for it wou'd be of great use both to your lordship and me, so I beg you may one way or other find it out, which I belive will be no hard matter, for I'm told he makes no secret of it. I'm apt to belive the storie because the substance of it is something like the truth, tho told with a malicious falss turne. Your lordship knows you was ordred with some others to give account of the circumstances of the prissoners, and in that account your lordship referrd to us at London to give an account of those who had apply'd to us, so I, being in waiting, was ordred to draw out an account of the circumstances and conditions of them all in order to respitt their comeing up. This I did as favourablie as I cou'd and upon it, as your lordship knows, I was ordred by the queen to wryt to your lordship to respitt the sending of them all, except a few of the Highland chiftains. The first sett being sent off long before this, it was thought by the councill that they cou'd not be stopt, else I belive most of them had been respitted too. As ill luck wou'd have it, it was long before a councill cou'd be got to lay this matter before them, tho' I and the queen's other Scots servants endeavourd it all we cou'd, and after the respitting orders were given I sent them immediatly by a flying pacquet, but notwithstanding it came too late, for which I was very sorie; but as soon as I knew that the prissoners were sent off before these orders arived at Edinburgh, I wrote back to London (being then on the road), beging that they might yet be stopt, and when I found that was not like to be done, I and severall others of the queen's Scots servants wrote earnestly that they might not be brought in to London with guards, nor put in prissons, and that the queen wou'd be pleased to admitt them to bail, all which they know was very soon comply'd with. This being the true and literall matter of fact, let any body consider whither or not that aspersion so maliciously throwen upon us of our being the cause of bringing up the prissoners be true. It is hard that when we were doing all we cou'd to get them respited that they shou'd belive us the authors of their comeing up on stories told by halves by people to excuse themselves, but I shall be glade that (as was promist them) this affair be inquir'd into when the parliament meets, tho' I'm affraid those who promist so will forget it before the parliament sit. After your lordship has inform'd your self what Auchterhouse sayes was told him of this at London, I shall be very glade your lordship tel him and the other prissoners what I have wrote to you of it, for I confess I 'm vext that I and others of our friends are so falsely blaimd for being the cause of bringing our country men up, which I 'm sure wou'd have been the last advice I or they won'd have given.

When I came from Edinburgh the good news put it out of my head to acquent your lordship of an order the queen was pleased to give me for a disabl'd brass gun in Edinburgh Castle, which was brought from Stirling when Edinburgh Castle was beseged, and disabled there. It is for makeing some things in my gardens. I have sent the order to Mr. David Erskine, and when he calls for the gun I hope your lordship will be pleased to cause it be delivered to him. I wryt this here expecting to meet the post betwixt and Northalertone. We are just a going, so I will not now trouble your lordship any more, but I shall be glade to hear from you, and I am, my dear lord, your lordships most obedient and most affectionat humble servant,   MAR.

I also forgot to speak to your lordship for a foreloff to my man Rait, but I beg you 'll be pleased to send it him, and to cause John Aitken acquent his colonel of it.

Earl of Leven.

271. JOHN, DUKE OF ATHOLE [to DAVID, EARL OF LEVEN]—Thanks for intimation of his liberty.

Blaire Atholl, July 23, 1708.

MY LORD,—I received your oblidging and kind letter with the acceptable orders you were pleased so soon to dispatch for my liberty, for which I return your lordship my humble thanks. The officers caried as discreetly as coud be expected, considering the strict orders were given. They have duly paide the soldiers quarters. They removed yesterday morning from this place, and all the time they were here there never was the least quarel hapened, or so much as a high word betuixt them and the country people, which I doubt not the officers nill acquaint your lordship off.—I am, my lord, your lordships most faithfull and most humble servant,   ATHOLL.

272. ATTESTATION of PHYSICIANS regarding the continued ill health of the DUKE OF ATHOLE. Blair-Athole, 10th April 1708.

WE, Mr. George Græme and Mr. John Murray, Doctors of Medicine, as we have already upon the twenty eight day of March last, so we do still by these presents, upon soul and conscience, testifie and declair that his grace the Duke of Atholl has been more than these twelve months bypast, in a very ill state of health and bad habit of body, and frequently seized with violent headachs, vomiting, and hot and feaverish fitts, for which he has already undergone several courses of medicine, yet, notwithstanding, his desease continually increases, and that his body was so low, and his desease so strong, that the least cold casts him into unformed, aguish like hectick fitts; so we do now, upon soul and conscience, further declair that his grace grows dayly rather worse than better, that his blood is very ill, and perfectly rheumatick, for rectifying of which his grace is at present under a course of medicine and a dyet of asses milk, which he has been making use of for a long time, so that his grace cannot travail without apparent danger of his health and life; witnes our subscriptions att Blair of Atholl, the tenth day of Aprile one thousand seven hundred and eight years.   G. GRÆME.

                                                                JO. MURRAY.

    Indorsed : Attestatione of phicitians concerning the Duke of Atholl, Aprill the 10th, 1708.

273. RIGHT HONOURABLE ROBERT WALPOLE, Secretary of War, to DAVID, EARL
              OF LEVEN—Recruits for Flanders.

                                        Whitehall, May the 31st, 1709.

MY LORD,—I have seen a letter of your lordship's to his grace the Duke of Queensborough, giveing an account of the disappointment the recruits for Flanders mett in their convoy, as likewise of severall recruits that have been rais'd by the commissioners, and are not yett deliver'd to any regiment; if I had sooner known of these recruits, they should not have been soe long without officers to receive them.   But orders are this night sent to Lieutenant Generall Farrington to send three or four officers to your lordship, who are to receive your commands, and goe for the severall recruits as your lordship shall direct them.

    The recruits for Flanders I hope will not be long stopt, for fresh orders are given to my lord high admirall to send them an immediate convoy. As for forrage I have allready acquainted your lordship that contracts were made with Sir Samuell Maclellan and others for provideing forrage for her Majesties troops in North Brittain, and I send you herewith a list of the severall places where the contractors have provided their grasse, and marching orders with blank routs, which I desire your lordship will fill up, with such places where the troops can be best accommodated in their marches, which I can have noe opportunity of being rightly inform'd of here.

I must desire your lordship will be pleas'd to transmitt to me copies of the routes to be euter'd in my office, and likewise the routes that you have allready made pursuant to the marching orders you had before from my office.

I acquainted my Lord Lothian before he left London, that it was her Majesties pleasure that Lord Dalhousie should command the battalion of Scotch Guards, if he insisted on it.—I am, my lord, your lordship's most faithfull humble servant,   R. WALPOLE.

P.S.—It will be necessary that every troop has an attested copy of the marching order, together with his proper route, when your lordship has inserted the quarters for every day in their severall routes.

Earl of Leven.

274. WILLIAM, EARL OF DARTMOUTH, Secretary of State, to DAVID, EARL OF LEVEN—Soldiers subject to church discipline.

Windsor Castle, September 10, 1711.

MY LORD,—The soldiers quarter'd in Scotland having made great complaints of the hardships they suffer from the judicature of that church, her Majesty is pleas'd to order that your lordship transmit hither a full account of the points at present in dispute betwixt 'em, and of the power which the church claims a right to exercise over them. In the meantime, I cannot but take notice to your lordship that her Majesty is inform'd the soldiers were willing to appear before the judicature, provided their adjutant was present, which would have been but a reasonable indulgence in regard of the ignorance of those poor men, and their incapacity to speak for themselves.—I am, my lord, your lordships most obedient and most humble servant,   DARTMOUTH.

Right honourable Earl of Leven.

275. DAVID, EARL OF LEVEN [to WILLIAM, EARL OF DARTMOUTH, Secretary of State]—Soldiers' submission to church discipline in cases of scandal. 27th September 1711. Draft.

MY LORD,—In answer to yours of the 10th instant, I have inquired into the ground of complaint made by the souldiery of the judicature of the church, and do find that it was by an innocent mistake that a young unexperienced minister presiding in the church session did not at all refuse, but only delayed, to allow the adjutant to be present with the souldiers convecned for scandal, untill he should advise with his bretheren. But that his bretheren ministers hearing of it, informed him of his mistake, and immediatly acquainted Collonell Breuse, the commanding officer, that any he should please to appoint to be present at the examination of souldiers questioned for scandal should be allowed to be witnesses to the procedure, and with this Collonel Breuse appear'd to be satisfied, which I hope may also remove the ground of this complaint, for that the souldiers should be subject to church disciplin was here judged expedient, both for the better restraining of immoralitys, and lykways for the better preserving of peace and good order, when the people should see no distinction made, and that none were exempted. But the church, on the other hand, have always been carefull to have their disciplin exerced with all charity and moderation, and particularly as to the souldiers have still, in the first place, been in use to acquaint their officers, so that hitherto the matter hath proceeded easily enough; and for hereafter I have caused make such an intimation to the ministers as I am hopefull there shall be no farder ground of complaint, but that, on the contrary, the officers shall remain fully satisfied.

Indorsed : Coppy of the Earle of Leven's letter to the Earle of Dartmouth, September 27, 1711.

276. ROBERT, EARL OF OXFORD, First Commissioner of the Treasury, to DAVID. EARL OF LEVEN—Hopes that Lord Haddo had let him know the care the queen intended to take of him.

August 8, 1712.

MY LORD,—I hope my Lord Haddo[1] (with whom I am proud to make a friendship) has done me justice to your lordship, and let you know the care the queen intends to take of your lordship. I shal very quickly have an opportunity of explaining that to your lordship. I hope the measure about Lord Findlater wil not be disagreeable to your lordship, and that a little time and patience wil produce a settlement to Great Brittain agreeable to the wishes of al honest men.—I am, with great sincerity, my lord, your lordships most humble and most obedient servant,   OXFORD.

Right honourable Earl Leven.

[1] Lord Haddo married Lady Mary Leslie, daughter of this Earl of Leven.

277. JOHN, DUKE OF MARLBOROUGH [to DAVID, EARL OF LEVEN]—That his
son's affair would be forwarded.

London, the   September 1715.

MY LORD,—I have had the favour of your lordships letter, dated the 16th
August, and did till I read it beleive your son's affair done three months agoe,
consequently whatever remains to [be] done in his favour shall be forwarded without delay.—I am, with great sincerity and truth, my lord, your most obedient
humble servant,   MARLBOROUGH.

278. WILLIAM DRUMMOND, VISCOUNT OF STRATHALLAN, to ALEXANDER, EARL
OF LEVEN AND MELVILLE—Demanding a requisition of £100.

Perth, 10 December 1745.

SIR,—As I am obliged for the subsistance of the Prince of Wales his army here
to apply not only to those I judge friends, but to others who may have the
happyness of their country less at heart, I desire of you to send in here the sum
of one hundred pounds, which I expect will be complyed with, within ten days
from this date, and thereby prevent any further trouble to yourself or me. You
shall have a receipt for the money, and your punctual complyance will oblige, sir,
your most humble servant,   STRATHALLAN.

    To the honourable my Lord Leven. In his absence to my Lady Leven, att
    Melvine.

279. SIR EVERARD FAWKENER to ALEXANDER, EARL OF LEVEN AND MELVILLE,
Lord High Commissioner to the Church of Scotland—The Camerons
submit.

Fort Augustus, the 27 May 1746.

MY LORD,—I hope your grace will have received his royal highness's letter in a
proper time. He arrived here the 24th. The men had a very fatiguing march
from the Lochend, but went through it very well. Lord Loudoun has been here
to give his royal highness an account that the Camerons and McDonalds, who were
got together to the number of about three hundred, dispersed immediately upon
the appearance of his advanced partys, and Lochiel orderd that every man should
shift for himself. The Camerons have since sent to submit and deliver up their

arms, which has been accepted.   Lord Loudon is now gone to Badenoch to oblige the people there to submit also; so I hope this troublesome business grows towards an end.   His royal highness goes to Fort William on Thursday and returns the next day.

Your grace wil give me leave to renew the assurances of that perfect respect with which I shall be always, my lord, your graces most obedient humble servant,

EVERARD FAWKENER.

His grace the Earl of Leven, lord commissioner, etc.

280. THE SAME to THE SAME—His Royal Highness to depart for England.

Fort Augustus, the 17th July 1746.

MY LORD,—The several letters your lordship has been pleased to write me of the 28th past, and 2d and 7th current, are all come to hand, nor can I perceive that any of those I have done my self the honor to write to your lordship have miscarried, for provost Cries information I believe was not exact as to time, for I had said to him I should write, which I did, and your lordship has own'd the letter.   It will be needless now to enter upon answers, as I hope soon to have the honor of seeing your lordship, as his royal highness will march as soon as this chase he is engaged [in] shall be over and his detachments returnd to the army, and this he has been pleasd to command me to communicate to your lordship, and to acquaint you at the same time that which way soever his royal highness should take, which he believ'd would be that of Stirling, he would pass so quick that he would not have you by any means put yourself to the trouble of attempting to meet him, nor will he make any stay at Edenburg if he passes there.   I shall go thither and must stay a few days, but they will be as few as possible.   If your lordships affairs should carry you thither, I should think it a most fortunate rencounter, as I should gain many useful informations, and be pleased with a new opportunity of procuring an increase of an acquaintance and confidence I so much value, and of indeavouring to convince you of the realty of the professions I take the liberty of making, of being, with the greatest respect and truest esteem, my lord, your most obedient humble servant,   EVERARD FAWKENER.

I am this moment commanded by his royal highness to acquaint your lordship that he desires you would meet him at Stirling on Tuseday evening.   You will not take notice of this.

Lord Leven.

FAMILY AND DOMESTIC LETTERS.

281. Sir Robert Melville to Sir William Douglas of Lochleven—To excuse
him to the queen for not sending her baggage sooner. *Circa* 1567.[1]

Sir,—Efter my hartlie commendation, I wnderstand that the quenes Majestie hes
send for sum baggage to be gewyn to the kyng, her sone, and sum to her cumers.
I pray yow haif me excusit to her Majestie that I haif beyne so long in sendyng,
for I wes absent from this town, and geue it be her plesure to wret to me
with her Majesties awyne hand quhat salbe send to that effect, and therefter it
salbe done, and ontrublyng yow forder, I commit yow in the tuytion of God.
At Edinbroughe, the xiiij   .—Yours at his pouar,

And quhaire hir Majestie dissirit to knaw quhow mony stayns theyre is of
the chayne quhilk wes brokkin, theyre is four hundrethe, lakkyng awght or nyne,
quhilk sall cum to the kunt I ressauit.

To the right honorable the Lard of Loughleawin.

282. James Melville of Halhill to Lord Melville—The character and
behaviour of Sir George Melville [of Garvock].   St. Andrews, 31st
May 1651.[2]

My Lord,—I gott an short viw of an peapir sent bee Sir Georg Melvill to Sir
Johne Broun, if it please your lordship to send me the coppie of it I sall answer
it punctwallie and trewlie bee the help of God.   In the mid tym, some circum-

---

[1] Copy by Mr. A. Macdonald from letter
in the Charter-chest of the Earl of Morton.
Compare with the lotter from the queen to
Sir Robert Melville, of date 3d September
1567, on p. 7 of this volume.

[2] Compare letter by King Charles the
Second in favour of Sir George, 6th May
1651, p. 23 of this volume.

stancis I thought good to glance att for the bettir information of your lordships honerable freinds that I hear ar to meet upon Monday nixt for your affairs. The truth is, this Sir Georg Melvill cam from Ingland, wher he left an wife and familie behint him, and stayed with Robert, Lord Melvill, who did intertain him kindly and pittied his hard condition, and thought to have don him good, bot the man his cariage becam to him so unpleasant that he took an grait disteast of him and all his wayes som moneths befor his death, the which being perceaved bee Sir Georg he deserted my unquhill Lord Robert Melvill his house and companie som litill tym befor his death. And wheras he alledgise that it was my wife hir practising with Robert Hammiltoun that caused my lord neglect him att his death, my Lord Melvill had his recidence that wintir befor his death pairtli in Bruntiland, pairtlie in Edinbrugh, comming and going betwixt the on and the othir. It was the tym of my Lord Balmirrinow his trouble, the which my Lord Melvill did carfullie attend. This wintir season I and my familie remained in Coupir becauce of childrin that was ther att schools. My wife did nevir see my Lord Melvill fra Michilmise that he went from Monnimeal, except once he cam upp and visited Monnimeal and his affairs ther, and stayed some ten dayes, att the which tym he sent for my wife from Coupir, who went to him; and that was the last of ther meeting, for aftir that she nevir saw him again. This was about the first of Januarie, and my lord died in Edinbrugh about the midst of Merch, att the which tym he did verrie kindly remembir an numbir of freinds with legacies, among tho which numbir Sir George his brothir was on; and some that wer about my lord did putt him in mind of Sir Georg, thinking that he hade forgott him; bot my lord answered he did not forgett him, bot thought him unworthie of annie remembrauce; nothing that could bee giving him wold doe him good; and this Robert Balfour cann testifie att mor lenth, because he was present and witnise to all that was done about my lord his seek bed. Aftir my lord his death Sir Georg cam to me in an verrie humble way, complainin of his hard condition, and delt with me not only to pittie him my selfe, bot to have interceded att the present lord his hand for him; att the which tym I gave him an hundrith crouns and an naig, for he resolved to goo to Ingland and nevir bee an Scotts man. He did indeed presentlie goe to Ingland and quiklie made his addresse to court, and chiflie to him who is now Duk Hammiltoun, then an youth attending court, and did show him of the death of the laitt Lord Melvill, and did inform him that all his esteat was loouse, and his successours hade no rights to brook his lands, and that the Lord William Hammiltoun, for then he was so called, that he might putt inn for his freindship and turn us all out of what wee had gotten; bot the noble young lord did apprehend the man to bee speaking without grounds, upon the which he did wrett hom to his wisist freinds, who returned him trew information that all Georg Melvill his wayes was lyk himself, false and deceaving, and so the noble man did quytt him. Aftir this he returned to Scotland, and bee the credit he gott with the bishop of St. Androwes, who was chanchlir for the present, and all the rest of that crew, with whom he had much credit, for they wer glade to find annie occasion to trouble us, both for the grait splenn that they carried to my laitt lord and to us his successours. Upon the hoppe of ther freendship he stealed out an false dative of the neglects of the testaments both of the laitt lord and of his ladie, who had died some three years befor him selfe, upon the which he intended action against us, who wer trew exequitours to my laitt lord, and it came befor the lords and was found altogethir unjust and rediculous, yit the chanchlir and his sonn, being president, carried things in so oppressing an way that aftir I had gotten an decreitt the chanchlir wrett and inhibit the clerk ethir from embooking or extractin of it; aftirward cam to the Toboth him selfe, and bee violence recalled my decreitt and broght the mattir to trysting against our desyrs, and all our freinds, and against all ordir of law, and caused us condescend to give him betwixt us five thousand merks aftir wee hade sustained so much trouble. As for that blank band he speks off, ther was such an peapir that Ro. Hammiltoun hade the keeping of, and pretended it was giving him bee the defunct to boe an awband ovir us twoo that wer left heirs and exequitours, that not on of us sould trouble anothir; bot the truth was, when the band was produced ther was no subscription of the defunct to bee seen att it; bot ther was not so much as an thought in annie mans head or an word in annie mans mouth that it relaited annie way to Georg Melvill. This shortlie for the present. I desyre your lordship to communicat with your honored freinds. If ye goe not yourselfe to the meeting att Kirkaldie, direct this peapir with an sur hand ether to Sir Johne Broun or the laird of Boogie. Wishing your lordship health and happinise, I am your lordships cusing and servant,   JAMES MELVILL of Halhill.

St. Androwes, Maij 31, 1651.

For my verrie noble lord, my Lord Melvill.

283. JOHN, DUKE OF LAUDERDALE, [to GEORGE, LORD MELVILLE]—Of the ward of the Earl of Tarras.

Ham, July 22d, 1676.

MY LORD,—By a letter from the Marquis of Atholl, dated the 13th instant, I was glade to heare of your lordships safe arryval att Edenburgh, and glader by a letter from yourselfe, dated the 15th (which I saw), to heare that your signator was past the exchequer. I doe nott doubt hutt the justice of the lords of the session will preferr yours. Butt the reason of my giveing yow this truble is to acquaint yow with a particular, which I thinke may concerne the Duke of Buccleugh and Munmuth. On Wednesday very late the Duke of Munmuth tould me he had some papers come out of Scotland which he desyred to show me before he wold doe anie thing in them. I received them from him, and found that itt was a letter from Sir William Scott of Hardin to the Duches of Munmuth, by which he informed her that the Earle of Tarras father, Sir Gideon, was dead, and that he besought her grace to desyre the Duke of Munmuth to move the king to pass the inclosed paper in his favours, and to speake to me for expediting itt with all speed. I found the paper to be a gift of the warde and mariage and non-entrie of the Earle of Tarras, in favours of Sir William Scott, for his behoofe.

On Thursday, in the forenoone, I went to waite on the duke and duches, butt both wer abroad, yett att the kings dinner I mett with the duke, and tould him what the papers wer he had given me, of which I found he knew nothing. I tould him that the paper was wholly for the Earle of Tarras advantage, who hes pretensions againstt his grace to a great value, and that I thought itt was nott for his interrest to putt the Earle of Tarras outt of the kings reverence ; that I had no concerne in the matter butt only for his interrest ; that I thought itt wold be tyme enough to doe such a favour to the Earle of Tarras efter his oune differ-ences wer removed, and that I should take care that no other should gett that gift. His grace seemed very wel satisfied. I have nott since mett with the duches, for shoe came and dyned here that day with my wyfe, and shoe was gone back before I came hither. Off this I thought fitt to give your lordship ane account, and shall ad no more, butt that on all occasions I shall studie to testifie how really I am, my lord, your lordships most humble servant,

LAUDERDALE.

My humble service to the Conntess of Weems and to my lord.

284. [MARGARET, COUNTESS OF WEMYSS], to ALEXANDER MELVILLE, MASTER OF MELVILLE—As to the defeat of the Duke of Monmouth at Sedge-moor.   [1685.]

MY DEAR NEPHEW,—I hope this shall not bring the first news of the unfortunat Duke of Monmouth, who, by all apeirance, is taken by this time or killd. I was unwilling to write to my sister least she know of it ; but if her business be not very pressing, I think she should come here and wait on our dear mother, who does not yet believe him in such hazard. Alas, the sad stroak will be heavy enough when it coms without the aggravation of groundles hops. The Lord comfort her. I ame in such confusion I can write noe more. Adieu, dear nephew.

For the Master of Melvill.

285. JOHN PATERSON, Archbishop of Glasgow, to DAVID, EARL OF LEVEN—
The book called the "Reformed Bishop."

Edinburgh, Agust 12, 1689.

MAY IT PLEASE YOUR LORDSHIP,—Not being able to attend your lordship my self, I have sent my brother to shew you the just copies of the Duke Rothes's letter, ordering me to cause destroy all the copies he sent to my house, without my knowledge, of these diffamatorie books called the Reformed Bishop, and telling he had seen the comittee of council's order comanding me to see them destroyd; after the elapse of ten years, this will seem ane sufficient instruction of my warrant for seeing those infamous books destroyd, which yet I never did, for these papers were brunt and destroyed without either order or consent from me. I begg your lordships favor and justice in it, after reading these letters in councill, to move, not onlie that I may be assoyld, but also the malicious accuser condignelie punishd for his injuries and indignities done to my credit and name, with the refunding of my expenss of plea. I expect this from your lordships friendship and justice, since I have always appeared ane friend to my lord your father's interest at all tymes, and that I am, may it please your lordship, your lordships most humble and obedient servant,   JO. GLASGOW.

The Earls of Crawfurd and Erroll will inform your lordship how in evrie article of my accusers alledgiances I confuted him vnder his own handwrittings befor the committee of council.

For the right honorable the Earle of Levin—these.

286. JAMES, EARL OF DUNFERMLINE (address wanting, perhaps to the EARL OF MELFORT)—Informing him as to Sir William Wallace. [An intercepted letter.]

Brea of Ranoch, August the 29th, [16]89.

MY LORD,—As I wrot to your lordship in my former desiring a speedy suply, soe now being dissipate, and the enemy grown stronger, makes me, with a great deal of regrait, trouble you at this time, beging it may immediately be sent ouer, as you

wish the king's interest to thriue.   My lord, I most likeways say there is a
bussines faln out that I cannot speak of without regrat, but howeuer most show
it to your lordship, that Sir William Walice, upon what accompt I know not,
hath taken such a prejudice at several of the officiers that he hath been making
caballs, which you know is uery prejudiciall to the king's bussines.   You will
know more of this then I can tell you; for certainly Sir William will be with you
befor this come to your hand.   He will likewayes shew you his instructions,
which are subscriued by fiue or six officiers, the rest never haueing seen them.   I
know alsoe Sir William is in expectation of my Lord Dundie's regiment; but
since I was with him from the first of this work, as I wrot to you formerly, I hope
you will doe me the justice not to let any get it but him who is, in all sincerity, my
lord, your lordship's most humble and obedient seruant,   DUNFERMELING.

287. LADY JEAN GORDON, COUNTESS OF DUNFERMLINE, to her husband, JAMES,
      EARL OF DUNFERMLINE—Mackintosh of Borlum imprisoned as a spy.
      [An intercepted letter.]

                              Fywe, the 3 of October [c. 1689].
I DOU not dout but you hau heard of yong Borlom's being laid in prison in
Irland, becaus my Lord Melfort said he was a spy, which he was no mor then I
am ; but it ples'd his lordship tou say so, becaus Borlom had not the good fortun
tou ples him.   I tell you this that you may consider well befor you send ouer to
the king; for if they be not in fauer with my Lord Melfort, you sie what they
may expect.   I must lykways put you on your gaird of an other thing, which is
that itts fear'd by seuerall of your frinds that thos iu your army who has ther
dependens on my Lord Melfort is cabaling against you and others, who they think
is not of the faction, and uou'd not cair tou be quit of you, that they might
persuad the king that the busines wear don by him and his frinds.   This is all
but supitiones, but we hau som reson tou think itt : whoeuer, itt's best for
you tou be upon your gaird, and not belue ther neues tou easnly, without good
prouf for them.   I heir som of them ar gon tou Irland, so I hop thel ether giue
you the king's comands under his oun hand or his secretors, that you may hau itt
tou show affterwards; but I'm in grett hops Melfort is from the king, the report
goes so constantly att Edinburgh without contradiction.   Lett me knou as soun
as posibell what way I shall send your mony tou you; for I uou'd hau itt att you.
Mr[s] Ogilbe was heir, but is gon from this tou Bamf eght dayes ago.   I expect her
heir uery soon agan.   The inclosed shou'd hau gon tou you with the last acation,

but was forgott : I dou not knou what letter I sent you in plac of itt. Lett me knou what you want, for itt's so far in the winter that I must mak haist tou send tou you, els nobody will go.—I remain yours for euer,

JEAN DUNFERMLING.

The chyld is uery well recouerd agaiu. This and that within itt ar all wreten att on tym; so dou not neglect tou read them all.

For the Earll of Dunfermeling.

288. GEORGE, DUKE OF GORDON, to [address wanting]—That he would not change his religion. 6th November 1689.

MY MASTER,—I receaud butt this day your letter off 10 October. I confess your adwys as to paganism and Turcks is good for thes tyms, butt yow most excus mee for all thatt to preferr Jesus Crist to Mahumett and Jupiter—quid retribuam Domino qui tantum tribuit mihi. As to my obligations to the poppish king, as yow call him, yow know long agon my rescutments; butt whatt I dooe in deutty is doon for God, and nott for men. I shall folow your adwys in nott suffring myself to bee imposd on by fals impressions, as yitt I am nott, I asseur yow, noe mor then I am apt to beliue legends, but sens in human things most reull as faith in what is abow humanity. I haw consulted verry good frinds off severall qualitys and perswasions, and I can show in wreett they all aprow my sentiments as to the queetting of that obligation I haw off Strathnavers, which is thatt as hee gaw itt so iff hee desyr itt back, he most ask itt himself; this in a vord is my resolution, and I'll stand by itt. Now, as to my religion, for I most answer all your letter, when I fynd on mor raisonable then itt, on my vord, I shall bee no more a catholicque or pappist; iff yow ples, raison better iff yow vold haw mee chang. I am glaid yow lyck your yong chiff, butt pray, my master, lett nott that maik yow forgett the old on. Adiew, my master, taik cair off your selff, and lowe your frinds, as they low yow. 6 November 1689.

Indorsed : Duke Gordon.

289. MARGARET, COUNTESS OF WEMYSS, to [GEORGE, FIRST EARL OF MELVILLE] —Proposed marriage of Lord Leven and Lady Anna Wemyss.

March 18 [circa 1691].
MY LORD,—Your letter of the 26 February came not to my hand till Thursday last, at which time my sone was verry ill; the small pox came out that night.

I hope this will excuse my not ansuering your lordships letter sooner. My lord, as for what I wrote formerly to your lordship concerning my Lord Southesk his proposals to my daughter, they were soe verry fair, and his offers soe great as his affection to her apeard to bee, that really I think it was noe great wonder that my daughter seem'd to incline to that match ; that which I do think a great deall more strange is that one soe young as shee should have been soe concern'd to have ane unjust right quatt, which might have ruin'd my familly if it had come to a competition, as I hope in God it never shall. I finde she has a great minde to have the persone she chuses for her husband should love her more then his interest, and have noe eye upon her brothers estate ; and I believe she will finde few if anie in Scotland that has a larger share of honour and generosety then your lordships sone my Lord Leven, who I hope by this time has persuaded her of his great affection to her ; but if neither I nor she did at first believe it was soe great, he may blame himselfe, and his friends who were against it. I have often and frily told him I think he should marry none that your lordship and his mother are averse from, since marriages seldome prosper when parents only give a forced consent. — I am, your lordships affectionat sister and humble servant, M. WEMYSS.

My daughter hops you will excuse her not ansuering your lordships letter ; she has a sore eye, and a sore heart too, for her brother was worse last night.

290. MEINHARDT, DUKE OF SCHOMBERG AND LEINSTER, to DAVID, EARL OF LEVEN—Recommending Monsieur Le Fevre.

London, 22d February 169⅔.

MY LORD,—This is to give your lordship the trouble in behalfe of the bearer, Monsieur le Fevre, who is a learned, pious man, but makeing some scruple to conform himself to the outward ceremonies of the Church of England, is desirous to go into Scotland to establish himself there, which obliges me to recommend to your lordships favour, I haveing knowne him many years. If your lordship can assist him in any thing I shall owne it as an obligation done to myself, who am, my lord, your lordships most faithfull and most humble servant, LEINSTER.

Lord Leven's.

291. DAVID, EARL OF LEVEN, to MARGARET, COUNTESS OF WEMYSS, his mother-in-law—His way to join the army. *Circa* 1693.

Antwerp, July 2,—always old still.

MY DEAR MADAM,—I wrot to yow from Heloutsluse the 23, and to my deareast, which I inclosed in your ladyships, which yow will make use of according as my dear wife knows of my jurnay, when it cums to your ladyships hand. I wreat from this lest the post be gone befor I cume to Brussells, which will be tomorrow morning, and I know yow will be anxious to hear from me, espetially if the newes be trew which is talked here this day, which is that yeasterday the armees did engeadge, but whats the event is not yett knoun. Yow will perhaps be glad it be trew, but I leve yow to judge how I will like to cume a day affter the markett. I know if I had not wreat yow wold have been concerned, [and I] judged it my deuty to give your ladyship [thi]s line. I am apt to think it has not been ane engeadgement of the wholl armee, but of a part only. However, this is my own conjectour, and I shall wreatt more fully from Brussells by nixt post. Yow have here on to my dearest, for I doubt not but she knows all ere now. I long to hear from yow and hir. I am in good health, and ever your ladyships most obediant sone and servant.

For the Countess of Weemys.

292. DAVID, EARL OF LEVEN, to ANNE, COUNTESS OF LEVEN, his wife—Injunctions as to her health. [27th November 1695.]

MY DEAREST HEART,—Wee came safe here this day, and are makeing ready for our jurnay tomorrow, which now wee intend to make in coach. Wee take a coach from this to Newcastle. Wee are to be ther on Saturday. I fear the coach be not ready befor Wednesday, in which cace wee will take our own horses to Hadington tomorrow, and stay ther till she cume on Wednesday. My dearest heart, yow have allways given so great proofe of your being a kind and observant wife to me, that I hop yow will not neglect anie thing yow promised to me at parting, which was that yow wold haue a good care of yourselfe and of my bairn. I assure yow I shall mind what I promised to yow, and shall not faill in anie part therof. Yow need not fear that anie thing will be able to hinder me from waiting on my dearest, when yow draw near your time, therfor persuad yourselfe that, God willing, I will help the cummers at the butter saps. I wreat this night lest I should be hurryed tomorrow. If anie new thing occure, then I shall add it.

Lundie goes with us. My Lord Stairs is dead this day. My father, brothers, and I wer at his likewake this evening. Mr. Funtain is also dead. I was to wait on my Lady Montrose, but she was abroad. They say the Lady Rothess had prepared a collation for us, and is mad at the disapointment she mett with. Let me hear from yow on Thursday, and direct it to be left at the postmaster of Newcastle, and on Saturday, and direct it to be left at the postmaster of Ferrybridge, and after that direct for me at London, wher I will expect to hear from yow at my arryvall. I shall wreat from the road to yow, but road letters are apt to miscarry, so yow must not be allarmed tho yow gett non, and it may be our post master at Edinburgh will keep them up, but when I am at London I can get them under the Master of Stairs cuver if I fear taking up. I heard this day that Mistris Cicill Augh. intends yow ane other visite, which I shall be sorry at, for I am told that she is subject to the fallen sickness, which is not pleasent companie. Be sure, my dearest, to have always sume of your frinds with yow. I spock to Bogie, that his mother might lett Mistris Margaret stay, which I doubt not but she will. Yow may tell what passed at Aiton when yow have occasion. My sister Raith will be with yow shortly. Yow may have the Lady Carny when yow please, or my brother James wife. Cause Charles wreat; its eneugh if yow end the letter. Have a good care of your selfe, my dearest heart, as yow love me. Adieu.

My blissing to my dear bairns. My humble service to my mother and to all your cumpanie. Send always your newes of us to Monimeall, and what letters are for them. Mind to cause wreat to Will. Patton, and if he will engeadge, cause hime cume speack to yow.

To the Countess of Leven.

293. ALEXANDER, LORD RAITH, to ANNA, COUNTESS OF LEVEN—Lady Ravelston's burial. *Circa* 1695.

Edinburgh, January 12.

DEAR MADAM,—I desire, if your coachman have a black coat, he may be over here with four of your coach horses and the postilion. I will get a coat to serve him, that I may haue the use of my father and brothers black chariots to my Lady Revelstons buriall Wednesday nixt, so they wold be here without faill once upon Twesday. My wife gives her humble service to your ladyship, and I am ever, dear madam, your ladyships most affectionat and humble servant,

RAITH.

For the Countes of Leven.

294. [DAVID, EARL OF LEVEN, to his wife, ANNE, COUNTESS OF LEVEN]—
Match with Carnwath. 1697.

MY D[EAR],—I have winne the race with my mare. I rune another by match
with my gelding against Carnwaths horse for fyve guineas, and win that. I have
matched him with the same horse this day moneth for 40 guineas to 20.—I am
yours, my d[ear].

To the Countess of Leven.

295. MARGARET, COUNTESS OF WEMYSS, to [GEORGE, FIRST EARL OF MELVILLE]
—Lord Tarbat's proposals.

Erroll, 6th of April 1700.

MY LORD,—I hear your lordship dessign'd the honour of a visett to my Lord
Northesk and my daughter last week, but was oblidg'd to goe to Edinburgh about
business. I shall be verry glad to hear you are not the worse of changing your
bed. My lord, I was earnestly intreted by your cousin, my Lord Tarbat, to write
to your lordship about a paper of propositions which I would not see till once
your lordship had consider'd it, for since you know his circumstances and estate
much better then I do, besides, that you are a better judge of the reasonablnes
of the terms offred, and being so neerlie concerned in both, your lordship is the
fittest person to give your oppinion and advice in the matter, which I beleive you
will do verry impartially, and I shall be glad to know your thoughts of it. I
finde my Lord Leven has heard a great many falce and malitious storys of me,
both anent this particular and other things. I did take paines to convince him
of the contrary, for I am conscious to my selfe I never failed in my affection to
him and his wife, and I don't take it well, they are so apt to beleeve what is saide
to my prejudice, whither it be by my enemys or of dessigne, to break, or att least
weaken my kindness to them and theirs to me. It is all alike upon that matter,
for both these kind of insendaries are wicked, and deserves noe creditt, neither
should they get anie from me, if they were the subject of their lys and storys as
I am. I have given you too much trouble, so I shall only begg your pardone for
this long scrible, and subscrive myselfe your lordships most affectionatt sister and
faithfull servant,   M. WEMYSS.

296. GEORGE, VISCOUNT OF TARBAT, to [GEORGE, FIRST EARL OF MELVILLE]—
Wishing his presence. *Circa* 1700.

MY DEARE LORD,—I proposed to be at Melvil Castl this day, but cannot, for Saturndayes journey hither from Edinburgh be the ferry, in so very ill a day, hath wearied me ; yett I would gone over that, had not my brother this morning caried my horse with him to Newtyle ; and heer there are no hors ether for money or favour ; no, not in Perth ; so I give my duty to my lady and your lordship by this.

I hope your better health ; and that I may [have] the honor to see yow heer ether on Wednesday or Thursday, this is my earnest desyre, tho with exception of hurting yow ; for I will rather want my satisfaction of your comeing (tho I doe most anxiously desyre it) then to prejudge your health. My Lady Weem exspects here three sonnes heer that day, I mean Thursday. Now my Lord Whithil told me that he suspects it as doubtful as to the Earl of Leven. I shall be very sorry if he doe so, not altogether because that would be the greatest indiguity he could put on me, as if I were too contemptible for his relation ; but likwise and cheefly because I should look on a good understanding betwixt him and the Lady Weems therafter as almost impossible, and any thing near that is very uneasy, and of uneasy consequences to both ; farr more so open a breach, and I am sure it would be so to, my dear lord, your most humble servant and faithfull coosigne,

TARBAT.

I could not desyre his presence on my accountt, because he justly declin'd that when I desyred it, on the accountt of his relation to herr and yow are one for all to me.

297. [DAVID, LORD ELCHO, afterwards THIRD EARL OF WEMYSS, to ANNE COUNTESS OF LEVEN, his sister]—Begging her to take charge of his children.

London, October 8th, 1700.

I HOPE you will not attribute my seldome writting, my dear sister, to any thing else but what it really is, want of what to say to prove diverting to yee. I was verry glad to hear from your lord of you'r all being prittie well, and wishes what you complain of about your own health to the doctor to have been what I att first supposed it, tho' I think there's noe great need of such a wish, unless it were to please you, for there is noe appearence, upon my word, but that you'l come in earnest to what you hoped for in jest when you was young, to have twenty hairns.

I am verry seucible, my dear, of your good wishes towards me, in your care and concern in what is most dear to me, my babies, and if ever it lyes in my power to show any returns of gratitude, there's nothing, I'm sure, could be more pleasing to me; but you are the only mother they now have, and they are by providence throun upon your care. I doe not encline to enter in compliments with you, seeing still they have too much the air of distrust, only what I could trust my all with is you, because we are so much one, that what belongs to one another we have a speciall tittle too. I have had thoughts of a good while to beg you to be att that trouble to look narrowly about the managment of my children: and that it may be the less trouble to you, and infinitely better for them, to take them to your own family. I know, my dear, you have told me you think it a trust, but as I said before there's noe body I could trust more with; so, my dear, when you please to take them they are yours. I'm affraid Margaret Caithness's coming to your family with the other necessary people about the bairnes prove but troublesome, so if Margaret Arthur be not immediatly going to be married, Mary is both as capable, and I'm sure full as willing, to look after them as any; so if you please order Caithness to get somewhat more than her wages, and let her dispose herself as she pleases; but doe in this just as you think best.

Give my humble service to Leven. Tell him there's a report over toun to-day which most people beleives, tho' it is but scarcely mentioned in the prints, that both the pope and the king of Spain is dead.—My dear heart, adiew.

298. ANNA, DUCHESS OF BUCCLEUCH AND MONMOUTH, to [KATHERINE, COUNTESS OF MELVILLE]—Death of the Countess of Leven.

Dalkeith, January the 14 [1702].

MY DEAR SISTER,—I can not bot lament the great loss you have hade of so good a daughter: indeed, I was much pleased to see my dear nephew so happy in so good a woman, but what pleases God must be born with submition. I shall be ever much conserned for what ever befalls you, or onie of yours; for besides my relation, I am mor oblidged to your lord and your children then to all the worald.—I am, most sincearly, your most affecnoat sister and humble servant,

A. BUCCLEUCH.

My son Dalkeith and his wif are your most humble servants.

Indorsed: Letir from the Duchess of Buccleuch when the Countess of Leven dyd.

299. GEORGE, EARL OF CROMARTY [address wanting, probably to the EARL OF
MELVILLE]—Expressive of friendship.

6th September 1704.

MY LORD,—Among the many dissatisfactions that I had in and of this parliament
the last was, that by continuall useless visits, and my owne frequent indispositious,
I missed of waiting on your lordship or yee went from town; tho as matters
have occurrd of late, wee have not spoke much of busines this year or two, yett old
kindnes and so great relation holds a gripp fast enough not to [be] puld away by
much more then what happend, especially since the causes (whether faults or
mistakes) have never been of nor from ether of our selfs, so all I will say untill
the mists clear some better, is that I doe with the old affection wish yourself,
lady, and children, weell and happy, and that now in our age wee may have quiet
and opportunity to see other oftner nor wee have done of late, and I assure yow
that to be at Elcho and Komes ill is more dessyrable, and truly more desyred then
the court by your lordships most humble servant and affectionate coosine,

CROMERTY.

300. ALEXANDER ROBERTSON of Strowan to [the EARL OF LEVEN]—Sending a
present of a Caper-cailzie.

Cary in Renunoh, May 14th, 1705.

MY LORD,—This is a busy time with such as can serve their country.   I therefor
thought a caper-keily woud not be unwelcome to your lordship, in regard it may
be a rarity to many who have the happyness of sitting at your table.   However
I may differ from your lordship in my perswasion, people need not wonder at the
profound respect I have for the Earle of Leven, unless they be ignorant of the
charitys my unfortunat family has receiv'd meerly from his good nature.   If your
lordship will lay your commands upon me I shall look upon my smal indeavours
as acceptable to you ; and shall uish for an occasion of showing my gratitude to
so generous a benefa[c]tor, because I am, in all sincerity, my lord, your lordships
most obliged humble servant,   AⁿR ROBERTSON of Strowan.

301. THE SAME to THE SAME—With a present of hawks.

Cary, June 11th, 1705.

MY LORD,—Business and recreation alternatly require one another, especially
when a man has a disposition for both ; a person of meer sport is useless in the

commonwealth, and he that is wholly for business is as litle to be indur'd in conversation. Neither of these can be charg'd to your lordship; and if the haukes I send you prove good, as they are likely, they'll unbend your mind from the worlds affairs, to think some times of no great matter, such as my being, my lord, your lordships most obliged and obedient servant.

A^{LR} ROBERTSON of Strowan.

My mother gives her humble duty to your lordship.

302. DAVID, THIRD EARL OF WEMYSS, to DAVID, EARL OF LEVEN—Sir George Byng to be recalled to the Downs.

London, March 29, 1708.

WHAT this express carrys Im not indeed wise enough to know; however, it shall carry my letter. My dear brother, you know I've not heartylie loved some folks you were in great friendship with, and now I don't find but I have reason so to doe. They make daylie, as I'm informed, some ridicolous foolish story or other about the proceedings of our Scots Councell and Scots Generall. Folks are very backward to impart any thing to me, as you may easiely guess. They have it in there heads that you was angry that Sir George Bing lay still in Leith roads, and they resent your finding fault with him extreamly. They never ask me any questions, because I'm told they say that I would speak as you would have me. I hate of all things to suggest any manner of way what may create a misunderstanding, but in this case, of this sett of people, who pretended so much fondness of yee, by God, I cannot be silent. There unmannerly ingratitude is past bearing. There favourites, they say, join in this; but I don't find but they doe it with caution. We are here now in as great tranquillity as we were before in confusion, every body beleiveing what they don't know. The Duke of Marlbrough went from this this morning. We are told the parliament rises on Thursday. Sir George will be immediately recalled to the Douns, and Briggadier Sabine to Ostend. I'm sorry you was not well when the express came away. I beleive Doctor Melvills affair will goe wrong. I'm sure I could doe noe more had he been my brother. There may be yet hopes if you be perremptory. I'm in great haste now, so my dear Leven, God bliss yee.

I think really you should dispose of Lady Mary, since her brother and I are so uncertain of ourselves. He keepes his health very well, and carrys himself very well when he's by me.

To the right honorable the Earle of Leven.

303. DAVID, EARL OF WEMYSS, to [LADY MARY LESLIE, daughter of David,
Earl of Leven] his niece—Good wishes.

London, June 27, [c. 1708].

I WISH yee, my dear, a great many years, a kind, a rich, and a loving handsome
husband, three sons and one daughter, which, in my oppinion, is somewhat better
then four daughters and one son.   I was in hopes you stood not in ceremony
about the return of letters, till my lord, your father, told me you did.   If it were
not for denying myself the pleasure of hearing from yee, I should give yee free
liberty not to answer mine, and yet you should see how punctuall a writter I
should be.   However, I think its better delay the experiment till another time.
We shall be with yee in four or five weeks, and whereever I am you have a most
affectionate uncle and faithfull servant,   WEMYSS.

Your father hes invited some of your friends to-night to drink your health.

304. PATRICK, COUNT LESLIE, to [DAVID, EARL OF LEVEN]—Recommending his
cousin James Leslie of Buchanstown.

Tullous, 14th July 1708.

MAY IT PLEASE YOUR EXCELLENCE,—Ther is non living mor unwilling to give
your lordship trouble then my selfe, yet the great necessity off my relationes, and
the esteeme I have off being judged in the honour off your lordship's favour,
obleidgys me at this tyme earnestly to recomend to your lordship's protectione
and assistance, my cusine James Leslie of Buchanstoune, whoise father and himselfe faithfully served the government for many yeares: and at last wer obleidged
as they say and as its generally esteemed, to sell the litle fortune they and thair
prædecessours hade injoyed for tuo hunder yeares at least, by the losse the father
sustained in being prisoner, and the want off ariers due both to father and sone,
all which I hope will pleid your lordship's pitie and charity to doe for him, which
is all the trouble I can offer your lordship on the heid, and does with a suire and
kynd heart subscryve myselfe, my dear lord, your lordship's most obleidged servant
and affectionate cusine,   PATRIK COUNT LESLIE.

305. THE SAME to THE SAME—Expressing a desire to see Lord Leven.

Tullous, September 27, 1708.

MY LORD,—Since my present infirmity of body hinders me from travailing, I am
obliged humbly to beg your lordship's pardon for not paying that duty I ow in

waiting of your lordship and your noble children; therfore let me humbly intreat your lordship will be pleased to allow me that honour in suffering me att any of your spare times, to waite of your lordship att this hermitage I was born att, and hes returned thereto, I hope in God, to dye wel, which will not only doe me a great deal of honour, but also add to the esteem I have in the countrie, and likways to the many and great obligations I have frequently met with, and confirm me in the honour I have to be esteemed, my dear lord, your excellence obedient and most oblidged servant,   PATRIK COUNT LESLIE.

306. DAVID, THIRD EARL OF WEMYSS, to DAVID, EARL OF LEVEN, Commander-in-chief of the forces in Scotland—That the Earl of Leven had enemies in London.

London, August 27, 1708.

HAVING nothing, my dear Leven, worth your while to write yee of from the road, I delay'd it till now. I had a very good journey, and came here last night, and am both angry and surprized to find noe letters from the Wemyss, but I beleive I shall never be able to reform that place. Earl Mar and Sir D. Nairn, both unaskt, assures me that the queen is to write to yee to-day, which goes by the Teusdays pacquett. By that you may conclude when it comes to your hands what justice is done yee by her servants, which I beg you 'l satisfie me of by a letter, that I may be the more capable of serving yee. By all I can as yet learn, the extravangt heat of the Juncto is not a bitt lessen'd, but encresseaces so much that I am possitively assur'd they must spare saill, else there party will never keep up with them. There spleen at you is particular, and they continue in assuring there party of there strict enquiry into our elections with a very particular manner. Its mightylie fear'd and surmized here of a great man's being more in there measures then ever was suppos'd of him. There's a great councell now att my Lord Sunderland's house in the country, where he is present. I shall be more capable to inform yee farther when I return from Windsour.

E. Leven.

We expect every minutt to hear of a battle in Flanders. Since the two armies are so near one another they scarce can escape fighting. The French are still about 1500 superior in numbers of brigads and squadrons, but they scarce ever are so strong as ours are.

Indorsed: Earl of Weemys, Agust 27, 1708.

307. THE SAME to THE SAME—Advising him to get a house in London.

October 12, 1708.

MY DEAR BROTHER,—Your lordship is pleas'd to be a very lazy writter. I've heard nothing from yee now a great while. I'm told your north-country journey was very splendid, and none but the great Lord Ross was ever treated with so great respect. I long to hear when yee intend to come away, for its pity you should loss so good weather; and the season now wears out apace. And I beleive to you'd think it proper to be in town sometime before the parliament sitts. If you please I think you should order some body to look out for a house for yee, for if you delay it untill yee arrive you'l find it difficult to please yourself, for the town beginns to fill very fast. I see Collonell Moncrief this morning, but he knows nothing of yee.

We still continue in great suspence about Lisle, tho all our letters promise very fair, so in all liklyhood we shall have a tedious campainge. It is beleiv'd when the seige is over that the armys can scarce shunn to justle one another, for the French seem resolv'd to dispute our retreat, and have been working hard upon a line with redoubts for that purpose. Every thing continues quiet here as yet, since most peoples heads are taken up with there diversions att Newmarcat. How soon that is over things may happen to open a little more, so I should indeed think it adviseable you were in the way. The Court is still att Windsour and may stay its thought so long as this fine weather holds. Give my most humble service to my Lord and Lady Haddo, and my Lord Aberdeen if you'r still there, and let me have your commands in any thing you want to know that I can tell yee, or any thing to be done here before your arrivall, which shall be punctually observ'd.—I am, my dear Leven, yours.

Indorsed : Earle of Weemyses letter, 12 October 1708.

308. SIMON, LORD LOVAT, [to DAVID, EARL OF LEVEN]—Giving an account of his imprisonment at Saumur, and alleging certain grounds of quarrel with Lord Leven.

London, the 23 of Apryle 1717.

MY LORD,—After the long and intimat friendship that was betwixt your lordship and me, it might seem very strange to your lordship that I had not the honour to writ to you since I came to Britain, and that I passd twice within a mile of your house without paying you a visit. But my reason for both was too

strong to be easily overcome. And it was this : James Fraser of Castleladers,
who was sent to France by my kindred to indeavour to bring me home, finding
me prisoner at Saumur by order of the court of France, he went to that court
to indeavour to obtean my liberty ; and the French ministers of state having
assur'd him that it was the court of St. Germans that keepd me prisoner, and
not the court of France, the said James Fraser adressd himself to the late Earle
of Perth, whom he had heard was my friend ; but the earle told him that I had
shown myself such ane euemy to his master that he conld not speak for me, and
as a proof of that the earle, as Master Fraser swore to me, show'd him a letter which
I had writen to your lordship with my brother before the queens death, in which
I told you that I had sent my brother to rise my kindred, and live and dy in
the Hanoverian interest, and that the Earle of Perth told him that your lordship sent that letter of mine to that court to show your zeal for that interest,
that they might put me in closs prison, and hinder my coming over because of
my interest in my countery. Tho' this, if true, as the gentilman swore to me,
and is ready still to declare the same, was a strange breach of friendship, yet I
protest upon honour that I did never speak of it to the king or ministry, nor
did never design to make use of it against your lordship, for I allwayes was so
jealous of my honour on the matter of true friendship, that I chuse rather that your
lordship should feal twenty tymes to me than I once to you. But what hes hapend
of late against me here by the direction of some that act for your lordship, is so
inhumain that I canot bear it without demanding satisfaction. I am too certainly inform'd that a very ungrat ill man of my name, whose unworthy charactere
is too well known in London, did impose upon Captain Niel McLeod to perswad
your lordship that I and others design'd you harm at this court, by a history of
medals from Barleduc, which I knew no more of than the man of the moon ; and
in short, it is as fals as hell that I or any other, to my knowledge, did design you
harm by those medals. But sinc your lordship has been so injust to me as to
belive the lyes that Fraser advanc'd, and that McLeod wrot to your lordship, if
your lordship does not treat them as they deserve, in ingadging your lordship in
a fals calumnious story to my prejudice, and do me the justice that I ought to
expect, all good men will excuse my leting the king and ministry and the publick
know all that ever passd betwixt your lordship and me, and when the proofs are
known, the world will than judge whether or not I allwayes was a man of honour
and which of us feald in the points of true friendship. I'le act nothing in this
any maner of way till I have your lordships answer, sinc the thing is so plain
that the Duke of Roxborugh told me, by the kings allowance, that those wittnesses
were examin'd by your lordships desire, which may do you bade service and me

no harm, sinc I defy all the universe to prouve the least defect in my zeal and fidelity to his Majestys person and government.—I am, with respect, my lord, your lordships most obedient and most humble servant,   LOVAT.

I expect your lordships answer under cover to Brigadier Grant, in his house in Dover Street.

309. DAVID, EARL OF LEVEN, to SIMON, LORD LOVAT—In answer to the preceding letter. Draft.

Balgonie, May 13th, 1717.

MY LORD,—I received a letter from yow, wherin yow seem to accuse me of breach of friendship. All I shall say to that is that I could never be capable of soe base a thing as makeing use of or exposeing your's or any other mans letter to his dissadvantage. And I ame a more dutyfull and loyall subject to his Majesty King George than to be guilty of corresponding directly or indirectly with any who were, or are knowen to be, his enemies. Therefore the breach of friendship seems to be on your lordships side, in giveing credit to what one Fraser laid to my charge. And I judged it proper, for my own vindication, to apply to his grace the Duke of Roxburgh to get one witness examined to shew my innocence in that matter, which was all I was concerned with.—I ame, my lord, your lordships most humble servant,

Indorsed : Coppy letter. The Earle of Leven to Beaufort, 13th May 1717.

310. SIMON, LORD LOVAT, to DAVID, EARL OF LEVEN—He had sent a friend to tell the story of his letter, which he accused Lord Leven of sending to St. Germains.

London, Agust the 20th, 1717.

MY LORD,—When I got the honour of your lordship's letter in the latter end of May last, wherin you denyd the sending of my letter to France that I sent to your lordship by my brother, with my resolution to stand by the Hanoverian interest, I was so satisfyd with that answer, that I never sinc spoke of your lordship, nor of those transactions, to any person whatsover; but resolv'd to go home your way, and that the gentilman that was in St. Germains, to whom the Earle of Perth shewd my letter might tell you the story out of his own mouth, and that he never did, or resolv'd to make ane ill use of it ; but now that my busines oblidges me to stay some tyme at court, and that the gentilman is going

home, I have intreated him and ingadgd him to see your lordship, and tell yourself the story as it really is, and I can get many worthy gentilmen that can atest
that he passes for a man of honour and truth where he lives and is known;
wheras the unworthy man that made up that story to the Duke of Roxborugh
to get some present subsistance, is known to have liv'd upon knavery, falshood,
and trick ever sinc he came to England. Your lordship sees by that how much
you have been in the wrong to me to give credit to a ly, made up by a notorious
lyar and cheat, and suported by my known and personal enemys. That very
villain Fraser that told that story, after his forging of it, gives out now that your
lordship wrot me a very threatening letter, and that you sent four copys of my
letters, attested by notars, to this place, and that you wrot very unbeseeming
expressions of me. I give no credit or faith to that villains assertion; but sinc
he publishes it every where, I am oblidg'd to ask of your lordship if it is so; and
incace you do not think fit to write to me, I send you this friend and relation of
mine to know it from yourself. Your lordship knows that I am born a gentilman, my graudmother being a daughter of the Earl of Weems, and that by my
father I can claime to as much birth as any subject, so your lordship may depend
upon it, that he was never born of a subject that I 'le suffer ane affront or
injustice of, without takeing the satisfaction that a gentilman ought to take
according to law. All the kingdom knows that my enemys have not much to
boast of their victorys over me in my lowest circumstance, tho' they had a great
power and authority to suport them. If my enemys forc'd me to do things that
put me in need of a remission, the king for my signal services was pleas'd to
give me ane ample pardon. But, my lord, if I was aue ill man, capable of being
ane informer or evidence, you know very well that I could put other people in
need of a remission for what hapend in the queens tyme, and what even this act
of grace seems not to take away; but as I never resolv'd to make my court to
any prince by witnessing or telling storys of my friends, which I think should be
the principle of every honest man, who never should say any thing disadvan-
tagious of his nighbour, except he sees clearly that it is the only meanes to
prevent the ruin of the government and countery he lives in, and of all mankind;
when your lordship reflects on all that passd twixt you and me, which is fresh in
my memory, and which I can convinc you of by tokens and witnesses yet alive,
I do extreamly admire that any man on earth could either make you think, much
less say or write, ane ill thing of me; and I dare say it would be the wrong way
to make your court to the king, who was so good to me as to give me proofs of
his justice and equity, even in the tyme that my enemys spoke most against me;
and I flatter myself that his Majesty will belive me as soon as any Scotch man,

sinc he knows I rather loose my head than tell him a ly.   I never spoke to the king or to any other of your lordship to your dissadvantage, and if you are just to me you will find me more really your servant than all those you beliv'd against me without exception, and its in that hopes that I am, with respect, my lord, your lordships most obedient humble servant,   LOVAT.

311. DAVID, EARL OF LEVEN [to COUNT BOTTMER]—Giving sketch of his
     history, and pleading with the count to recommend him to the king.
     Circa 1717.   [Copy.]

MY LORD,—It is but very lately that I heard of your lordship being made a count of the impire, therefor I beg leave to take this occasion to wish your lordship much joy thereupon.   I have so frequently addres't your lordship in my small concerns, more especially in desireing the honour of your assistance to put his Majestie in mind to provide for me, that nothing could induce me to give your lordship any trouble of this sort so soon, were it not the great disappointments I have met with, and which are the more discourageing, considering it 's near three years since his Majestys happy accession to the throne, and yet hitherto nothing done for me, notwithstanding of many others being put in their former posts, or otherways provided for, therefor pray, my lord, give me leave to lay befor your lordship the grounds I had to hope I should have been provided for befor now.   And, first, I must begin at the time I had the honour to be known to your lordship at the court of Brandyburg.   I had then the honour to be imployed by the Prince of Orange (afterwards King William) to negotiat his interest at that court privately, and I was so happy as to be the instrument of perswadeing his electorall highness to make his journey to Cleve, to have ane interview with the Prince of Orange, in order to concert measures for undertaking the revolution, which was the foundation thereof.   Thereafter I made severall journeys from Berlin to the Hague with private commissions upon the same account, untill that matter was ripe.   And a little before that I raised a regiment upon my own expense in Germany and Holland by a commission from his electorall highness, which I carried over with the Prince of Orange to Brittain.   And few days after his arrivall in Brittain, the governour of Plymouth being ready to submitt to the Prince of Orange, his highness was pleased to acquaint me thereof, and told me that he reposed so much trust in my regiment, that he design'd to order them to march and take possession of that place (being the first that surrendered after his arrivall), which accordingly was done.   I 'll forbear mentioning what part I acted in the convention of estates of Scotland, after King William's accession to the throne of England, save only that I had the honour to be intrusted with carrying his Majestys letter to that convention; and next I cannot omitt to acquaint your lordship that in the year 1689, when his Majestys troops marched against the Highlanders, that my regiment being amongst the number of those troops, I did myself the honour to appear at the head of that regiment at the battle of Gillycranky, and what my conduct was, and the behaviour of my regiment in that battle (altho' the battle went against his Majesty), I wish I were so happy as that even my enemys were to give their account thereof, for that was so well known and so full in the publick prints, that (without my presumeing to give her royall highness Princess Sophia ane account of my small appearance) yet she honoured me with a letter upon that account, wherin she was pleased to take notice of my behaviour, which letter I have yet in my custody. However, this regiment was taken from me by the influence of a Tory ministry (without allowing me any consideration therefor), and is still commanded by the Lord Shannon. What I have now mentioned will, I hope, convince your lordship of the truth of what I have formerly told you in generall concerning my early appearance for the Revolution, and I have so often acquainted your lordship of my zeall for the Protestant succession, and my firm adherence to his Majestys interest and service, that I need not again mention it. What I am now to mention to your lordship is that in which I most depend, which is, I have two letters, one from his Majesty, wherein he is pleased to accept of my offers of service, and assures me that he will be mindfull of it. The other letter is from his royall mother, in which she is pleased to assure me of her protection and care; and in the same letter she is pleased to give the same assurances to my father and my self at her son's desire. If I were not affraid it might give offence to his Majesty, I would willingly transmitt to your lordship coppys of both the letters, to enable your lordship the more to support my pretensions when your lordship allows me your good offices. His grace the Duke of Marlborough has been always my patron and very good freind. I lately wrote to him, intreating his good offices to put his Majesty in mind of me, therefore I am hopefull, if your lordship pleases to mention me, that his grace will concur with your lordship to represent me favourably to his Majesty, and to give your lordship a full view of the posts I enjoyed in the last reign, and the reasons of my being laid aside. I presume to inclose a coppy of my letter to his grace the Duke of Marlborough. My lord, I might plead for something to be done for me on account of my father, the Earl of Melvill, his sufferings and forfeiture before the Revolution, the part he acted in the foundation thereof, and his zealous

adherence thereto during his wholl life. But I have presumed so much on your
lordships patience that I forbear it now, and humbly beg your pardon, and that
you will do me the honour to believe that I am,

312. [MR. JOHN EDMONSTONE, Writer in Edinburgh], to ALEXANDER, FIFTH
    EARL OF LEVEN AND MELVILLE—His reminiscences of the history of the
    earl's father, David, third Earl of Leven. Written *circa* 1735.

MY LORD,—The early notice taken of me by my lord your father, my being
imployed by him and trusted in all his affairs, and my almost constant attending
about him in town and countrey, gave me better access than many others to be
well acquainted with a great deal of the remarkable occurrences in his life. As
your lordship was too young when some of these happened to remember them, or
may have had them told you imperfectly, I have presumed to give you the trouble
of this, which if, at some of your leizure hours, you will peruse, it may possibly
bring some things to remembrance which have escaped your memory.

Many and many a time have I heard the Earle of Leven, with inexpressible
pleasure, relate the early part he acted under the direction of the Earle of Melvill,
your grandfather, and in concert with the Elector of Brandyburg, to bring about
the ever glorious Revolution, the blessed effects whereof all the Protestants of the
present age now enjoy. Your father and grandfather came over with our deliverer.
Your father brought over his regiment, and carried the letter from King William
to the convention of estates in Scotland. The Earl of Melvill was made commissioner to his first parliament, and president of the privy council of Scotland.
These are undeniable evidences of the honour and trust King William (who was
never thought a bad judge) bestowed on them, and are proved by the records of
parliament and council.

As there was no hopes of issue betwixt King William and Queen Mary, and
as little of Queen Anne, the hearty revolutioners never believed their work compleat untill the succession to the crown was solemnly fixed and setled on the
present royall family, and therein with unwearied diligence did your father act
his part, preferring that grand affair to all other earthly concerns, and God only
knows how much of his private estate he willingly bestowed in accomplishing that
great work. His conduct in this most memorable transaction, upon which all
that's dear to the subjects of these dominions doe depend, was most conspicuous ;
as it drew down upon him the wrath and indignation of all the enemies of the
Revolution and opposers of the succession in the house of Hannover, so it reached

the ears of that most illustrious family. For proof of this take but the trouble to cause search your father's repositories, and there will be found convinceing documents of the truth of what I have said. If my memory serve me you will find a course of correspondence by letters betwixt the Princess Sophia, Dutchess Dowager of Hannover, the present kings grandmother, and my lord your father, and in some of her letters to him she expresses the sense she had of your father's zeal for the Protestant succession, yea, promising if ever she, or any descending from her, should sway the scepter of these realms, he or his family should reap the fruits of his then faithfull services. These, my lord, are honourable evidents, and well deserve to be preserved and kept in remembrance by your family, especially since I know well you steadfastly tread in the footsteps of your forefathers, and think nothing can reflect greater honour on your family than to support and vindicate the just rights of your king and countrey against a lawless tribe of insolent rebells. But to shew your lordship the vicissitude of all humane affairs, and that the strictest honour and sincerest faithfull discharge of a man's duty is not always able to stand the shock of envy, malice, and calumny, suffer me to inform you—

That in the year 1714 I was called on by your father to accompany his lordship and my Lord Balgony, your brother, the length of Berwick, in their way to London to wait on the late King George his arrivall, and congratulate his Majesty on his accession to the throne. Your lordship will remember at this time the Earle of Leven was stript of his imployments of commander in chief, master of ordinance, and governour of Edinburgh Castle, as not being a person fitt to be trusted, about the latter end of Queen Annes reign. All the gold of Peru wou'd not have tempted him to embark in the scheme then in view. In our way to Berwick, having staid a night by the road, your father took occasion to inform us of the way and manner how the revolution was brought about, and the succession to the crown establisht in the present royall family, and albeit my lord was then well advanced in years, yet I can't remember ever to have observed him in greater spirits, or undertake a London journey with greater pleasure; often did I hear him, in our way to Berwick, with tears of joy in his eyes, thank his God who had spared him to live and see his long labours crowned with success, that when he was to be called to the other world, a Protestant king was left on the throne of Brittain, bidding us frequently be thaukfull to Almighty God, who had brought about so great a blessing to these lands, wherof we might be more sensible long after he was dead and gone. No doubt my lord himself, as well as every body else, expected that he wou'd be amongst the very first objects of the king's favour, which surely would have been the case, had not the king upon his landing at Greenwich, hearing the Earl of Leven named, lookt out for him, streacht forth his hand to him, and brought him within the circle of the guards that surrounded the king, and leaning his hand on your father's shoulder, told him how long it was since they had been together last at the Elector of Brandyburg's court, askt how it was with him, what family he had got, etc., all in the most friendly manner. This accident, which was greatly to your father's honour, proved, however, very hurtfull to him; for some of his countreymen observing the distinguishing notice the king had taken of him, resolved if possible to deface the good opinion they were feared the king had of him, and for this purpose that very night a most hellish plott and contrivance is laid against your father's character, and the fittest man liveing found out to furnish a proper person to execute their wicked scheme, to witt, Lord Lovat, who quickly brought one Captain or Major Frazer, to make oath before one of the contrivers of this villanous design, that he, Frazer, was sent from the pretender's court, somewhere in France, with letters and credentials and a great quantity of medalls to his friends in Scotland, and particularly that he was charged with a large packett to the Earl of Leven, which he delivered at Balgony, with a certain number of the medalls, and from thence proceeded to my Lord Perths house at Drummond Castle, and so on according to his directions, and ways and means were fallen on to have this discovery laid before his Majesty, as well backed as was in the contrivers power. This being the work of darkness was carried on with the utmost secrecy. Your father continued all that winter in London, often endeavoured to obtain an audience of the king, but was never allowed it; all avenues were shutt whereby he cou'd have access to his Majestie. So he returned home, and spent the remainder of his days privately at Melvill house. I do verily believe, and am fully convinced in my conscience, that this usage dispirited, and at length broke the good old man's heart. You know he could not well brucke disappointments, and when he reflected that he had spent the best part, both of his days and of his estate in the service of the family then reigning, saw himself quite neglected, and those who had strenuously opposed the succession promoted to the highest stations of trust and profit in the government, it cou'd not miss to embitter his life, and sit extremely heavy upon his mind.

Some old friend of your father's about court at last discovered the before-mentioned execrable plott, and I think transmitted to him a copy of that villanous false oath of Frazer's, and some short time after he fell dangerously ill, insomuch that physicians were called from Edinburgh and elsewhere to him at Balgony, where I was then staying with him, and upon their intimateing to him the imminent danger they thought him in, he desired the curtains of the bed might be drawen to the stoops; and in the hearing of the whole physicians and other gentlemen present, he, in the most solemn manner, takeing the Almighty God to witness his sincerity, declared that every word in the said affidavit, which he caused me read, was absolutely false and without foundation ; that he never keept the smallest correspondence in the course of his life with the pretender, or any of his aiders or abbettors, or had ever in thought, word, or deed, swerved in the least degree from his duty to his only rightfull and lawfull sovereign, King George, and in presence of all the company in the room he desired me to reduce to writeing what he had declared, to the end it might be signed by him, if able, that so all in his power might be done to wipe off that most unjust calumny and reproach, which I did, and helpt to support him in his bed when he signed it. This declaration (which was also signed by all of us present as witnesses) or a copy of it, I daresay you will find among your papers.

By this time your lordship will be wearied reading this piece of history. You know I am grown old, but as I am convinced I have been reserved to the present reign to do justice to your family, I could earnestly wish to live to see you thereby enabled to purchase lands equal to Cassingray, Drummeldry, Inchmartine, Westfield, Raith, and Carden, which your father spent serving the governments that establisht this.—I am, with great respect, my lord, your lordship's most humble and most obedient servant.

Indorsed : Letter from J. E. concerning the hellish contrivance to ruin my father.

313. The REV. GEORGE WHITEFIELD to ALEXANDER, EARL OF LEVEN AND MELVILLE—Preaching arrangements, and other matters.

Edinburgh, October 2d, 1741.

MY LORD,—Last night I returned from the south country, and received your lordship's kind letter. My invitation to Cupar was in the name of many. Who the persons were that signed the letter I cannot tell. I have sent it enclosed in this. Had I known it would have been more agreeable to your lordship I would have apointed the meeting at Melvill, but I fear now such publick notice is given that will be impracticable. I cannot possibly stay with your lordship all Tuesday, being to preach at Dundee, but in my return from Aberdeen, hope for an opportunity of being at yonr lordship's house. I am glad your lordship intends to be at Kinglassy. I shall have both sermons very early, and hope the glorious Jesus will be with us in our going to Melvill. Oh ! my lord, I want a thousand tongues to set off the Redeemer's love. Having Him, tho' I had nothing else, I find I possess all things. I have not forgotten your lordship since I wrote last. You are and will be much upon my heart. I have heard of the piety of your lordship's ancestors, and hope many prayers are yet laid up in store for you. Above all, I trust Jesus prays for you, and then you cannot but be conqueror—nay, more than conqueror, over the world, the flesh and the devil. Take courage then, my lord, and fear not to follow a crucified Jesus without the camp, bearing His sacred reproach. Beware of honour falsely so called. Dare to be singularly good, and be not ashamed of Jesus or His Gospel. Oh that you may find it to be the power of God to your salvation ! Look but to Christ by faith, and your lordship's great possessions will not retard, but further and promote, your progress in the Divine Life. What sweet communion will your lordship then enjoy with God in your walks and gardens. It will then be a little paradise to your soul, and every thing you meet with will only draw you so much the nearer to that Jehovah in whom alone all fulness dwells. This I find by dayly experience. That your lordship may dayly experience the same is the earnest prayer of, my lord, your lordship's most obliged, obedient humble servant,   GEORGE WHITEFIELD.

314. THE SAME to LADY DORLINGTON [DIRLETON]—That her house might be a household of faith.

Bristol, November 22d, 1741.

HONOUR'D MADAM,—At length I have gotten a little leisure. I must improve it by writing a letter to your ladyship. The many favours conferred on me loudly call for a more speedy acknowledgement, but hitherto busyness for my Master has prevented. Dear Mrs. Cambell's letter will inform your ladyship how I have altered my state, I trust for the better. For I think my soul is more intimately united to Jesus Christ than ever. I would humbly hope your ladyship can say so too. For there is no happiness till we feel an union of soul with God. That, and that only, as your ladyship hath often heard me assert, is true and undefiled religion. Your own experience will best convince you of the truth of it. Your ladyship enjoys great advantages and glorious means of making a progress in spiritual things. You are rich in this world's goods : may God make you rich in faith and good works.

My Master will not let the kindnesses you have shewn to one of the least of all his servants go unrewarded. It gives me comfort to think what sweet freedom of spirit I have enjoyed when opening the Scriptures in your lady-ship's house. Surely God was with us of a truth. The savour of it is not yet gone off my own soul, and I hope neither from your ladyship's also. Since I left Edinburgh I have put up many hearty prayers for you and your family. The Lord make it an houshold of faith, and make you perfect, entire, lacking nothing. The glorious Emanuel seems to be repairing the breaches of his tabernacle which were fallen down. In Wales we had much of the Divine presence. The people there are so hungry, that they are resolved not to cease wrestling with the Most High till He shall be pleased to send me thither. Oh that God may incline your ladyship to intercede in my behalf. For I long to be humble, to lie low as a very poor sinner at the Redeemer's feet, and wrap myself in God. I think I can say He brings me nearer and nearer to Himself dayly; and I will not rest till I am wholly moulded into the image of my bleeding Lord. I pray God your ladyship may be content with no degrees of holiness, but may be dayly pressing forwards till you arrive at the mark of the prize of your high calling in Christ Jesus. My dear Luke desires to join with me in sending our most affectionate respects and thanks to your ladyship and all friends. Our particular love awaits dear Mr. Macviccar. I trust he will yet live to see glorious days of the Son of man. Surely Christ is getting Himself the victory. May He alone reign King in your soul, and reward you a thousandfold for every token of love shewn to, honour'd madam, your ladyship's most obliged, humble servant,

G. W.

To the right honourable The Lady Dorlington, near Edinburgh, to the care of Mrs. Trail, bookseller in Parliment Close.

315. [LADY ANNE LESLIE] to her brother DAVID, LORD BALGONIE, afterwards SIXTH EARL OF LEVEN. Edinburgh, May 26, 1746.

DEAR BROTHER,—I dare say you are sensible that it is more than you deserve my writing so oft, when I never get so much as a line from you; nay, you have now left off even giving your service to Titty in papa and mama's letters. If it were not for my writing to you, I believe you would forgett there was such a body in beeing. You may think what you please, but I asure you a letter from me at present is a very great complement, considering how much of Lord Crawford's bussiness I have to doe. He goes over to the camp this day. I cant go, as he has left me some despatch's to send of (for I am both secretary and aid de camp), but I follow him Thursday or Fryday, and then too I shall have the pleasure to conduct Lady Leven the lenth of Kinghorn. I wish Lord Crawford had gone to Flanders by land, for I'm afraid I shall be dreadfull sick at sea; but there is no help for it; when one turns a soldier they must doe what they are bid. When you read this I know there is another thing, you will think I'll be in as great danger of turning as sick, but I asure you no; I have been the most couragious creature in the world for some weeks, and I wear a sword and will make it revenge me upon any body who dare brand my name with such a peice of injustice. As I am but a young soldier I have not try'd the fighting yet (deuls excepted), but I know I can bragg as well as any man.

Papa has got a prodigious bad cold; he has slept none these four nights with coughing and the asthma. Mama says she never remembers to have seen him worse; he goes to Melvill about by Stirling in a day or two.

The Prince of Hess did us the honour to dine with us on Fryday, drank tea, and at five waited on papa to the General Assembly, and the ladys waited on his highness there and sat in the loft. He staid an hour. On Fryday we had a fine dancing assembly; his highness got the first set to dispose of; he gave me the first couple, but he began with dancing a minuet with his partner, Mrs. Kinloch, and then he danc'd one with me. My partuer was Sir Patty Murray; we led down the country dances. There was four setts and a vast crowd of company. Every thing was derected with the utmost prudence and discretion, and no petts that I can hear of. Papa says if you are to stay in Scotland he would wish to have the lend of one of your horses, as he has none at present of his own. He begs you would send it with the first good opportunity; any gentleman that is coming this way will allow his servant to lead it. Now, my dear brother, I have no more to say, but to asure you I am not grown so fat as Mrs. Skeen said. I 'll just give you a discription of myself, and you may depend upon it: I am neither ugly nor hansome; I am neither well shap'd nor ill shap'd; I am neither tall nor short. I would not have troubled you about my persou if Mrs. Skeen had not said you was so concerned about it; but I have told you what you are to expect— just an ordinary course lass, seldom neat but always clean. The half of the town makes their compliments to you. As I have a little time at present, I shall give you a sample of some of the most conspicuous names, and shall take two columnes, one for plain compliments, the other for compliments in the kindest manner.

Kindest manner.	Plain compliment.
Lord and Lady Leven.	I have given you a short abrigement,
Lady Dumfrise.	but I could find no plain ones. Nobody
Mrs. Skeen.	can speak of Lord Balgony but in the
Anna Home.	kindest way. Every body loves you and
Mrs. Mar. Thomson.	esteems you. I long more to see you
Lord and Lady St. Clair.	then I can tell. Some folks says I am
Balgarvy. Mr. Makay.	grown like you, but I dare skarce flatter
Mr. Steuart.	myself with these vain hopes.
Lady Dirleton and	
The Miss Nisbets.	
etc. etc. etc.	

Poor Lady St. Clair is very ill; Docter Clark has very little hopes of her. She was very sorry that she did not see you when you was in town.—I am, my dear brother, ever most affectionately yours,   COUNT LESLIE.

I just now hear there is a messenger come down from London to carry Mr. Ratry and Mr. Lauther, the surgeons, there.

To the right honourable the Lord Balgony, in General Handasydes Regement, to the care of the post master of Inverness.

316. PROFESSOR AARON BURR to the EARL OF LEVEN AND MELVILLE—A plea for the college of New Jersey.

New Jersey, Newark, November 20th, 1751.

MY LORD,—I have been encouraged by a worthy friend and correspondent in Scotland to address your lordship in this manner, for which I can make no other apology, but that tis with a view to promote the most valuable interests of mankind, and to put it in your power to be still a more extensive blessing in the world. For this purpose I beg leave, humbly and earnestly, to recommend to your lordships kind notice and patronage the college of New Jersey, some account of which, I suppose, before this has reach't your ears.

We entred on that important design some years ago, having obtained for that purpose a charter by favour of our excellent governour, Mr. Belcher, who, on all occasions, has distinguish'd himself for his friendship to religion, liberty, and learning; done great honour to the king's commission by his wise, steady, and uncurrupted administration, and been a signal blessing to this province in its late confused and divided state. There comes enclosed a copy of this charter, to give your lordship a fuller view of our design.

When the college first came under my care, by the death of the late worthy Mr. Dickinson, there were but 8 students belonging to it; their number is now increased to between 40 and 50. We carry on the instruction of the youth in the best manner we can under our present disadvantages; but we have not undertaken to build an house, for want of money. We are attempting what we can by way of subscription for that purpose, and for a fund to support the charge of it, but dont expect to be able to answer our ends without considerable assistance from abroad. The province is poor. The ruling part of our assembly are either Quakers, or such as are no better friends to learning, so we expect no assistance from that quarter. Some of our friends in Scotland have proposed to attempt getting an act of the General Assembly for a national collection. Should your lordship be so kind as to countenance and encourage such an attempt, 'twould doubtless take effect. And as it would meet with the most gratefull acknowledgements, and be esteemed by us a very signal smile of heaven on our infant college to have so noble a patron, so I doubt not you will have the pleasure to hear that your generous designs for the advancement of religion and learning in these parts (where tis so much needed) have had their desired effect.

A consciousness with what view I mention these things to your lordship persuades me I shall obtain any easy pardon for the freedom I have taken.

May my hearty prayers and good wishes for your continual prosperity and usefullness be acceptable, and allow me to subscribe with all due difference and much respect, your lordship's most obedient and most humble servant,

AARON BURR.

The right honourable the Earl of Leven.

317. ALEXANDER MELVILL of Balgarvie to PROFESSOR CHARLES MACKAY—
Announcing Lord Leven's death.

Melvill, 3d September 1754.

DEAR SIR,—This serves to give you the melancholy account of my Lord Leven's death, who died yesterday about four of the clock in the afternoon, at my Lord Balcarras's house, where he had gone that forenoon from Balcaskie to dine. His lordship had been seised with a fainting fit on the Saturday before as he was comeing from Mr. Thomson of Charltons house to Balcaskie. However, the fainting fit went soon over. He was alarmed, and sent for Dr. Rigg next morning early, who, when he came, found him considerably better, and so well as to take an airing in his chaise. He continued pretty easy all Sunday, and eat his supper tollerably well, and on Moonday thought himself so much better as to propose to make his visit to Lord Balcarras, whither the Dr. attended him, along with Lady Leven and Lady Betty. He bore the little journey very well, and was tolerable cheerfull till dinner, which [he] eat as usuall, but about a quarter of an hour afterwards he was suddenly seised with another fainting fit, which carried him off in less than 3 or 4 minutes with very little struggle. The Dr. attempted to bleed him, but to no purpose. The Dr. imagines the occasion of my lords sudden death was a polypus of the heart. His corpse was brought to Melvill last night. My Lord Balgony has his compliments to you. He desires you may bespeak as many escutcheons as you think will be necessary. He enclines to have one for the house of Melvill, one for the isles at Melvill and Balgony, and one for the

lodge at Edinburgh, if it be thought needfull, which he leaves to you. I make no
doubt of your kind sympathy with Lady Leven, Lord Balgony, and the other
friends.—I am, dear sir, your most humble and obedient servant,

AL. MELVILL.

DEAR SIR,—Forgive me for not writing to you more fully on this melancholly
occasion, but a multiplicity of letters has prevented me. I know how much you
will be affected, so you may judge of what passes here. There is no time fixed
for my lords funeral, but Saturday will be the sooncst. Any day before that I
expect to have the pleasure of seeing you. Kind compliments to Mrs. Mackay,
and I am, with sincere regard, dear sir, your faithfull   BALGONIE.

To Mr. Chas. Mackay, at Leswade.

318. ALEXANDER BELSCHES, Advocate, to ALEXANDER, LORD BALGONIE—
A gossiping letter. [Excerpts.]

Kings real birth day. Edinburgh, Saturday, 4th of June [1768].

* * * *

The General Assembly and Commission are now up, and all the black coats
are generally gone to their respective abodes. By the bye, did your lordship
hear of the commissioner's speech, wherein he disapproved of the proceedings of
the Assembly? Some say it is unconstitutional, others that he could not do
otherwise, seeing they had overturned all preceeding Assemblies with regard to
settlements. When I enquired who was thought to have made his speech, I was
told that as Wilkes said the kings speech was always that of the minister, so his
was wrote by his minister, Gilbert Lang at Largs.

They say Sir Laurence Dundas has wrote a letter of thanks to Mr. Traill
of Hobister, a Caithness minister, for his good conduct in prosecuting Lyall,
inviting him to Kerse, and desiring him to name a successor to Lyall.

Mr. Townsend, I'm told, is to be here next week or some time soon. Have
you seen Mr. Whitefields letter to Dr. Durell on the expulsion of the six students
from the university? It is well worth your perusal, boing very spirited, lively,
and clever; 'twas indeed a very odd affair on the side of the university, as
represented in the news papers.

The justice clerk is to be married to Miss Annie Lockhart of Castlehill next
week, as is her sister, Miss Tibbie, to a Mr. Muirhead, of whom you'll probably
have heard; he got 60,000 l. lately from an uncle, who was governor to some
young gentleman of fortune, who left his whole fortune to him, as his heir was
some worthless fellow or other.

Provosts Laurie and Stewart are just now gone out to the canal to consult and direct the proper place for beginning their operations, so it will certainly begin now; when it will end, or how it will end, nobody knows.

Tenducci it seems is to settle here, and is gone over to Ireland to bring his wife here. The players are now at Haddington, where they go on pretty well, having made 7 or 10 l. the first night, which being that of a market day, all the farmers about went there, being the first I dare say ever they saw in their life; no less than the company belonging to our Theatre Royal, with the addition of Mr. Stayley, being the performers.

The Duke of Buccleugh's only son is dead, you'd hear; that family have always suffered greatly by the small pox, so they tried inoculation when he was only 2 months old, and of this he died: very melancholy indeed! but you well know neither rank nor riches, nor any other thing, can withstand the all conquering hand of death, for he

> Æquo pulsat pede pauperum tabernas
> Regumque turres——

Did you know Mr. Andrew Home who died lately? Your grandmamma did, I'm sure. He had a very great library of books. Everybody thought Provost Laurie would have been his heir, tho' no relation, but he has left all he had to his sister, unmarried, of 70 years of age, which is 3000 l. They say Bob Chalmers gets his post, one of the general accomptants in the excise. * * * When shall I end or how? Why, the old formal way, and from time immemorial, by subscribing myself with all sincerity, my dear lord, your most affectionate and most humble servant till death us do part (to use the phrase of the common people),   ALEX^R BELSCHES.

Monstrous! what a packet of stuff!

To Lord Balgonie at Melvill.

319. THE SAME to THE SAME.   Edinburgh, June 8th, 1768.

THE letter with which I was favoured by my dear lord this morning, 48 hours precisely after your receipt of mine, filled me at the same time with pleasure and pain—with pleasure, that it had been in my small power to amuse for ever so short a time—with pain, that your lordship should have been so liberal in your acknowledgments for such an insignificant trifle as that of one in town writing to a country correspondent the little news, chit chat, and clishmaclaver occasionally going—so no more of this I charge you.   * * *

This is the marriage day of Miss Louisa Whytt, a sister of Bob Whytt's, to

Mr. Ruat, Lord Hope's governor that was, but I suppose you'll have heard it already; a man 30 years older than herself, but strong, healthy, and agreeable, has seen a deal of the world, an income of 800l. a year, bought an estate of 300l. a year or 200 l., at the head of Lochlomond, has, they say, 500 l. a year from Lord Hopeton, which you'll know better, and 50 l. a year from a Sir John or Sir Something Maxwell, having been formerly governor to one of that name; so there, you see, is his 800 or 850 l. a year.   A very handsome fortune, say you!

The justice clerk was married last night, but Miss Tibby Lockhart's intended spouse is at London.   It seems he got a grand house in Cavendish Square by his uncle, which he is going to dispose of, having bought the estate of Herbertshire, in Stirlingshire, belong[ing] to Lady Stirling of Glorat, and being to settle in Scotland, for which I greatly commend him, don't you, too?

They have a clatter that Miss Jessy Chalmers is to be married to Nabob Swinton, but I don't believe it. You know our people here are very fond of match making and bringing together folks who never beheld each other.   Witness their marrying that very gentleman to one of the Miss Renton's before he saw her. Nor do these goodnatured people find the smallest [difficulty] in marriage articles, but draw them up in a trice to the satisfaction of both parties.

Lord Deskford has been very bad of a fever at Cullen, which no doubt would greatly trouble and affect Lord and Lady Findlater; he, however, is now out of danger, and a good deal better.   I 'm told, in case any thing were to befal him, the title of Seafield goes to the laird of Grant, that of Findlater to Col. Ogilvie, formerly of Inchmartin.   Is it not so?

One Thomson, a musick master, gave in a petition t' other day to the magistrates, wanting a tack of Heriot's Gardens to build an orchestra, and make it another Comely Garden, with dancing, etc.   Did you ever hear such madness? They refused it very proper, as not chusing such a thing to be near an hospital.   Had they granted it, the man would have infallibly ruined himself, since that which we have already scarcely supports itself, so that 2 tenants have already broke by it, how much less would two of the same kind do in this place?   Apropos, Monday being Heriot's day, I went to the church, where was the whole world, and heard the sermon and singing.   Mr. Brown of the New Gray Friars had a suitable sermon from 1 Kings 6-12, " I fear the Lord from my youth."   The singing was exceedingly good.   They sung, after all, the 133d Psalm as an anthem. Franks, the New Kirk precentor, led the boys, and our precentor led the girls of the 2 Maiden Hospitals, the other precentors sat by themselves singing the bass; but it was very agreeable to see so many young creatures in their new clothes, and hair dressed, and flowers in their hands, so happy and so contented.

So great is the patriotism, the unwearied, unremitting patriotism of Bowed Joseph, that, not contented with having formerly hanged J. Wilkes in such a solemn manner, he has got an effigy of Sir W. Wallace, the head all made of white iron, and painted naturally enough, I 'm told, and all the body clad in armour, whom he is to carry in procession thro' the town on the king's nominal birthday, with Wilkes's head on his spear. Joseph says it cost him 6 sh. before it went to the painters, so you see this great patriot spends not only his time but his money to shew his great amorem patriæ, which I am much apt to question if Wilkes himself does, and that, too, without any hopes of a place or a pension, so great and so laudable is the disinterestedness of Joseph! cedite Heroes Romani, cedite Graii! Did you see the elegant description of Castlesteads in the news papers? quite à la mode Angloise. I suppose Baron Grant imported the style of it from London, or rather from the Grenades, where you know he has bought an estate of 2500 l. p. ann., payable on the 'Change of London. I 'm told he asks 1800 l. for his 240 English acres, and holden too of a subject superior. Meantime he has taken his friend and fellow musician, Mr. Callender's house just close by his own.

Is not that a melancholy story? One Walter Pringle, a brother of the late Lord Edgefield, and governor of St. Kitt's, after dining aboard the Phœnix man of war, drowned when coming ashore in the boat. What a sudden, what an unexpected, and what an unprepared for (I fear I may say without great breach of charity) death! His secretary was drowned with him.

There was a meeting of the canal gentry yesterday, the proceedings of which have not yet transpired, to use a borrowed phrase.

What shall I say more? My stock is quite exhausted, so much so that you see I have had recourse to the news papers for the 3 preceeding articles ; but stop, What do you think of our principal and his 4000 l.? Will your lordship or I ever make so much of our brains? 'Tis amazing! I hear Dr. Ramsay has the best chance for being physician to the infirmary, thro' Lord Roseberry, it seems. If so, he 's very lucky. Still more! I thought I had finished, but whatever is uppermost come out, is always my maxim in letterwriting.

What think you now of our correspondence? When this comes to your hand there will have passed 5 letters betwixt us in less than a fortnight ; pretty well, say you! But where shall I go next? My paper is done, but turn over I must somewhere— * * *

You seem to be wondrous gay in your part of the world, nothing but horse and foot races and balls. Quite the reverse is the case here, they are all flown over the water.

You would be greatly taken with Mr. Barclay, for he is a very sensible, agreeable man as any I know; but why should I be your echo, repeating just what you said before.

Need I now assure you that my father and mother join, at least if they knew of my present writing they would join, me in most respectful compliments to Lord and Lady Leven, and in best compliments and wishes to you and all others of your good family. Happy am I, happy should I always be, if any thing I can do prove agreeable or acceptable to you.

And now, may that God who hath hitherto preserved and blessed you continue still to preserve and bless you all with all manner of blessings, and may you all at some distant period be severally received into everlasting habitations thro' the merits and mediation of a blessed Redeemer, is the sincere and ardent prayer of one who subscribes himself with the greatest esteem, your lordships humble servant,   ALEX^R BELSCHES.

I hope that when writing to you, my dear lord, I need make no apology for my very serious conclusion, especially as I cannot conceive a reason why such serious sentiments should be always excluded from our letters, and considered as no where proper but in the pulpit or in letters professedly serious and devout.

To Lord Balgonie, att Melvill.

320. THE SAME to THE SAME. [Excerpts.]

Edinburgh, 17th August 1768.

*   *   *   *   *

MATRIMONY seems to thrive apace. I'll tell you of another marriage, one Miss Mary Hay—her father is John Hay the accomptant—is to be married, or was yesterday married, to Mr. Alexander Farquharson, a young man, nephew and heir to the late Mr. Francis Farquharson, of whom I daresay you have heard, and whom he succeeded both in money and business, so 'tis a fine match for her in that respect.

The Duke and Duchess of Buccleugh were a jaunt to Inverara for some time, and returned to Dalkeith on Friday evening, where they will stay a good while.

The Earl and Countess of Holdernesse arrived at Newbottle, either yesterday or Monday, on a visit; you know well the relation there.

There is also a Welch judge here, one Judge Barrington, a brother, I think, of Viscount Barrington. Nor must I forget Mr. Strahan, his lady and daughter, who are also here. He went up to London from this a poor 'prentice boy, but by degrees got into great business, and has acquired a very great fortune; he is one of the law printers to his Majesty. An Irish bishop and his lady are soon to be here, one Dr. Traill, bishop of Downe and Connor. He was first a Presbyterian student of Divinity, but turned Episcopalian, and got this see from Lord Hertford when lord lieutenant, which is between 2 and 3000 £ per annum. He is a north country man, cousin german to Professor Traill at Glasgow, and has a brother minister at Panbride, Lord Panmure's parish church.

Is it not very hard that Johnston and Smith have not one person here who sympathizes with them? Every one either disbelieves their story, or think it a very silly way of losing their money, saying that nobody but themselves would keep so much, or indeed any at all, in a place where nobody sleeps. That affair, too, of the porter's finding the 225£ at the council chamber door, puzzles people more than ever, as they cannot conceive where it should have come from, unless from the porter himself, as it was so long after the robbery. One Macfarquhar, a printer, laid claim to that money as being his, and condescended on a 50£ and a 20£ British Linen Company note; however, there were none of that value among that cash. Some say the porter was put in prison.

The man who really shot Mr. Allen is here just now, at least was here on Saturday se'ennight, for on that day there was a man who wanted to enlist and take the King's money, pretending he was no soldier; but on enquiry it being found that he really was a soldier, and being at that time somewhat intoxicated, he was put in the guard, and then carried for examination before Baillie Miller, when he told who he was, and that he had come here upon a furlough, having been sent out of the way of purpose while that affair was trying. I suppose he is the man mentioned in the summary of the trial as having actually deserted, and whom they call Maccloughlan, so no wonder they acquitted Maclane.

Mr. Townsend, I hear, is to be made one of the governors to the Orphan Hospital, and to have his picture drawn at full length, to be hung up there. He was to preach as last night at 6 o'clock on his return from Glasgow, but I did not hear him, being obliged to be elsewhere, nor do I know whether he did so or not.

Dr. Macqueen grows daily better and better.

Did you hear of the waterspout or prodigious deluge which fell at Duplin that terrible Saturday? You know the situation! Well, the rain came almost instantaneously down the slopes before the house, running 3 or 4 feet deep in the court, you know, before the house, which it would certainly have run into and spoiled the whole furniture, which, on account of the repairs, is mostly in the ground floor, or else might have washed away part of the house itself, had they not had the presence of mind to open the windows which lead down to the kitchen, and so let it run down to the court of offices below, where it met with more water, and carried off the slaughter house and another house, hurling them down the brae.

Thus you have got everything that I know, even the most trifling, so 'tis unnecessary, as well as almost impossible, for me to give you a longer letter. I ought only to answer such parts of your letter as I can with all brevity. I have seen that Miss Lindesay you speak [of], she is a genteel, well looked, agreeable young lady. She used to stay, I believe, with Mrs. Nicky Murray. I daresay Allen's trial is not yet published, at least not come here; when it does you may depend on having it. I dont know the price of Mr. W. and his grace of C., but shall send you word by J. Russell, as I shall Macintosh's proof, if I can possibly get it. I have not seen Rush since Strang's ball, at least not spoken to him. Miss Mary is very well just now; they will all do themselves the honour of waiting on the noble family at Melvil when they go home, which will be the beginning of next week, I suppose; but I dont think your humble servant can be of the train, as he must be cloister'd up with the law. My most respectful compliments and best wishes attend all whom I am forever bound to remember at Melvill. I herewith send you 2 old North Britons which I got but lately, only for want of something better, for they are abominable stuff, not worth your reading, so I have desired my brother to send no more.—I am, my dearest lord, your lordship's most obedient and humble   ALEX. BELSCHES.

To Lord Balgonie att Melvill.

321. THE SAME to THE SAME. [Excerpts.] Innermay, 30th August 1769.

Wednesday.

MY VERY DEAR LORD,— * * * With regard to other news, one who is in the country cannot be thought to have any worth communicating; only what I heard just before I left town was, that Mr. Oswald was to be soon married to Miss Gray, to whom her uncle, G. Ross, certainly is to give 5000£. The 2d Dutch Miss Crawfurd was married to young Mr. Maclood of Genzies, and gone to his fathers. One Col. Grant was to be married to a Miss Nelly Murray of Jamaica. Lord and Lady Dunmore were just sailed, or about it, from Leith for France, to get the fresh air. Mr. Drummond had been attack'd and almost assassinated. Mr. Davidson had got his 370£ stolen out of his house, and no tidings concerning it; and the bridge had fallen as you heard. All these things had happened or were to happen, and [of] all these you have probably been informed, so that you 'll have no very great cause to think you have got a pennyworth for your money, since you 'll pay 2d. for this ; but remember that 'tis this considera-tion which makes me send this to Edinburgh by a private hand, of which I have now the opportunity ; else I might have made you pay other 2d., being the post-age from Perth to Edinburgh.   That, however, would have been too much— more indeed than any of my letters deserve.   As to Byrom, I shall try to get a secondhand one when I go to town, tho' I formerly tried it for you without success.   So it seems you have not yet desisted from your design of learning short-hand !   Were I to give an opinion in the matter, it would be that it is utterly useless ; nay, in one sense, hurtful, as it teaches one negligence and sloth, and hurts the memory, as it takes away all dependance upon it, withdraws the attention from the spirit and connection to the mere words of the speaker, and entirely prevents what, in public speaking, it is very material to notice, the tone and gesture and other circumstances.   To this you may reply, one is for the most part at no great loss tho' he does not observe all this.   Very true, but even from the worst something may be learnt.   J. Bonar told me he proposed to wait on you some of these days, and I wanted him to fix Friday first, as I might have a chance of doing myself the same honor about that time, but now find that it will not do ; but I have told Jack he must go with me soon ; I hope it shall be some time next week, as those of this family who were at Tullybanacher came down last night ; at any rate it shall be very soon.   You see I 'm now got to the end of my paper as well as of my matter, so 'tis now time to close with offering my most respectfull compliments and best wishes to your papa, mamma, and all your family, and am, my very dear lord, yours,   ALEX^R BELSCHES.

Lord Balgonie att Melvill, by Cupar in Fife.

322. THE SAME to THE SAME—News and Court gossip.

London, Panton Square, Mrs. Laurence's,
19th April 1771, Friday night, ½ past 10 o'clock.

MY DEAREST LORD,—You must indeed forgive my very long silence, and impute it not to the want of inclination, but of opportunity.   You may easily indeed believe that one who comes here for a few weeks, and especially when he goes about with others, who never were here, will have but little leisure to sit at home, if he pays his duty to those who have the greatest title to demand it, and to require an account of what he does, that is all which is to be expected, at least for some time. That has been my case. I have been so much hurrying about from place to place, that I have never yet had time to write to any body, but my father: and I now take the first opportunity of enquiring after the welfare of your lordship and family. Having thus introduced myself with an apology, may I not take the first word of flyting, and ask why I have not had the favour of a line from you? Why have you stood so much upon ceremony, as not to write me first, had it been only to let me know that you were well, and that Lady Jane was, as I hope she is, almost quite well? especially as I take up such a deal of time with my letters, that I can never sit down unless I have about 2 hours before my hand; whereas you write as fast as can be, and half an hour is as much to you as double that time. But a truce with flyting and recrimination!—you want something more agreeable. I need not tell you, for 'tis so long ago, that I was a good deal with H. Hope and his sister, when they were here. He and I walked one day for 5 hours together—a pretty comfortable walk for a young man going abroad for his health! Indeed, he was vastly the better for his journey from Scotland: he both looked well and his cough was very little. I accompanied them to the Magdalen Chapel, and I was with them just before they took chaise to depart. I have not heard of 'em, however, since they arrived at Dover: after that time yours will be the better and more authentic intelligence. There is not much news to be had at present. The commitment of the Lord Mayor and Mr. Oliver, which happened the very day I arrived here, put an end to most of the political disturbances in this capital. It was surprising, indeed, how little tumult upon the whole it occasioned, for the news paper accounts of the insults offered to his Majesty in going to the Parliament House about that time were greatly exaggerated and unfair. I have been several times in the House of Commons. I was particularly lucky to be there on the day of the opening of the budget, when my Lord North made a fine appearance, and, to my apprehension at least, vindicated his own administration, and exposed the conduct of opposition in a very able manner. The opposition, except Mr. Dowdeswell, did not enter into the merits of the budget, but lugged in a deal of trite, commonplace topics of abuse against government, with which our ears have been so often dunned by the coblers of our constitution as well here as in a certain society, which shall be nameless. It seems these topics are brought in heels over head in every general debate to the no small consumption of the time and lungs of our hungry patriots, but unhappily to no effect. I was present, too, at most of the debates on the India Bill on Friday and Monday last, as also a little while on Tuesday. You see it has gone so far, but the scheme of employing foreigners has been dropt, so that, instead of 2000, only 1600 men are to be raised. The debates were very warm, and every inch of ground was

strenuously fought. It was no ministerial affair, and yet the whole, at least the
principal leaders of opposition were against it, as were the whole army people,
except General Conway and Lord George Germaine, both of whom spoke very
well upon the occasion. Sir Gilbert Elliott was a great man for it, his son being
to get some good commission in case it passes. The house was on the whole very
thin—shamefully thin—for a matter of such importance. I have been present at
no other debate, but in those I have mentioned, I heard the chief, at least most
of the chief, speakers on both sides. Col. Warrender's election, which has been
depending for these 3 days, was determined to-day in his favor, tho' he was in
great fears, and his adversary had great hopes. I have heard no particulars. Sir
L. Dundas espoused Capt. Ogilvie's interest, but it seems he must not always win.
Mr. Adam, you'd hear, has carried the affair of the Durham Yard Embankment
in the House of Commons. It is now in the Upper House. Council was heard
for the City of London yesterday, and to-day the House was to examine some
witnesses with regard to it, so I did not attend. The City will make nothing of
it ; they only render themselves more and more ridiculous. You'd hear how the
Lords behaved some time ago in the Anglesea affair. It was brought again before
the House on Wednesday, on a petition from Lord Anglesea for leave to bring more
evidence. Lords Mansfield and Camden were clear of opinion for allowing it.
Lord Denbigh was clear against it ; he urged that it was highly indecent in that
House, after having named a day for determining the cause, and after having
actually upon that day proceeded so far, as that, if there had been but 6 lords
who would then have voted, it would have been determined, now to require
further evidence.   Lord Camden said that the very circumstance of there being so
few lords who would vote upon the evidence already brought, induced him to
grant the prayer of the petition ; accordingly the House divided, and further
proof was allowed. It is a very intricate affair, and there has been a vast deal of
perjury, particularly on the side of Lord Anglesea, I mean of him who assumes that
title, and who is married to Lord Lyttleton's daughter. The Lords seem in
general to think that he is a bastard, but would wish, if possible, not to decide upon
the matter. He, in bringing his proof, has brought too much. The point at
issue is, whether his father was married to his mother before he was born. That
he was married to her is certain, but whether before, or after, the birth of this
lord, is the question. To prove that it was before his birth, he, not contented
with the declarations of his mother and others, has produced what he calls the
certificate of the marriage, and upon this a number of witnesses are examined ;
30 swear one way and 30 the other, but they say the Lords rather incline to
think that it is forged. Another instance of his having proved too much is this :

one of the evidence, I forget whether it be his mother, or some other body, being asked as to the particular time of the marriage, swore positively that it was at such a time; and being asked why she was so positive, she said because such a deed, which she produced, was granted at that time, and for the greater security, as well as that it might be the better known again, she had put a sixpence under the seal. The deed was accordingly opened and the sixpence found, but when Lord Mansfield came to look at the sixpence, he found it was coined several years after the deed was said to have been wrote. Was not that shocking? It seems it is Lord Mulgrave who is competing for the honours and estate with the other. I have not seen any of the evidence; it seems to be a curious affair. They all wish Lord Anglesca to carry it. Lords Mansfield and Camden spoke in his favor on that day when it was to have been decided. The Kir[k]cudbright peerage is soon to be heard. The appeal of Lord Chatham about the Pynsent estate comes on upon Wednesday, I think. I doubt whether he 'll find as much favour as Lord Pomfret did. I shall certainly attend that day. I wish his lordship may do so, that I may get a sight of him. The law people here seem not to be much pleased with the present chancellor. He is indeed a very good sort of man, but never speaks in the House, either in debates or in private business. I was assured yesterday that Jeremiah Dyson is the author of the letters signed Creon in the Gazzetteer. I was at court yesterday, where I saw both their Majesties; it was not a great drawing room, tho' there was a good deal of people there, but none of 'em remarkably dressed. Not a single green ribbon was there, only 2 or else 3 blue ribbons, and 5 or 6 red ribbons; except Mr. Stuart Mackenzie, Lord John Murray, and young Charteris, there was not a Scotchman of note. The bishop of Chester was the only bishop there. He kissed the queen's hand on his late appointment. He is exceedingly well spoken of, and thought to be very fit for his present employment. He is much versed in history, ancient and modern, and in the different constitutions of various states: he is, in particular, an excellent geographer, and has a most notable memory; not a place in ancient or modern times but he knows and can describe with the greatest exactness. General Wolfe used to say that he gained more military knowledge from Dr. Markham than from all the officers he ever conversed with; before he went to America he used to go to him two or three times a week of an evening, and sit with him till 3 o'clock in the morning, conversing about military affairs. With all his knowledge he is a silent reserved man in company, unless when put upon certain subjects. He is a moderate man both in religious and political principles. His appointments, as preceptor to the Prince of Wales, are 1000 or 1500£ a year. He, as well as the rest of the household, were appointed without Lord North being consulted; this is certain.

Indeed he was made a bishop against Lord North's inclination, for he was for one Dr. Dampier, who had formerly been his tutor when at college. They said Lord North was really to go out, but nobody believes it. The Lord Mayor and Mr. Oliver are still in the Tower; it was said they were to come as this day to the Court of Common Pleas, to apply for a Habeas Corpus, but they did not do so. I heard Dr. Fordyce last Sunday afternoon: he preached a sermon of an hour and 4 minutes, in his usual style, from these words, " What fruit had you then in those things whereof ye are now ashamed ?" It was one of a series of sermons to young men, a work in which he has been engaged these 3 months. I liked it much, and would have liked it still more, if it had been better suited to his auditory, most of whom were not young men. Dr. Dodd has published his sermons to young men, but I have not seen them; I dare say they 'll not be so good as those of the other. I have called twice on Lady Mary Walker : the first [time] I saw her, but t' other day I did not see her, as she was not very well; she is just at the down lying. What sort of weather have you had lately : our weather here has been most bitter cold ; we had a deal of snow on Tuesday and Wednesday. They say there is not the smallest appearance of spring in the ground. There is a great number of Scotch people here now, and more are daily coming. I heard lately that Mr. Alison and his wife were on their way up. I saw Principal Robertson t' other day, he talks of moving about the 10th or 12th of May. I, too, shall move about that time, so as to be down soon enough to the General Assembly, whereof I hear by C. Stuart I am chosen a member. I was at Guadagni's concert t' other night, where we had all the music composed by Signor Vento for the Harmonic meetings. I cannot say that I was much taken with it, but then I have no gusto. I am quite a Goth in the matter of Italian music. Last night was a most brilliant masquerade, the finest, they say, that has been known for a long time ; but I have heard no particulars, as every body present would, no doubt, be in their beds most part of this day. Lord Findlater was there for one, so his governor told me. I must now conclude with offering my most respectful compliments, and best wishes to Lord and Lady Leven, Lady Jane, Lady Mary, etc. etc. etc.—I am, my dearest lord, yours, ever yours,

ALEX^R BELSCHES.

P.S.—What do I not deserve for such a long letter, and full of such intelligence ? Write one, a long one, in return and remember if you answer me soon, the reply shall be soon. Be so good as to let me know particularly how Lady Jane does. I trust by this time she is quite free from all complaints. In case you be at Hopetoun House when you get this letter, be so kind as to offer my most respectful compliments to Lady Hope, and tell her ladyship that, when I have picked up some court tales, and some anecdotes about the coterie, I shall do myself the honour of writing to her. If Lady Leven has any commands for me, they shall be punctually performed, provided I am acquainted therewith. Did not your honour propose that I should get, or that you would procure for me some franks from Mr. Wemyss, addressed to you? But I must have done, for the hour of eleven approaches.

Lord Balgonie.

323. ALEXANDER, LORD BALGONIE, to his Father, the EARL OF LEVEN AND MELVILLE—Sketch of his travels.

Tours, 3d May, Teusday, [1774].

MY DEAR FATHER will permit me to write this one letter in our native language, which is however for his particular inspection, who is intreated to preserve it from the sight or ears of the ladies, like the mason word.

I had the pleasure of yours of the 31st March, just before setting out for Hatton. About the same time I wrote to you, begging to know your opinion in regard to Marshall remaining with me some months longer, etc. etc., which I hope reached you in safety. I have waited for an answer to that letter, before I proposed any scheme for the summer's campaign, which not being arrived, I am prompted, tho' in the same uncertainty, in order to gain a little time, to mention to you that, after a month or six weeks, this town is by no means a desireable residence, from many circumstances. I need only mention the eternal stink that reigns here in all quarters of the town, especially in warm weather, and which proceeds from the most horrible of all causes, viz., from the cimetieres, which are all full to the surface of the earth, in number about 16, scattered about in the center of the town. Every creature that can, crawls out to their country houses, which is the prevailing passion of the inhabitants of this town during the summer; in winter, eating and gaming employ much of their attention. Our abbé has a mighty pretty one about 3 miles from hence, but his attendance upon St. Martin does not permit him to go there except a month or two in the vintage. However, we go all there for 8 or ten days upon the 16th. Now, my dear father, do you approve of our going from hence to Paris, or rather in the neighbourhood, to spend a couple of months? Our style will be as much as possible more that of improvement than of pleasure, and our time and expences regulated accordingly. If this scheme is not agreeable to you, you have only to name any other provin-

cial town to the northward, as they are all alike. But from our present knowledge of the language, and perhaps no other oppertunity of seeing Paris and its
environs may return, I should hope our time there will not be mispent. From
hence we may go southward, perhaps as far as Lyons together, where it is probable we may part, if I go into Italy, as Marshall says himself that his own
affairs will oblige him to go home before the winter, and I now know enough of
traveling, etc. etc.

Our promising season still continues, an inexpressible blessing to this country.
We have roses, honeysuckle, etc., and strawberries already red ; a good deal of
rain, but no appearance of frost.

I received yesterday a letter from mother, which she dates most seriously the
20th, but unfortunately the postmark is 19. As she knows that you and I are
rather apt to be thick at the uptack, I must beg of her to explain at large who
the hen is that was not crammed in the infirmary, as I do not comprehend a
single word of it. In the night between the 30th and first instant we had the
most violent thunder ever heard by Marshall, Cunnynghame, or any English
person here. Such a night is even rare in France, which continued with a constant lightning between two and three hours. It has happily done no harm we
have as yet heard of ; and what will perhaps surprise you is that I did not hear
it, but outslept it fairly. Next morning I was out on horseback, one of the [most]
pleasant mornings I ever felt. Upon calculation you will perhaps discover that I
was out upon Sunday. To tell you the truth, any other [day] except by accident,
I am not out of my room but to go into another to take a fencing lesson at
10 o'clock, from between 6 and 7 that I rise, till a ¼ from two that I go down
to dinner, and am never out of the house till four or half an hour after, when
we take a long walk for a couple of hours. However, tho' I have an archbishop
at hand, I must send for absolution to Fife, where I am certain, from various
reasons, it will be granted me, even by Cardinal Moody himself, to whom, as well
as his wife, Mr. Johnstone, etc., I desire to be kindly remembered, and to all our
worthy neighbours. I intend to surprise Madame Rig with a letter one of these
days, but am afraid she will be also surprised at the postage. I am this instant
informed that an express is arrived here in his way to Madrid, and that by him
the archbishop is ordered to have prayers said in all the churches for the king,
who is seized with the smallpox in the 64th year of his age. None of the royal
family has ever had them. The eruption made its appearance upon Sunday, after
frequent bleedings, and so far as they can as yet judge, promise no bad symptoms. I have nothing to add to this intelligence, you will surely see enough of
it in our English newspapers. The reason that the royal family and very few

families in France are not innoculated is because there is no convincing the French people that one has not the smallpox oftner than once. By my calculation of your motions you should reach home to-morrow or Thursday. Mon Dieu, you will be at Wingates and Keltons this night; how distant I am from those friends I love best in the world. Mothers letter mentions your being to go by Glasgow. Absolutely if you have not given Jane and Mary a peep at Lochlomond, you are quite intollerable. You will forgive my freedom, but you know my partiality for that scene, and I assure you I do not expect to see such another in all my travels. You would be at Cardross sans doute—a horrible place.—Adieu.   BAL.

    The Earl of Leven, Melville House, near Edinburgh,
          per London.

324. THE SAME to THE SAME. Tours, 15th July, Friday, [1774].

I HAVE been this fortnight past taken up in making a journey into Bretagne, in which the half of the costs were defrayed by Mr. Wauchope, Nydries eldest son, a sensible and worthy man as any I know. As I undertook this voyage in a warm season, and having left Marshal behind me, I thought it better finished before I should mention any thing about it. The 27th of June we set out after dinner, and got to Saumur, which afternoon was the only warm weather we saw. This may surprise you, but I do not believe that except that afternoon, when the thermometer was at 76, we were ever, in 16 days we were upon our journey, in the heat of 60 degrees. We agreed we never felt the weather at this season so cool in Scotland, and, upon the whole, our journey was, and not a little owing to this circumstance, one of the most agreable we could have made in France. I will now only mention to you our route, which you may trace in any map by going along the coast of Brittany, and mention a few of the most striking circumstances we met with. 28th June—Got to Angers by 11 o'clock, where we went to see the academy. The grandson of Pignérolo, who was Lord Broadalbanos master, keeps it. The buildings are much better than they were at that time, but the academy much fallen off. He has, however, 24 horses seemingly in good order. Here we spent the rest of the day in seeing the château, walking about, etc., and next morning, 29th, proceeded to Nantes, where we arrived about 2 o'clock. This is an immense town, contains from 80 to 100,000 inhabitants, who are all in trade, and concerned in every species of [commerce] with all quarters of the globe. The road from Tours hither is delightfull, almost the whole way upon the banks of the Loire, which is a noble river. The port of Nantes, however, is at Painbœuf, but very considerable ships come even to the porte of Nantes. The quarter of the town called La Fosse is superb, and the Isle Feydeau is like an inchanted island. Here, as indeed all over Bretagne, the subjects pay no fewer than 114 additional taxes since the year 1771. This province is, however, as yet free from the duties upon salt, 14 pounds of which they have here for a liard (or half a farthing), and for which one inch over the limits of this province costs the poor inhabitants 14 sous per lib. At Nantes we remained till the 2d of July. Here we received the greatest politeness and attention from Monsieur Babut, Harris's correspondant, whose wife is one of the best women I have seen in France. 2d July—We set out from Nantes, and in the evening reached Vannes a Roche Bernard, cross'd the Vilaine in a boat, a little below which Monsieur Conflans thought proper to shelter his fleet, after the defeat he met with from Sir Edward Hawke. But I find I am getting into a particular journal, which shall be carried on in some degree in my next letter. Suffice it to say, we went on to Brest, where we were guarded par tout; could hardly go to the commoditie without a serjeant. From hence we came round to Morlaix, the name of a place I suppose David knows from its tobacco trade with Glasgow. So by St. Brieuc to St. Malo, from whence we saw St. Cast. Thence to Rennes, and so by La Flêche to Tours, where we arrived Teusday the 12 in good health, and not ill pleased with our tour. I have much to say of the bas Bretons, who speak Welsh, and are entirely a different race from any other French, or even any other inhabitants of this earth I have as yet seen. Our Highlanders are civilized in comparison of these savages. I leave this place Monday se'enight, the 25th, spend a few days with our friends at Orleans, thence get to Paris by the first of August, where you may send my letters to the care of Messrs. Germany Gireriiot & Co., Harris's corespondants.—Adieu, my dear, dear father, mother. Love to everybody.

The Earl of Leven, at Melville House, near Edinburgh, par Londres.

325. REV. JOHN NEWTON to MRS. THORNTON—Reflections on the duty of gratitude to God.

Hoxton, 9 September 1780.

MY DEAR MADAM,—This waits upon you, I hope, in due time, to congratulate your safe and happy return to Clapham, and likewise to thank you for your very obliging favor of the 5th from Buxton.

To be preserved in the course of so long a journey, not only from real harm, but even from the appearance of danger, is a mercy indeed, a great mercy, if considered in the lump, and an assemblage of millions of mercies if considered in detail. Every moment of time you have been abroad you were liable to illnesses which might have rendered your progress impracticable. In every step of the way the fall of a horse, or a thousand unexpected events, might have been attended with grievous consequences. And when a journey is performed in company, that every one should escape the evils to which each one was equally exposed, renders the Lord's care and protection still more evident and striking. Then to have all at home preserved in safety during your absence, so as to find nothing to distress you upon your return, is the crowning circumstance, which heightens the sense of His goodness, which will, I trust, draw forth acknowledgments and praises, not only from you and yours, but from me and many who feel themselves nearly interested in your concernments. It is a singular priviledge of your family, that whether yow are abroad or at home, asleep or awake, numbers in different places are engaged both by gratitude and affection, in prayer for you daily as for themselves. May the God who hears prayer, make us all truly thankful for His late goodness.

Could you have a history, madam, of all the persons and families who have left their homes since you set out, you would be greatly affected by the comparison. Some who went abroad in health, have been arrested by the hand of death. In vain the tender mother expects the return of her beloved child, or the wife counts the days and hours till she shall see her husband again. In their room, the post or the messenger arrives to tell they must meet no more in this world. Others who left all well at home were followd by painfull news, and calld hastily back to a house of mourning. The desire of their eyes has been taken away with a stroke, or some heavy calamity like a sudden flood has broken their schemes and swept away their expectations. Such is the uncertain state of human life, from which no situation is exempt ; and therefore to be preserved in such a state—to stand as upon a field of battle, to see many suffering and falling on the right hand and the left, and we and ours to be kept, not for a day or two, but for a course of years, as if we were quite out of the reach of danger and of change, what a call is this for gratitude, what an engagement to love and serve and trust our great Preserver, what a strong argument should it prove to reconcile us to the lighter trials which He appoints us, and to teach us to bear them not merely with submission but with chearfulness.

Still more endearing our sense of obligation will be felt, when we consider that the protection and blessings we receive are afforded us by Him who once bore our sins and sorrows in His own person, and now, in that nature of ours in which he sufferd, exercises all power in heaven and in earth. It is He who

upholds those who stand, and raises those who are fallen ; who gives us as much
prosperity as we can bear, and who is our stronghold in the day of trouble. Many
who love Him not, because they do not know Him, are fed by His bounty, and
preservd by His care ; but *they* have a double, a tenfold relish of temporal
blessings, who can say—

> He sunk beneath our heavy woes,
>   To raise us to a throne ;
> There 's not a gift His hand bestows,
>   But cost His heart a grone !

I have read very animated and picturesque descriptions of the hills and dales
and lakes in Westmoreland.   But how different is my idea of what I have read,
from yours of what you have seen ? It was, however, I suppose, the account you
had received of them, which induced you, when opportunity offerd, to view
them yourself upon the spot.   Thus the Queen of Sheba was excited by the report
she had heard, to visit Solomon, but when she saw him, she found the half had
not been told her.   And thus the Holy Spirit, by the good report of the gospel,
engages poor sinners to set out, and thro' a thousand difficulties to press on to see
Jesus.   There is a twofold view of Him attainable.   He is to be seen by faith in
the present life.   This sight is imperfect, we behold Him but in part, and darkly,
as in a glass.   It is, however, sufficient to convince us that, in comparison of Him,
there is no other object deserving our notice.   Experience is the best, the only
competent expositor of what the Scripture means by joy and peace in beleiving.
that joy which is unspeakable and full of glory.   When we actually taste and see
how good and gracious He is, when we are favord with some suitable apprehensions of His glory and His love ; when the eye of our mind, anointed with the
holy unction, and furnished with spiritual light, can view Him as He was prostrate
in Gethsemane, as suspended upon Golgotha, as rising from the tomb, and as
reigning in glory, as the Lamb upon the cross and the Lamb upon the throne,
then the Queen of Sheba's acknowledgment is ours,—not the half, not the
thousandth part was told us.   If words cannot give us the idea of a taste of a
pine-apple, much less can they describe the nature, privileges, comforts, and supports of a life of faith in the Son of God.   They who see Him thus by faith here,
shall in due time see Him as He is, without a vail or cloud.   And compard with
this blissful vision the largest discoveries of faith itself amount to little more than
meer description.   What the Apostle saw and heard when he knew not whether
he was in the body or out of it was unutterable, and beyond the power of human
language to express.   We must die before we can rightly understand many passages of Scripture.   How desirable should death (in the Lords time) appear to us

in this view of it! The happiness designed for those who love the Savior, is too great for the utmost exertion of our faculties in the present state to comprehend.

We shall with great pleasure and thankfulness accept your permission to wait on you during Mr. Thorntons absence, when we know you are at leisure to receive us. We join in best respects.

I am with sincerity, madam, your much obliged and affectionate servant,

JOHN NEWTON.

Mrs. Thornton, at John Thornton's, Esquire, Clapham.

326. DAVID, EARL OF LEVEN AND MELVILLE, to ALEXANDER, LORD BALGONIE, his son—Family news.

Edinburgh, Saturday, May 17th [1783].

MY DEAR BALGONIE,—I heartily condole with you on the death of our worthy friend; with much truth I can say she has always been so to me in a very [high] degree from my infancy.

I arrived here to-day with George at 2, left every body well at home. Found your letter of last Tuesday, always most acceptable. I dont think you have much occasion to make an apology for not writing.

Dont be vexed at mothers not liking the spring velvet; all I said was that the red would have been more showey. I have a history of another suit to tell you. I have not seen it yet myself. The few hours I have been here have been employed in arranging my ladys funeral, which is fixed for Tuesday at the West Church, as it was impossible for me to go to Fife. What with this mournfull operation and the others of next week, I have been in a state of confusion since Thursday night.

All my matters are well, and I hope properly advanced. Sir John and Jane came on Monday. I stay here at Walkers till Wednesday night. You have had a world of trouble about the warrants.

A letter this day from David; he has been seriously ill, first a fever and then a flux, but recovered. Love to John. I am afraid to miss the post.

Yours most affectionately,

LEVEN.

P.S.—Remember I dont expect you here on my account.

327. DAVID, EARL OF LEVEN AND MELVILLE, to ALEXANDER, LORD BALGONIE—
Proceedings in Assembly.

May 29th [1783], 8 morning.

MY DEAR BALGONIE,—The last time I wrote I complained of having no letters from you or John for 3 posts. But I now find that the blockheads in the post office sent all my letters and news papers to Fife, the consequence of which was sending for Davie Ross, and giving him a hearty set down. I continue to enjoy perfect health, and if I wrote it before, I continue to write it now, that there is not a single thing happened in any shape whatever, that has given me a moments disquiet in all the course of this bussiness, and I trust it will continue. Every commissioner must meet with respect, but sincere friendships and good will I have experienced in a high degree. One wish indeed I have had, that the Assembly did not sit so late; on Tuesday from 11 to 8, upon the immoralities of a minister; and yesterday from 11 to 6, on the overture concerning patrounge, which was dismissed by the small majority of 9.

However, I write letters and read news papers when a dull speaker holds forth, otherwise, much entertained with the debates. The president and chief baron have been with me both days. I had to advise them on a knotty point of my own, about a Fast and Thanksgiving.

I have ordered Jane, Keyden, and George to write. John and you would be happy to hear of dear Mary. I expect my brother on Saturday.

When I began this letter I intended to set out by saying that I had received back yesterday morning all the letters, &c., from Fife; and also your letter and newspapers of Saturday night from London. For my own part, I have desired you before not to hurry yourself for me, so that I certainly have found no fault with your not being here, and I wrote yesterday to your mother in such a manner as that she must be satisfied, especially when I told her that I had informed you that I dispensed with your presence.

As to dress, I am satisfied that the gold lace is quite the thing, and a handsome suit it is as can be seen. I have besides, unknown to you, the finest and most fashionable suit in Scotland. This has made me delay making up the velvet, as it will be new next year, if so be, etc. I am perfectly satisfied with it. The barons sign the orders for cash to-day; I shall send a remittance on Saturday. John and you will [have] an accountt of every thing bought for the occasion. Since the change of ink, all is wrote upon the throne. For a little amusement I propose to go out and sleep at Barnton to-morrow night. It is now near 4, and I dont expect to dine before 8. Another bad cause against a minister. Kind love to John ; remember me kindly to Lord and Lady Hoptoun. I have wrote to Lord Privy Seal.—Yours, with great affection,   L——

328. DAVID, EARL OF LEVEN AND MELVILLE, to his Sons—Attending the Assembly.

Saturday, May 31st [1783.]

MY DEAR SONS,—An hour ago I had the pleasure of receiving both your kind letters. I continue to have the pleasure of telling you that [I] am still in perfect health, in spite of walking bareheaded in this bitter cold weather, and that every thing goes hitherto to my wish ; except long sederunts, for four successive days have not dined till 7. Yesterdays business was so long, and not finished, that out of indulgence to me they resolved to meet this morning at 9 in a committee of the whole house, and the Assembly not to be resumed till one o'clock. I availed myself of this, and went out last night for a little recreation, *and slept with Lady Glenorchy and Lady Harriot.*

Much obliged to you for the articles of news in your letters and for the profusion of newspapers, which you know well when to stop.

Till I see how matters turn out, I have ordered Mr. Russell to send this night a remittance of £60 to Captain Leslie, 1st Guards. I forgot to say before, that the pages swords and every thing arrived in perfect order and time. I hear every day from Melville, and happy to get so comfortable accounts of dear Mary. Ruth[ven] came last night back, having gone the first day after all was over. Mr. R. receives the drawback for the warant from the agent for the Church.

I am just called upon to go to the Assembly, so must conclude. My plan is to stay Tuesday to return visits, and the birthday being Wednesday, I hope to get to dear Melvill on Thursday.—Ever, ever your most affectionate father,

L——.

P.S.—I expect a list of every thing bought at London on this occasion. Sir John and Jane and Georges love. Sir John goes on Tuesday to see his new estate at Fettercairn. Martin behaves well, and Keyden most usefull. Donaldson and Bonar both here, and have been honoured with several Fife gentlemen on purpose.

My dear John, you never told me of your tooth ; I hope it is not a fore one, and that you are now free of pain.

329. Mrs. Thornton to [Wilhelmina, Countess of Leven and Melville]—
Character of Miss Thornton.

Clapham, 14 May, Thursday, [Indorsed 1784].

Madam,—Were I to judge by my own feelings, your ladyship will not be sorry to receive a sequal to my last, at least I am sure I write in continuation with much greater pleasure. Lord Balgony seems quite well and in spirits ; the family super went of very well, and to the sattisfaction of all partys, and yesterday the same, which would have been somewhat tremendous a fortnight ago, on account of an introduction to Mr. Cornwalls family, Mr. Thorntons old partner of 42 years standing, and just ended, and also my sister Wilberforce, a plain, good woman, who spends a hansome income in doing much good, and who was leaveing town on Tuesday, and who much wished to see Lord Balgony, also dined with us, and all easy and happy, tho chance or rather Providence brought all togather somewhat unexpectedly.   Your ladyship will perhaps think I wrote before in my sleep, but it was not so, nor any thing that I know of exagerated ; but it pleased God so to involve us in a mist of doubt and perplexity, as I am persuaded will never be forgotten by my daughter at least, who is so affraid of the like scene coming again, that I was constrained to confess to her yesterday the bold step I had taken in writing to your ladyship, tho I have not named it to Mr. Thornton, and she was very happy on the occation and only wished I had done so a week or two before, and added she could and would confide in your reply, from her confidence in your integrity and perfect knowledge of the truth.

And here, my dear madam, while investigating one party so narrowly, do I find my self, as it were, in justice constrained to deleniate another, with all the exactness I am able.   It is said affection is blind ; I sometimes think it a wrong phraise, and that it would be better exprest by being partial, at least I think I sometimes see faults in my young ones, which would escape another.   Janes person is rather strong and musculine than elegant and delicate, and her mind a little accords therewith, she bears pain, disapointment, and the losses, cross accidents of life, better than most I know, from not either feeling them so keenly or partaking of her fathers natural courage, yet at the same time that she is not unhappy from her friendships and a thousand fears about them, she is warm enough in them, her sence and judgment are rather useful than brillient, by which she avoids getting into scrapes, nor do I once in my life recolect her haveing the slightest quarrel with any human being   Blest with a good constitution, her temper has been also uniformly chearful, nor till this last twelvemonth of anxiety on Lord Balgonys account did I ever hear her complain of broken rest ; she uses much walking exersise, nor would her health keep up without it, drinks only water, eats plain but with good rellish, and has nothing of the fine lady that distresses herself by over refinements and delicacys; she is fond of employment, nor have I ever made a point of being always togather in our gentlemens absence; a circumstance that makes mother and daughter often go on ill togather, when they might do well, were more latitude allowed to sit in what room they chuse, and to this I think has been owing that Jane is often her own mantua maker and milliner, and upholsterer, and the inventer of many things in her own apartment, which have been a source both of amusement and usefulness, and where time never seems to hang upon her hands.   I wish she read rather more, but have the comfort to hope that frivolous books are not her choice, and plays, as she never saw one acted, so have they come seldom in her way to be read, nor have the run of romances so pernicious to youth poisoned her mind with ideas of love and intriague. Were any one very ill, as was the case when my mother died, she is not a bad nurse, and spares no pains, but from her own natural habit she is not soon allarmed either for others or herself, which may and I think does take of that appearance or reallity of tenderness which is so amiable in a friend.   In the things of God, I have had many fears that she may be over high rated at present, tho I do think from narrow inspection were it to please heaven to deprive me of her I should not be uneasy as to her safety, tho' I wish her to be more free in conversing on the best subjects, and do not know how it is with other familys, but tho' our young ones seem to have turned their faces Zion ward, yet their is a shyness in talking over doctrins as their own experiences of any work of grace on the heart, which some would think prognosticated ill, but Mr. Thornton as well as myself are thankful for the day of small things, and that they have hitherto been preserved from runing to the same degree of rioting.   How unsuitable this letter is for any inspection but your ladyships.   I trust we have similar wishes for our offspring, and had rather they built up a house for God than headed a kingdom.   That these wishes may be gratified if the present plan takes place is the prayer of, madam, your ladyships obliged servant,   LUCY THORNTON.

I am impell'd to say a word conserning a little Dolly, my daughters maid, who has behaved exceeding well in this family for 7 years past; she washes her fine linnen, dresses her, and cleans her rooms, and attends to my sons linnen, and is no fine lady, tho' a pritty neat figure, but not very sensible, tho' clever in what she does, and good tempered, and of a serious cast, very fond of her mistress, and I think suits her well, that [I] should be sorry they parted as she has her interest at heart, and is learning to improve herself in a family way.

330. REV. JOHN NEWTON to JOHN THORNTON, Esquire—Congratulations on the marriage of Lord and Lady Balgonie.

Priestlands, Lymington, the 12 August 1784.

MY DEAREST SIR,—I am too well acquainted with your activity as a traveller to wonder that you did not stop till you reached home. I desire to be thankful for your safe journey, and that Mr. Warner has so good an opinion of your toe. It is a very great satisfaction to us that you consulted him. Such consequences have often followed from a lame toe, that I could not help having some apprehensions, tho' in my better judgment I beleive your life is the special care of Divine providence, and I hope will yet be prolonged for a blessing to many.

Mrs. Newton delivered your letter at Mrs. Godfroys. The answer is, that the lodgings are yours upon your terms, and will be ready at your time.

I delegated this business to Mrs. Newton, that I might be more at leisure to attend to the important business of the day. Accordingly, I mounted your horse and rode a little beyond the house you told me was Mr. Rooke's. I went and returned very softly, and was greatly pleased with the prospect of the island, the sea, and the shore westwards towards Poole. My time, thoughts, and prayer were much employed about the bride and bridegroom, and the families now so nearly allied. May the Lord, the God of the families of His people, crown the alliance with His blessing to all concerned in it. I could moralize on the occasion, as I did in a letter I wrote to Mr. Samuel Thornton on his marriage. But I could say nothing that is new, nothing but what is well known. I beg, however, you will present my congratulation and Mrs. Newton to my Lord and Lady Balgony and to Mrs. Thornton. I am now rather an old man, and have never been much acquainted with the higher walks of life. But I have much to be thankful for with respect to the comforts of domestic life upon a smaller scale. I believe no situation in life can afford perfect happiness, but that they are likely to be most happy, who seek and depend upon the Lords blessing, and are most devoted to His service.

I am not likely to grow hoarse with preaching here, or to be ask'd to preach at all. But I am Mr. Ettys chapel[ain], and expound to the family every evening. Mr. Gilpin was here yesterday. He is an amiable agreeable man, but nothing particular passed at the visit. We are to return his visit on Monday next.

I shall rejoyce to see you next week as you propose, and am glad Dr. Conyers will come with you, as my time will then be drawing short.

With Mrs. Newtons best respects and Elizas, I remain, my dear sir, your most obedient and obliged servant,   JOHN NEWTON.

Mr. Etty and the two ladies desire me to mention their respects to you.

John Thornton, Esquire.

331. WILHELMINA, COUNTESS OF LEVEN AND MELVILLE, to ALEXANDER, LORD BALGONIE, her son—His approaching marriage.

August 10th, [1784].

MY DEAR BALGONIE,—This is to bid you adew at London. Hope you'll have left it before another could reach. Kiss the young wife for me, and tell her I wish her as happy as you can do, and mean always to contribute all in my power towards it. Tell her I am not good at making a show upon any occasion, even where my heart is most interested, that she may not be surprized when I do not utter any many fine speeches. She must consider me as her Scotch mother, and sincere freind ; therefore, may trust me upon every occasion, and be persuaded that I will consider every word and action with a partial eye—which, alas ! with regard to my own freinds, has ever been a failing of mine. I shall think of you all Thursday.

Wednesday—The above was intended for the post yesterday, but finding that Wednesday was not a post day, and that we have a servant going to Edinburgh to-morrow, delayed sending letters till then. This is our fast day. We have heard 3 excellent sermons. Wish we could improve such a blessing. We think to drink your health at the dinner on Monday, where the ministers, you know, conveen. Mr. Lyon, Glamis, paid us a visit of thanks yesterday. A very good young man I dare say, and well behaved. Had an excellent prayer at night. Mr. Thomsons is to be proposed to the heritors to-morrow, but your father will tell you this.

Adeiu, my dear batchelor. Wish I was with you, yet better absent. My strength is too small for such interesting scenes. My heart sympathizes with and pitys the worthy parents, as it must be a hard pull. My best wishes attend all. No letters yesterday. It is realy wrong. Lady Balgonie's dressing room will be very empty, but we think it is better she should have the ordering of some things for it to her own taste. Indeed, I do not know properly what it should have. Once more, my dear Balgonie, adieu. I hope the church ceremony will be easier gone thorough than you expect. It is realy not easy to me to think of it.

This day exceeding warm—much needed, indeed. The season here has been cold of late, to a degree very uncommon, and every thing backward.

I cannot conclude without one additional word of advice, and, at same time, express my hopes, that whatever you have been, or done, that it is now your firm intention, by the help of God! (without whom you can do nothing) to live soberly, righteously, and godly in this evil world; to have your conversation as becometh the gospel, which uniformly hath appeared unto all men, teaching them that, denying ungodliness and worldly lusts, they should live soberly, etc. etc. Self denial is a Christian duty—an indispensible one—tho little known or practised in our——, what shall I call it? Christian or unchristian land. I have wrote this almost in the dark.

Lord Balgonie.

332. DAVID, EARL OF LEVEN AND MELVILLE, to ALEXANDER, LORD BALGONIE, his son—Marriage of the latter with Miss Thornton.

Wednesday, August 18th, [1784].

MY DEAR SON,—The Clapham packets arrived yesterday. May God Almighty pour down his best blessings on you and your wife, and may you long enjoy together much happiness. I have wrote to Lady Balgonie to assure her of my tender affection.

I have received copies of the contract and entail, and with pleasure observe the marginal notes, which shall be particularly acknowledged in my letter to Mr. Thornton.

Sundays post brought me your letter of the 10th. Your accounts of the presentation give me very great pleasure, and I heartily thank you. After having wrote to the heritors, I find that they are by no means under promise to Mr. B., that is Mr. Fidler and Capt. Lindsay, who are hearers, and Mrs. Bethune. The two first have expressed a desire to hear Mr. Thomson, who I have wrote for. The only 2 elders exclaim against Mr. Paton, as does all the parish. There are other 2 elders, Mr. B. himself, a nominal one, and an old, infirm, deaf creature, who is not able to officiate.—Ever, my dear son, your most faithfull and affectionate father,   LEVEN.

P.S.—The first announcing of this happy event was to the clergy after dinner on Monday, where the joy was very general.

Direct the inclosed to Banff; I dont know his address, or where he is.

333. GEORGE, SIXTH EARL OF NORTHESK, Admiral, to his nephew, ALEXANDER, LORD BALGONIE. Kinross, 16th September 1784.

Kinross, Red Lyon Inn,
Thursday, 7 o'clock P.M.   September 16th, [17]84.

DEAR LORD BALGONIE,—In obediance to your lordships request, I have the honor to inform your lordship, etc., that after a thorough survey of the road (Lady Mary Anne Carnegie and the noble Captain, navy) on horse and mare back, surveying without board, and the old admiral looking sharp out ahead and on each how, and we hereby certifie and declare that the road is a good road and nothing to pay. We arriv'd safe and sound here at 3 o'clock, dined well, fine troutts, etc. etc. etc., tho no small shoulders of mutton. Evening, a pleasant voyage too and from the famous island, alas, Queen Mary of Scotland's prison; but her charms and address procured her escape, tho, hard to tell, only from one prison to another, and so we say no more on so tragical a tale. As to news (tho' have not consulted the barber), a sister of Mr. Grahams (Kinross) to be married next week to a Captain Park (India sea service), so a merry meeting, etc. etc., and we hope and believe it may bee. The best respects of this company wait and attend the family at Melvill House, and believe me to be with truth, affection, and esteem, dear Lord Balgonie, most, etc. etc. etc.,   NORTH-EAST.

Lord Balgonie.

To the right honourable the Lord Balgonie, Melvill House, Cupar, Fife.

334. THE REV. JOSHUA GILPIN to JOHN THORNTON, Esq.—Death of Rev. John Fletcher of Madeley.

Madeley, 19th August 1785.

DEAR SIR,—I have 2 motives for troubling you with this letter. The first is gratitude for your continued kindness to my father, and truly I am at a loss to say anything suitable to my feelings on this occasion. What joy will it give me when I return with the talents in my hand which you have now so generously afforded us. But I have a second motive, and a melancholy one it is, for writing at this time to acquaint you with the death of my spiritual father, John Fletcher, who died on Sunday evening last. My heart is so dejected that I can scarcely speak on the subject. He had enjoy'd a much better state of health lately than for several years past, and was enabled to go thro' his duty without feeling any symptom of his old complaiut, so that we had some reason to hope for a long continuance of his valuable labors. But all our expectations are now blasted at once by a sudden stroke. A violent putrid fever has raged much, and been very fatal of late in this neighbourhood. Mr. F. was entreated not to throw himself in the way of danger, but no danger cou'd keep him from the doors of the sick. He was a constant attendant on their death-beds, till the same dreadful disease confin'd him to his own. On the evening of Thursday, the 4th, he spent some time in visiting infected houses about two miles from his home. He then preach'd to a number of people in a small room, and after being excessively heated, return'd home on foot thro' a very heavy rain. It is no wonder he was immediately seiz'd with a violent cold. The two following days dangerous symptoms appear'd, but he wou'd suffer no help to be call'd in. His soul was kept in perfect peace. On Sunday morning he was worse in body, but strong in spirit. I entreated him to suffer me to stay at Madeley instead of going to my own church, but he wou'd not permit it. That day's work made his case remediless. Surely he had some presentiment of that Sunday's labor being his last. He went up to the house of God to magnify His mercy. " How excellent is Thy mercy, O God " (part of his text). It was sacrament day ; and as he approach'd the altar with faltering steps, he cryd out, in an animated tone, " Here, I hide myself under the wings of mercy." The whole sermon was peculiarly awful. Mrs. F. and some others attempted to lead him out of church, but he burst from them into his pulpit, exclaiming there, "We confer not with flesh and blood." How often he appear'd exhausted and fainting during his last service, which continu'd about 4 hours, will never be wip'd away from the remembrance of his people. The next morning he seem'd a little reviv'd, but soon relaps'd again. On Tuesday we insisted on sending for a skillful apothecary, who gave but little hope of his patient. He grew weaker dayly, but his soul was constantly rejoicing in God. While he could speak, this short sentence dwelt on his tongue, and was an answer to every question we ask'd, "God is Love." He substituted a motion of his hand for the same expression, against the time in which his voice should fail, and he continu'd to use it as often as he look'd upon us. He was speechless for more than two days, to our unspeakable grief. He preach'd only by his patience and resignation, which were wonderfully conspicuous thro' the whole of his illness. On Sunday, 14th, while preparing to set forward to my own church, I was sent for again, and found him in a dying state. I determin'd not to leave him while he continu'd in this world. It was with unutterable anguish that I stood over my dear friend, and yet there was something in his appearance that consol'd my agitated heart. He continu'd till ½ after 10 in the evening, and then fell asleep without a sigh. Mrs. F., tho' deeply affected, was not absent from his bed a single moment. She still suffers greatly. May the Comforter return and wipe away all tears from her eyes. Yesterday we committed his poor remains to the earth. Oh! how sad a day was it to me! How did his sorrowful people press upon one another to get a last look! Every circumstance so reminded me of past scenes, that I was wholly lost in a flood of sorrow. He always insisted there shou'd be no funeral pomp or order at his burial. We remember'd his words, and bore him to his grave in a plain oaken coffin, without any nominal mourners. Indeed, many of his dear friends and myself wish'd to follow him close, but when we got into the church yard, thousands of his sad parishioners, with tears and loud bursts of sorrow, throng'd about their dead pastor, and divided us from his bier. It was a solemn and affecting time, and I trust his death spoke as loud and effectually to some as his life had done to others. And now what will become of this poor deserted place? I fear the day of visitation, which has lasted 26 years, is now past. One circumstance is truly distressing, that several valuable works, scarcely half compleated, must be totally suppress'd. I might have written a much longer and more full account of his last scenes and of our extreme sorrow, but my heart is so much dejected that I can add no more, but that I am, dear sir, your afflicted and greatly oblig'd humble servant and poor debtor,   JOSHUA GILPIN.

It would have given me great happiness to have paid my respects as you lately pass'd through Madeley, but I knew not that our village had been honor'd by such a visitant untill you was gone from it many a mile.

To John Thornton, Esq., Clapham, Surrey.

335. SAMUEL THORNTON to ALEXANDER, LORD BALGONIE—Death of Mrs. Thornton, Lady Balgonie's mother.

London, 14 November 1785.

MY LORD,—Your sundry letters after receipt of the express and that of my sisters to me were all duely received on Friday last, and it gave us all much satisfaction to hear that she had not suffer'd more by the melancholy tidings we sent and which you had so properly communicated.

It was Henry's own act to send off the express instantaneously, of which my father would otherways have consider'd a little; indeed I perused and approved it, as I thought my two letters might induce you to set out as I meant they should have done. It appeared to me when they were written that my brothers had perhaps varied in their accounts, and lest you should not know what to make of them it was better for me to write decisively.

As things were order'd by Providence that you could not have been up in time, it was well that you did not set out; had it happened that you had staid in London this summer as you once hinted to me, it would have been very providential as affording Lady Balgonie the last opportunity of her mothers society and would therein have doubtless been a satisfaction.   I really, however, believe that my mother had nothing particular to communicate, but what she may have done by letter, which I mentioned to Jenny for her satisfaction.

We had yesterday a very affectionate funeral sermon from Mr. Urwick on 13 Acts and 36 verse, of which I may send you the heads another opportunity.   I now enclose you one of Watts's odes which she got my brother Robert to read to her a little before her dissolution, and which was sang in the parlour after her decease.

Mr. Bentley made mention of the event yesterday at Camberwell, as has been done at many other places, and I have the satisfaction of saying that we have seen a great number of very sincere mourners and many of them much affected.   Mr. and Mrs. Bewicke, and their son and daughter, were at the meeting yesterday, and all the servants of both families, with many other extra attendants, which made us very full.   I have had a very affectionate card from Dr. Trotter, desiring his particular compliments to you and Lady B.   Mr. Jonas Hanway has also sent the same.

Mr. Wilberforce and his family are come from abroad, and paid us a visit on Friday ; he looks but very thin tho' [he] thinks himself better.

Our cousin, Captain Shore Milnes, was married to Miss Bentinck (niece of the Duke of Portland) on Saturday ; we have just sent our congratulations, and shall go to see them if they stay in town.

We conclude from your letters that you will not now travel much before Christmas ; when the time is fixed you will doubtless let us know, and if it is more agreable to you to come to Clapham before you go, I repeat we shall be ready to receive you, or my father has said the same, if Lady B. would like better to go to his house.   The coach horses will be in readiness against you come up, and as to a coachman I do not fear finding one easily at the time, but can be enquiring if you will mention what you gave your last.

My wife joins with me in best respects to all your household, and I beg you will believe me, yours affectionately,   S. THORNTON.

336. THE REV. JOHN BERRIDGE to MRS. WILBERFORCE—A friendly letter.

Everton, 28 March 1788.

DEAR MADAM,—I thought the matter had been well settled before I left Blackheath, that no coffee or chocolate should be sent to Everton ; but a parcel of both found its way thither before me, and sent, I suppose, by your private order. To you, therefore, I must return thanks for this unexpected favour. If it be pleasant to receive a favour from a living friend, how much more from the dying Saviour, whose gifts are purchased with his blood, and come as free as air, and sweet as light, when the heart is prepared to receive them. You are happy in a share of these gifts, which have opened your heart, and made you ready to communicate, and to feel the greater blessedness in giving than receiving. You have been active in the Lord's work, as far as you could, to him be the praise, and are now come to the Christian's latter stage, suffering work, the harder part of the two; but grace can make hard things easy. You see, no doubt with thankfulness, the Lord's mercy in giving faithful servants to wait upon you, and sending faithful ministers to pray and converse with you; but chiefly is his mercy shown in giving you a calm, composed spirit, with tokens of his love, and a sense of his presence, to enable you to bear a long affliction, and heavy pain at times, without repining. Nothing makes the Christian meek and mellow, like a furnace, when blown and sanctifyd with grace. It brings a crucified look and temper, and prints the Saviour on the soul, and stamps him on the conduct. Grace appears with glorious lustre in afflictions undergone with sweet resignation: not my will but thine be done. These trials will be over presently. Jesus says, tarry for me, lo, I come quickly, when I will become your everlasting light, and your days of mourning shall be ended. One hour spent above will make you quite forget all earthly sorrow; and the prospect of eternal joy before you will fill your soul with inexpressible delight. In the mean time, your work is to lay still, and may everlasting arms be underneath you, neither wishing for life nor for death, but calmly waiting for the Lords pleasure; if it be a restoration to health, that it may redound to Gods glory; if a release from sin and sorrow, to your own eternal blessedness. And now, dear madam, I commend you to the care of the Good Shepherd; may his presence be with you, and his dying love cheer you, living or dying; so prayeth daily your affectionate servant,   JOHN BERRIDGE.

For Mrs. Wilberforce, Blackheath, near London.

337. THE REV. JOHN NEWTON to MRS. WILBERFORCE—Reminiscences, and notes of his travels.

Weston, near Olney, Bucks, 22 July 1788.

MY DEAR MADAM,—You are not farther from my thoughts at this distance than when I was in London. Indeed the place reminds me of you, and brings to my remembrance things that occurrd in past years when we were favord with

your company at Olney. Your first visit was in the year 65, with Mrs. Conyers.
She and Mary Lambert, Betty Abraham, and several other of the Olney people
whom you knew, have been long since removed into a world [where] they have done
with sin, sorrow, and pain for ever. Your time of dismission is probably not far
distant, and I am following, for tho' I am still favoured with good health, I grow
older apace. It is well. Our times are in the Lord's hands, and our part is only
to pray for daily supplies of grace, that we may glorify him by our services or
sufferings according to his will, and wait with faith and patience his appointed
hour of calling us home. Then every evil shall cease, and all our best desires shall
be abundantly satisfied, and, so says the Apostle, We shall be ever with the Lord.

Who can expound these words? We must die before we can understand
them. At present we little know what is included in being with the Lord. But
we know that when he is pleased to be with us, and to lift up the light of his
countenance upon our souls, one such hour is worth a thousand of the worlds
hours, yet here there are many abatements. The vile body debases and pollutes
our best services and our best enjoyments, as it is sinful, and restrains them as it
is weak. It is needful that the Lord should proportion not only our trials but
our comforts, to our weakness. We cannot bear much of either. When Moses
desired to see his face he said, No man can see me and live. Here he shews
him by glances, as it were, in part, and as thro' a glass—he communicates his
goodness by means and ordinances, and by intervals—there is a vail between us
and the Sun of our souls, or we should faint and die beneath the full brightness
of his beams. But hereafter every vail and interposing cloud will be removed,
and we shall see him face to face, see him as he is, see him where he is. Thus
we shall be with the Lord. It was a good time with Peter when he said, It is
good to be here, and with John when he contemplated the prints of the nails in
his Saviours hands and feet, and cried out in a rapture of devotion and love, My
Lord and my God, but they were still in the body. To be with the Lord, and to
behold him on the throne of his glory, will be unspeakably more than any of his
saints were capable of in this world.

And when we are thus with the Lord it will not be for a visit, and then to
return to a state of warfare again. No, the Apostle says, We shall be *ever* with the
Lord. The inhabitants of the heavenly city shall go out no more ; their sun
shall no more go down ; it will be a long, an everlasting day, an eternity of
wonder, love, joy, and praise. Well then may our Lord say to us, as he does by
his word, Fear none of the things that thou shalt suffer, when he has promised
to enable those who trust him to be faithful unto death, and then to give them a
crown of endless life.

We came hither by the way of Bedford, where we staid 3 days with Mr. and Mrs. Livius, in which time I paid 5 or 6 visits to my dear friend Symonds. His family is well, but he himself is very poorly, seems much altered since I saw him in London, and I think is not likely to live long. He is resigned and pretty chearful. He still preaches. I calld likewise to see his daughter Bettsy, now known by the name of Mrs. Emory. She seems comfortably settled, and they say she has a very good husband, but I did not see him. The Lord brought us hither in safety, and preserved us from any alarm on the road. We found Mrs. Unwin and Mr. Cowper in pretty good health (they desire me to present their respects and best wishes), and the journey agreed well with Mrs. Newton. The Olney people are glad to see us, but our residing at Weston makes it rather fatiguing to her to visit and call upon them all, and yet not one, if possible, must be omitted, especially of the poorer sort : we wish to comfort them, but we shall grieve them if any think we neglect them.

Next week I purpose seeing my Northamton friends for 2 or 3 days. I have not fixd the time for my return to London yet, but think I shall be in my own pulpit the third Sunday in August at farthest. I thank God I am comfortable abroad, but home is home still.

Mrs. Newton and Betsy join me in affectionate respects to you and to any of your family or friends who may occasionally be with you—Mrs Bewicke or Miss Hannan, particularly to Miss Maria.

I wrote last week to Mr. Thornton, but beg you to mention me respectfully to him when you see him.—I am, my dear madam, your obliged and obedient servant,   JOHN NEWTON.

Mrs. Wilberforce, Blackheath, Kent.

338. HENRY THORNTON, M.P., to ALEXANDER, LORD BALGONIE—Mr. John Thornton's illness.

London, 21 Sep[tember] 1790.

DEAR BALGONIE,—I have a short letter of yours to answer, but I think of delaying to send your account till Robert comes to town, which will be in a few days, when I will desire him to settle the money transaction you bid me remind him of, which he had not time to do before.

My father has been poorly for some little time, and a few days ago the account which Samuel sent me to the seaside was such as to bring me up again, but I thank God he is now tolerably, and I feel no scruple in going again for a few days to the sea.

He is, however, so much broken without any one very particular complaint, that I cannot help considering him as really declining. Under these circumstances you will not be surprised at our expressing a wish that you should make a journey to London this year; and indeed it might be well to do it rather sooner than usual. We will keep you and my sister fairly informed how he is, and if anything should arise to give occasion for a hasty message on this, or indeed any other account, I wish you to observe that I can take the liberty with Mr. Simpson (William Simpson, Esqr.), cashier of the Royal Bank, who is always on the spot, to make him the channel of conveying any intelligence.

At Newcastle and Stilton you will always remember that we shall accustom ourselves to direct to you on the road. Do not imagine I am making these observations on account of my now expecting to have occasion for alarming you. I really trust my good father will go quietly on in his old way, tho' a little more feeble, and will yet for some time continue to have his capacity for usefulness, and to furnish us with that good example which he has so long done; but it is better in every event to adjust such little matters as I have touched upon.—Believe me, dear Balgonie, yours always very affectionately,   H. THORNTON.

Lord Balgonie, by Edinburgh.

339. MR. WILLIAM COWPER, the poet, to   THORNTON, Esq.—A short poem
on the late John Thornton.

Weston Underwood, November 16, 1790.

DEAR SIR,—Lady Balgonie having done me the honour to express a wish in a letter of hers to Mr. Bull, that I would write something in remembrance of your late excellent father, I have endeavour'd to express my sense of that honour by doing it as soon and as well as a violent cold and my necessary attention to my Homer, now in the press, would permit.

Should the lines be favour'd with your approbation, you will oblige me by forwarding them to her ladyship, to whom I beg you to present my most respectful compliments, and to believe me, dear sir, with much esteem, yours,

WM. COWPER.

Mrs. Unwin sends best compliments.

340. JOHN ERSKINE, D.D., minister of Old Greyfriars, Edinburgh, to ALEXANDER, LORD BALGONIE—The loyalty of the seceding ministers.

Lauriston, 17 June 1794.

MY DEAR LORD,—Many thanks for your kind letter. I am concerned to hear you have been indisposed, but hope it is now over. I should be sorry you took any personal trouble as to the parcel for Dr. Rippon. It would suffice to drop him a line, and direct him to call at your lodgings for the trifle.

The present crisis is truly alarming. Indeed, Lord Howes victory, and the discoveries made both at London and here, call for our warmest gratitude. But surely we should rejoyce with trembling. Depraved as mankind is, I could not have suspected any numbers in this country were so lost to religion and humanity as to frame such horrid plans of massacre and desolation ; and the discovering none of the deadly weapons at Glasgow, Paisly, Perth, or Dundee, where, from the proportion of the disaffected, probably they could not be wanting, is, I'm afraid, a proof that much of the intended evil yet remains unknown. It also gives me pain that, thro' unjust suspicions artfully raised by interested, party-spirited, and malicious men, some of the greatest worth have been keeped out of stations where they might have been highly usefull to government. The heritors of Falkirk solicited the presentation for Mr. Robinson of Gargunnock, a pious and popular minister; but they were disappointed, it is generaly thought, thro' slanders of Mr. R. as a democrate being sent to administration, tho', in fact, no minister in Stirlingshire had been more bold and warm in recommending loyalty and good order. Was Mr. Wilson the person presented as zealous for our happy constitution, which, from his intimacy with Dr. Priestly, many doubt, yet for want of popularity, he would not be of half the use to government. Some of the seceding clergy have nobly stood forth and recommended subjection to rulers from the press as well as the pulpits, particularly Shanks at Jedburgh, Young at Hawick, who has just published essays on interesting subjects—government, revolutions, etc.—which is thought one of the ablest political pieces of Scots production, and Sheriff of Kirkaldie, whose address is in a more old fashioned stile. Mr. Sheriff, in a late sermon in Mr. Hall's meeting house, observed that ascending to heaven, there he found beautiful order and subordination, God ruling supreme, under him cherubims and seraphims, angels, etc. Descending into hell, even there was a prince of the devils. Travelling to every quarter of the globe he found authority and subjection. Coming home to his closet, and consulting his Bible, he found repeated precepts that every man should be subject to the higher powers, but could not discern one trace of modern equality. Some of the people both of the burgess and anti-burgess oath seceders, are undoubtedly chagrined. They observe that soon after the first seceding ministers had been deposed by the General Assembly the rebellion 1745 took place, when no party was more zealous and active in support of king and constitution than theirs, and yet that not only the marks of favour bestowed on papists and non-jurants have not been showen to them, but measures pursued as to settlements which put them to the expence of paying their own teachers. I believe, however, the number of malecontents among them bears a small proportion to their numbers.

With kind and respectful compliments to Lady Balgonie, I remain, my lord, your lordships affectionate and obedient humble servant,   JOHN ERSKINE.

Right honourable Lord Balgonie, Spring Gardens.

341. MRS. LESLIE (probably wife of Hon. David Leslie) to LADY BALGONIE— Her Irish experiences.

Cookstown, Wednesday, November 22d, 1796.

MY DEAREST LADY BALGONIE,—Tho' I address this to my lord, I know he will have the goodness to pardon the Irishism, as my last was to his lordship ; and since that, I have been favoured with your kind letter, which was a real treat ; we go on pretty well here, tho' the peoples minds in general seem seized with a kind of panic. Several families have left Cookstown, amongst whom, to my great regret, were Mrs. and Miss Stuarts, daughters and wife to a member of the Irish parliament, who is one of the most gentlemanlike men I ever saw. They burnt the summer house in their garden, and wrote anonymous letters to Mrs. S. threat'ning her own life and the lives of her children, so that she was seized with hysterics, and they made a precipitate retreat to Dublin, bag and baggage, the day after we came here. Every night some bodys house or other in the town or neighbourhood is robbed of fire arms ; but all the inhabitants are not equally timerous. A lady who called here to-day said she was learning to fire off a pistol that she might shoot at the United Irishmen. Mr. Leslie says I drew my chair a little way farther from her ; to be sure I thought her a little of an Amazon. Every body is kind and civil to us, and we have got tolerable lodgings here, which Mr. L. prefers greatly to Stewartstown ; we have a parlour with 4 windows, a bedroom with 3, and a dressing-room, and servants place ; but they are very dear, being £1, 4s. a week. However, government allows five shillings of that and fuel, with one pound of candle, which last is rather short allowance. I have got a Roman Catholic maid of all work, who hitherto does pretty well, with some of my assistance and advice in the cooking way; we had 4 officers at dinner yesterday, and you would have smiled to have seen how I bestirred myself, and after all so many things went wrong that I was obliged to laugh them off, tho' I could much easier have cried; but in these cases, putting on a good face on the matter is half the battle.

I am afraid poor Lady Ruthven will be very uneasy about Lord Ruthven, as I see the firing is begun at Gibraltar from our people, and I likewise fear our dear kind friends at Melville and Balgonie will be uneasy about us from the accounts which come from [this]; but indeed we are far from being uncomfortable, and I believe and trust that God will be with us and protect us; for my own share I feel much more easy to be on the spot than I should have felt at a distance with my husband here. I was at the Presbyterian meeting here on Sunday, which the people told me was completely filled with United Irishmen. Mr. Leslie says I want to make friends of the mammon of unrighteousness; but I hope I have a better motive, as their minister was an excellent one; gave us a Gospel sermon (which I have not heard in Ireland before), and pray'd heartily for the king. Tho' I must own his audience were terrific looking figures, mostly all men. The English clergyman is a great puppy, nephew to Lord Inniskillen, and so violent and bloody minded that he quite disgusted me from going to church. We have many visitors, and I have great funds of laughter in store if ever it shall please God that we meet again. I long to hear again of dear dear Lully. I hope her eyes are now much better, and that all the rest, with my lord and you, are as well and as happy as my heart wishes you. I have got no new bulls, except that one lady talking of another assured me "She was a United Irishman." My husband is made a justice of peace by the commander-in-chief, which gives me great uneasiness, only I hope if it please God he will not be called to act as such. He jokes and says his Scotch friends will mention their relation, "The Irish Justice," with much veneration. I smile when they call him "your worship."

The right honourable Lord Balgonie, Custom House, Edinburgh, via Donaghadee.

342. ROBERT THORNTON, Esq., M.P., to his sister, LADY BALGONIE—Visit to Admiral de Winter after his defeat at Camperdown.

27 October [1797].

MY DEAR SISTER,—I have just been at the Russia court, where we have come to a very liberal resolution in favor of Miss Meggotts. The Russia company have agreed to give 200 gs. towards the support of the young ladies. I left a frank with Mr. Foster, the governor, that he might acquaint them with the particulars.

Last Monday I went with George Eyre and Henry Bewicke to the Nore to see the ships that were come in of Lord Duncan's fleet. I went on board the Venerable, the gallant admiral's ship, and eat a cold repast and drank some wine with Admiral de Winter, who was prisoner on board. Mrs. Lutwidge and a very pleasant lady from her house at Sheerness went with us. Captain Fairfax was on board, who made every thing very pleasant to our party. I took with me an introduction to Lord Duncan from Mr. Elphinstone, which I delivered on the road, as he was going up to London with Lord Hood. I afterwards eat a 2d dinner with Sir Richard Onslow at Admiral Lutwidges, who gave a full account of this very severe engagement. He has 2 admirals on board his ship the Monarch, which we sailed round, and saw the dreadful damages she has sustained. We had not time to go on board her, tho' Admiral Onslow particularly asked us. We also sailed round the Powerful, Captain Drury's ship, who fought in the most gallant manner. These were the only 3 then arrived ; the Dutch prizes were not come in.

Admiral de Winter is a very well looking man about 40 years of age—as tall as Admiral Duncan, with a very spirited countenance, and manners the most pleasant and easy. He talked pretty good English and French with us. He went over the deck of the Venerable and shewed the damages his shot had made, and hoped it would never be said that he had given away his ship. He desired I would admire two little pug dogs that were taken prisoners with him. He played a rubber at whist the evening he was taken, and frequently since with Admiral Duncan. De Winter fought his ship most desperately ; every man on the quarter deck but himself was killed or wounded, and he was obliged to strike the colours with his own hands, walking over heaps of dead men. I saw little Watson on board, Lord Northesk's nephew, who was very well, and is a very fine lad, and said he knew you.

The Venerable was wounded chiefly in her hull, as the object of the Dutch admiral was to sink her, and we saw symptoms of the most dreadful slaughter, tho' the wounded were taken out. Sir Richard Onslow told us that when all the men were killed at one of the guns of his ship, a woman came up and loaded ; she soon had her leg shot off. A little boy, 10 years old, also on board the Monarch, had his hand shot, and could hardly be persuaded to go below to get it dressed. After they had made him get it dressed, he returned to one of the guns, and soon had his leg shot off. He is getting better and is in great spirits, and describes the action as if himself, some other little boys, and the woman mentioned, had gained the victory.

Sir Richard Onslow told us one man with him at first was shy of fighting and his comrades threw him down the hatchway.

Captain Drury, a very gallant officer, took a singular sailors method of calling upon his men to do their duty. The Monarch had been a most notorious ship at the time of the mutiny, and he had never spoken to his men since, nor been on any terms with them. When they came in sight of the Dutch, Captain Drury called all his men on deck, and said—You are all a pack of scoundrels and rascals, and hardly deserve the name of Englishmen. You are a disgrace to humanity, and you know I have never spoken to you. I have flogged you unmercifully, and meant to continue flogging you. I dont know whether you are cowards or not; but, he said, I must further add, there is the Haarlem, a 74 gun ship, along side of you, if you make her strike in 10 minutes I think I must forgive you, and we must be friends again. On this they flew like lions and tygers to the guns—he took out his watch—and they made the Haarlem strike in ten minutes. This story was told us at Admiral Lutwidges.

After dinner, while Sir Richard Onslow was with us, his captain came in, and said they had had a curious adventure on board the Monarch.

The 2 Dutch admirals made a complaint that some of the Dutch prisoners had stolen some of their knives and forks and spoons. As it was their own men, the captain desired the Dutch admirals themselves woud search into the business and they shoud have a rope, if necessary, to hang as many as they pleased. When he came away they had been 3 hours employed in searching for their spoons.

I rather think, if I can find leisure, I shall go again Monday next, to see the Dutch prizes and the grand sight of manning the yards, saluting, etc., etc., etc., when the king will be there. It is expected to be the finest thing of the kind ever exhibited. Samuel talks of going with me. He had a slight cold, or woud have gone before.

I took the East India Company's yatch with me. This has intervened, and I must hereafter give you some further account of our Welsh travels.—Yours affectionately, in haste,   R. TH.

Remember me to Balgonie.

Viscountess Balgonie, at Balgonie, near Edinburgh.

343. Mr. George Chalmers, author of "Caledonia," to Lord Balgonie—
Progress of his book.

Office for Trade, Whitehall, 20 April 1802.

My Lord,—I have had the pleasure of receiving the letter which your lordship had the goodness to write me on the 5 curt.

I owe your lordship a good many thanks for your kind inquiries about the forwardness of my great work on Caledonia, and still more for your wish to give me further assistance.

By constant perseverance I have certainly made a great progress. I am now bringing it forward for the press. But even this will require much time and attention from a man who has much public and private business to attend to. I mean to press it forward, however, as it begins to hang heavy on my shoulders. If I should want any additional information from Fife I shall freely apply to so good and helpful a friend as your lordship always has been.

Pray give me leave to inquire if my Lord Leven has any manuscript collections that would throw any light on the history of Scotland. If he has, I should regard a communication of them as a very particular favour.

I thank your lordship for sending me Dr. Jamieson's prospectus of a Scotish Dictionary. He had before written to me, and I had engaged to help him though I differ with him in some points of antiquity.

I appear from the inclosed receipt, which I had forgotten, to have paid for your lordship to Malet Duvan, 1½ guineas.

We are in momentary expectation of the ratification. The heralds have orders to be in waiting to make the proclamation of peace. Every body is preparing for illuminations, and every one is happy.

Accept of my best wishes, being, with unalterable esteem, your lordships most faithful and obedient servant,   Geo. Chalmers.

Right honourable Lord Balgony.

344. Alexander, Earl of Leven and Melville, to John Francis Erskine, afterwards Earl of Mar—Recommending Melville House as a winter residence.[1]

Balgony Castle, 16 July 1802.

Dear Sir,—At the moment I was going to express my regret for not having had the pleasure of seeing you and your family here, which I was led to hope for from

[1] Original in the Charter-chest of the Earl of Mar and Kellie at Alloa.

a note left here by your servant, directed to Miss Erskine, I have very accidentally heard you paid some visits to Lesly House, with a view to take it for a residence. Let me then intreat you, with as much disinterestedness as you can expect from me on such a subject, to pause in concluding a bargain for Lesly till you look at Melville, where it will be a particular gratification to me to have a person of your taste and turn for improvement for its tennant, and where, barring the advantage of the two streams at Lesly, and perhaps the article alone of situation, you will find, on examination, Melville House a preferable residence. As a furnish'd house —Lesly is it not—Melville you will find far more so in point of accommodation. They are both fit for a large family ; and as I think you pass your winters in the country, Melville is warm, early, dry and sheltered, whereas Lesly is well known to be cold, wet, damp, and late. The rides, too, at Melville have all the properties of the place as above described, and of late the country around here has been opened up by very capital lines of gravel turnpike roads, and the neighbourhood you will soon find abounding in game. Only favor me by seeing it—and let me know when Lady Leven and I can have the honor to meet you there—if not too late, say the 28 or 29, or sooner, if you have the goodness to name it.

Lady Leven unites with me in offering every good wish to you and the young ladies.—I am, sir, at all times, with true regard, your faithfull h[umble] s[ervant],

345. DAVID, LORD BALGONIE, to his father, ALEXANDER, EARL OF LEVEN AND MELVILLE—Account of an attack on the French convoy at Rosas.

H.M.S. Ville de Paris, off Roses, November 2d, [1809].

MY DEAR FATHER,—The French convoy from Toulon and one of the storeships had run for protection under the batteries of Roses ; it is the place Lord Cochrane defended so gallantly, and the troops were well aware they would not remain there long without an attack from the British fleet. Every precaution was taken to prevent our success, and since Sunday [they] flattered themselves they were ready for our reception. Lord Collingwood allowed three lieutenants to volunteer, and take three mids with them to any ship of the squadron intending to attack. I chose the Topaze, Captain Hope, who gave me an excellent boat, and nineteen famous fellows under my command ; we were ordered to board the storeship with our division of the boats, which was done about a quarter past four in the morning, after a row of near four hours from the ships. In ten minutes we carried her with great slaughter on both sides. We wished to bring her out, but the commanding lieutenant thought it of more consequence to finish our job. We therefore proceeded to destroy the convoy, while we burnt the prize. Almost every vessel proved armed, but they were taken one after another, under showers of shot from four batteries. I seized one fellow, who, with the assistance of some boats and Clifford, of the Tigre, who I mentioned to my mother some time since, we brought her out, and was clear of the batteries by six in the morning. In less than two hours there were ten sail burnt and four towed out. The explosions were grander than anything I ever saw. The French must have lost an immense number of men, as we have not taken more than a hundred prisoners, and they had not less than four hundred when the attack began. Some may have swum on shore, as we were close to the batteries. We had between 400 and 500 men in the boats. Our loss, 1 Lieutenant, Tait of the Voluntaire, and 14 men killed, and about forty wounded, most of them severely.

346. The Same to The Same—His promotion.

Gibraltar, December 30th, [1809].

My dear Father,—I have deffer'd writting to you upon my promotion till my brig arrived, and I could give some account of her, but as an opportunity now offers, and she seems determined not to make her appearance, I shall no longer postpone it.

Upon first hearing of it I thanked Lord Mulgrave in a short letter. He hardly deserved it, but it will shew how gratified I was when it arrived. The news here is not very pleasant, and therefore difficult to find the true account. Gerona has at last fallen, and the governor died two days before the capitulation. We have curious accounts of some proposals made by Boney to Ferdinand the 7th ; they, however, will be known in England before this arrives. I have been engaged this forenoon conducting a famous female officer about the Rock and on board the ships. Her name is Augustina Saragossa, who wears three insignias of merit for her gallant conduct in three battles, where she was as often wounded. I would bring you her portrait, but I cannot get it done under 14£. I had a letter yesterday from John, who is in England before this. I was extremely anxious to hear of him, as an officer told me how ill he was. As my outfit will cost me a good deal of money, I must beg you to let me have four or five hundred pounds placed in the hands of Austin, Maude, and Austin to defray it. I will get Purvis's things if possible, and make an auctioneer value them. General Colin Campbell commands here, he is extremely civil, and says he knows you. Give my kind love to all.—Your most affectionate son,   BALGONIE.

Right honourable Earl of Leven and Melville, Melville House, Edinburgh.

347. JANE, DUCHESS OF GORDON, to ALEXANDER, EARL OF LEVEN AND MELVILLE—Regretted she was to leave Ireland.

Phenix Park, August 14, 1810.

I AM most unfortunate, my dear lord ; your son arrived to-day, and to-morrow I leave Ireland for England. With much regret I must give up my loved cottage this year, it is impossible to be there as the building is wet. As that is the case I propose visiting my children's children,—and the most amiable and best of men, the Duke of Richmond, goes to-morrow to shoot, and he regrets much he wont be here when your son returns, but I have recommended him to Lord Harrington. I hope Lady Melvile and your lovely family are in good health. This· is the loveliest country in the world, the most populace, and I believe the happiest if left to themselves, but a few *malignant stars* do much harm. The Richmonds are adored, indeed their publick good and charitable institutions occupies their whole time. He neither grants senecures nor promises. My best wishes to Lady Leven. Poor March at 18 was with Lord Wellington in the last fatal affair. Heaven protect our brave army, but I can see no good can arise from all they can do.—Yours ever, my dear lord, with affection and esteem, etc.   J. GORDON.

Indorsed : Duchess of Gordon.

348. THE HON. WILLIAM LESLIE MELVILLE to DAVID, LORD BALGONIE, his brother—Of his occupations in India.

Commercolly, 1st December 1811.

MY DEAR BROTHER,—I yesterday received a packet of newspapers and pamphlets despatched by you from Portsmouth some time back, and a fleet being just on the point of sailing, I hasten to thank you for the same. I am in a sad solitary station here, about 150 miles from Calcutta, and scarcely ever see a white face, so your packet came particularly apropos, and indeed I know not how to thank you enough for your kindness and attention in thinking of it. You still talk of coming here, I find, but I now apprehend all my hopes of so happy an event are terminated. We have completely expelled the enemy from these seas, and there is not a hostile flag flying to the eastward of the Cape. There has been some tough work at Java, as you will see by the newspapers, but thank God it is all happily over, and in consequence, I suppose, the squadron in these seas will be reduced. One cannot but rejoice at the success of our arms, tho' I feel a little disappointed that I shall not see you. There is an old acquaintance of yours who about a month ago arrived at Calcutta, Mrs. Gowan, quondam Helen Abercrombie, and her husband. They staid with me for the first week after their arrival, and then I most hospitably ran off and left them to shift for themselves. The truth is we are under as strict discipline as you are, and duty very inconveniently summoned me up here. The lady seems as if she would probably give birth to something soon.

I am busy up here superintending some of John Company, my honourable masters commercial concerns, and by the way I do an odd job now and then for his Majesty and your honor. There is a considerable *sunn* (the Indian hemp) concern which I overlook for the king, and pray mention what sort of a character it bears in the navy, a considerable quantity of the rope and canvas used by you naval gentlemen is imported unwrought from this country. I know not what sort of a paymaster you may find his Majesty (God bless him), but not a sous of his money do I see for my trouble. It is all, like a good patriot, for the honor and glory of my country, and the truth is, tho' I dont get it, a handsome allowance is given which as I rise in the service will come to me also. I have not a manufacture up here like folks at home of 50 or 100 people, but by the best accounts I have some 50,000 employed more or less for the Company, and for all my trouble I only get £600 a year ; however, next month I am to have double that allowance and one-tenth part of the trouble and responsibility, and some 15 or 20 years hence, if I live as long, when you are an admiral, I mean to be a country gentleman of moderate fortune, and hope to have realized the wherewithal to give you a good bottle of claret when you visit me, so mind that. In the meantime, suppose you was to take a spouse. John has set, I think, a praiseworthy example to the family, which, however, I don't mean to follow till I get home, for divers good reasons. Robert when he gets seated in a fat living must have something of that sort to help him in the manufacture of gooseberry wine and other delicacies, and you certainly ought to be thinking of this matter.

I hear a good character of your Romulus, but I wish he was not en flute. However, long ere this you must doubtless be Post, on which step I congratulate you, and hope my anticipation may not be ill-founded. Good bye to you, my dear Balgonie, most affectionately yours,   W. L. MELVILLE.

Viscount Balgonie.

349. The Rev. Thomas Chalmers to the Earl of Leven and Melville—
His call to Glasgow.

Kilmany Manse, December 14, 1814.

My Lord,—I am indeed greatly touched by the kind and condescending interest which your lordship is pleased to take in me.

My letter of acceptance was sent off to Glasgow a few days ago, and not without a very painful struggle on my part from the variety of arguments which weighed on each side of the question. I am now in a tumult of tenderness among the regrets of a people whom I love, and from whom a separation will be far more distressing than I at first anticipated.

The consideration respecting my health which your lordship is pleased to notice has not been overlooked by me. I had a consultation with an able physician on this subject and his report was encouraging. Should I find it hurt, however, by the confinement of a town, my views will in all likelihood be directed not to Edinburgh but to the country, and I will have one reason more for looking back with regret on the pureness of the air I now breathe, and on the peacefulness of the valley I am now to abandon. Your lordship's offer to promote my future views will ever be recollected by me with gratitude. I have been the object of much unmerited and unsolicited kindness, and it will go far to alleviate all the regrets I may feel in my future situation that I have not moved a footstep myself for the purpose of obtaining it. There is something wonderful and unexampled indeed in the whole history of the appointment, and if the will of God can be at all collected from the progress of events or from the opinions of his most eminent ministers, I have had much of both to fix my present purpose, and to pour a light over the path of my duty and the leadings of his providence.

May his blessing rest upon your lordship's home and family. May every individual under your lordship's roof experience the rich supplies of his grace and spirit, and be made meet for that happier home where there is no sorrow and no separation.

I beg leave to offer my respectful compliments to my Lady Leven and the other members of your lordship's family.—I am, my lord, your lordship's most obliged and obedient servant,   Thomas Chalmers.

Right honourable Earl of Leven and Melville.

350. GEORGE DEMPSTER, Esq., of Dunnichen, to ALEXANDER, EARL OF LEVEN
AND MELVILLE—Sending the present of a Skibo cow.

Dunnichen, Forfar, 2 January 1815, Monday.

MY DEAR LORD,—I beg leave to offer my respectfull compliments and the very
best wishes of the season to your lordship, to Lady Leven, the Ladys Melville,
and all the family. The bearer of this has also in charge a *Skibo* cow, or more
properly *Cat*, of last years importation. Let it have the run of your ample
domains. It wont be fat, I hope, before it be wanted on the occasion of a
wedding at Melville House; but a lean Sutherland cow is said to be better than
a Smithfield monster for fat. If this little new years gift shall be kindly received,
it will make me very happy.

A rumour of peace with America has reached this place. Should the report
prove true, what a new years gift to the two empires! Believe, my dear lord,
that I have the honour to be, with the most sincere respect and attachment, your
lordships faithfull humble servant,   GEORGE DEMPSTER.

Please mention me kindly to the Reverend Dr.

Right honourable the Earl of Leven and Melville, etc. etc.

P.S.—Just as I was warming the wax to seal this letter, your lordship's letter
of the 27 instant reached me. It has happened to me very often when thinking
of friends I respect, to receive proofs of their not being unmindfull of me. This
is the most recent instance of the truth of that observation. It would seem you
had not only thought of me but knew my thoughts, for I was actually wavering
in my mind and full of doubts if so paultry a new years gift would be taken in
good part. Your letter remov'd all doubts by swelling my gift to five times its
present value. Its chief recommendation is its colour. It may pass for a deer
that has strayed from the herd, and if not doom'd to the *buulk*, would make a
pretty gentle pet for a lady—a pad indeed if the lady lived in Astracan.

351. ZACHARY MACAULAY, Esq., to ALEXANDER, EARL OF LEVEN AND MELVILLE
—Death of the writer's brother, and of Mr. Henry Thornton.

London, 13 April 1815.

MY LORD,—Owing to some inexplicable cause your lordships letter of the
29th of March reached me only the day before yesterday. I am much grieved at
this delay lest I should have appeared to your lordship to have been wanting in
the respect I owe, or insensible to the kindness which dictated your lordships
communication.

I had early heard of the sudden death of my brother in your lordships neighbourhood; but until I heard of that melancholy event, I was not aware that he had been in Fifeshire. He was one of those unhappy men who defeat all the efforts of friends for their benefit, and who had latterly estranged himself from his family; and this may in some measure explain my reasons for having forborne to avail myself of your lordships experienced goodness in giving him an introduction at Melville.

I feel exceedingly indebted to Dr. Marten for his benevolent and Christian offices on this occasion, and should rejoice in any opportunity of testifying my gratitude to him.

We have indeed sustained a loss in dear Mr. Henry Thornton, which is not to be repaired. My individual share in it is unspeakably great. He was and had long been "my guide, philosopher, and friend"—all that the most indulgent parent and the most affectionate brother could have been to me; and every day that has passed since he left us to mourn his loss has only added to my sense of its extent. Mrs. H. Thornton and Marianne have been the admiration of all who have observed. They have shewn in its best form the union of Christian tenderness and Christian resignation.

I have been urging our friend Mr. Wilberforce to give to the world a detailed view of Mr. Henry Thornton's character. I shall continue to urge him. Such an example should not sink into forgetfulness.

I beg to present my very respectful remembrances to Lady Leven and your lordships family, and to your lordship my assurances of unfeigned respect and gratitude.—I have the honour to be, my lord, your lordships obliged, obedient, and faithful servant,   ZACHARY MACAULAY.

The Earl of Leven and Melville.

352. LADY MARY WALKER [or HAMILTON] to her nephew, ALEXANDER, EARL OF LEVEN, etc.—A description of her residence in Jamaica.

June 15, 1815, from the Bank of Newfoundland.

MY DEAR LORD,—I take the advantage of a calm (after a storm which sank one of our ships) to write you this, intending to go on shore at Portsmouth, and the captain has engaged to give it and a turtle for your lordship to the first vessel he shall meet in the river bound for Lieth. Finding I had been so cruelly duped by my trustees (who paid me only four hundred pound per annum), and that since the Court of Chancery had decreed that I should receive my rents myself, that the estate had produced annually three thousand pound, I found by experience that, in the affairs of this lower world, that it is not faith, but the want of it, that saves us.   I determined, at the age of seventy-five, to go out to Jamaica to make myself acquainted with my own affairs, correct abuses, etc.   This voyage has succeeded entirely to my satisfaction; and this year, being a very favorable season, the sugars will make seven thousand pound, and the rum fifteen hundred pound.   The voyage agreed perfectly with me.   I was too grossiere ever to have been sea sick, or to have had the vapours.   I have always endeavour'd to preserve the same degree of spirits in every situation.   My mind is amphibious, and can subsist in different elements.   Of all the beautiful situations I ever saw, I prefer that of Success (the name of the estate).   The house, calculated for the climate, is placed on the side of a hill on a platform, surrounded by orange trees, from which there is a gradual descent of three hundred yards to the sea, which, rounding the grounds, forms an amphitheater, and ships and boats often passing, gives life to the picture.   The hills behind the house are finely wooded, and majestically rise with variety on the unequal summits.   A gully at one side of the house, in which there is a rivulet, becomes a river after rain, and the rushing impetuously of water from the hill over trimendious rocks, forms a most magnificent cascade.   Had I possessed the talent of drawing I should have taken several views, some as wild as those of Salvator Rosa, others placid, and, with the setting sun, worthy of Claude Lorrain.   The estate being on the north side of the island, one can keep themselves tolerably cool ; and I might have been tempted to have remained had I relished the society ; but having had the advantage some years of my life of conversing with men of the first rank of literature, taste, and wit, could not find myself at home with them.   They are a set of modest, inoffensive people, who pretend to no other sense but that of making money.   Every gentilman, from the lowest to the highest, is as solicitous in the pursuit of gain as a tradesman on Cheapside.   The conversation always turns on money.   The moment you name a man you are told what he is worth, the losses he has had, or the proffit he has made.   They eat and drink to excess, to which succeeds loud peals of laughter, vociferous mirth, and knocking on the table.   Their hilarity is a kind of storm, and the most moderate only enjoy a jovial sort of dulness.   I think, of all the places I have seen, one may live there at the smallest expence of wit, as by all rules of economy, the disbursements bearing proportion to the receivings, one ought to lay out very little.   My mind was in a palsy, and its faculties benumbed !   As I cannot now return to France, where I meant to have gone to publish a French book, I shall take a house in London ; but not having had the precaution of chusing my friends young for fear of losing them, I have survived many of them.

I hope your lordship may be able to read this letter.   My writing engine is more like a toothpick than a pen. It has been an ancient inhabitant of the standish, and I verily believe has been subject to no flight since it left its mother's wing. Faithful narrator of the log-book, it has defaced much white paper on dull matters of fact. It can never deviate less from its usual habits than when it enables me to assure you of my esteem, and of my constant wishes for the welfare and prosperity of your family, and that I have the honor to be, my dear lord, your lordships affectionate aunt and obedient humble servant,   M. HAMILTON.

Indorsed : Lady M. Walker, 15 June 1815.

353. ——— LESLIE WALKER, C.B., to his cousin, the EARL OF LEVEN AND MELVILLE—Paris during its occupation by the allied armies.

Paris, Camp aux Champs Elysees, [November 1815].

MY DEAR LORD,—I had the pleasure of receiving your lordship's two kind letters, with another enclosed from Lady Ruthven, two days ago, and I beg leave to assure you that I feel most gratified at the satisfaction therein express'd in so flattering a manner at my promotion ; but observe with concern that both Lady Leven and Lady Jane have been suffering for a considerable time under the pressure of severe indisposition, but hope the latter may derive immediate benefite from a change of air and the advice of a London physician.

My late promotion will not in the least influence my return to Glasgow, where the 2d battalion now is ; and I am inclined to beleave that the final departure of the allied troops from this distracted country will be protracted much longer than has hitherto been expected. However, we were a few days ago review'd in the Plaine de Sablons by the Duke of Wellington, as, it is surmised, a preliminary step to our removal into cantonments in the provinces of Normandy and Picardy, or of occupying barracks in and about the immediate vicinity of Paris. It was anticipated that the Russians and Austrians would break up for the frontiers two days ago, but the immediate intended departure of the sovereigns, which was some days ago announced, is again postponed to an uncertain period. En attendant, the allies are possessing themselves of their former property wherever they find it, and have considerably thin'd the gallery of the Louvre, the walls of which have assumed a very bare and cold aspect, strongly contrasting with the rich and splendid appearence they made last year. We have taken nothing ourselves, but in consequence of our furnishing, since a few days ago, a captain's guard to protect the removal of the Ecole Flamande by order of the King of the Netherlands, we bear the odium of the measure without reaping its benefit ; but it is said the pope has given Great Britain the

Venus de Medicis, Laocoon, Apollo de Belvedere, and all of the paintings taken from the Vatican. The Spaniards will this day strip it of those taken from Aranjuez, the Escurial and St. Ildefonso ; and the Emperor of Austria claims the Venetian horses at the Place du Carousel. A report prevails that the triumphal column, on the model of that of Trajan at Rome, now on the Place de Vendome, is to be pull'd down by order of Blucher, who return'd yesterday to Paris, and the Prussians have completely gutted several fine museums, taking from them the beautiful models of the fortresses, particularly that of the artillery in the Rue du Bag, which was on a most magnificent scale, and which must inevitably suffer from the very act of transportation, which is much to be regreted dagli conoscenti and admirers of the fine arts. Much effervescence and discontent prevails not only in the cabinet but in the public mind, on account of the uncertainty of the future fate of the country, and the procrastinated though anxiously expected proclamation of the sovereigns respecting their final views and intentions ; and much alarm exists least the integrity of the country should not be preserved. It is said that the treaty bears so hard on the country that the ministry have refused to affix their names to it, and that in consequence Tallerond, Fouche, and the Ministre de la guerre have tender'd their resignations.

I have selected a set of caricatures, many of them contro il nostro paese, which I will take an early opportunity of forwarding, agreably to your wishes, and which I daresay will prove a source of entertainment at the expense of John Bull et sa gaucherie. My mother, when I last heard from her, was in good health and spirits, and had, en attendant her fixing on a residence in London, taken for a short time a small cottage at Staines, No. 11 Lower Kennington Green. Since a few days I have had the satisfaction of seing myself gazetted by the recommendation of the Duke of Wellington, a Companion of the order of the Bath, for my services at the battle of Watterloo, and my brother is also gazetted a Companion. I am happy to observe that Lord Balgonie is quite recover'd, and hope that e'er this Lady Leven is out of the invalid list. With best respects to her ladyship, and kind remembrance to all the family, and to all at Freeland, Gask, and Egerton, I remain, my dear lord, with great truth, your lordships affectionate cousin and obedient humble servant,   LESLIE WALKER.

The right honourable the Earl of Leven and Melville, Melville House, near Cupar, Fife, Scotland.

354. CHARLES KIRKPATRICK SHARPE to ALEXANDER, EARL OF LEVEN AND
MELVILLE—That he had caught cold at a dance.

93 Princes Street, Edinburgh, [c. May 15, 1816].

MY LORD,—I should much sooner have troubled you with my thanks for the
honour which you were so good as to do me in a letter that I lately received,
had I not been confined pretty constantly to my bed for near a fortnight past
with a very severe influenza, which I verily believed would have landed me at
last in the other world. A certain Lady Campbell of Arkinlass, who has apart-
ments in Holyroodhouse, had the goodness to send me a card for a party which
she gave one very rainy evening; in an evil hour, God wot, I went, and after
dancing a great deal on a carpet, and in a room hot enough to have baked all the
mutton pies in the Cannongate, when I came to take my departure, I found that
somebody had made free with my great coat. Some of the 42d who were at the
party took me a little way in their hackney coach, and very civilly set me down
without giving me the Scotch fiddle, for which I am greatly beholden to them,
but I had to walk a good part of the way home in a shower of rain, the consequence of which was such a concatenation of aches in the way of rheumatism as I
never before sustained in my life. My eyes swelled beyond my temples, and my
mouth beyond my nose, and my ears met at the top of my head; my cheeks—but
no power of language can describe them. I will make no use of vulgar simili-
tudes respecting haggisses or those parts of little children which the wholesome
birch is sometimes wont to visit, but merely hint that a head of Fame, with the
trumpet broken off, may convey some idea of the huge inflation. Thus swolen like
a bagpipe, I lay groaning and screaming for many days in a thousand pair of
blankets, and even now, after being boiled and roasted selon les regles, I am still
far from well; an extreme lassitude and weakness render me almost incapable
of motion, and I outcough all the old women in the Cowgate. In such a situation, I shall take care, my lord, not to trespass upon your goodness by carrying a
chorus of sighs and groans to Melville at present; but when I deem myself
capable of enjoying the most agreeable society there, and well enough not to annoy
any body except with my usual dullness, I will certainly avail myself of the
invitation to wait upon your lordship and Lady Leven, with which you have been
so obliging as to honour me. I am quite greived that you had any trouble about
that tiresome book of caricatures, which is used to travel, and always finds its way
home again, like those ugly fairy children that nobody can lose. The Duchess of
Beaufort carried it away from town to Badminton three years ago, and after some

time it reappeared, but without the portrait of Lord Worcester, which that imperious princess chose to appropriate to herself; she said she 'd restore it when Worcester returned from Spain, but I have never seen it since. Apropos, my lord, to any one curious in extremes, and studious of human ingenuity, the exhibition of Edinburgh pictures, now open, is one of the most interesting and delightful scenes in the world; no imagination, tho' ever so much versed in sign posts, can conceive the perfection of the thing. The portraits of great black haired, red nosed old men, with snouts like hot pokers sticking through the hearth broom, and of fair haired, interesting young ladies, as flat as pancakes, well garnished with roses and pink ribbon. Then there are landscapes coloured from a dish of fresh spinnage, nicked down with a knife here and there by the cook, to represent hills; and sea-pieces, taken from the puddle at the Cannymills in a high wind. I shall say nothing of the miniatures, save that they appear to have been done from the human face divine seen in a silver spoon, sometimes turned the long way, sometimes the broad.

I am extremely glad, for the sake of our national credit, that Allan's picture is so much approved of in London. I was unlucky enough not to see it when here; but I have seen some of his sketches, which struck me as being very pretty; and I am quite certain that if he will study nature much, and *the antique* little, he will prove an excellent painter.

It is quite a relief to one's mind that the Princess Charlotte is married at last; the put offs were as tiresome as the prosings about the marriage in Richardson's Pamela, when one is wearied through twenty pages with Pamela's doubts, fears, and numberless reflections on the contingencies of her approaching state; but if the poor lady got not her favourite brother after all, she is much to be lamented, tho', indeed, if she takes after the rest of the family, she will quickly find consolation in other quarters. It is a marriage that has passed over with wonderful little eclat; one dont hear even of a single knight being dubb'd, far less of those dozen or two of dukes that were talked of, so I begin to fear that Lord Stafford will not be Duke of Cleveland after all, not that to my virtuous ears is the title of Cleveland tolerable. Lady Stafford her grace of Cleveland. Oh, fye! to what volumes of " chambering and wantonness " doth that name entice the imagination !

My lord, I do think that people are not in a safe neighbourhood, residing so near a certain Circe whom you mention; one should wear mountain ash and holy water to guard one from the spells of her witchcraft; but perhaps she only, like Thalestris, sets her cap at decided heroes, of whom, by the way, we have had one here, who has suffered terribly from the furious pursuit of our Edinburgh Amazons. They plucked the feathers from his cap, and the hair from his head, and the whiskers from his cheeks, and God knows what beside, to keep by way of relicks, and flocked after him at all the parties like pigeons after a plate of salt, or cats winding a bush of valerian. The poor man, who chanced to be modest, actually blushed his face into St. Anthony's fire, and has retired to London for a little cool ease and comfort. The person I allude to is Colonel Dick of the 42d, who has a great many orders, and is really a very good, unassuming sort of a hero.

But it is full time for me to assume no more of your lordship's leisure to my-self, on which I have already trespassed far too much. Have the goodness, my lord, to present my best respects to Lady Leven and the Ladies Melville, and to believe me your lordships ever obliged and faithful servant,

CHAS. KIRKPATRICK SHARPE.

To the Earl of Leven, Melville House, Cupar.

355. DAVID STEWART, EARL OF BUCHAN, to ALEXANDER, EARL OF LEVEN AND MELVILLE—His views on political opinion in courts of justice, etc.

Dryburgh Abbey, Berwickshire, June 22d, 1816.

MY VERY DEAR COUSIN,—Your letter of the 18th, which came to my hands this day, marks the great grandson of my worthy uncle the Black Colonel Erskine, and my own good old friend.

Lady Buchan desires her kind compliments to you and good Lady Leven, and love to all your family, in which I heartily concur.

I sincerely hope my Alma Mater's shores may prove propitious to the health of my dear Lady Jane, your daughter, who, I know, will make a good use of that and every other blessing.

I have always advised my partisan acquaintances who are not in parliament, and are professionally engaged at the bar in Scotland, to take their routine of promotion to the bench as a soldier ought to do in his regiment, and thinking, as I have always done, that political opinions ought not [to] mingle with courts of justice, Adam, Gillies, and Cathcart, not to speak of others, I think are not to be blamed for accepting, or even solliciting, their places, but I blame those greatly who have been instrumental in blinding their superiors to the opposite opinion, and losing their opportunity of an honourable preferrment.

The world consists, my dear Lord Leven, of two great classes of men, the dupers and the dupees. Thank God I belong to neither of these.

I have taken various opportunities arising from my correspondence with the royal family of England to promote the plan adopted by some of them, and lately by Prince Leopold, and I dare say that prince will hereafter find occasion to be glad he did adopt it.—I am, my very dear cousin, yours most affectionately.

BUCHAN.

Earl of Leven and Melville, etc., etc., etc., Melville House, by Cupar, Fife.

356. GEORGE DEMPSTER of Dunnichen, to ALEXANDER, EARL OF LEVEN AND MELVILLE—With good wishes.

Dunnichen, Forfar, 3d September 1816.

MY DEAR LORD,—I receiv'd last night your lordships obliging letter, dated Airdit, 29th August, in some measure answering my letter to the owner of that place, and mentioning your ladies had left St. Andrews, and had found the lodging there not unsuitable to their residence. If you had told me the bath had agreed with the ladies, and that all the family at Melville were well, it would have afforded me still more pleasure. I hope the best. Should the cow be suffer'd to breed, the park of Melville might have a herd of animals little less ornamental than deer, and nearly as delicious as the deer kind. I am forced to abandon all thoughts of ever returning to St. Andrews, or leaving our county, as our burring place is in it, where were I now to be laid, it could hardly be murder, for I am alive, and that is all. These may be called letters from the dead to the living. I wish you may be able to read our dead mens scrawls. If you be, they will tell you I send my compliments to Melville House, and that I have the honor to be, my dear lord, most respectfully yours,

GEORGE DEMPSTER, Aetatis 84.

To the right honourable the Earl of Leven, at Melville House, by Cupar, Fife.

357. CHARLES KIRKPATRICK SHARPE to ALEXANDER, EARL OF LEVEN AND MELVILLE—His memoirs of Viscount Dundee, and Kirkton's History. *Circa* August 1817.

93 Prince's Street, Edinburgh, Sunday evening.

MY LORD,—I should long ere this time have begged leave to thank you for the honour you did me in a few lines conveyed by General Leslie, had I got anything but mere acknowledgments, the climax of dulness, to offer, and now, though greatly encouraged by your goodness, I should make a thousand apologies for the freedom which I am about to take; but you were kind enough, in your last, to say that you would extend your aid to me in my late literary undertaking, and I now assume the confidence to solicit it for a little work with which I am (privately) very busy just at present.

It is long ago since, after reading a vast quantity of romances, and falling violently in love, I set myself to write the memoirs of Grahame of Claverhouse, Viscount Dundee—of course, under such circumstances, my work, which I then deemed excellent, was most intolerable stuff—after the lapse of a few years, when I had forgotten Amadis and Palmerin, and discovered that love was a physical sensation, I could not read a single sentence of it without blushing. But now, I have resolved to rewrite my memoirs, to crop all their rhetorical flowers, prune their luxuriant conjectures, demolish their clipt yew periods, and relate mere matter of fact (if that be ever possible) in homely language, alias, my mother tongue. I am told that your lordship some time ago sent into Edinburgh a great many family papers, among which were several letters written by the hero in question, and I would take it as a most singular favour if you could afford me a sight of these papers by giving an order to whomsoever you have honoured with so great a trust. Though a *borderer*, I can assure you I am honest, and appeal to Lord Lothian, who lent me some very valuable papers lately, and many others, for the truth of my assertion. I know very well that the politicks of Lord Melville and Claverhouse did not exactly agree ; and I confess that I myself am an *old* Tory, but I know how to respect dignities, and to refrain from a railing accusation. Moreover, were there any just ground (and there is none) for a Tory attack upon your lordship's ancestor, I am already too much indebted to his representative to be guilty of such abominable ingratitude.

I have at last finished Kirkton, after much trouble in transcription, squabbles with the press, and destruction of my eyesight in etching some very coarse embellishments. Your lordship will find Master James an author of considerable spirit, and possessed of more candour than could well be expected in a person of his time and profession ; but it is a sad pity that his History breaks off at so very interesting a period, and it is wonderful, talking of his genius, that a man who could write such reasonable memoirs should compose such ridiculous sermons.

I think I have got very little Edinburgh news wherewith to trouble you. Our last tea-table sensation was caused by the marriage of Miss Mercer Elphinstone, a ceremony which took place in Mr. Murray of Henderland's house, the bride with green gloves and ribbons, and not one of her near relations to countenance her folly. It is said that the count is very gentlemanly as to manner, but that is all. I have had the honour of being known to the lady all my life, and never imagined that she would marry for love. She was a person who always flirted with what was fashionable for the moment—Lord Cochrane—Tommy Moore—Sir Godfrey Webster's moustache, etc., etc.,—but seemed unmade for softness.

> " In life's last scene, what prodigies surprise,
> Fears of the brave, and follies of the wise."

An heiress in her teens is excusable for pleasing herself as to a husband—at thirty she should in decency have some respect for the world; however, our Scottish heiresses don't trouble their heads much about making great matches, witness Lady Hood, whose husband is a very good sort of man, and was once good looking; but (alas!) resembles a Jew in face more than in fortune. I suppose it was an innate love of old cloaths that made him admire Lady H., who never wore a new thing in her life, and is herself the left off surtout of old Sir Samuel; they are to rusticate in the north for three years, and then they come forth rich, and she gets the family title. Such is the present plan, which will, most probably, be realized at the Greek calends,

> " When mussel shells turn silver bells,
> And cockles grow on ilka tree."

To-morrow is the first day of our races, which, as to sport, are to be good, I am told, but I hear of nobody coming in to them, save the Kennedies, on their way to Colzean. Lord Kennedy called on me to-day, full of the same blushes and bashfulness he exhibited while a boy, which dont become the papa of two lusty children. What a pity it was that he did not first marry Alma Mater and then go abroad, in place of espousing Miss Allardice and growing mouldy at Dunotter! however, neither his aukwarduess, nor that of a country tailor, can spoil the look of *blood* and a very pleasing manner. His factor in the country is at present prosecuting him here for calling him *rascal*, which term Lord K. assures me was very properly applied—but truth is one thing and law another—the man has got Jeffrey on his side, so I fear Lord K. will have but a bad chance with them.

Lord Elcho is on the point of being married to Lady Louisa Bingham, the *intended* wife of Michael Stewart; his friends, who cannot, internally, be very well pleased, put a good face upon it. I remember the lady's elder sister, Lady Elizabeth Vernon, giving a supper to the Duke of Devonshire, before her marriage, in Lord Lucan's house, the father being absent, at which I was. It was a curious scene; for putting the oddness of the thing itself out of the question, the duke was as deaf as the chair on which he reposed, and as cold as the ice he devoured. Cupid's dart was weak as the javelin of Priam. Lady

Anne Murray and her husband are here, she being so unwell as to require the medical aid of Edinburgh. I am told that she is very pretty and accomplished ; but what is strange, her husband, who is a bastard, drives a barouche adorned with a pair of stout supporters to the arms, which I am assured he has had regularly granted by the unworthy herald's office here. This should certainly be noticed ; but it is full time for me no longer to trespass on your lordship's patience ; so, without making any farther apologies for my bold request, or the tiresome verbiage of this long winded epistle, I beg leave to subscribe myself your lordship's ever faithful humble servant,   Cha⁵ KIRKPATRICK SHARPE.

358. THE SAME to THE SAME—Memoirs of Viscount Dundee—Edinburgh gossip. 3d August 1817.

93 Prince's Street, Edinburgh, Sunday morning.

MY LORD,—I have so very much to thank you for, that I am actually at a loss how to attempt it, and think it better to leave my gratitude to imagination, as the Greek painter did the face of Agamemnon, than to express it very clumsily. What you have had the goodness to entrust to me I shall take the greatest care of, and restore them safely to your lordship's hands by the first proper opportunity.

Tho' there is nothing very material in Lord Dundee's letter, yet every scrap of his is interesting, to his biographer at least, who, generally speaking, is a very partial person ; however, if I can contrive to complete these memoirs so as to reach the press, I shall endeavour to give a fair account of his faults, and also I shall have the confidence to ask your lordship to add one favour to so many, by allowing this trifle the honour of being inscribed to you. If one cannot testify one's respect and gratitude in great things, one must in small, and I shall rely on your experienced good nature to forgive whatever of stupidity and nonsense (there shall be no fault as to good morals or good manners) the life of Lord Dundee may contain.

But it will be many months before I can lick my bantling into printable shape ; for besides Mr. Law's memorials, I have engaged to edite some correspondence (by letters) of the 1st Duke of Queensberry. I believe I once saw the portrait of Archbishop Sharp, which your lordship mentions, in the possession of Miss Melville while she resided in Edinburgh. It appeared to me then to be extremely well painted, and made him out a much more *comely carl* than he is usually represented. I should like very much to know whether there be still extant a

picture of his daughter, who behaved so well in that dismal scene on Magus
Muir.   She married a Mr. Cunningham of Barns in Fife; apropos, I heard
lately that at Mr. Beaton's there are many curious old portraits, and, among
others of the family, that of Mary Beaton, who was maid of honour to Marie
Queen of Scots.

I lately was lucky enough to discover an original of Mass David Williamson,
the dainty Davie of song, and long minister of the West Kirk of Edinburgh.   He
was so celebrated from his adventure at Cherrytrees, and for possessing a trio of
what niggardly nature is wont to distribute in pairs, that when he went to court
to present an address to King William, the circle was like the black hole at
Calcutta, from the croud of ladies.   He married 7 wives, the last of whom buried
him in his 70th year.   The picture belongs to his great-grandson, Colonel
Williamson, and is done by Sir J. Medina.   Alas! it represents this squire of
dames, antient, but still there is a twinkle of a dark eye, and the smile among
wrinkles, that denoteth a snake in the grass.   I have borrowed it to take a
copy.   .   .   .

Talking of heroes, I hear that there never were two such happy people as
Countess Flahault and her husband; 'tis the billing of the eagle and the solan
goose, the entwining of the fleur-de-lis with the thistle; but from this auspicious
junction I am assured no issue can proceed, for the count is so worn out, that
he's like an over-milked cow on a common, or our Edinburgh pumps in a dry
summer.   However, the countess may find ways and means, so let us hope the
best.   Sir John Sinclair wrote to him the other day, begging as full an account
of the affair of Waterloo as he was able to give!   I forget if I told your lordship
that when the count and countess were at Drummond Castle, before they went
home, a female friend of mine happened to call upon them one day while a bagpipe player was in the courtyard.   The countess called him upstairs and placed
him in the passage, but the door was very soon shut upon him.   When my friend
saw him afterwards, she said, "Weel, Donald, how did the count like your
music?"   "No very weel, madam, he had enough o't the last time he heard it."

The Wemyss family are here at present on a very melancholy occasion.   Poor
Walter, whose strange illness you may have heard of, is now threatened with the
loss of power in his legs.   He walks with the utmost difficulty, and seems
altogether very weak and languishing.   It is a sad spectacle to see a young lad
scarcely beginning life in such a helpless (and, I fear, hopeless) condition.   His
parents flatter themselves that the pressure of the instrument he wears upon the
upper part of his thighs occasions this want of power in his limbs; but I doubt
much if that be the true reason, as one has heard of this imbecility frequently

following the distortion of the spine without the aid of instruments. A person here is employed to alter his collar, etc., and it is that which brings the family into Edinburgh.

I suppose that Elcho is married by this time. His rival, young Gilbert Heathcote, is at present in Edinburgh, but denies to me all sober sadness in his admiration of Lady Louisa, who is pretty, tho' marked with the small pox, and having a broken front tooth. The young couple have not as yet got a house, for Needpath and Seton are not habitable, and they are not to reside at Gosford, which I think a pity. We have had, and have still, the most dreadful weather imaginable. Sunshine one moment, merely to entice the beaus and belles forth, a deluge the next, to the utter destruction of new hats and great coats, French bonnets and pea green pelisses! not to mention poor Lord Murray's shrubbery wall, which has given way, owing to a settlement of water, towards Queen's Street, and fallen in upon the shrubs and walk. I suppose we shall all shortly be obliged to build arks, if we do not starve owing to this ruinous harvest.

Before I relieve your lordship from the tedium of this scrawl, I must beg leave to return you my best thanks for what you honour me by saying in your last respecting a visit to Melville, but I deem it very bad policy, as well as bad manners, to carry aches and pains and sad grimaces, and a waggon load of flannel and a hamper of opodeldoc into the houses of those who honour me with their kindness. 'Tis, according to the Scotch law term, the very worst kind of hamesucken, for who can endure an animal more troublesome than a breeding woman at an occasion, or a bilious child in a stage coach? My lord, I am resolved, if possible, to retain your much valued patronage, and so I will deny myself the gratification of waiting upon you in your own house.

I beseech you to excuse all this stuff, and to allow me to subscribe myself your ever obliged and faithful servant,   CHAS. KIRKPATRICK SHARPE.

Poor Madame de Staël! We shall have no more dull metaphysicks gilded with gallantry, and great ignorance covered with the spun sugar of very pretty French. The memoirs of her namesake, which your lordship was so kind as to afford me a loan of, are written with great vivacity, and all that knowledge of the world which French people are so rich in. She was fille de chambre to the Duchess du Maine, the great Conde's daughter, basely married to a bastard of Lewis 14. And her account of the Duchess's political intrigues, and of her own confinement in the Bastile, is particularly interesting. French women write memoirs eternally. They seem ever to have a pen in one hand and a —— fan in the other!

The Earl of Leven and Melville, Melville House, Fife.

359. The Same to The Same—Edinburgh gossip—his literary work, etc.

93 Princes St., 20th July 1818.

My Lord,—From a great many circumstances, such as domestic sickness and many mental distresses, with the tedious details of which I shall not trouble your lordship, I was resolved not to encroach upon your time with a chorus of sighs and groans in answer to your last obliging letter; but now that the election of the Scottish Peers approaches, I begin to be apprehensive that you may suppose me fairly under ground in the Greyfriars' churchyard, and so that I shall lose the honour of seeing you when here; therefore I take the liberty of signifying that I am still as much alive as I have been for several years, that is, I am like the unfortunate prince in the Arabian Nights, half man, half black marble, or rather a sort of galvanised mummy escaped from its gums and cerements; but your lordship will perceive that I have in some measure preserved my hieroglyphicks, when attempting to decypher the pestilent scrawl of this uncouth epistle!

You do me much honour by inquiring as to the progress of my literary labours, which, in truth, proceed slowly, for bad health is a sad impediment to everything; however, Law is very nearly finished (all but a sheet or two), and I think that I shall be able to complete Lord Dundee in the spring. Meanwhile Master Kirkton has been most hugely lauded in the *Quarterly*, with many flourishes, which, as dairy-maids say in letters to their sweethearts, is more the author's goodness than my desert; however, such compliments are very convenient, for there are a number of people who believe every thing which they see in print. The sale of curiosities, etc., which your lordship mentions, was of rubbish belonging to Hatton, the carver and gilder, who made frames for two prints you entrusted to him. He employs people to send him prints and toys from Holland. But Ballantyne is the great monopolist in that way, and 'tis really wonderful what prices are given—for china principally—such as you, or any other judge of what is rare and curious, would scarcely permit to deck the mantelpiece of a dressing room.

The hurly-burly of our gaieties is now concluded, tho' this is the first day of the races. The winter past, as other winters have done, with many parties—a few merry, most dull,—some love,—and a great deal of cold. Three unfortunate youths were sent into sudden banishment, on account of fair ladies, who were supposed to possess the qualities of Tasso's Armida, and deal deep in the witcheries of tenderness. The first luckless knight who was carried off by that cruel giant, the adamantine *Papa*, who figures so harshly in most romances, was Mr. Davidson, the rich merchant of London's son—him the fair Inglis, daughter to the scribe in Queen Street, held a month in flowery chains ; but, alas, her bosom friend, the nymph Anstrutheria, daughter to the Ephesian matron of that name, contrived, as Fame reports, through malice dire, to have notice sent to Papa, who forthwith ordered off the sighing youth in a fiery chariot, *alias* the mail coach, to London. The second victim to parental cruelty was the juvenile Bowes (nephew to Strathmore's Earl), whose sire is pent within the enchanted walls of Holyrood, where he clasps to his bosom the widow of Ardkinglass's knight, now his third dear helpmate. Young Thomas, like that animal Silenus loved, between two bundles of hay, was in a dismal state through love of Miss Brown and Anstrutheria ; but again the direful Papa cut short the sweet dilemma, and sent the swain to bray amid the luxuriant pastures of Yorkshire. The third child of despair was a young warrior of the Greys, who at present valiantly defend the fortress of Piershill. He seemed to have been nursed in the bosom of Flora, and taught quadrilles by the Graces themselves. In evil hour Anstrutheria exerted her charms. Under the midnight moon she and Hecate, her mother, composed philtres and amulets, which fixed the hapless youth. But the commander of the regiment stepped forward, and the lover was ordered off to a distant quarter, there to weep his melancholy doom, and sigh o'er scenes past bye. My lord, I can proceed no further, else I shall outdo Cassandra or the Grand Cyrus, both in pathos and prolixity.

I am told that the races are to be good ; but I shall not taste of their sweets, for I never ride, and my mother has given up her carriage. It is wonderful to observe from these windows the number of tawdry bucks who are riding towards Musselburgh to deck the strand with their fashion—"stant littore puppes." I shall always regret that the scene of action is changed from Leith to Musselburgh, as the spectacle at Leith, whatever the sport might be, was really charming.

The Countess de Flahault and her husband are here at present ; she, under the care of Dr. Hamilton, having had a very bad fausse couche. I sit with the Count and Countess every night, and find him a most agreeable person. But it is now high time for me to relieve your lordship from my load of impertinence, so I hasten to conclude, being ever your most obliged and faithful servant,

CHAS. KIRKPATRICK SHARPE.

To the Earl of Leven and Melville, Melville House, Fife.

360. Mr. DAVID WILKIE, R.A., to ALEXANDER, EARL OF LEVEN AND MELVILLE
—Proposed portrait of Lord Hopetoun.

Kensington, February 17, 1817.

MY LORD,—I had the honor of a letter from you yesterday, which gave me great pleasure. Your lordship was particularly kind in giving me accounts of Mr. Walker and his family at Collessie, and of my little nephew now under their charge.

My family and myself were much gratified by receiving a call from your lordship's youngest son, Mr. Alexander Melville, with two ladies, about a fortnight ago. I had not seen him for a long time, and was much prepossessed, I assure you, with his appearance and manner.

What your lordship has mentioned about the proposed portrait of Lord Hopeton for the county, gives me real pleasure, and I cannot help noticing that it is the first time our county have, to my knowledge, ever thought of possessing a picture. They will, however, in following your lordship's suggestion of employing Lawrence, make a good beginning; and in order that he may know what is expected of him, I shall have great pleasure in mentioning to Sir Thomas what your lordship has said, as an inducement for him to exert himself.

Our countryman, Sanders, continues to go on, I believe, in full employment. He paints portraits of the full size in oil, but I am not sure that he has yet given up miniature.

I have not yet had the honor of an introduction to the Grand Duke Nicholas. It gives me great pleasure to hear of the encouragement he has given to my friend Allen in Edinburgh.

With most respectful compliments to the Countess of Leven and to my Lord Balgoney, I have the honor to be your lordship's very obedient servant,

DAVID WILKIE.

The Right Honourable the Earl of Leven.

361. THE SAME to THE SAME—The South of Scotland—the author of "Waverley."

Phillimore Place, Kensington, London,
November 10th, 1817.

MY LORD,—Being desirous of the honor of hearing from your lordship, and of learning how my Lady Leven continues in her health, I take the liberty of obtruding this letter upon your lordship, and it will give myself and those about me very great pleasure if it is in your power to give us agreeable accounts of her ladyship and the family.

The occasional visits I had the honor to make at Melville House, and the excursions in company with your lordship to some places in the neighbourhood, I now look back to with great delight. The ride to Balfour, Balgonie, and to Leslie House, was exceedingly interesting to me. The places were entirely new, and presented objects in the way of art that, like many of the pictures and curiosities you showed me in Melville House, become to an artist a sort of stock in trade.

After leaving your lordship and my friends in your neighbourhood, I took my course towards London. In the south of Scotland I stopt in a district where music and song have become indigenous. The Tweed, the Galla water, the Yarrow, the Etrick, and the Cowdenknows, were all within my view, and seemed almost to be ringing in one's ears. What also contributed to add to the poetical interest of the place was the means I had of seeing the minstrel himself, whose writings have given an interest to that as well as to many other districts of our country. You may believe, my lord, that the question of whether Mr. Scott is the author of Waverley, so frequently discussed, occurred to my mind often when I had such means of observing the suspected person. It was to little effect, however. He seemed so completely unemployed, and appearently so little capable of concealing anything of the sort, that I thought it impossible. To my surprize, however, I found his family were as much in the dark as any body, and almost as uncertain. They hoped most anxiously that he might be the author, and felt provoked that he had not discovered it if he was.

Of the long expected Rob Roy I heard nothing, and if it is still in hand and had anything done to it when I was in his house, it must have been when everybody else was asleep.

Besides many other interesting objects, the ruins of Melrose Abbey struck me much. It is one of the finest instances of the florid Gothic I have seen. From this quarter I took my leave of Scotland, and came by the way of Carlisle and Manchester, through a rich, and in some places, romantic country. But manufactures are here the order of the day and the indications of improvement, and they present to the mind a very different object for contemplation from what I had left behind me in our own native land of tradition and of poetry.

In London, for the short time of my absence, I have found various changes. One of the most impressive to me was the death of Mr. Barclay of Conduit Street, which your Lordship would hear of with regret.

Of my friends and relatives at Collessie, and the venerable and worthy pastor, I have heard nothing, but I hope favourably of them. Your lordship, I hope, will excuse this long letter. It will give me very great pleasure to hear of your lordship and family, and with most respectful compliments to the Countess of Leven, to the Ladies Lucy and Mary Ann, and Mr. Alexander Melville,—I have the honor to subscribe myself, my lord, your lordship's very devoted servant,

DAVID WILKIE.

The Right Honourable the Earl of Leven and Melville,
  Melville House, Fifeshire.

362. THE SAME to THE SAME—Portrait of the Duke of Wellington, by
Sir Thomas Lawrence.

Kensington, June 24th, 1818.

MY LORD,—I have often wished to write you since hearing of the loss your lordship and family have met with in the death of the much respected Countess of Leven, to express my concern at an event with which both I and those about me were much affected. I was most happy in receiving a pleasing account of you all from Mr. Melville, who I met with some time ago, and I have since that been much gratified by the letter which your lordship has done me the honor to write me.

The town has been much taken up about the Arts this spring, and the Royal Academy Exhibition is reckoned better than usual, and has been very attractive. I have made up a catalogue to send your lordship, which will show what it contains. There is a fine equestrian portrait of the Duke of Wellington, by Sir Thomas Lawrence, in the dress he wore on the field of Waterloo, arranged in a very masterly style. Such a picture of the Earl of Hopetoun would have been a great acquisition to our county of Fife. As it is, however, I hope they will have one not much inferior. There are also two very fine pictures (sea views), one by Turner and the other by Callcott. I have only got two small pictures in the exhibition. One that I have been engaged upon through the winter, of a Scottish wedding, is not yet done.

I was much interested lately by meeting a review, in the *Quarterly Review*, of the book your lordship showed me, by Mr. Kirkpatrick Sharp. I suppose it to be by Mr. Walter Scott. It speaks handsomely of Mr. Sharp, who, I believe, is a friend of your lordships; it has also a most humorous allusion to our worthy friend, Colonel Wemyss, in respect to his zeal in avowing himself as the descendant of Burley.

I am happy to hear from your lordship that the popularity of Dr. Chalmers still continues. I understand it has lately obtained for him another promotion in Glasgow.

Your lordship's good report of my little nephew at Collessie gives me great pleasure. I beg to be most respectfully remembered to the Lady Melvilles, and to Mr. Alexander Melville, and with sincere esteem and regard, I have the honor to be, my lord, your lordship's very obedient servant,

DAVID WILKIE.

The catalogue shall be sent to Miss Brown as directed.

The Right Honourable the Earl of Leven and Melville, etc.

363. LADY MARY WALKER [or HAMILTON] to her nephew, ALEXANDER, EARL OF LEVEN AND MELVILLE—Her own literary works.

London, 14th September 1818.

MY DEAR LORD,—I recieved the favor of your lordship's letter, and was surprised Lord Northesk cou'd afford you any information on my subject; for though his lordship and family have been frequently in town, he never condescended to visit or inquire after his aged aunt. The neglect of those with whom we are connected becomes painful and mortifying to our feelings, yet the poignancy of the sensations we experiance are regulated by our ideas of the injury we sustain by their neglect. Flaxman said that "no head or face had its duplicate." I believe the same thing can be said of the mind. Naturalists have taken pains to class the different kinds of plants and animals, but moralists have left three parts of mankind without any particular character, though man exhibits in his race the whole scale of animal intellect, from the orang-outing to the oyster. My temper is not susceptable of strong resentment on common occasions. I have always made it a rule not to see insult where none is meant, and we must be sensible of accepting consequence from others before they can take it from us. I have valuable friends and inducements to enter society, where the old woman is sometimes the gayest of the group, but I can dispense with nominal friends, and numerous acquaintance now near four score. I am flattered by your lordship's approbation of my reveries : flattery is doubly dangerous when offered by those whom our reason teaches us to esteem. I have met, indeed, in both languages, encomiums I never cou'd have deserved. It is better to be beloved than admired, and consequently, commendation is the more welcome from our consciousness of its partiality ; but perhaps that passage in your lordship's letter was designed as a supplement to the Moria of Erasmus's Encomium in praise of folly. I find by yours, that you have already got all my English books but Munster Village (which last I think the best), as the different additions were all bought up, and the books out of print, after three years. I have been able to recover, at a circulating library, the three first, and hope to get the last : as to Popoli, I had a set for your acceptance, and by letter inquired from you how they should be sent. Not recieving any answer, I gave them away, but shall send to Paris for others.

Having been unhappy in marriage, instead of dissipation I had recourse to literature for my consolation, but I never presumed on the idea of becoming an author! Notoriety to women is destructive, at least collectively and generally speaking; but with a family of young children left on my hands, abandoned by their father, I was necessitated to hazard the effronterie of publication to cloath, feed, and educate them! and there are few persons so weak as to be incapable of understanding a subject if they devote their constant and undivided attention to it. It is now fashionable to take a tour to Greece. I make no doubt my nephews, Balgonie and Rosehill, will be very much amused by visiting that classic ground : to explore those regions which have produced such scenes of the greatest actions, perform'd by the greatest hero's, and recorded by the greatest poets. To see a people whose ancestors were the founders of literature must ever be interesting. I was glad to hear that Lord St. Vincent had given a thousand pounds on this occasion. I had the pleasure of seeing the General John and his lady, who I think a very pleasing woman, as also Mrs. Rutherford. My daughter, Mrs. Alderson (now a widow, who resides with me), excells on the harp, and played to them. I am sure your lordship would be delighted to hear her. Rapidity of execution, not delicacy of expression, constitutes the scientific perfection of modern music; but I prefer the touching melody of a ballet to the scientific combinations and ambitious beauties of a bravura. I am sorry to say that Leslie's widow had no fortune; it was all for love, etc., etc. He might have married an agreeable young woman of family and fortune, a friend of mine; had I been apprised of the circumstances I should not have gone to Ireland. He was grateful to Lady Ruth[ven] and much mortified she had not answered his letter.—I remain, my dear lord, your affectionate aunt, and obedient humble servant,

M. HAMILTON.

To the Right Honourable the Earl of Leven, Melville House, Fife, by Edinburgh.

364. SIR CHARLES EASTLAKE to DAVID, EARL OF LEVEN AND MELVILLE—
    Picture commissioned by the Earl, etc.

Rome, November 4, 1820.

MY DEAR LORD,—It is high time that I should give some account of myself and of the picture. When I last heard from you I was hard at work at it, and then wanted a week or ten days' work to complete it. Your kind permission to take my time about it (in your last letter) induced me then to lay it by for a while, and to accept an invitation from Lady Westmorland to accompany her to the country for a fortnight. The place was twenty miles beyond Tivoli, and so fine in point of scenery, that I worked all day long in the heat of August, the consequence was that on my return to Rome I had a violent attack in my eyes, from which I have suffered before, and could do nothing for some time. After this, poor Kirkup came from Tivoli with a fever, which brought him to death's door, and which still confines him, altho' he is rapidly getting better. His illness took up the time of all his friends, but without their assistance he would have sunk under it. Having been so long without working for money, I now began to find it necessary to turn my attention to some works which would put something in my pocket, and am now about two or three things to send to England in order to recruit my finances. Such are my excuses for having yet 10 days' work to do to your lordship's picture; and as it is now the season when the English begin to come, I should wish, even when it is finished, to keep it a week or two, as it is the best thing I have done, and might be of use to me. As I am upon this subject, I will beg you to direct any of your friends who are coming here to pay me and my studio a visit. Some used to come to see your picture when I had not got it to shew; now they may see it and report their opinion to you. I have heard of one Scotch nobleman who is coming here, Lord Blantyre. If he should be an acquaintance of your lordships, perhaps you will be so good as to give me an introduction to him. You must not fancy I am in a very bad way because my finances are low at present. I have plenty to do, and have made it a point to receive money for nothing (your picture is the only exception) beforehand, so that I have only to work and have, but delay just now might be productive of serious inconvenience, and I must occupy myself on two or three commissions first. You have perhaps seen Mrs. Graham's book; the engravings from my sketches are very bad, and, I am afraid, hurt the book as much as me. The book itself is very good. I hear nothing of Lord Ruthven, and as I have no means of sending money to Dorville, I wish to wait to see whether Lord Ruthven goes by way of Venice, when he could undertake to settle your little account with Dorville. Are you likely to come here again? I should be delighted if it were probable. Kirkup is now making sketches for some subjects for you. He has not quite decided on one yet. Campbell has taken the marble cutter's place under me, and has got a bust of Miss Campbell and Miss Guthrie, very good. Miss Campbell, you have perhaps heard, is to be married, if not already so, to Lord Tullamore, and one of the Ladies Bruce to Mr. Anderson.

Now that Rome is filling with new faces again, I shall perhaps have something to talk to you about, and shall not fail to send you any amusing news.   The people who are now here are Sir G. Talbot (who called on me some time ago at your request), Sir Thomas Gage, two Sir Drummonds, or one, I am not quite sure, the Misses Berry, Mr. and Mrs. Craufurd, Col. Bonar and family, the Duchess and Lady Westmoreland, besides a number of lesser luminaries, and greater too, perhaps, whom I have not heard of. Two princes are to be here, I think, of Denmark and Bavaria. Naples is for the present quiet, and Rome likely to remain so. Nothing more is said of the Austrians, tho' they are ready to march on any fresh commotion in Naples. I have heard nothing about my picture of Paris, and don't whether it is in the stable at Melville or in London. I desired my brother to send it (having first obtained your lordship's permission), but he has said nothing to me on the subject. If you think such an ornament worth the expense of carriage, you will do me a favor by desiring G. Eastlake, junior, Plymouth, to send it. It is a picture I cannot possibly sell now, and do not know where to put, so that it would be only taking in a houseless wanderer.—I remain, my dear lord, your lordship's sincerely grateful and obedient servant,

C. EASTLAKE.

To the Right Honorable the Earl of Leven and Melville,
    Melville Castle, Fifeshire, Scotland.

365. THE SAME to THE SAME—Death of the artist's father.   His commissions, etc.

Plymouth, February 28th, 1821.

MY DEAR LORD,—If you don't know that I am in England you will be surprised at hearing from me from this place. The occasion of my visit to my friends, that of my father's death, is one in which your own feelings, at no very distant period, will enable you to sympathize, and will, I have no doubt, excuse me in your eyes for the additional delay your picture will be subjected to. When I came to England a few weeks ago, I was not without hopes of paying you a visit ; but I am so much behindhand in my works at Rome (owing to a complaint I have had in my eyes), that I am anxious to return thither as soon as possible, to fulfil my promises to many, and my duty to you. I have brought Lord Guildford's two pictures with me, and shall leave them in town for him. I left him in Rome. Captain and Mrs. Graham had been at Plymouth some time before I came home, and while I was longing to be with them and my friends, I little thought that so severe a calamity would so soon call me here. They are still in lodgings in the neighbourhood, the Captain being promised a ship in March, perhaps for the East Indies. It is long indeed since I have heard from you, but I often heard in Rome of you from persons who were introduced to me thro' your kindness. The last, I think, was Lady Warrender; she was going to sit to me for her portrait just before I was called away, so that I did not begin it.

Rome is become so completely the theatre of my exertions, such as they are, that I cannot but regret having left it, tho' only for a time; but my anxiety to see my mother and brothers after more than four years, and after such an event, determined me to lose no time to come home. I only now remain to do a portrait of my mother and a little landscape, and shall be ready to go back, I hope, in about 6 weeks, for I must stay some days in London. Are you likely to revisit Italy? It would be a happiness indeed to accompany you thither. The last news I heard of Lord and Lady Ruthven was from Miss Talbot, who corresponds with Lady Ruthven. They were then at Naples and talking of coming to Rome. I brought a letter of introduction from a Mr. Craufurd, who is in Rome, to Miss Carew of Anthony. Miss Amabel Carew I find is an old friend of your lordship's: she will be married in a few weeks to Mr. F. Glanville of Catchfrench.

I must now beg the favor of your sending me a line, for it is possible you may be in London when I go thro' it; and I hope it is not impossible that we may meet again on the Continent. The affairs of Naples and Austria will, I hope, not interfere with the English travellers. I had a letter from Kirkup a few days since, who does not speak of any prospect of disturbance. Next to seeing your lordship, I shall be delighted to hear from you, and therefore entreat you to reply to this soon.—I remain, my dear lord, your sincerely grateful and obedient servant,   C. L. EASTLAKE.

To the Right Honorable the Earl of Leven and Melville,
    Melville Castle, Fifeshire.

366. THE SAME to THE SAME—Hoping to meet the Earl.

Plymouth, March 24, 1821.

MY DEAR LORD,—Your letter gave me great pleasure, and I am glad to find that you are soon to be in London. I shall look forward to the pleasure of meeting you there on my return from Rome, whither I am going in a few days, and whence I hope to return immediately. I am alarmed for the safety of my possessions there, and begin to fear that Italy will be unquiet for some time, and as I must settle in England at last, I have made up my mind to do so at once.   I did not like to set out on a journey even for so short a time without letting you know, but I have so much to think of that you must excuse the shortness of this letter. Captain Grahame has a ship, the Doris, and goes to South America; he is just gone to London, the ship is at Sheerness.   My resolution has been so suddenly taken that there is no time, owing to your being in Scotland, for me to receive any commission your lordship may wish to have executed in Rome, but every day is of importance to me, and I shall therefore set out immediately.   A poste restante letter might find me there, so that that will be the best plan to adopt if you wish me to bring home anything.—I have the honour to be, my dear lord, yours most obediently,   C. EASTLAKE.

P.S.—An old acquaintance of your lordship's, Miss Amabel Carew, is just married to Mr. Glanville, junior, of Catchfrench.

To the Right Honourable the Earl of Leven and Melville, Edinburgh.

367. REV. THOMAS CHALMERS, Professor of Moral Philosophy at St. Andrews, to DAVID, EARL OF LEVEN AND MELVILLE—A chemical lectureship at St. Andrews.

St. Andrews, March 12, 1825.

MY LORD,—I thought much of our chemical lectureship after your lordship's conversation with me upon that subject, and was led in consequence to take a decided view of what was best to be done in our peculiar circumstances.   My opinion, however, has been overruled by that of the majority of my colleagues.

I beg to express the very great satisfaction which I felt in observing the interest which your lordship took in the welfare and reputation of our university. I shall be ready at all times to give my sincere though humble endeavours to the object of turning to its most beneficial account the connection which has now been established between your lordship's family and the college of St. Andrews.—I have the honour to be, my lord, your lordship's most obliged and obedient servant,
                                                              THOMAS CHALMERS.

To the Right Honourable the Earl of Leven and Melville,
        Melville House, Cupar.

368. MR. DAVID WILKIE, R.A., to DAVID, EARL OF LEVEN AND MELVILLE—
Portrait of the Earl of Kellie for the County of Fife.

Geneva, June 18th, 1827.

MY LORD,—The portrait of the Right Honourable the Earl of Kellie, which the gentlemen of the county did me the honour to commission me to paint for the county hall of Fifeshire, has, from an illness that has required me to travel abroad, been interrupted for the last two years. But having lately in Rome been able to recommence in a moderate degree my labours, and meaning next winter to return to London, it is my intention, this picture being already advanced, and more near completion than any of my other works now on hand, to proceed with it, that it may be forthwith brought to a conclusion.

With this view, may I take the liberty of addressing myself through your lordship to the gentlemen who are acting for the subscribers, to know whether they could favour me by advancing one hundred pounds of the price, such advance being not uncommon in similar undertakings, and would, in the present instance, from my protracted absence on the continent, be to me a particular accommodation.

If agreed to, [I] should be glad the sum might be paid to Messrs. Sir William Forbes & Co. to my account, and should your lordship be pleased to honor me with any communication, my address will, till the 12th August, be Poste Restante, Geneva.

With respectful regards to the Countess of Leven, to whose family I felt indebted for many civilities in Rome, I have the honour to subscribe myself, my lord, your very faithful and obliged servant,   DAVID WILKIE.

The Right Honourable the Earl of Leven and Melville.

369. THE SAME to THE SAME—The same subject.

Kensington, London, September 8th, 1828.

MY LORD,—I take the liberty to state to your lordship for the information of the subscribers for the portrait of the late Earl of Kellie, that the picture is now finished, and that as soon as the frame (which I have ordered, after submitting an estimate of size, price, etc., to Mr. Horsburgh, who is on the spot to compare it with the other) is completed, which will take a month, it will be all ready to send to Scotland.

The time I engaged with your lordship, and those gentlemen who act for the subscribers, to complete this picture, was in three years. This, by my unhappy illness, has been lengthened to four years. My regret for this delay, as well as to gratify a wish that I understand has been expressed by the Countess of Kellie to see the portrait to " retrace in it the features of him whom she mourns," furnish an inducement to send it with as little delay as possible. I fear, however, that to keep it till I see it in the frame, which I wish to do, it cannot reach Cupar before the 20th of October.

I have just one request to add regarding this picture for the subscribers. My friends here, both professional and otherwise, urge me to put this (the only picture of the kind I have yet painted) in the Royal Academy Exhibition next year in Somerset House. As I conceive the subscribers will not object to allow me the picture for this object, may I request, if such is their pleasure, that you will inform me whether they would do me the favour to return the picture to me in London by March next for this purpose, to remain here till the close of the Exhibition in July.—I have the honour to be, dear Lord Leven, your lordship's very devoted and obliged servant,   DAVID WILKIE.

The Right Honourable the Earl of Leven and Melville.

LIST OF PORTRAITS AT MELVILLE HOUSE.

MELVILLE PORTRAITS.

1. George, first Earl of Melville; in armour, with a red scarf coming over the right shoulder and passing round the waist; three-quarter length; by Sir J. B. Medina, 1691.

2. The same; also in armour; three-quarter length; by the same artist.

3. The same; half-length; by the same artist.

4. The same; head and shoulders; small; artist unknown.

5. Catherine, Countess of Melville, his wife; in an orange-coloured dress, with a lilac mantle, fastened over the breast with a jewel, a portion passing over the lap, in which she holds some flowers; three-quarter length; by Medina.

6. The same; in a tan-coloured silk dress, with a large blue scarf covering the knees and part of the body; also three-quarter length; by Medina, 1691.

7. The same; in a slate-coloured silk dress, with a red scarf gracefully thrown over the right shoulder; half length; by Sir J. B. Medina.

8. Hon. James Melville of Cassingray, his younger brother; artist unknown.

9. Hon. James Melville of Balgarvie, third son of George, first Earl of Melville; in armour, without a scarf; three-quarter length; by Medina, 1696.

10. The same; in a coat of mail; half length; by Medina.

11. The same; artist unknown.

12. David, third Earl of Leven, General of Ordnance and Commander-in-Chief of the Forces in Scotland; in armour, with a red sash; three-quarter length; by Sir J. B. Medina, 1691.

13. The same; in a coat of mail, and large flowing wig; half length; by Sir Godfrey Kneller.

14. The same; half length; small size; artist unknown.

15. The same; half length; artist unknown.

16. Lady Anne Wemyss, his Countess; attired in a red dress, with short slashed sleeves, lined with blue and fringed with gold; below are large white sleeves tied round; in one hand she holds an orange; three-quarter length; by Michael Dahl.

17. The same; a head; by Medina.

18. George, Lord Balgonie, eldest son of David, third Earl of Leven; in armour, with a helmet and red scarf beside him; three-quarter length; by Jervas.

19. The same; half length; artist unknown.

20. Lady Margaret Carnegie, his wife; attired in a white gown, with a large red scarf enveloping a great part of the body; three-quarter length; by Jervas.

21. David, fourth Earl of Leven; a boy; blue coat, red scarf over left shoulder and round back; full length; artist unknown.

22. Hon. James Melville, youngest son of David, third Earl of Leven; a large half length; by Medina.

23. Mary, Lady Haddo, daughter of David, third Earl of Leven; dressed in a green velvet gown, with a red mantle thrown over the lap; three-quarter length; by J. M. Wright.

24. Alexander, fifth Earl of Leven; attired in the robes of a Lord of Session; three-quarter length; by Bellucci, 1739.

25. The same when twelve years of age; in the dress of an officer of the Guards; full length; by Medina.

26. Mary Erskine, his first wife, d. 1722; artist unknown.

27. Elizabeth Monypenny, his second wife; in a blue gown, with a light lilac coloured scarf, with her right hand under a fountain; three-quarter length; by Bellucci, 1739.

28. The same; and beside her a child, Lady Ann Hope, daughter of James, third Earl of Hopetoun; a small half length; by Allan.

29. Lieutenant-General Alexander Leslie, second son of Alexander, fifth Earl of Leven, Colonel of the Ninth Regiment of Foot; a head; by Ramsay.

30. David, sixth Earl of Leven; a head; by Ramsay.

31. The same; half length; by Martin.

32. Wilhelmina Nisbet, his Countess; a head; by Ramsay.

33. The same; half length; by Martin.

34. The same, with Janet, Lady Banff, when children, on a couch; by Aikman.

35. Alexander, seventh Earl of Leven, when Lord Balgonie; half length; by Martin.

36. Jane Thornton, his Countess, when Lady Balgonie, along with Master David, her son; half length; by Romney.

37. David, eighth Earl of Leven and Melville; attired in brown overcoat lined with black silk, and black under coat; three-quarter length; by Capalti, Rome, 1851.

38. Elizabeth Anne Campbell, his Countess; three-quarter length; by Buckner.

39. Hon. William Leslie Melville, his brother; three-quarter length; by Phillips.

40. Lady Lucy, his sister, wife of Henry Smith, M.P.; by Thomas Ewins.

41. Lady Marianne, his sister, wife of Abel Smith, M.P.; by the same artist.

LESLIE PORTRAITS.

42. General Sir Alexander Leslie, first Earl of Leven; three-quarter length; by G. Jameson.

43. Agnes Renton, his Countess, when fifty-five years of age; a head and shoulders; by G. Jameson, 1642.

44. Alexander, Lord Balgonie, their son, when twenty-three years of age; half length; by G. Jameson, 1643.

45. Lady Margaret Leslie (Rothes), Lady Balgonie, his wife, afterwards Countess of Buccleuch and Countess of Wemyss; attired in a white dress, the sleeves looped up to diamonds; a large blue scarf brought over the right shoulder falls over the lower parts of the dress; she is dipping her hand in a fountain; three-quarter length; by Sir P. Lely.

46. The same; a head; by G. Jameson.

47. Lady Margaret Howard, Countess of Alexander, second Earl of Leven; a half length; by G. Jameson.

48. Margaret, Countess of Leven, her daughter; half length; by Medina.

OTHER PORTRAITS, RELATIVES, ETC.

49. Gustavus Adolphus, King of Sweden; attired in a yellow leather surtout and boots; full length; by Francis Pourbos the younger. Presented by the King to General Leslie.

50. Mary Queen of Scots, when young; attired in a black and orange bodice, and wearing a necklace and cross of pearls; bust; artist unknown. Bought in 1819 at the sale at Kinross House, Lochleven.

51. King William the Third; attired in his robes; three-quarter length; by J. J. Bakker.

52. Queen Mary, his wife; attired in her robes; three-quarter length; by J. J. Bakker.

53. William Bentinck, first Duke of Portland, K.G.; dressed in his robes; three-quarter length; by Sir John Medina.

54. David, second Earl of Wemyss; a large half length; by Medina.

55. Margaret, Countess of Wemyss, daughter of him and his Countess, Lady Margaret Leslie (See Nos. 45 and 46); a large half length; by Medina.

56. James Wemyss, Lord Burntisland, her husband, d. 1685; a large half length; by Medina.

57. David, third Earl of Wemyss, their son; in armour; three-quarter length; by Sir Godfrey Kneller.

58. The same; a large half length; by Medina.

59. Lady Anne Douglas, Lady Elcho, his wife; a large half length; by Medina.

60. David, fourth Earl of Wemyss, their son, when Lord Elcho; a large half length; by Medina.

61. David, fourth Earl of Northesk; in armour; three-quarter length; by Michael Wright.

62. The same; a large half length; by Medina.

63. Lady Margaret Wemyss, his Countess; a large half length; by Bourgignon.

64. George, sixth Earl of Northesk, vice-Admiral; a head; by Ramsay.

65. Lady Anne Leslie, his Countess, daughter of Alexander, fifth Earl of Leven; a head; by Ramsay.

66. Lady Christian Carnegie, daughter of David, fourth Earl of Northesk; large half length; by Aikman.

67. John Graham, Viscount Dundee; a head; artist unknown.

68. James, third Marquis of Montrose; in armour; in his thirtieth year, d. 1669; by Walker, 1659.

69. George, first Earl of Cromartie, Secretary of State for Scotland; d. 1714; a large half length; by Medina.

70. John, first Earl of Breadalbane; in armour, and a large flowing wig; half length; by Sir J. B. Medina.

71. James, fifth Earl of Perth, called Master of Drummond; a large half length; by Medina.

72. James, Marquis of Drummond; in armour; with a black serving boy; three-quarter length; by J. M. Wright.

73. Margaret Nairn, Lady Strathallan; in a yellow dress, with a large red scarf, on which she is seated in a garden; three-quarter length; by Sir Godfrey Kneller.

74. Mary Steuart, Lady Strathallan; a large half length; by Medina.

75. Robert Lundin of Lundin, heir to the family of Perth; in armour, with left hand resting on his helmet; three-quarter length; by Michael Wright.

76. Jane Bennet, called Lady Dirleton, wife of William Nisbet of Dirleton, and mother of Wilhelmina, Countess of Leven [Nos. 32-34 *supra*]; a head; by Ramsay.

77. William Bennet, her father; a head; artist unknown.

78. Mrs. Bennet, her mother; a head; artist unknown.

79. Janet, Lady Ruthven, wife of James, third Lord Ruthven, and sister of Wilhelmina, Countess of Leven; full length; by Medina.

80. John Thornton, Esq., founder of the Marine Society; in drab clothes; half length; by Russell in 1790, after Gainsborough.

81. Murillo, the Spanish artist; a head; copied by Sir David Wilkie from a picture at Seville.

82. Lady Margaret Skeffington, daughter of Lord Massarene, wife of Sir Charles Houghton, Bart.

83. Sir Islay Campbell, Bart., of Succoth, grandfather of Elizabeth Anne, Countess of Leven and Melville.

84. Arthur, first Duke of Wellington; head and shoulders; by Phillips.

85. King George the Fourth, on horseback; painted on china.

86. The Queen, as Princess Victoria; by Sir David Wilkie; an unfinished picture. In the background are the Duchess of Kent, Duchess of Northumberland, and Baroness Lehzen; Leopold, King of the Belgians, in armour; Prince Lichenstein; and the tutor, Mr. Davis.

COLLECTED MELVILLE SIGNATURES.

No. 1.

No. 2.

No. 3.   No. 4.

No. 5.

No. 6.

No. 7.

No. 8.

1. Sir John Melville of Raith, 1502-1548.
2, 3. Sir Robert Melville of Murdochcairnie, first Lord Melville, 1527-1621.
4. Sir Robert Melville of Burntisland, second Lord Melville, 1621-1635.

5. Sir James Melville of Hallhill.
6. John Melville of Raith, 1548-1605.
7. John Melville of Raith, 1605-1626.
8. John Melville, third Lord Melville, 1626-1643.

No. 1.

No. 2.

No. 3.

No. 4.

No. 5.

No. 6.

No. 7.

No. 8.

1. George, fourth Lord and first Earl of Melville, 1643-1707.

2. David, third Earl of Leven and second Earl of Melville, 1660-1728.

3. George, Lord Balgonie, his eldest son.

4. Alexander, fifth Earl of Leven and fourth Earl of Melville, 1729-1754.

5. David, fourth Earl of Leven, as Lord Balgonie, 1723.

6. David, sixth Earl of Leven and fifth Earl of Melville, 1754-1802.

7. Alexander, seventh Earl of Leven and sixth Earl of Melville, 1802.

8. David, eighth Earl of Leven and seventh Earl of Melville, 1832.

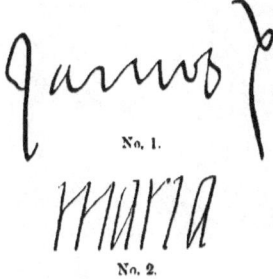

No. 1.

No. 2.

No. 3.

No. 4.

No. 5.

No. 6.

No. 7.

1. King James the Fifth, 1534.
2, 3, 4. Mary, Queen of Scots, 1556, 1566.
5. King James the Seventh, 1689.

6. William, Prince of Orange, 1689.
7. The same, initials as King William the Third, 1690.

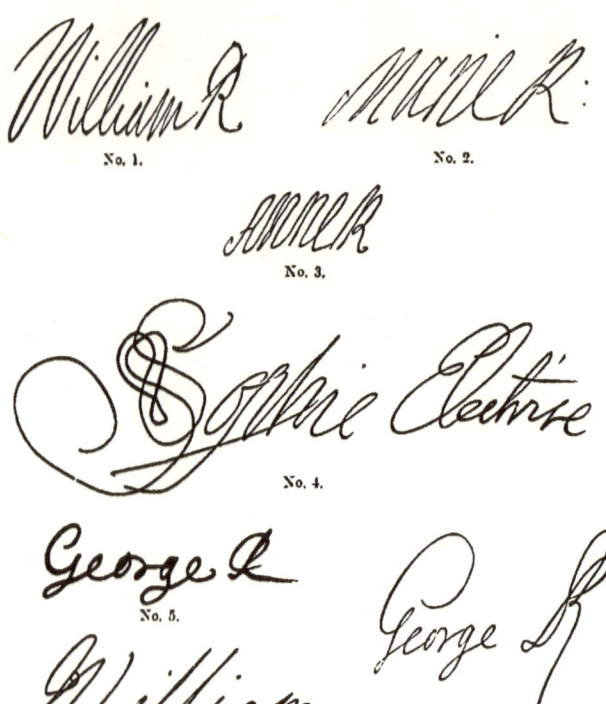

No. 1.

No. 2.

No. 3.

No. 4.

No. 5.

No. 7.

No. 6.

1. King William the Third, 1690.
2. Queen Mary, his wife, 1690.
3. Queen Anne, 1706.
4. Princess Sophia, Electress of Hanover, 1702.

5. King George the First, 1714.
6. King George the Second, 1734.
7. William, Duke of Cumberland, 1746.

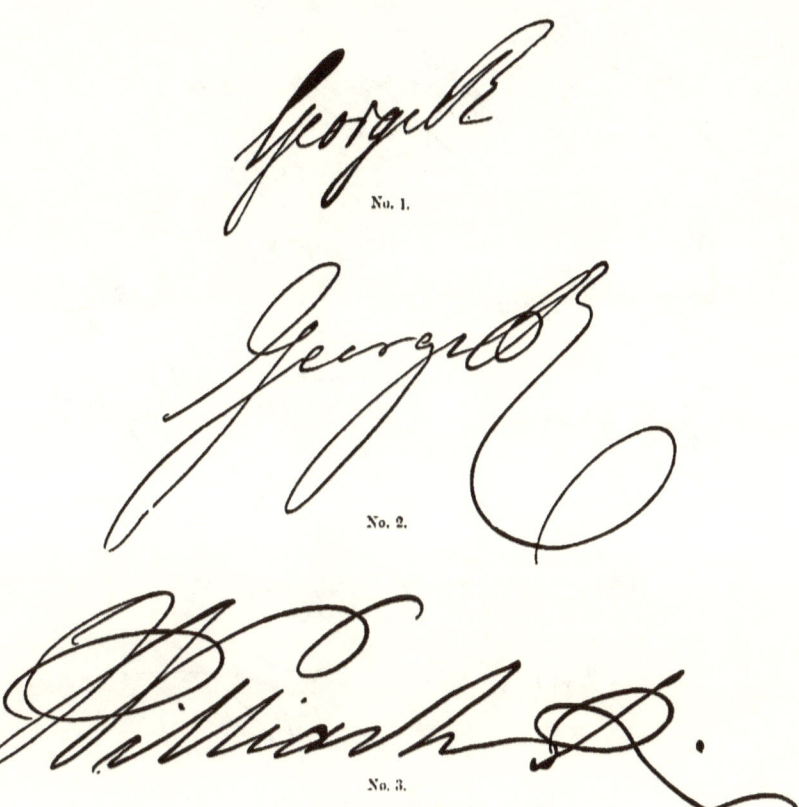

No. 1.

No. 2.

No. 3.

1. King George the Third, 1761.
2. King George the Fourth, 1820.
3. King William the Fourth, 1831.

1. Gustavus Adolphus, King of Sweden, 1631.
2. Sir Alexander Leslie, 1631.
3. The same, as Earl of Leven, 1648.
4. John Erskine, Earl of Mar, Regent, 1571.
5. James Douglas, Earl of Morton, Regent, 1577.
6. David Beaton, Cardinal, Archbishop of St. Andrews, 1540.

No. 1.

No. 2.

No. 3.

No. 4.

No. 5.

No. 6.

No. 7.

No. 8.

1. James Stewart, Earl of Murray, 1565.
2. Andrew Leslie, Earl of Rothes, 1565.
3. Andrew Stewart, Lord Ochiltree, 1565.
4. Sir William Kirkcaldy of Grange, 1565.

5. James Haliburton of Pitcur, 1565.
6. John Wishart of Pittarro, 1565.
7. Mr. Thomas Craig, Advocate, 1586.
8. Mr. Alexander Peathine (Peden), 1674.

No. 1.

No. 2.

1. Seal of John Melville, first of Raith, 1400-1427.
2. Seal of John Melville of Carnbee, 1509.